Heartburn

Kylee Minus

Dedicated to my family, for all of your support and love

Prologue

"And they lived happily ever after. The end."

"That's how all your stories end," I said. Sitting atop the counter, my legs thumped against the cabinets rhythmically, a spoon dripping with cake batter in my hand.

Mom chuckled as she shook her head knowingly, pouring the batter she had just finished into a large cake pan. "Every story ends with a happy ending. Even stories with wizards."

The word "wizards" seemed to ring in my ears. The mention of what Dad had forbidden in the house caught me off guard. I hoped I hid my shock well, trying to act casual as I spoke again. It wasn't the first time Mom had hinted to me about Dad's hatred of wizards, and though I knew it wasn't allowed, I couldn't help but feel encouraged by Mom's constant reminders. Ever since the war against the wizards began, such talk was not permitted in the house, yet Mom and I seemed to constantly break that rule.

"But I thought wizards are bad," I countered with the most innocent tone I could conjure, adding a slight tilt of my head for extra effect. Though I was young, I had enough mischief to challenge an imp.

"I know you don't believe that, Ivory," Mom said.

As I tried to cover my surprise, my mother slipped me another chocolate chip, her lips settling into a relaxed smile. She continued with the cake nonchalantly, leaving me to wonder how she knew of my wizard infatuation. I thought I had hidden the newspaper clippings well, but apparently not well enough.

Just as she parted her lips to add something, she was cut off when the door burst open. I heard Dad and my two older brothers walk in, their boots pounding on the wooden floor, their earthly aromas covering the sweet scent of cake.

"Not a word to your father," Mom whispered in my ear as she lifted me from the table. She set me down gently, using a thumb to wipe the cake batter from my cheek.

I nodded with a sudden triumph, her mischievous eyes matching mine. With playing eyes like hers, one wouldn't help but question if perhaps she too had something to hide. A second later, Dad, Layton, and Dean came through the kitchen entryway, smiling with a familiar victory painted on their faces. They clearly had a good hunting day, the scent of death wafting in after them.

"Silver, you wouldn't believe it! This little bugger got a stag today." Dad ruffled Dean's hair, and the three of them fell into a fit of bursting laughter.

"Did you, Dean? You better start hunting something else before you get them all." Mom smiled and grabbed a towel, wiping the dirt from his pudgy face.

"There's quite enough stags out there." Dad pecked her on the cheek and eyed the cake batter with a growing smile. "Now, I wonder what this cake is for. Ivory, could you tell me?"

"My birthday!" I beamed.

Dad laughed and scooped me from off the ground with his huge, lumberjack hands. "Right you are. I have something for you."

Mom frowned as he set me down. "Jakob, not yet."

"She can have one present now. She's been dying to open something all day," he insisted, and retrieved a package wrapped in a thick brown paper, dropping it into my arms.

The sight pushed any dwindling thoughts of wizards from my head. Bouncing with excitement, I tore through the paper to reveal a wooden bow, along with a few dull arrows. I marveled at the weapon in my hands, my first bow, but with a gasp that cut through the air, I thought perhaps that wasn't the appropriate reaction.

"You got her a bow? Jakob, that's not what you get a young lady! She's only four years old!" Mom exclaimed, swiping the present from my hands.

"Oh, let her try it out. I bet she'll be great at it," Dad pleaded, swiftly plucking the bow from Mom's grasp and setting it back in my arms. "C' mon, Ivory. Dean and I can show you how to aim. You'll be out hunting with us in no time."

Before my mother could fit in another sentence, I was herded outside. Instead of helping Mom finish the cake as we planned, I spent the rest of the afternoon shooting arrows at distant targets Dad had set up for Layton on his fourth birthday.

That night, after the cake had been eaten, the presents opened, and Layton, Dean, and I were sent to bed, Mom and Dad slipped in my room, whispering one last happy birthday as they bid me goodnight. They kissed the top of my head and backed out of my room, but as Dad disappeared into the darkness of the hallway, Mom lingered. She whispered something quick to the other side before she gently eased the door closed. She came back toward me, sitting beside me on my bed. I instantly perked up, eager to hear what she had to say.

"I have one more thing for you, but this is a secret," she said.

Even through the dimness of the room, her wide smile stuck out like a diamond glittering in gold. Her smile, one that nobody could miss, even from miles away, contradicted the raging sickness in her lungs. With a smile like hers, nobody would guess something beset her like a plague. Her sickness was one of an enigma, a sickness that I always forgot she had. I expected it to disappear just as fast as it appeared, but it had lingered like winter's frost coating petals in the spring.

From inside her cloak, she pulled out a heavy book. Written in thick golden letters, *Wizards* decorated the front cover, bound with leather that almost seemed homemade.

"I got this from someone very special. He wanted you to have it when I told him about your birthday." She had a sort of dreamy look in her eyes as she spoke.

I gaped as she handed me the book, throwing words of thanks her way. She hushed me with one more reminder to keep it a secret. With one last kiss, she backed out of my room, bidding me a final goodnight. As soon as she was gone, I flipped through the pages, filled with curiosity as my eyes flicked over the words and pictures. On the back of the book, a small initial written in the corner caught my attention.

G.K.

I smiled and flipped back to the first page. I had been planning to crawl through my window to retrieve my bow with an intention to practice all through the night, but instead I decided to stay inside and read every word of the book. And I did.

The next morning, I woke with a cluster of muddled thoughts, a sick feeling raging in the pit of my stomach like a ravenous monster. I clambered from my bed with a panic of losing the cake I had eaten the night before, clutching onto my torso as I stumbled to find the comforts of my mom. Instead, I found that both my parents were nowhere to be found, and though I banged on my brothers' doors for an explanation, they remained hidden and silent.

Eventually, as the sun had begun to set, Dad returned with nothing but war propaganda clasped in his hand. My questions seemed to go unheard by my father, who resolved to pop the cap off a bottle I had been told never to touch. I watched as he chugged the contents, the liquid dripping down into his dark beard. He pulled the bottle away slowly, like he yearned to keep it to his lips. And that was when he finally answered my question.

"Where is Mom?"

The answer was worse than anything I could've imagined, spilling from Dad's lips with dulled ease.

Her illness had claimed her.

1

Littered among the outskirts of the small village of Cyrene, my arrows hid in the dirt, long swallowed by weeds of dark green and yellow dandelions. I had lost many to the ground beneath my feet, never having the pleasure of slipping them back in my quiver again. Some I'd walk right past, emitting a crack almost as loud as lightning as I accidentally tread over them. And some had seemed to disappear right under my nose, perhaps snatched by a lone god or goddess with an interest in human weaponry.

Whatever the case was, my arrows were steadily dwindling, and as I withdrew the worn string of my bow, the disappearing number of arrows taunted the back of my mind. I opted to ease my grip instead of letting the arrow fly off to worlds unknown. With one last exhale of cold air, my numb fingers slipped from the string and the arrow shot into the darkness, hitting the dirt across the field with a distant thud.

I dropped my stance, the corners of my lips twitching up as I moved to retrieve it, my quiver of old wooden arrows strapped to my back clunking with each step. My boots suctioned to the black mud, ruined. Weighing down my pocket, a rusted key bundled for warmth in the folds of my skirt, bouncing against my thigh.

It would seem quite irregular, for lack of a better word, to know I worshipped that key almost as much as the pantheon of divine entities in the sky. The key, of which I had stolen from its hiding place, unlocked the chains of my isolation.

When my mother's flame flickered out, snuffed by her mysterious sickness, it seemed my old life died with her. No longer would I roam the town, or climb trees, or jump in ponds like normal children. Because after she had gone, she left her sickness behind. In me.

My father noticed the way my fingers never grew warm, even in the presence of a raging furnace. Along with the empty hole in my chest where my heart was supposed to live, and my strange, witch-like appearance, Dad couldn't risk letting me step past the threshold of our house ever again.

I grew up with the silver glints of locks mocking me every time I passed a door or window. The years flew by in solitude, my time used up with cleaning, or reading, or filling out Dean's schoolbooks. Prone to colds and infections, I spent many days in bed, hand resting against my unbeating chest, dreaming of the day I would perhaps sense a little flutter in my palm.

Dreaming of the day I could discover what it meant to love.

My state of living was just as confusing as Mom's illness, my cold blood rushing underneath my skin, but with no heart to pump it. The concept of love was unknown to me, even as words of my mother's funeral filled my ears, I remained rather apathetic and distant, even though grief and sorrow surrounded me.

But I wasn't the only one who had grown distant.

Dad, whose name filled me with muddled memories of bursting laughter, warm smiles, and booming voices, lost his previous mirth. Sometimes I wondered if I even remembered him correctly. The father that I remembered wasn't like anything of these flashes of the past.

Stripped of all jubilance, I grew up purposefully avoiding him, locking myself in my room, drowning out everything beyond my door with the words of books. So many books, all inherited from my mother. Stories of princes, kings, heroes, dragons, and thieves. I might've lacked a heart, but when I was a child, my imagination ran wild.

Over time, I noticed even Layton and Dean steadily began distancing themselves from our father, afraid of saying one wrong thing, one wrong move, one wrong glance. It was almost a relief when he told us he had drafted himself in the war raging in Embrasia. His hatred of wizards finally drove him to the battlefields, and it left us alone. With not much more than pity, the three of us watched him disappear.

Layton wasted no time. He became a blacksmith's apprentice the same day Dad walked out the door, never to return. At twelve years old, he had taken up the responsibility of supporting what was left of the Morrow family. Dean, on the other hand, had learned so much from Dad, he regularly dragged home a bloodied stag or walked through the door with mangled chickens hanging over his shoulders. I nearly got sick the first time he came home with a turkey, its severed head bobbling limply by threads of veins and arteries.

Back then, I possessed enough hope to believe that the rule Dad had set would be disbanded with him gone, but I was wrong. In fact, Layton proved himself to be almost even worse than Dad, with a set of eyes on the back of his head, it seemed. I spent even more time cutting myself off from my brother, the mischief inside me growing as I did.

With my mother's gift, *Wizards*, my interest in the war sparked, and in those days, I would do anything to get my hands on a newspaper. The book told of wizards that could fly, or even vanish into thin air. I thought, surely, the king of Embrasia would taste defeat by the wizards' hands, but yet again, I was wrong.

The king promised the citizens of Embrasia safety against any magic-wielding specimen during the war, pushing out anyone displaying magic, and when the Embrasians pushed the wizards out, they stayed out. Stranded near the coast of D'Erricoe, miles away from the borders of Embrasia, the wizards crafted their own city, which eventually became known as Naxos, The Wizard City.

And yet, some wizards remained in Embrasia. The turning tide of the Embrasian War had been King Cathair's most elite and powerful league of wizards, or Magicians, as he called them. With grants of land, families of wizards were allowed to stay in Embrasia. And while some possessed these grants, most didn't.

I plucked my arrow from the mud, flicking it clean before returning it to my quiver. Wisps of silver hair slipped from my loose bun, twirling in the wind like streams of snow. I hastily shoved them behind my ear.

If Layton or Dean knew of my occasional nightly excursions, I believed they would ensure I never saw the light of day ever again. Though I turned sixteen in only a few short hours, they treated me like the same four-year-old I had been after Mom died. Always a little afraid I would fall ill, a cough resulting in hours of demands to stay in bed. They pretended Mom or Dad never existed, as they pretended the war and the wizards didn't either, as well as the fact I couldn't love them back as a sister.

They never mentioned my heartlessness. They tried to avoid it as much as they could, in fact, but it seemed that that factor about me had created a barrier around us that not one of us could break. They stayed on one side, and I on the other. And even when I pounded on my side, my efforts always ended up in vain. Eventually, I stopped trying altogether.

Just as I reached behind my shoulder to grab another arrow, a distant light appeared in the dark expanse of the night. I squinted, taking in its red glow, a flicker of fear bubbling up in my stomach. If anyone caught sight of my silvery locks, snow-white complexion, and iridescent crystal eyes, I could've found myself facing an angry mob. If I were mistaken for a witch or wizard, I could've found myself run out of Cyrene.

I scrambled back as a figure darker than the night stepped into my line of sight. Tall and thin, it appeared to be several meters away from me, the red glow surrounding the figure with disturbing brightness. My breath hitched as it seemed to turn in my direction.

Shivers ran up my spine as I whirled around, letting my legs fall into a sprint. Glancing behind my shoulder, the figure grew smaller and smaller the more I ran through the field, the tall grass scratching my legs, mud splattering up on my skirt. My blood rushed with adrenaline and panic as I cursed myself for choosing the one night someone else wandered the fields. If I were seen. . . . If I were recognized. . . . I couldn't imagine the outcome, and I didn't want to.

With labored breath, I stopped upon the front steps of the house, scanning frantically for the glow of crimson taunting me in the distance, but it was gone. Though, whoever it was could've still been out there. I wasn't out of the woods yet.

I threw off my quiver and bow, gingerly returning them to their exact place among the discarded pile of Dean's broken bows and arrows. With trembling fingers, I silently unlocked the door, slipping through like a shadow, hoping I wasn't leaving a trail of mud in my wake. I rushed past the living room and into the hall, passing Dean's room, my door growing ever closer, and—

"Ivory?" The door to Layton's room flung open, revealing my older brother, fully dressed, wavy brown hair tamed, freshly shaven face, and ironed clothes. He looked down at me with a stern, yet slightly confused, look in his eyes.

"Layton! I was just—"

"Don't you know what time it is?" he questioned, and I stepped aside lightly to allow him to pass me.

"I thought I heard something. A man," I sputtered quickly, my stomach rolling. "I was coming to get you."

"A man?" Instantly, he turned and started toward the door. "I'm already late for work but tell Dean about it. I'll be home later."

I watched as he rushed out the door, exhaling a long breath of relief. Getting rid of Layton had never been so easy. I returned to my room, easing the door closed behind me. I kicked off my muddy boots, hiding them deep in my closet. I buried the key away in a drawer, concealed by loose papers and abandoned schoolwork, though only after I had bestowed a kiss to the rusty metal. Grime stained my hands, the scent of the outside world following after me.

I entered my bathroom, flicking on the lights, the wood underneath my feet sending cold tingles up my spine. Purposefully avoiding my eyes in the mirror, I washed my hands three times, grime and dirt swirling down the drain and staining the white sink. Replaced by lavender-scented soap, all traces of fresh nightly air disappeared from my skin.

It had become a routine for me to sneak back into the protection of the house moments before Layton left for work in the town, and never had I been so close to being caught. I took a few breaths just to calm the last of my adrenaline, forcing a grin on my lips.

But the small smile disappeared as a flash caught my eyes. My head shot up to face the mirror, but something more than my reflection filled the glass. I whirled around in shock, my eyes wide.

Blocking the door, a creature of pure ebony stood seven feet tall, gangly arms nearly grazing the floor. It had no distinct features, a mere figure of a man. The same man I had seen outside. Glowing red eyes sunk into the center of its face, filling the room with scattered crimson. The edges of the figure blurred in and out of reality.

I froze, sickly fear gripping onto my senses, a gasp caught in my throat. I had never seen anything so otherworldly, the creature like something straight from a nightmare. My knees buckled as I realized what the creature must've been.

A ghost.

And just as the thought passed through my mind, it attacked. Lunging with its languorous arms reaching for my neck, it moved like a bullet. I shrieked, shooting backward to avoid its outstretched fingers. My back rammed into the mirror, and the glass wobbled dangerously before it crashed to the ground.

The ghost grabbed me tight, flinging me to the ground, where the broken shards pierced my skin. The pain sent a wave of adrenaline my way, and before I knew what I was doing, I had a shard wrapped tightly in my hand. But with whatever efforts I tried to fight, the ghost proved too fast.

Its hands found my throat, grasping tightly, stealing away what little breath I had left. I choked, sputtering as my chest tightened painfully, agonizing bursts spreading through my lungs. With panic flowing through my veins, I gripped the shard in my hand tight, using it to drive into the dark creature.

A hiss escaped the ghost, and it clenched my throat tighter. Just as the edges of my vision blurred, the door burst open and as it did, the ghost withdrew its hands. It faded out of sight, leaving me gasping on the bathroom floor. Air returned to my scorching lungs, my pounding head easing with each deep intake.

"Ivory!" Dean exclaimed, rushing to pull me to my feet. "What happened? Ivory, calm down!"

I shook my head rapidly, drawing in violent gasps as I stumbled to regain my balance, my head swaying. "A ghost! Dean, a ghost! Did you see it?" I rambled on, gesturing dramatically to the spot it had just occupied.

"You're bleeding." He caught my flailing hand, inspecting the beads of crimson dripping down my palm, a cut gained from holding the shard too tight.

"So? You saw it, didn't you? Oh, tell me you saw it!" Along with fear, the creature stirred something else in me. A jolt of some emotion, something like curiosity, like excitement, struck. And I couldn't ignore it.

"You're bleeding everywhere," Dean said, swiping a hand towel from a cabinet and throwing it across the room to me. He stepped around the broken glass cautiously. "Get out, Ivory, I don't want you stepping on any of this."

"But—"

"*Now*, Ivory."

I clasped my mouth shut, watching as he began scooping the broken glass into a pile, his eyebrows knitted together. Curls of dark hair fell into his black eyes.

Thick, red liquid slid down my wrist, the stinging pain in my palm steadily growing more and more noticeable as my adrenaline wore off.

But the taste of adrenaline still lingered, and I wanted another bite.

2

I sat on the edge of my bed, cradling my throbbing hand in my lap.

Dean had tied the bandages too tight, suffocating and cutting off the blood flow to my hand. Trapped in a familiar silence, my reeling thoughts attacked my conscious. It was like the house had inhaled a deep breath, waiting anxiously to release it. But when was the right time? If it was too soon, would the house come crumbling down?

Stuck on my supernatural encounter, I couldn't get my thoughts to slow down.

I'm sure Dean saw it, I mean, he was right there! Why would he avoid my question though? Maybe he really didn't see it. Perhaps he thought I lost my mind. Or, perhaps that's what he wants me to think.

Wracking my brain for some type of explanation, the memory of the ghost replayed over and over, like a broken record. If I concentrated hard enough, I felt I could still feel its tight grasp on my neck, its touch like the kiss of burning embers, and the ephemeral fire in my lungs. It was the most painful thing I had ever experienced, but as the minutes passed by, I found myself wishing for another encounter. It *had* to mean something. Ghost attacks didn't just happen spontaneously. Why, on my sixteenth birthday, did a ghost capriciously decide to commit attempted murder?

I slipped from the edge of my bed, urging myself to ignore the throb in my hand and crossed the floor, facing the wall of bookshelves lined around my room. I lifted my good hand, hovering above the spines, combing through the shelves. However, as I pulled out book after book, flicking through the pages, I found nothing including information on ghosts. Not one page.

With a deafening chime of the clock that sliced through my concentrated silence, I dropped the last book in my hand, all the others strewn about on my floor. I took a deep breath before I picked it up and finished scanning the last remaining pages.

I scurried to return each book back to their rightful place on the shelves, my body heavy with disappointment and defeat. However, I wasn't going to forget about the ghost. Nothing could possibly make me forget about it, and I wasn't going to stop searching until I knew everything there was to know.

As I slipped the last of my book collection back in place, a knock at my door startled me.

"Ivory, I have breakfast ready." The voice of Dean rang from behind my door.

"Alright, I'm coming," I called back.

As my brother's footsteps faded away, I tore myself from my books, useless for the first time in my life, and threw myself into a bland green blouse and skirt. I buttoned the black buttons, slipped on a pair of white stockings, and tied a black ribbon into my silver hair, pulling it away from my ears. With a half-contented sigh, I pulled my door open and left to greet Dean.

The popping of bacon, along with a sweet aroma, led me straight to the kitchen, where Dean was busy with pans of bubbling pancakes and sizzling bacon. Only on my birthday did Dean ever make pancakes.

"Go ahead and sit," he said, his full attention still on the food.

I complied, settling down in my wooden chair. Ever since Mom died, the rest of us seemed to always sit in the same seats, a strange assigned seat game we played but never acknowledged. All I knew was that Dad's chair stood on the far left, untouched for years, the wood blanketed with a thin layer of dust.

I flicked my eyes away as Dean set down a plate in front of me. He joined me at the table, in the seat across from mine with his own plate.

I watched as he scarfed down the food, though mostly leaving the pancakes untouched, abandoning them sadly soaking up syrup in the corner of his plate. My brothers preferred savory over sweet, but I craved sugar more than actual food, more than water, sometimes more than air. Just another difference to keep us apart.

But, that morning, I wasn't interested in the sugary pastries. Even as I chewed slowly, my mind barely registered the sweet taste, instead still wired on the black ghost. I knew Dean couldn't aid in the mystery, having no expertise on anything other than hunting and cooking. The only way to learn more about it was through books, but none of mine included the information I needed. I would need a new book. I would need a place with countless books.

I needed a library.

"Ivory, your food is getting cold," Dean said, his voice snapping me out of my thoughts.

I hadn't realized how much time flew by, and sure enough, when I stuck my fork in my mouth, my pancakes were indeed cold. I bashfully tried finishing my breakfast as fast as I could, my mind racing.

It's not possible. Even if I asked, Dean would never get me a book about ghosts. Neither would Layton. Not even on my birthday.

"Layton will be home tonight. He told me he has a surprise for you." Dean stood up and carried his plate to the sink, dumping half-eaten pancakes in the trash. "I think you'll really like it."

I heard a slight smile in his voice, and his tone lifted the previous tense atmosphere. Though, his change in voice only encouraged me further. He was pretending that it never happened as if that would make the memory disappear from both our minds.

"Oh, yeah? Mind giving me a hint?" I asked.

"You'll just have to wait until Layton gets back." A smirk spread across his face. He grabbed my plate and dropped it in the sink.

"Oh, c' mon. Please?" I chuckled, pushing myself out of the chair, tailing Dean as he exited the kitchen. "I promise I won't tell Layton."

Out of my two brothers, Dean was my obvious favorite. He did something Layton never even tried to do. He took my side. He heard me out. He defended me. If I begged enough, he would eventually crack a smile and whisper to me obvious hints. Out of the very few people I knew, he was the only person I could count on.

"That'll ruin the surprise," Dean insisted, sticking his nose up as he tried to ignore my gaze.

"Please?"

"No."

"Please?"

"Ivory."

When he turned to face me, a stone look set on his face, I grinned innocently and batted my eyelashes. His expression melted in an instant, replaced by a smile he had been clearly fighting to keep from his face.

"Go cause trouble somewhere else. I'm not telling you this time." He shoved me in the direction of my room, shaking his head jokingly. "Read your books. Do some math. Something other than pestering me."

"But Deeeeean," I groaned, "I've read all my books. I've solved a thousand equations. All there is left to do is pester you."

"I've got work to do."

"Hunting isn't work."

"Sure it is. How else are we going to get dinner?"

"Oh, I don't know, buy something in town? There's other food than meat, you know." I rolled my eyes, crossing my arms.

"Why waste money when there's a whole forest right outside?" He shrugged. "I'll be back soon. Don't go anywhere."

He says that like I have a choice.

"So," I said casually, strolling into the hallway as I made my way back to my room, "how long exactly will you be gone?"

"Two hours? The same amount every day, I don't know exactly." He shot me a strange look. "Why does it matter?"

"Right, you're right." I chuckled nervously, tugging on my hair as I backed further and further down the hallway. "See you when you get back."

I dove back into my room to avoid any more questions, shutting the door swiftly behind me. A plot was hatching in the back of my brain, but I was trying desperately to ignore it. The rule said I couldn't leave the house. I had followed that rule ever since it was set, respected my father's last request, except the few nights I stole in secret. Besides, it increased the chance of getting caught.

Even though it drove me insane when Layton did it, I paced. Back and forth across my room, spinning on my heels.

But I never needed to break the rule before. This time, it was a matter of ghost murder. I wouldn't be able to understand the reasoning behind the attack if I didn't even understand the ghost itself. I needed that library. I needed to break the rule again. It was the only way.

With a bout of guilty determination, I retrieved the key from its hiding place among my messy drawer, clasping its cold handle tight in my hand, rubbing the rust with my thumb.

I slipped on a pair of black slippers, tying an old cloak of Deans around my shoulders and leaned precariously from my doorway, scanning the empty hallway with rising anticipation.

"Dean?" I called out, though I knew he was already gone.

I waited for an answer; only silence responded. Chewing on my bottom lip, I slipped through the hallway like a ghost myself, treading lightly on my feet. With each step, the temptation to turn right back around pushed harder, until I was sure I couldn't possibly go through with my plan.

I painfully crossed the living room, some invisible force driving me back. Escaping during the hours of the night, the darkness smuggling me out, the shadows hiding me away, a sense of security accompanied me. But with the sun lighting the world, scaring away the shadows I had grown so reliant on, my resolve was breaking.

If I want to know why that ghost attacked me, I have to go. I have to do this.

Taking a deep breath, I pushed the key in the lock with trembling hands, the click slicing through the silence like a knife. I released a breath I hadn't realized I had been holding, lightly easing the door open. Rays of light spilled into the house, a flash of white blinding me momentarily. A rush of fresh air filled my lungs. I blinked until my vision returned, gazing into the eyes of a world unknown to me.

I pocketed the key and stepped out of the house.

3

The morning air smelled of pine needles and rain, the dew coating the grass soaking my black shoes. I held my skirt up slightly to keep it from getting wet, drawing in deep intakes. Anxiety had burrowed into my blood, my pace quicker and quicker with each step. I threw nervous glances behind my shoulders every once in a while to ensure nobody followed my path.

My feet hit a stone road. I glanced up, shaking my troubling thoughts from my head and spotted a town in the distance. I had only seen it cloaked in darkness, when all was unmoving and quiet. In the daylight, I could see people, tons of people, in large crowds and flying past each other.

As I got closer, I tightened my cloak, throwing the hood over my abnormal hair. A twinge of anticipation entered my mind, causing my hands to shake slightly. Without realizing it, I had picked up my pace dramatically, keeping my head down as I stepped into the town. I had spent countless hours wishing to be one of the crowd, but finally being there, all I wanted to do was go home. I felt like everyone's eyes were on me, like they knew there was something wrong with me, like they knew I was different.

The town was cramped, the shops hugging each other, stands and carts getting in people's way, the cobblestone sidewalks so cluttered with pedestrians, they were barely even visible. An occasional carriage would stroll down the street, pulled by tall horses, causing the crowd to disperse. Smoke bustled from the chimneys like fluffy clouds, filling the sky with a gray tint that tinged the beautiful blue above. Sounds boomed in my ears like the cannons of war. Colors of beige and brown mashed together as I flew past. Sellers shouted out, trying to draw people in. A hundred faces blurred together, a hundred voices, a thousand eyes.

So many sounds, so many smells, so many people. I listened to the sellers, curious, as I walked past, ignoring the overwhelming wave washing over me. Bread was half off. Salmon was fresh. Someone even claimed they had the rarest gems in the world. I stole a glance to find what was obviously fake gold and forged diamonds.

I moved on, not staying in one place too long, afraid someone would somehow recognize me as a Morrow, though I shared no defining features similar to my brothers. I passed a cart displaying knives, arrows, and jewelry, recognizing some of the handiwork and carved with an "L", I figured out why. They were all made by Layton.

I jumped as I glanced up to see my older brother himself nodding to a man speaking to him. The man was huge, wide and tall. The blacksmith, Linus. Quickly, I darted away, allowing myself to be swallowed by the crowd, tightening my cloak once more. A surge of panic shot through me full force like a bullet shaking my insides. I could only hope Layton didn't see me. I was jostled around, leaving me stumbling and tripping over people's feet. I swung my arms in an attempt to regain my balance, but with so many people everywhere, moving so fast, nobody watching where they were going, shoulders bumping into me, it was an impossible task.

Just as I was about to fall, a pair of hands grabbed my arm. My head shot up to find a boy around my age steadying me. Determination shone on his face as he directed the two of us out of the haphazard bustle in the streets. He led me to the sidewalks and we ended up standing in front of a small bakery, sweets and pastries displayed in the front, the sugary scent wafting through the thick smog of the cramped town.

"Are you ok?" he asked. His voice was bouncy, traces of a child still there. He couldn't have been very old.

"I'm fine," I answered shortly. "Thank you."

"No problem. This place is so small, I was sure I knew everyone, but I'm not sure I've ever seen you around," the boy said, bending his knees as he tried to get a better look at my face.

I turned slightly, reaching up to tug at my hood. "I'm, uh, just visiting."

"Oh, I see. Well, my name's Dulce." He jerked his thumb at himself. "I can show you around if you want. This place may be small, but it sure can get confusing."

My first instinct was to decline. The longer I spent in his presence, the higher the chance he caught sight of my strange looks and mistake me for an illegal witch. Being run out of Cyrene was not on my agenda for my birthday.

But *I* didn't know where the library was. He did. And I was running out of time.

"Actually, I was looking for the library. And, I'm in a bit of a hurry, so if you wouldn't mind telling me where it is," I said.

"Of course. Follow me." He gestured to me as he set off walking.

I drew in a deep breath, pulled on my hood once more, and took a few long strides to catch up with him. Out of the corner of my eye, I studied him, his unruly black hair, dirty apron tied around his waist. His face was tan and pudgy, his blue eyes wide, and his grin strangely lopsided. He caught me staring and smiled, revealing at least three chipped teeth.

"So, how long are you staying?" he asked.

"Oh, uh, not much longer. Gotta get back to—" I cut myself off, realizing my knowledge on other towns was severely limited.

"To?" Dulce's eyebrows rose as he peered down at me.

I swirled my head away from his gaze. "To, uh, Lockdale."

"Ooh, so you're from Lockdale. What, does Lockdale not have a library?"

"No, no, it does. It just doesn't have what I'm looking for," I answered. *Can you just shut up and show me where it is? Why do I have to tell you my whole life story?*

"What are you looking for?"

"Do you work at that bakery?" I asked instead of answering, hoping I hid my scoff well.

He blinked quickly as if processing the sudden change in conversation. Maybe he would get the hint.

"Yeah, my parents own it." He nodded. "They want me to take over."

I heard the dismay in his voice, loud and clear. He obviously did it on purpose, trying to draw some pity out of me. I figured listening to him whine was better than trying to make up lies.

"And you don't want to."

"No, I'd rather join the king's military or something dangerous like that," he said with drastic simplicity, batting his hand in the air.

My eyebrows shot up in surprise. So, he wanted to die?

"But the last war was so deadly. What if the next one is even worse? What if the wizards decide they aren't done fighting?"

"Then I die." He shrugged. "What about you?"

"What about me?"

"What do you want to do with your life?" he clarified, smiling.

I paused, at a loss for words. I didn't have much say in how I wanted to spend my days. Surely, my brothers would let me find my own life . . . right? They couldn't keep me cooped up like some type of prisoner my whole life. They'd have to let me go eventually. And then what? What would I do once I was out in the world, alone?

"An author, maybe." I shrugged.

"Ah, that's boring. What do you *need* in life? What do you want more than anything else in the world?"

I huffed quietly and thought for a few more moments, but the answer was an obvious one. "I want to go to Naxos."

"Naxos?" He sucked in a breath. "Isn't that one of the most dangerous cities in the nation? I've heard wizards just roam the streets and do whatever they want, literally. Anything." The way he spoke sparked a flame of anger in the pit of my stomach.

"Says the one who wants to join the king's military." I narrowed my eyes at him.

He smirked, nodding. "Good point. So, what's wrong with Payne?"

I nearly groaned at the mention of the name. Peyton Payne was the name of the one legal wizard in Cyrene. He was a wrinkly old man that wore a suit of pure silk, actual crystals sewn into the hems. He was the only person that knew about me. Layton and Dean paid him in an attempt to fix me, but he was never able to help. In his words, I was devoid of a heart because I "must've developed a magical deformation in the womb" and he "couldn't do anything about it". He didn't deserve to be called a wizard.

"I've read about wizards that can fly or disappear. Have you ever seen Payne vanish?" I responded sharply.

"No, but that doesn't mean he can't," Dulce shot back.

The day Payne flies or vanishes is the day Layton will let me get a tattoo. I resisted the urge to roll my eyes.

"So, when do you think you'll go?"

"I don't know," I replied dismissively.

"I think I want to leave soon. My brother should be old enough to manage the bakery on his own. And it's not like I'm getting any younger."

"What about your family? You're just going to leave them? Won't you feel guilty?" I asked, the questions slipping out of my mouth so fast, I couldn't stop them. I couldn't imagine actually feeling guilty the day I left my brothers for good, but then why did I hesitate so much for just leaving for a few secret hours?

"No, it's my life. I can do whatever I want." He shrugged, sticking up his nose.

My words caught in my throat. How could he possibly think that? Nobody could do whatever they wanted; it just wasn't possible. Even someone living with normal circumstances.

"There it is," Dulce said, his voice tearing me from my thoughts.

I looked up to see a modest-sized building composed of wood, like the majority of Cyrene, a stone path leading up to it. In the glass windows, the spines of a hundred books faced the world. And on the front, in big, crumbling letters read *Cyrene Library*.

4

Dulce pulled the door open and moved aside so I could get in. I stepped past the bakery boy, forgetting him the second I walked through the threshold. Inside held the most books I had ever seen in one place, countless shelves, almost tall enough to reach the ceiling, spanning from wall to wall.

I practically dove into the maze of shelves, running my fingers along countless spines as I walked past. That nostalgic book smell entered my nose, better than air. I felt like I was floating as I maneuvered around the library hopelessly.

"Can I help you pick something out?"

I looked up to see an old woman smiling down at me. I made sure to tug on my hood before I smiled back.

"Can you direct me to the . . . uh, supernatural section?" I stuttered.

"Of course, though I must admit that is our smallest section. Ghost stories just aren't as popular as they used to be," the woman replied with a sigh.

I followed her to the back of the library, and hidden by the towering shelves, was one mini shelf, harboring a sad collection of books. I tried to keep a smile on my face, but I couldn't help but let the corners of my lips drop.

"Uh, thank you," I said, bending to one knee in front of the tiny shelf.

The woman said something else, but I was already too busy pulling out books to listen. I heard her footsteps fade away somewhere in the back of my head. My full attention was on the words, new words, words I had never read before, about things not in any of my books at home.

But, much to my dismay, most of them were fictional. Some of them were even children's books. I needed a guide, not a story.

I continued rummaging and reading, but nothing matched what I had seen earlier. Soon, stacks of books surrounded me, the shelf empty. A tight knot had risen up in my throat, tears of anger threatening to fall.

"Oh, there you are. Find what you were looking for?" The sound of Dulce's voice startled me.

I jumped, then quickly reached up to pull my slipping hood. I shoved each book back on the small shelf and pushed myself up on my feet, biting the inside of my cheek and taking subtle deep breaths.

"No."

"Oh, that's too bad. Did you try looking by author?"

"What?"

"Was there a specific author that you were looking for? It might be put in the section with all the books written by that author," Dulce explained.

"No. Uh, wait, actually, yes," I sputtered. "G.K.?"

"G.K.? I've never heard of that one," Dulce said, frowning.

"I know where those books are."

Dulce and I jumped at the sound of the man's voice. We whirled around to find a pale, narrow man wearing a simple buttoned shirt and tan trousers staring at us with dark eyes. How long had he been standing there? Had he been there the whole time? How did I not hear him? I nervously tugged on my hood as I watched him approach.

"Who are you?" Dulce questioned, glancing around as if also unsure how long the man had been right next to us.

It was almost as if he appeared out of thin air.

"Oh, me?" Even his accent was strange, as if he were awfully trying to impersonate an Embrasian. "I'm just a fellow who likes books. I couldn't help but overhear. You're looking for G.K., right?"

I nodded, and I couldn't help but lift my face to meet his. His eyes held a strange swirling of colors. I gaped as he blinked and the pigments in his irises halted.

He smiled widely. "Right over here."

Unsure, we followed after the strange man, who glanced over his shoulder every other second just to make sure we were still following him. Dulce subtlety stepped closer to me, almost close enough that our shoulders touched, but for once, I was glad he was with me.

The man moved quickly, his strides confident. A strange sweet scent wafted from him, almost as if he had doused himself in vanilla. He stopped abruptly in front of a shelf, and Dulce and I stumbled to avoid crashing into him. We waited as he studied the spines, but it didn't take him long to find a book. He clicked his tongue and pulled out one book, his hand unwavering. How did he know what I was looking for?

He turned and handed it to me with a graceful smile. I accepted it gently, slightly in shock. I hadn't expected to ever find another one of G.K.'s books, but there I was, holding one. It seemed to be made from the same leather *Wizards* was made from. I held my breath as I read the title.

Creatures of the World Beyond: A Guide.

"Is that what you were looking for?" the man asked, but his tone signified that he already knew the answer.

I nodded. "Exactly what I was looking for."

He smiled. "I'm glad I could help. But a little word of advice, most things aren't what they appear to be."

Dulce and I glanced at each other in confusion, but when we turned back toward the man, he was gone. Vanished.

"Where did he go?" I asked aloud, his advice just as strange as he was.

Dulce whirled in a full circle, scanning the isle. "I don't know. Let's just get out of here before he comes back."

I agreed hesitantly, wishing I didn't have to abandon the library so quick, following Dulce back to the front. Quickly, he helped me sign up for my own library card. I signed under Layton's name, not allowing Dulce to see the way I scribbled his name in a quick, nervous flourish.

I checked out the book and tucked it into my cloak, where it would be safe. Dulce and I waved goodbye to the old librarian before we thrust ourselves back into the chaotic bustle of the town. I shook the thought of the strange man from my head. I had more important things to worry about.

Now all I needed to do was lose Dulce and make it back home in time without being caught. Piece of cake.

Just as I was about to tell Dulce some made-up excuse, he sucked in a breath, words already on his tongue, prepared. It seemed he too had forgotten all about the strange man.

"So, what's with the cloak? Are you a fugitive or something?"

"Why would a fugitive want a book?" I shot back, self-consciously tugging on the hood, glaring at him from under the folds of the frayed fabric.

"I don't know. Why would a baker want to join the military? Are you hiding something?"

"No," I spat, attempting to pick up my pace.

Dulce matched my speed easily. "Then take down the hood. You don't see anyone else covering their faces."

"Well, everyone else isn't me."

"What's that supposed to mean?" A poisonous irritation drowned in his words.

I glanced over at him to see him glaring at me, as if I were the one in the wrong, as if I were the one asking personal questions to a stranger. What was his problem?

"Look, I helped you out today. Least you can do is let me see your face. Or, at least tell me your name!" he exclaimed.

"Why?" I cried.

"Why?" He blinked. "Because I want to see you again, that's why! I just spent all morning helping you, the least you can do is tell me your name."

I took a step back as his shouts began to attract the crowd. People had stopped to stare, obviously listening. I pulled on my hood again, glancing at the hundreds of faces in panic. The pressure of their eyes weighed down on me, whispering, aware of what I had done, aware of who I was.

"Dulce, please, be quiet," I whispered, stumbling backward as I shushed him, my eyes darting every which way.

"Why won't you tell me? Don't you want to meet again?" he shouted, quickly filling the gap I had made between us as he reached out and grabbed my shoulders.

My panic shot up at the touch. I wretched myself away and broke into a sprint. Dulce called for me to wait, but I was already gone, my black shoes pounding against the hot cobblestone as I slipped through the crowd like a snake. I kept one hand grasped around the hem of my hood, ensuring it didn't fall off. People glared down at me as I flew past them, my shoulders accidentally bumping into countless strangers.

Eventually, the crowd began thinning, easier to dodge, the shops and carts disappearing behind me. Soon, it was just me and that stone path leading out of town, the chatter, clatter, and clang fading. I finally allowed myself to release my hood, sucking in deep breaths. I slowly eased to a walk as it seemed I had lost the bakery boy, my panic steadily fading away. Just as I was about to wipe my sweaty forehead, a hand grabbed my arm.

"Wait, please! All I want to know is your name!"

I whirled around to face Dulce, his large, pleading eyes boring into mine, gasping as I tried tugging my arm from his grasp, mind racing. I tried to hide my face from him, burying my eyes into my palm.

"Please, leave me alone," I begged, fighting against him the best I could without letting my hood fall. "You don't want to know who I am!"

"You don't know that! Please, just let me see your face. Then, we can go back to my bakery. You can tell me all about that author you love so much," he said, his voice falling soft.

I quit struggling as my thoughts refused to pass through my head. I was frozen, stuck staring at his face, trying to comprehend his persistence. *Why does he even care so much to know me? We just met!*

He smiled as soon as he realized I had stopped. Perhaps he thought I was really going to listen to him. With a steady hand, he reached out toward my hood. Before I could stop myself, I flipped the hood in one swift motion, revealing my silver hair, crystal eyes, and deathly pale skin splattered with freckles.

Retracting his hand from my face faster than a bullet, he let go of me, his eyes widening in shock. His jaw slightly hung open as he recoiled back.

"Y—You're—" He didn't finish his sentence. He just stared with those large eyes of his, before he turned and ran back toward town, not looking back once.

I sighed as I watched him disappear into the bustle of the town, a tiny speck compared to everything else. I knew I would get that reaction, and yet I let him see anyway. It was the reaction I wanted, but it still didn't hurt any less. People just couldn't understand my looks. They couldn't understand me. I wasn't sure if I even understood myself.

After all, who would love someone who couldn't even return the favor?

5

When I returned to the house, I found Dean waiting for me just beyond the front door, his arms folded tightly across his chest. He narrowed his intense, dark eyes at me, fuming. Somehow, his curly dark hair seemed even more disheveled than it had been that previous morning.

"Town," I said before he could ask, too mentally exhausted to care that I had been caught.

"Town!" he repeated, his eyebrows shooting up in anger.

I nodded, eyes downcast as I tried to slip past him, the book clutched in my hand calling to me, but he stepped in front of the hallway swiftly, blocking it off.

"Do you have any idea how much trouble you're in? How did you even get out?" he thundered, peering down at me with slanted eyes.

I recited the lie I had composed during my trek back to the house. "You left the front door open."

For a moment, he looked dubious, but he quickly shook it off. "What is the one rule we have?"

I winced at his tone. "No leaving the house."

"Then why did you leave?"

"Maybe," I started sarcastically, "because of the bloody ghost trying to kill me!"

My brother paused for a second, shock flicking in his eyes. The expression, immediately switched back to anger.

"There was no ghost. You hallucinated it," he finally said.

I glanced up to meet his face, my mouth almost dropping open as a wave of familiar anger rose up in the pit of my stomach. He was there! He saw it with his own eyes! What did he mean it was a hallucination?

"But, you—"

"Enough, Ivory. I've had enough of your overactive imagination!" Dean shouted, swiping his arm through the air. "Did anyone see you?"

When I hesitated, he sucked in a sharp breath. He stepped toward me, grasping my shoulders tight, his fingers digging into the flesh through my sleeve.

"Who?"

"It was—was just some—"

"*Who*, Ivory?"

"His name was Dulce. At the bakery." I decided against including the strange man at the library.

Dean shoved me aside, pulling on a cloak of his own. "I'm going to find Layton. You better *stay here*, or else you'll be in even more trouble."

I stared wide-eyed as he rushed out the door, slamming it loudly behind him. The slam seemed to echo through the air. I released a breath I hadn't realized I was holding, unmoving for a long time. I almost expected him to come back, for whatever reason. Maybe to tell me I was right, or to scream at me that I was crazy. Maybe to apologize.

But, he didn't, and I was left alone in a house that seemed strangely silent. I glanced around as if expecting something to happen.

Though, of course, nothing did, and soon my rushing blood calmed. I wandered back to my room like a lost soul, unclasping the old cloak and letting it drop in a heap on the floor. I plopped down on my wooden chair and pushed a stack of books from my desk. They crashed to the floor with a loud thud, but I didn't wince at the sound. With anger running high, I felt no sympathy for anything, not the books, not my brothers, not Dulce.

I dropped the library book on the desk and threw it open to the first page. A signature that I recognized was written just below the title. *G.K.* I had read G.K.'s work my whole life, all of his facts and opinions about wizards. I knew his writing style, the quirks in his words. In a way, I felt I knew *him*.

I thumbed through the pages just so I could get a feel for the old paper. The smell of the library sank into the pages, intoxicating. When I couldn't hold myself back any longer, I flipped to the first chapter.

Sirens.

I flicked through to the next.

Faeries.

I combed past that one.

Dust.

I recognized that one. I had seen Dust before, tiny specks of multicolored crystals in long vials. Peyton Payne had once given me a vial of Healing Dust, golden and bright. It didn't do anything to help me, but it did cause me to feel all tingly for a couple of hours. My eyes glanced over a few of the words, then jumped to the next chapter.

Ghosts.

My anger evaporated quicker than the blink of an eye. I leaned forward, peering over the page anxiously, and began to read.

The most common speculation about these intimidating apparitions display ghosts as maliciously evil, waiting to tear you apart one by one, but in many instances, that is not the case. Some ghosts roam the living realm, memory distorted, half-convinced they never died, appearing like any normal human, save a scent of death, cold skin, and slight glow. Some know fully well that they died, and are left wondering why they are still among the living. The answer? Well, my dear readers, after so many years surrounded by the creatures of other worlds, you start to pick some things up. What do you suppose happens to those stabbed? Dismembered? Thrown into a lake? Where do their mind and soul go, their body being crushed by the water's surface, or their mangled parts flung into the streets? Their mind and soul stay here, waiting for their cold bones to finally find refuge in a coffin, awaiting some tears to be shed for them, waiting to be marked by a gravestone. Or, perhaps they remain here because they are in search of something. It can be an item as simple as a ring or a doll, or it can be something a lot more complicated, like their murderer, or even love.

They may be rough or even cruel, but they only want to rest, as everyone does, and the longer someone stays up past their bedtime, the crankier they get. Believe me, I have four young sons.

So, if you come across a ghost, be quick to discover the way they died. No ghost will be able to tell you directly where their bones are, but they can give you hints and clues. It's up to you to find the bones and bury them properly, host a funeral if you can, it doesn't even have to be a large one, and mark where you buried them. If their bones are already off the face of the living realm, help them seek out what they are staying here for. Lastly, don't forget them.

I leaned back in my chair, blinking for the first time since I started reading. It was better than I ever expected, his words like a lullaby, lulling me into a state of curiosity. As I read, I felt I could hear Mom's voice reading the words to me, like she used to do. Somehow, I felt the book held her in the pages.

Alright, but does this help me? According to G.K., ghosts look close to human, and they can communicate. The thing that attacked me doesn't match that description.

I hummed as I flipped through the short chapter, scanning the words once more just to make sure I didn't miss anything. I clicked my tongue in slight irritation. Nothing in the chapter matched what I had seen.

I got up and paced across my room, lost in thought. The chapter said very little about ghosts, leaving a big space for doubt. I bit my bottom lip, my feet slapping against the wooden floorboards. The book said ghosts stay because they wanted to be buried, or because they were looking for something. Was my ghost wanting its bones to be buried, or was it looking for something? And if it was looking for something, what could it possibly be searching for in my house?

Still with a hesitant mind, I strolled into the bathroom, where my encounter took place. Feeling slightly foolish, I examined everything in the room, checking under every nook and cranny, hunting for something that seemed out of place, strange, that didn't belong.

When I didn't find anything out of the ordinary, I wandered back to my room, scanning underneath my bed, combing through my books, and sifting through my closet. I even thought to check the folds of my dresses, the insides of my shoes, the pockets of my nightgowns. Nothing.

I huffed in frustration. *This is getting me nowhere. Think, Ivory, what happened this morning?* I paced awhile longer, my mind a jumbled mess. I took a few breaths to calm myself down, to quiet and control my thoughts. I needed to focus. *Well, it disappeared when Dean walked in, so maybe . . .*

I peeked out of my room. I had no clue how long Dean would be, or what my punishment would even be, but I urged myself to ignore those thoughts. I hoped I still had a while until he came back. At least, enough time to search his room.

I crept down the hallway, easing myself to a stop in front of Dean's door, my mind exploding with warring thoughts, an inward battle of right and wrong. I wasn't really allowed in my brother's room, but with a bit of internal convincing, I told myself it was for an important reason. With an intake of breath, I turned the knob.

Dean's room was about the same size as mine, perhaps a bit larger, lacking in decoration, a plain wooden square. For whatever reason, Dean liked to mount the heads of his hunts high on his walls. I thought it was barbaric, dead animal heads for decoration, but he explained it as "claiming his prize".

His closet was left wide open, practically screaming out to me. I stepped through the closet doors, exploring the interior, glimpsing everything I could. I checked the few clothes and shoes he kept there, ultimately ending empty-handed.

Standing on the tip of my toes, I tried my best to find something in the mounted heads, but yet again, I found nothing. I checked under his pillows and blankets, my blood rushing faster and faster with each second that passed by. The pressure of time weighed down on my shoulders, but I didn't want to give up. I wanted to see this through to the end, wherever it would take me.

I climbed down to my knees, scanning the dusty floor beneath his bed. At first, I was convinced that nothing was there, like everything else, but at the last second, a shadow caught my attention.

Pursing my lips, I reached under the bed, stretching for whatever the object was, dust clinging onto my skin. My fingertips came in contact with the object. It seemed like a box. My fingers curled around the edges, trying to get a good grasp. I pulled it out, and sure enough, it was a little rectangular box, one crafted from shiny metal baring one too many scratches. Layton's craftsmanship, it seemed.

I wiped the dust from the lid, studying it thoughtfully. I had never seen it before. What was it doing hiding under Dean's bed? Such a beautiful box didn't deserve to be treated like that. With a shaky breath, I pulled the lid off, a mix of anxiety and excitement brewing in the pit of my stomach.

Inside, the box was stuffed with paper. A stack of yellowed envelopes caught my eye, tied together with a small, fraying ribbon. I pulled the stack from the box, eyeing it curiously and set it down next to me. At the bottom, a photograph rested. I managed to free the photo from the box, careful not to rip it, though it was already torn at the edges. However, the longer I studied it, the more confusion clouded my mind.

It seemed like a family photo, the color faded by age. A large family stood in front of a modest, brick house, a yard full of flowers and bushes behind them. A man, a woman, two young boys, and one very little girl posed in front of the house. I squinted at the man in the photo. He seemed so familiar, broad-shouldered, short beard, wide chest.

It can't be. Is that . . . Dad?

My eyes flew to the woman holding his hand, her naturally tan skin, her brown hair long and wavy, like Layton's, full face, slim frame. She wore a casual beige dress, her eyes lit up with a smile. It was an infectious smile, one that people miles away could see.

I couldn't believe I didn't recognize her at first, calmly reminding myself I hadn't seen her for so long. But there she was, my mother. Seeing her again reminded me of how much I didn't look like her. Nobody would ever be able to guess that I once belonged to that woman.

I studied the young boys, Layton and Dean. They were so small, I hardly recognized them as well. Their faces were pudgy, their eyes wide with wonder that every little boy seemed to have. Both of them held fake wooden swords in their hands. I wracked my brain trying to remember seeing such swords, but none came to mind. They seemed so small, so happy, it was impossible that my brothers could have possibly been the same boys as the two in the picture.

Then, there was the last little girl, but the moment my eyes fell on her, I knew she wasn't me. For one, she had that same natural dark skin Mom had, and dark brown hair that curled around her ears and neck. She wore a frilly, pastel pink dress that fell to her knees, her stockings white as linen. When I examined closer, I noticed that she too had dark brown eyes.

Who was this girl? Clearly, she wasn't me, so who? Where was I? And where was the photo taken? We had only ever lived in Cyrene, in the wooden house that I had been stuck in over the years. I searched for clues signifying the identity of the girl, her and the house behind them unrecognizable. I was sure I had been born by the time the picture was taken, so where was I?

With a dull panic, I flipped the photograph over and found something scribbled on the back.

17703, Lockdale.

An address.

Lockdale was just a town over. It wouldn't be hard to find and wouldn't even take me long to get there. Suddenly, this wasn't about the ghost anymore. Whatever I had uncovered, it was a lot bigger than the ghost. Swallowing, I took a deep breath in an attempt to calm down, telling myself that I would figure out the meaning behind the picture. I kicked the box back under Dean's bed and picked up the envelopes, hoping to find some explanation. I gripped them tight against my chest as I returned to my room, telling myself not to draw conclusions.

But what if I never belonged in the first place? What if that girl was—

Stop it, you do belong. This is your house. You are right to be here. Layton and Dean are your brothers. Mom and Dad are your parents. Or, are they?

I slammed my door behind me and practically tore the ribbon from the envelopes. They all had already been opened long ago, each one torn and ripped. I plucked the first one from the stack and let the rest drop on my desk.

My fingers tingled as I slipped them through the ripped envelope, pulling out a folded paper. It too was yellowed with age and wrinkled like an old shirt. I unfolded the crisp paper, trying to smoothen the wrinkles and found a page full of words written in black ink. With trembling hands, I read the first line.

Dearest Gethan Kementari,
Gethan Kementari.
G.K.

6

My blood seemed to run cold as I read over the name again and again. This whole time, Mom knew G.K.? How had I never heard of him or seen him before? I forced my racing thoughts to quiet in order to read the rest of the letter.

Dearest Gethan Kementari,

Thank you for sending that book, I plan it to be the perfect gift for my youngest. Her mind works differently than the rest of my children. I'm sure she would love to meet you. She's not tainted by the lies of the king, unlike my sons and husband. I hope to keep her that way forever. I wish I didn't have to leave her behind, she's like me in so many ways, but she's young and naive. I want to tell her, explain, but I don't think she'd understand. None of them would. Perhaps if she came with me. I know you're leaving your sons behind, but I don't want her being influenced by Jakob any longer. I know she would grow to love you more than she ever loved him, and we could start a new life, just the three of us, somewhere far away. Whatever your answer, there is one thing I'm sure of. I can't stay here any longer. This will be my last letter. I'm ready for you.

Confusion swarmed my head. What did Mom mean she was "ready for him"? I frantically searched for a date, trying to put the letter in perspective to the day she died, but no date caught my eye. The letter seemed scandalous, but surely it wasn't what I was thinking. Surely, it couldn't have been.

Reaching for the next letter in the stack, I urged myself once more not to jump to conclusions, fear dripping into my stomach like drops of acid. This one was from G.K. himself.

Dear Silver Morrow,

You must wait a little longer, I'm afraid. I know how many times you've asked me, and I know how many times I have replied with the same answer, but please, I promise you it won't be much longer now. Everything will fall into place. Just think, a bit more time waiting versus an eternity with me. Trust me, it'll all be worth it in the end. Those soldiers are getting closer to knowing our whereabouts. It won't be much longer until they are found. After all, my family is composed of illegal wizards. Even if they are young, they'll be arrested, and the two of us will be long gone. It'll be perfect, and I only need a little more time. You can manage that, can't you? I'm sending you a book I wrote, perhaps that will speed the clock. Know the book well, it will explain things you'd never learn from anywhere else. Until I see you again.

G.K.

With panic steadily rising, those words nowhere near as comforting as G.K.'s usual words that I had come to know, I rummaged through the rest of the letters, discovering all of them were written by G.K. Written by him, but received by my mother. Why was Mom's last letter to him still at the house? Why was it not sent? Did she die before she even got the chance to send it?

Who cares? She tried helping an illegal wizard! And maybe more than just help him. . . .

Yet, one part of me still wanted to believe it was not what it seemed. There had to be some explanation. A brother, an old friend, a cousin twice removed, anything other than what I was suspecting. She had always told me wizards weren't the villains; I had to trust her. I thought the other letters would surely explain everything, but as I reached for the next one in the stack, I heard the unmistakable slam of the front door. I froze, a melody of footsteps approaching.

With blood rushing, I threw the letters in the one drawer of my desk, covering them with loose sheets of long-forgotten math. Just as I slammed the drawer closed, a knock at the door resounded through my room.

"Ivory, may I come in?" Layton's voice. *And he doesn't sound mad. Oh, that's bad. That's really bad.*

"Y—yeah, go ahead," I said, eyeing the drawer apprehensively.

In walked my older brother, his face suspiciously blank. I stood awkwardly against my desk, my hands behind my back in the most innocent manner I could think of. Panic thundered in my chest like a raging storm, my thoughts a spiral of sirens and alarms.

"Come to the kitchen with me," he said, almost monotone. "We brought back pastries."

I nodded, swallowing as I followed Layton into the kitchen, wringing my skirt around my hands. Dean was already there, seeming to be purposefully avoiding eye contact. On the counter, a bag filled with sweet-smelling cakes sat, but at that moment, cake was the last thing on my mind.

"Sit down, Ivory. We need to talk."

I took a subtle deep breath before I slid into my chair, glancing down at the pastry already waiting for me.

The two of them sat calmly, causing my anxiety to rise steadily. They had never taken the calm approach with me, albeit, I had never broken the biggest rule set in my life. Or at least, I had never been caught.

"Look, is this about the—"

"The *what*, Ivory?"

Yup, definitely angry.

"The, uh, rule-breaking, and the whole, uh . . . ," I trailed off, my cheeks burning as the word "ghost" came to mind. Thinking about it, the whole notion seemed a little foolish, but I had reason to believe it. I saw the creature with my own eyes, and so did Dean, no matter how much he refused he did.

"What's the one rule we set?" Layton asked, reaching into his pocket and fishing out a small flask. His emergency flask.

"Actually, Dad was the one who started it," I mumbled, gripping the edge of my seat tightly. "You're only following in his footsteps."

"Will you stop being a child? You're sixteen now, gods!"

"If I'm so old, then why can't I leave, like every normal human being?" I exclaimed, throwing my arm in the direction of the door.

"You can't, Ivory. If you haven't noticed, you aren't normal. You never *were* normal, and you never will be!" Layton shouted.

"Layton!" Dean cried, gripping onto Layton's shoulder tight. A look passed between the two of them before Layton shook his hand off and slumped into his seat, sipping his liquor quietly.

I watched this transaction in confusion, as though there was something I was missing. Layton took a small intake of air before he spoke again.

"I didn't mean it that way."

"What Layton was *trying* to say was that you know why you can't leave. Do you know how quick people could react to someone who looks like you? And if they somehow figured out about—" he cut himself off, his eyes flying to anywhere but me.

"About my lack of heart," I finished for him, my tone impatient and cold.

"Yes, about, uh, that. If we don't know where you are, then we can't protect you. That's why you can't leave. Not until we find a solution."

"And where is this solution going to come from?" I knew I was just being cruel, but I found the anxiety in my stomach had turned into burning anger, and it was easy to allow my temper to take control.

"Peyton Payne, of course." But even as he said it, he didn't sound too sure of himself.

It took everything in me not to roll my eyes. Instead, I picked at the pastry absentmindedly, the sugary scent barely registering in my brain. I knew a punishment was not far off. I wished they would just tell me so I could get back to the letters. The letters, hidden in Dean's room, in a box crafted by Layton. Mom's words suddenly filled my head, along with the photograph of the little girl who was clearly not me.

Perhaps if she came with me. That girl who clearly wasn't me. *I know she would grow to love you more than she ever loved him, and we could start a new life, just the three of us, somewhere far away.* Just the three of them, far away.

"I thought you liked sweets. Why aren't you eating?" Layton asked, tearing me from the storm of thoughts raiding my mind. He lifted the flask to his lips.

"Was I . . . adopted?"

Layton's eyes grew wide as he choked on the liquor, coughing and sputtering. I leaned back in my chair, shocked. I had never seen Layton choke. He set the flask down quickly and stood up, drawing in a deep breath, his hand on his chest. Dean stood, too, his eyes glazed over with worry. They caught each other's eyes, a silent conversation passing between them. Layton cleared his throat a few times, before chuckling slightly. Dean joined in, clearly trying to fight his oncoming fit of giggles.

"Where did you get that idea?" Dean asked, shaking his head, his smile more full of ridicule than amusement.

I opened my mouth to say something, but nothing came out. Instead, my cheeks began to burn, and I wished I hadn't said anything at all in the first place.

"I—uh," I stuttered, my eyes flicking around the room, "I found something. A picture."

The laughing ceased, the room suddenly so quiet, I felt I could've heard the heartbeats of my brothers standing all the way on the other side of the room. The two shared a quick, perplexed glance as if they knew exactly what I was talking about.

But the picture looks so old. Surely, they don't know. It looks like it hasn't been touched for years!

"Where did you find it?" Layton questioned, his voice set like stone.

His sudden change of tone frightened me, the hairs on the back of my neck standing up straight. When I spoke, my voice was quiet, wavering.

"In a box. I found it—"

"Were you in my room?" Dean thundered.

I shrunk back in my chair, fear seeming to swallow my stomach. There was no way to escape the conversation now that I had brought up the box. They already knew. My silence answered his question.

"What were you doing in my room?" Dean's face twisted with anger as he took a few quick steps toward me.

I jumped out of my chair and whirled around it, using it as a shield. "I was just—"

"Where is it?" he demanded, and before I could say anything, the two of them were marching straight toward my room.

I rushed to slip past them and block my door. "Wait, please, I didn't mean to—"

"Get out of the way, Ivory," Dean growled. He grabbed my wrist roughly and pried me from my door, shoving me to the side as if I were a mere rag doll.

I stumbled as I tried to regain my balance, rubbing my wrist softly, traces of shock flickering in the pit of my stomach. Whatever the photograph and the letters meant, Dean and Layton clearly never wanted me to know. My panic rose higher. Was I right about Mom? Why would they want to hide something like that from me?

I shook the thoughts from my head, forcing myself to calm my breathing as I stepped into my room. Of course, Layton was the one who found everything; the letters, the photograph, and it only took him approximately a few seconds to locate them. Clever Layton; I hated that he was so clever.

He pulled them out and observed the paper for a few seconds. He turned toward me.

"You read them, didn't you?" he asked, shaking the envelopes at me.

"I—I read a few of them. Not all of them," I sputtered out, holding my hands up in a surrender of some sort. I inhaled, mustering up the little amount of courage that I possessed. "Why? What do they mean? Why have you hidden them from me?"

"Why were you in my room?" Dean shouted instead of answering.

I gulped, my previous anger rushing back into me. "Who is G.K.?"

"How many of them did you read?"

"Answer my question!"

"Answer *my* question!"

"Don't you get it, Ivory? You want to know, then fine, we'll tell you." Dean pushed past Layton, a finger pointed at me.

I immediately backed away as he approached, stumbling out of my room. I had never seen him so angry. His cheeks flushed red, his eyes wide and bulging. His hands trembled. I rushed to create space between the two of us as he grew closer.

"Dean, no—" Layton reached his hand out to Dean, following us out of my room, but Dean just shoved it away.

"Shut up, Layton, she was bound to figure it out sooner or later!" Dean screamed, throwing his arms up in exasperation. "You want to know the truth? Fine! Those letters are from Mom's secret lover! The lover she's with right now!"

"Dean!" Layton roared, but it was too late.

The whole world seemed to halt, time nonexistent, Dean's screams echoing through the air. I clasped my hand to my mouth, afraid of being sick, the small dash of color draining from my face. *I was right. Mom did have an affair. But, did he say "now"?*

"What?" My voice faltered. "Mom . . ."

"She's a cheater. She left all of us for a wizard. She hated us, Ivory," Dean finished, his eyes flickering with contempt.

I glanced at Layton for some reassurance, but he was looking away, his eyes downcast. Dean was telling the truth.

I took another step back and ran into a chair. I plopped down, holding my head with one hand.

"Why didn't you tell me?" I squeaked, my anger long gone, dried up by Dean's words. Instead of being full of a raging fire, I felt cold. Freezing, empty.

"We thought it would be easier that way. You were so young, you wouldn't have understood. Dad wanted you to remember her as someone good. He wanted one of us to still think of her as our mother." Layton wavered.

His voice broke at the end of his sentence, and he whirled his head from my gaze, his hand hiding his eyes. I had never seen him break, or at least break right in front of me. He was supposed to be my older brother, wise and strong, clever and unbreakable. He was supposed to be the backbone of our family. At least, what was left of our family.

"So, Mom, she's still alive?"

They nodded.

"In the picture . . . who's that girl? The one in front."

Layton glanced down at the photo, studying it for a few moments. His head snapped up to me, blank. When I turned toward Dean, he wouldn't look at me, pain plastered on his face. I waited for the answer, the one I wanted to know more than anything else about Silver, but the answer never came. So, I chose a different question.

"Who is Gethan Kementari?" I asked, swallowing roughly.

"We don't know," Layton replied, defeated.

My eyebrows knitted together in suspicion, but I didn't have enough fire in me to push. I wasn't sure if I cared anymore.

"Were you ever planning on telling me?"

They didn't answer once more, just stared with regret in their eyes. I scoffed bitterly as I stood up, yanking the photo and envelopes from Layton's hand, striding past them silently. I retreated to my room, where I knew it was safe to cry, but instead of letting my tears flow, I grasped the letters and threw them across my room with all my might.

7

For hours, I raged. I ripped every last letter from G.K., as well as the unsent
one that Mom wrote. No, not Mom. She was Silver, now. She didn't deserve
to be known as Mom. She didn't deserve to have any recognition from me.

I flung myself across my room and kicked *Wizards* again for the fifth time,
sending it flying under my bed. I scowled, grumbling as I knelt down to
retrieve it in order to kick it again. I couldn't believe Silver gave the book to
me, a gift from her secret lover to pass the time until they ran away together,
leaving all of us behind. How could she have possibly thought that it was an
appropriate gift? Letting me believe for so long that wizards were the good
guys, that they were misunderstood, that they deserved my pity and interest.

I couldn't decide who I hated more. Silver, wizards, or my brothers.

How could Layton and Dean do that to me? They told me she was dead.
They let me believe the beautiful lie that she was a wonderful woman, that she
loved us, that she loved her life with us. They let me believe a lie my whole
life. I realized, with a drop in my stomach, that was why I never remembered
her being sick. She never was.

I gripped my hair in frustration. How could they do that to me? I kicked
the book again, watching it fly. What else could possibly go wrong? It wasn't
like my birthday hadn't been terrible enough!

I stomped toward the book, but instead of kicking it once more, I plopped down on my bed. My throat felt tight, like a hand had clamped itself around my skin, my chest feeling like it was full of flaming cotton. I bit my bottom lip, attempting to draw tears. Perhaps if I cried, I would've felt better, released the anger inside me, but my eyes remained dry.

"Ivory?" Layton's voice called through the door, hesitant.

I had locked it, though I knew they had a key to every door in the house. Still, they hadn't entered, even when they insisted to be let in. At least they had enough kindness to pretend I had privacy. I buried my face into my pillow, trying to silence my ragged breaths.

"I made dessert. Your favorite, banana pudding."

I glared at the door. Did he think banana pudding would fix this? There wasn't enough banana pudding in the world to fix what they had done. I heard a sigh from beyond my door.

"Please, Ivory, we're sorry. We should've told you the truth a long time ago, it's just . . . complicated."

Complicated? It would've been a hundred times less complicated if they had just told me the truth in the first place. It wasn't my fault it was "complicated". Layton continued on, babbling, but his words died at my threshold, never entering my room. Finally, after some time, his tuneless voice faded away.

I slipped from my bed, drowning in thoughts. In all the years spent behind doors, I had never felt so confined before. It wasn't just the locked doors and windows; it was my mind. I tried recalling my life before everything was ruined, but the more I tried to think, the more I seemed to forget. It was almost like my mind had holes blown through it, and my memories were scattered all over the wide expanse of my brain, into the dark cracks, never to be seen again.

I felt, somehow, I should've known the little girl with my mother's eyes, my mother's hair. Somehow, I should've known the house in Lockdale.

The house in Lockdale. The address.

I rushed to the pile of demolished letters, rummaging through until I found the photo, willing myself to ignore the faces of my parents. Somehow, I felt everything was connected to that little brunette, and I was going to figure out why. I studied the numbers of the address, a combination I swore I had never seen before. The only possible way of making sense of the picture had to be by my own hand. Layton and Dean would never tell me, not even after they told me about Silver. Perhaps I really didn't know everything. Yet.

I strode over to my closet, pulling out the darkest coat I owned and a pair of black slippers. I shoved my arms through the sleeves and stepped into the shoes. My mind, a never-ending spiral, captivated by the key still jingling in my pocket, finally focused on one thing. Escape.

I marched into my bathroom, photograph in hand, ignoring the light switch. A window suspended high on the wall, locked with the same lock every other window and door was equipped with, called out to me like the song of a lark. And that song would be my escape.

I shoved my laundry basket against the wall and climbed up, my free hand clasped around the cold key sheltered in my pocket. Fingers trembling, I rammed the key into the lock, and with a relieving click, the lock popped open, falling from the handle. With my knuckles, I pushed the window open. Instantly, a strong breeze flowed into the room, as well as a chorus of a thousand chirping crickets. I threw the photo into my mouth, biting the torn sides, needing a free hand.

For a moment, I wavered, glancing over my shoulder. I tightened my lips, thinking of Layton and Dean. I couldn't imagine their reaction when they realized I was gone. But what good would staying be? Would they tell me what I wanted to know? Probably not. Nothing would stop them from lying to me again. I swirled my head back around.

I hauled myself up on the ledge and swung my legs over the windowsill. With a shaky push, I fell from the window, landing on the edge of a flooded ditch. I lost my balance, my knees buckling from underneath me. I stumbled backward, my feet submerging in the muddy grass and dirty water. Shivers shot up my spine as my face scrunched up in disgust with the shock of the freezing muddy water. I exhaled a shaky breath, picked myself up, my shoes sliding right off my feet as I freed myself from the mud.

I tumbled forward, swinging my arms for balance, my once white socks plastered to my feet. I glanced back, but my shoes had already disappeared into the muck. I willed myself to forget about them and continue on, sticking the photo in my pocket along with the key.

My journey to town was brief, my walk more like a jog. I didn't care to marvel at the world around me. I just wanted to get to Lockdale.

As I neared the town, I spotted a few fading lanterns illuminating the streets, but the shadows of the shops and houses almost overruled the light. I shivered as I stepped upon the road, hugging my body tightly, my eyes darting at the slightest sound or movement. The song of chirping crickets filled my ears, the night's air chilling my fingers. In a matter of minutes, a pink hue dusted over my cheeks, nose, and ears. The walls of houses and shops seemed to close in on me, growing closer and closer until I was sure I would be crushed by doors.

Everything seemed so quiet, but now knowing the true manner of the town, it felt strange that Cyrene could ever be so silent. For a moment, I was sure I couldn't possibly have been in Cyrene any longer. After my day excursion, I never thought Cyrene held the capability of possessing so much peace.

The peace, however, abruptly ended as a barrage of noise cut through the silence. I jumped at the sudden commotion, whirling around to see a door swing open. I squinted, cautiously taking a few steps backward. A boy fell out of the doorway and faced me, his eyes wide with shock. Our eyes met and locked like we had put a spell on each other. It was Dulce.

I tore myself from his gaze, continuing on toward the edge of town quickly. My mind thundered with confusion. Why was he following me when he ran away from me just hours previous? I urged myself to ignore him, walking faster. First I only heard his distant footsteps, then his breathing, and suddenly, he was right beside me, drawing in deep breaths. I felt his eyes on me, or rather, my silvery hair. I didn't acknowledge him. Instead, I kept striding forward, quicker and quicker with each step.

"Are you . . . going to Naxos?" he asked, hesitant and quiet.

I considered to leave him unanswered. Maybe if I pretended he wasn't there, he would get the hint. However, somewhere deep down, I almost wanted to tell him where I was going. I wanted someone to care. To know.

"No."

He stayed silent, expecting me to continue. I sighed and pulled the photo from my pocket.

"I'm going here." I flashed him the photo.

He took it from my hand cautiously and examined it. A few moments later, he handed it back and I returned it to my pocket, tucking it safely inside the fabric of my skirt. The edge of town appeared in distant view, growing rapidly closer. I spotted a wooden bridge, moving to cross it, but stopped short as Dulce's voice vibrated through the chilly night.

"Is it true?"

I spun on my heels to face him, studying his wide eyes, his trembling hands. Whatever he thought of me had to be wrong. Why did I want to correct him? Why did I want him to know I wasn't going to hurt him? Anger lashed at my stomach.

"Is what true?" I snapped.

"That you're," he shifted from one foot to the other, "a witch."

I stepped on the bridge leading out of Cyrene and paused. "So what if I was? Would you stick me to a pole and burn me to a crisp?"

"I . . . ," he hesitated, "I don't know. I thought witches are bad. I thought they steal people's hearts."

My hand lifted to my chest, where I should have felt a thunderous heartbeat, but instead, it was as still as freshly fallen snow. Nobody had ever told me about witches stealing hearts. Was that even a thing, or just another stupid rumor? I knew I'd find the answer in G.K., but I suddenly trusted his words no longer. Now, I didn't know what to believe.

"I'm not a witch," I finally said. "I'm not anything."

"What do you mean? You're standing right here in front of me." His face scrunched up in confusion as he took a step forward. "Is there something wrong with you? Is that what you're saying?"

I resisted the urge to step back. "Have you ever met someone without a heart?"

His eyes widened again, not from fear, but surprise. "You mean you're . . ."

"Heartless," I finished for him.

He paused in stunned silence, his lips clasped together tightly. I waited for him to say something, the seconds ticking by. A voice inside my head told me to forget about him, to move on, but my feet remained planted. Deep down, I wanted to know what he had to say about me. The first villager of Cyrene to know my existence. Would he hate me just because I lacked a heart? What was I even expecting him to do?

"Did a witch steal it?"

"No," I replied slowly.

"Wizard?"

"No."

Again, he offered no other words. The voice in my head increased in sound, louder and louder until it was thundering in my brain. *Leave. Leave. Leave!* I gave in to the voice, turning my back on Dulce and stepping further down the bridge, disposing of all thoughts about him.

"Wait!" he cried.

I forced myself to stop, but this time, I didn't turn. I merely shifted my head to indicate I was listening.

"You never told me your name," he said quickly, breathless.

I glared at him through the corner of my eye. "Ivory."

"Ivory," he repeated. He seemed at a loss for words, scanning my face as if looking for some clue. A clue for what? I didn't know, and neither did I care. I took the opportunity to take off again. I was certain he wasn't going to stop me, and he didn't.

8

The sun peeked up from behind the hills, filling the sky with pure, scattered light, its hue illuminating every crevice of land. With breath paused in my lungs, I wished time would pause for a single second so I would have a little more time to gaze upon the shimmering horizon. Scarlet and violet painted the sky, mixed with a splash of bright yellow and deep orange, making it into a masterpiece.

Without even realizing it, my feet had stopped in the wet grass, my mouth hung agape in awe, my eyes widened in marvel. Of course, I had seen a sunrise before, but never at such an angle that made it seem like the sun was rising mere inches away from me. I felt if I just extended my hand toward the sky, I could've caught some light in my palm, letting it pour from in between my fingers like golden grains of sand. Watching it rise, I couldn't help but be overtaken by the thought that it was rising for me, and only me. That it knew my struggles, and despite its own struggles, it rose for me.

What a selfish thought. The sun rises for no one, and especially not me.

I glanced behind my shoulder to find Cyrene had long disappeared, but Lockdale still far from sight, though I knew it was close. I dragged my feet as I walked through the tall stocks of wet grass, the scent fresh in my nose. The field reminded me of Cyrene. The thought of my brothers slipped into my mind despite my constant struggle to keep them out.

Had they noticed I was gone yet? Maybe. Will they come after me? Probably. Was I going to let them find me? Definitely not.

A flash of rusty red caught my eye in the ocean of green grass. I shook my thoughts out of my head and hurried to approach it. I stooped down to find a lone brick, cracked and losing its color. My eyes examined each edge of my surroundings, but with no avail of finding where the brick could have come from.

I continued on and found myself running into more and more bricks, scattered about the grass like dandelions. A mix of curiosity and confusion swarmed my head as I walked. Where had they come from? Why were there so many and so far apart? It was almost like the bricks were forming some sort of path, but to where? And why?

I pressed my lips together, my eyes glued to the grass and my mind wandering. I almost missed the shape in the corner of my eye. My head shot up, and a house greeted me. Or, perhaps a cottage, in the far distance.

A smile burst on my face as a surge of triumph rose up in my chest. I retrieved the photo as I jumped through the grass, my feet wrinkled and cold. Finally, I had found it! Finally, I would get some answers!

But then I got my first good look at the place.

I slowed to a stop, smile waning, chest heaving. The house, one story, looked as though not a single person had lived there for hundreds of years. Half the windows were shattered, the other half majorly cracked, the front door barely hanging from the hinges. The brick interior was falling out of place, swallowed up by climbing vines and thorns, barely hiding the wooden structure underneath. It was destroyed. Demolished. Gone.

I glanced down at the photo in panic, but there was no doubt about it. They were one and the same. I shook my head slowly in disbelief, anger igniting in the pit of my stomach. I had spent so long trying to find it, even managed to break out of my own house, for *this!* It would serve me no answers.

Taking deep breaths, I approached like a wolf stalking a deer, full of hunger and malice. I allowed a thought, one hopeful thought, to slip into my mind. *Maybe I will still find an answer.*

I stepped upon the bricks leading to the house, and with a wavering hand, pushed the door aside, earning a long, eerie creak. The wood was wet to the touch.

I found the inside as hopeless as the outside, the walls peeling away, emitting a sharp scent of must. As if I were walking through snow, my feet left footsteps in the dust, the wood moist and sunken in slightly, moaning under my weight. It was barren and small, not a trace of life to be found in the dimness.

With my hope diminishing like a dying flame, I ventured on, fear slipping into my mind like a venomous snake. I knew I would find nothing to soothe my disheveled thoughts. Nevertheless, I ushered hope to keep its place in the tight corners of my head.

I blindly made my way through what used to be my family's house until I edged myself into a hallway. Groping the walls, I stumbled down, knees trembling. I wouldn't admit it, but I was scared. Terrified, in fact, and cursed myself for it.

I found my way into a room that might have once been painted blue but had faded so much, discerning the color was nearly an impossible feat. The curtains were torn beyond belief, and some type of singed wooden stand stood alone in the corner. Upon further inspection, I discovered it wasn't a stand. It was a bed. Or, at least, it used to be.

Panicked, I hurried out of the small room and into the next, which was in even worse shape. The walls were stained with black, and only one thing occupied the floor.

An upturned cradle.

My breath caught in my throat, and without another glance, I threw myself out, the barrage of panic pounding in my head breaking free. I ran down the hall, away from the room with no rational thought guiding my way. Across the main room, the door seemed to taunt me, so far away when all I wanted to do was get out.

When I claimed another step, the wooden panel beneath me gave out a shriek and I felt myself lurch forward. My right foot plunged downward, sending me crashing to the wet floor. The wood bit through my once white stocking, piercing the skin underneath like knives. Pain tore into my flesh like the claws of a wolf.

I trapped a scream in my throat, swallowing it back down, though the pain urged me to let it go. I remained crumpled on the floor, trembling, one foot dangling through the house. Tears pricked in my eyes as I used every ounce of energy to pull it free, yank it out, but it wouldn't budge. I was stuck.

I heaved in the musty air, attempting to organize my thoughts. I needed to be smart. Crying and screaming would get me nowhere. With agonizing slowness, I inhaled, counted to five, exhaled, and repeated until I could control myself again.

Try again, slow.

I listened to my thoughts, twisting my leg and driving myself up. The broken wood scraped at my skin as I pulled myself up, but I didn't let it stop me. When I was free, I rolled away, cold blood trailing down the side of my calf. I wiped my eyes, leaking with tears, and waited patiently until the panic coursing through my body subsided.

Once I finally felt in control again, I clambered to my feet. Pain shot up my right leg as I put pressure on it. I cried out, whimpering as I balanced myself on one foot. I hobbled past the puddle of blood I had left, toward the door.

I reached out and pulled it open, and found myself gazing into bright crimson eyes, the same eyes I had just seen hours ago. The ghost.

This time, I let myself release a shriek. The ghost, as tall and dark as I remembered it, reached out for me blindly, also as quick as I remembered it. I dropped, dodging its outstretched hand, and swung myself underneath its arm, ramming it into the door. With a loud crack, the door broke from its hinges, sending both me and the ghost hurtling toward the ground.

In a flash, the ghost vanished, leaving me crashing to the grass alone. In an instant, I was on my back, rolling out of the ghost's way. I scrambled backward, but I was too slow. It grasped onto my right foot, my blood soaking its hand. I screamed out in pain as it dragged me back into the rotting house, and I felt my feet lift off the ground. Black spots clouded my vision as my body slammed against the wall.

I crumpled to the floor, blood running down from my nose. The taste sent me grimacing in disgust, but as I reached up to wipe the cold liquid from my lips, a pair of hands clasped around my throat. Its eyes, deep and mesmerizing, burned into my gaze. I never expected them to be the last thing I saw before I died. I couldn't believe I actually wanted to find the ghost again. Of course, I would be that stupid.

If only I listened to Layton and Dean.

But then a barrage of noise entered my ears and suddenly I was back on the moist wooden floor, my vision fading in and out, gasping for air. Heaving, I blinked rapidly, searching for the ghost, but it was gone. In its place stood a blurry man.

The man rushed forward, gently resting his hands—unnaturally warm—on my back. He held a cloth against my bloodied face, muttering to himself in a language I couldn't distinguish. His voice, however, was unlike anything I had ever heard, a thick accent drowning in his words. Deep and raspy, it was the one thing keeping me breathing.

Where had he come from? I was too disoriented to really question it.

"Are you ok? You're bleeding pretty bad."

Finally, words I understood. I blinked a few more times, shoving away the cloth soaking up my blood. My sight returned to me slowly, but as everything cleared, I couldn't quite believe my eyes.

He was the strangest man I had ever seen, though I hadn't seen much men at all, with dark magenta hair that flowed down to his shoulders and a fuchsia jacket concealing a buttoned-up white shirt. His shoes were polished black, and I felt if I looked hard enough, I would've been able to see my own reflection in them. Glittering gems decorated his ears. His eyes, terrifyingly bright, glowed green.

"Who are you?" I choked out, struggling out of his gentle grasp. He swiped his hands away in an instant, scooting back a few inches.

"Alright, alright, take it easy. I'm just trying to help," he said, lifting his hands in mock surrender.

I scrambled to my feet, or rather, foot, and hissed in pain as I tried to steady myself. The man rushed forward, but I threw up my hand and he immediately stopped. His earrings jingled as he moved.

"I won't hurt you." He offered out his hand. "And I trust you will do the same, yes?"

I narrowed my eyes. In the state I was in, how could he possibly believe I had the power to harm him in any way? I wouldn't have been able to protect myself from a mouse.

"Not much of a talker, are you? Or are you worried I'll turn you over to the police? Well, rest assured, you are safe with me, whether you're legal or not," he continued, a smile spreading across his face.

"Legal? What do you mean legal?" I demanded. Did Layton and Dean already send a search party after me? Was I illegal now?

The man's face twisted with confusion, his smile fading, his white teeth hidden by his lips. "You . . . what are you doing here?"

"I—I—" I sputtered, then cleared my throat. "That's none of your business. What are you doing here?"

The man opened his mouth but closed it a second later, his eyebrows furrowed together. I waited for an answer, but instead, he merely flicked his eyes up and down, as if studying me. I took a hesitant step back, grinding my teeth together. Finally, after what seemed to be ages, he inhaled softly.

"You . . . you are a wizard, right?"

Shocked, I shook my head rapidly. "Of course not! What made you think I was?"

"Well, first of all, most humans don't go wandering abandoned houses crawling with Incarti!" the man exclaimed.

"Incarti?"

His mouth hung agape for a second. "You don't know? You were just attacked by them!"

"You mean the ghost?"

"Ghost?" He laughed, and his voice rang like a bell. "I was sure you were a wizard, but everything makes sense now."

Suddenly, something clicked in my head. His strange appearance, his voice, his clothes all piled up against me. He wasn't human, I realized. He wasn't there to help me. He was a wizard.

"You're an illegal wizard, aren't you? You'd be lucky if I didn't turn you in!" I didn't know what came over me, but anger filled my being as I spoke with him, a real wizard, the same as Gethan Kementari.

I had wanted to scare him, but instead of cowering in fear, the man laughed once more, and this time, it was filled with malicious ridicule. Shivers ran up my back and I instantly regretted my words. Of course, I would be smart enough to insult a wizard.

"I'll have you know I'm not illegal." He reached into his coat and pulled out papers—documentation and identification. In a flash, he tucked them back in place, smirking. "Apologies for mistaking you. I've just never seen a human with silver hair and crystal eyes. I just naturally assumed . . ."

My cheeks flared red, heat rushing to my face. He was messing with me now, I knew, but I still wanted the last laugh. However, I had run out of things to say, my mind fuzzy and frantic. Blood had begun to run down my feet. My anger was steadily being smothered by pain and fear. I realized I had no one to help me, and the only person around was a wizard I had already insulted. He was the only one who had the power to help me.

I dropped my glare, shaking my head, doing my best to avoid his burning gaze. "I didn't mean to be so rude, I just . . . don't like wizards."

"Have you ever met one?"

I considered his question. "Not really."

His eyebrow arched up, and I could feel myself blushing again. I had made myself a fool in front of him. All I wanted to do was get out of the house. To where? I had no clue.

"Well," he chuckled and extended his hand out to me, "my name is Alexei. A pleasure to make your acquaintance."

I resisted the suspicious glare fighting to take over my eyes, instead hesitantly holding out my hand. When he grasped onto mine, I felt his hands were still warm, inhumanly warm. I pulled away, my skin glowing hot red.

"Ivory Morrow."

His smile flickered for a second. "Morrow? *Morrow.* I feel like I've heard that name before."

I waited for him to continue, but he elaborated no further. I couldn't say the same. I had never heard anything like his name. It was just as strange as he was.

"Well, I'll remember sooner or later." He shrugged. "You should get out of here. The Incarti usually don't attack humans, I mean, unless they have a reason to."

"Wait, you know about them?" I asked, attempting and failing to keep my desperation for answers out of my voice.

"Of course I do. I'd be a lame excuse of a wizard if I didn't," he answered shortly.

"Please, can you tell me? Why is it following me? Why is it attacking me? How does it even know where I live, or where I've been going?" I rambled, spewing words out faster than the fall of rain.

"Woah, woah, calm down. What do you mean it's following you? Attacking you?" Alexei questioned, shaking his head, puzzled.

"I mean what I mean. You want the long story?" I crossed my arms, fighting to keep my tone from sharpening like a knife.

"Alright, alright." He huffed. "So that's why you're here. You're hiding from them."

"That is not why, and as I said before, it's none of your business. Please, just tell me how to get rid of them." I hated the slight beg in my voice, but it was impossible to maintain my pride when fear was steadily bursting in my stomach.

"Well, Snowflake, the question isn't how to get rid of them, it's what you did to anger them. Incarti never attack people randomly, especially humans. They only go after someone who had wronged them. They only want revenge for the sins of the people," Alexei explained.

I ignored his stupid nickname. "But I've never wronged a ghost before."

"Please," he huffed, "would you listen? They are Incarti, not ghosts. I guess I'll have to break it down even further. Incarti aren't physical beings. They are fragments of magic controlled by someone. Probably a wizard. Maybe a sorcerer. I don't know."

I closed my gaping mouth. "But I've never met anyone with magic either."

I wanted to add that I had never really met *anyone*, but I didn't want the strange wizard to know my life story. However, if he was capable of helping, I wanted him to know as much as he could about the situation.

He released a sigh, brushing his hand through his hair. "Then I don't know what to tell you. I guess just go home. Maybe they'll leave you alone. Where do you live?"

"Ha, like I'd tell you. You'd probably find my house and—and—"

"And what? Rob you? Eat your heart, or whatever you humans say about wizards? Well, sorry to disappoint, but I'd rather face the wrath of the Incarti than see you again."

Just as the words left his lips, the house began to tremble. I shrieked as the roof came caving down, dropping to my knees with my arms clasped around my head. When the dust subsided and I opened my eyes, I found Alexei's wish had come true.

All around, the Incarti filled the dim space of the crumbling house, eyes glowing blood red.

9

In the time it took me to blink, Alexei was by my side, hauling me to my feet. My mouth hung open in terror as I stood. They were everywhere, blocking off every possible way of escape. Alexei stepped in front of me, holding out one arm in a defensive manner.

"Stay back," he whispered and held up his other hand.

With a flash, his fist burst alight, flames licking up his fingers. I gasped and stumbled backward. I wanted to yell at him to run as the Incarti closed in on him, but my silent concern didn't reach him.

"As much as I'd love to see you terrorize this girl," he smirked and glanced back at me, "you've started to become really annoying."

The Incarti hissed in response, a high and shrill sound that seemed to rupture my eardrums. I clasped my hands over my ears, pitching forward. Alexei barely winced at the sound.

"Fine, be like that." He shrugged, and before I even realized what was happening, he had thrown himself at them.

My breath caught in my throat as I watched, helpless. The Incarti, fortunately, weren't good fighters, but they were large in number. Very large in number. However, they obviously weren't fireproof.

Alexei's fire spread like a plague, catching onto anything in sight, the walls, the floor, the Incarti, even Alexei himself. Smoke soon tainted the air, burning my eyes and filling my lungs. The monsters' shrieks resounded through the burning house.

Then, all of a sudden, the screams stopped and only the sound of the house being engulfed in flames filled my ears. My eyes watered, but every time I wiped them, new tears would spring up quicker than I could keep up with. I tried listening for the wizard, guilt weighing down my stomach, but all I could hear was the popping of the fire. Was he dead? He couldn't possibly be . . .

"Alexei!" I cried, blindly stumbling through the yellows and reds. Sweat poured down my face, the heat seeming to close in on me. "*Alexei!*"

A figure burst from the flames, pushing them out of his way. His chest rose and fell rapidly, sending my panic to accelerate. He rushed toward me, his breathing labored. His coat, caked in ash, was slipping down his shoulders.

"Are you ok?" I screamed.

"Aw, worried about me now?" he sneered.

A flicker of anger ignited in my stomach, but I forced myself to swallow it down. He was a wizard, after all. It was merely in his blood to be terrible.

He glanced down at my trembling hands and his sneer instantly melted away, his features softening, sparking confusion instead of anger inside me.

"C' mon, let's get out of here before it collapses," he said, the bite in his voice gone. "Let me help you, I don't think you can walk with your foot looking like that."

He reached out for me, but I pulled away. I didn't care about the blood sliding down my leg, I didn't care that there was no way for me to get anywhere by myself in the state I was in. I didn't want his help. Or pity, for that matter.

"I don't need your help," I spat. "Not from a wizard."

"Are you serious?" He scoffed. "I just saved your life! You'd be dead if it wasn't for me!"

I opened my mouth to retort something back, but a loud crack cut me off. The two of us paused and slowly turned our heads up to the ceiling. Fear froze my body.

"Run!" Alexei screamed, but I couldn't move. He screamed again, his deep voice echoing in every crevice of my mind. "Snowflake!"

He grasped my wrist and practically shoved me out the doorway, knocking the air from my lungs. We collapsed upon the grass as the house came tumbling down, sparks flying from the wood. I sucked in as much air as I could, trembling, coughing and staring wide-eyed at the house. If there had been anything else inside, I would never know. Nobody would. My stomach plummeted, sending a wave of emotion through my head, swelling and tightening my throat.

Beside me, I heard Alexei crawl to his feet, steadying his breath until his chest rose and fell naturally. He took a few steps toward the house slowly, and I didn't know if I was seeing right, but I saw him shaking his head, his mouth slightly hung agape. Something deep in his eyes flickered.

I pushed past my exertion to sit upright. "You know this house?"

"No." He hesitated, then turned to face me. "Do you?"

I glanced up at the house. Did I know it? My family lived there for years, but I never did. Alexei hummed lightly, his eyebrows raised.

"No," I finally responded.

I felt Alexei's gaze burning in my eyes for a couple of moments before I forced myself to look away. I could still feel his eyes, however, but I ignored him. Yet again, a wizard had stolen something from me. Dad had been right the whole time.

Wizards truly were disgusting thieves.

I clambered up to my feet, grinding my teeth in pain. Alexei moved to help me, but I instantly pulled away from him, glaring with the hatred of a thousand cobras.

"I told you, I don't want your help."

"Sure, you might not *want* it, but you need it."

"I don't ne—"

"Shut up, won't you? You're literally three seconds away from falling over," he snapped. "Why won't you let me help you, stupid girl?"

I took a deep breath, biting my lip to keep from recounting everything Dad had said about wizards. I already knew he had insane power—I didn't need to be the one at the receiving end of his flames.

"Fine, don't tell me." He sighed, then took a few steps backward. "Tell you what, if you can make it all the way over here, then I'll leave you alone, but if you can't, you have to accept my help."

"That's absurd!" I exclaimed, mostly because I knew there was no way I could make the few steps. "Why don't you just leave me here and go on your way? It's not like there's an audience you have to prove your unyielding kindness to."

"Because you're pathetic and I pity you," he answered simply, harsh and without missing a beat. "Now, what will it be? Can you make the walk?"

I clenched and unclenched my sweaty fists. My blood had begun to dry against my leg, but that didn't mean it hurt any less. Pain like knives drove up my leg as I prepared to take a step. My foot collided with the grass, a fiery agony shaking my body. Before I could prevent it, my knees buckled, and I crashed to the ground.

Like a crack of lightning, Alexei laughed, but I was too busy groaning to really take notice. My whole body felt like it was on fire, my vision unfocused. I sucked in a few deep, shaky breaths, trembling.

In a fit of anger, I slammed my fist against the grass. If I had been stronger, gotten out of my house more in my life, I would've done it. I would've been able to take the couple steps. I would've been able to prove to that stupid wizard that I was strong. I didn't understand exactly why I wanted him to think of me as strong, but I couldn't help it. I knew he didn't matter, that he was just a stranger and I'd never see him again, but the daunting thought that he would remember me as a pathetic, daft, little girl sent me driving my legs up.

"Hey, hey, wait!" Alexei exclaimed, and before I could shove him away, he had his hands grasped around my arms, hauling me to my feet. "Do you live near here? I'll help you home."

"Let me go! I'm not telling you anything!" I thrashed, but his grip was tight.

"You want me to drop you?" he asked, a dangerous edge to his voice. He loosened his grip on me, causing pain to creep back into my feet.

"Wait, wait, please—" I stammered, and he grabbed me again, supporting even more weight than before.

How was it that he was cruel and kind at the same time? He sent my mind reeling in confusion. What good what it do to help me? He obviously disliked me and didn't even try to hide the fact, but that didn't explain why he was so willing to help.

"Cyrene. I live in Cyrene."

He clicked his tongue in irritation. My stomach dropped.

"I can't get in Cyrene."

"Why not?" I asked.

"I don't have the documentation and papers. I never bothered, Cyrene is the hardest village to get papers for. Well, other than Embrasia. And I don't intend to break the law today."

"Oh," I uttered, and a faint, familiar flicker of anger returned to me. Not anger for wizards. Anger for the king. For a second, I was back on the wizards' side, like how my mother taught me to be. "That's . . . stupid."

"I thought you didn't like wizards." Alexei chuckled.

"I—oh, never mind! I guess I'll have to go alone, then," I said, the moment of Silver's influence on me over.

"How? You can't even walk," Alexei said. "It'll take all day and night to walk to Cyrene. The best bet is to go to Lockdale. We can figure something out there."

"No!" I cried, then awkwardly cleared my throat. "I mean, I—I can't go."

"What, why? You need identification and papers to get in, too? I thought you said you aren't a wizard." Alexei's eyebrows rose as he shook his head in confusion. In his voice, I could hear a trace of exhaustion.

All at once, I remembered my brothers, how their voices always sounded like that. They had lost patience with me too.

"No, no, never mind. Lockdale's fine," I said, ignoring the blaring sirens in my head. My whole life, I had been told to never let anyone see me. Going to Lockdale would completely contradict everything I grew up with. Dad's rule would no longer matter.

Alexei studied me for a moment, the corners of his lips pointed downward. He sighed and shook his head. He shifted me to his left side, one arm curled around my waist. Out of panic, I wrapped my right arm around his shoulders for extra balance. Up close, he smelled of whiskey and something else. Something incredibly sweet.

As I was distracted with the scent, he pulled out a large crystal from his jacket. Translucent, it glittered in the sun. I gawked at it, curious.

"What is that?" I inquired, peering forward slightly to get a better look.

"A magical artifact," he answered, and with a disappointed sigh, added, "my last one."

"Can't you get more?"

"No."

"Where did you get it?"

"That doesn't concern you." A twinge of irritation slipped into his voice. Clearly, it was a touchy subject.

"Well, what does it do?" I asked.

"You're not going to like it, but it's the only thing I can think of right now," he responded. "This crystal is connected to anything the owner chooses. When used, it'll transport you to the spot you chose, but only that spot, and it can only be used once. The spot I chose is in Andros."

I blinked, fighting to keep my fascination from taking over. I struggled to remember I hated wizards. When I spoke again, I tried to keep my voice even.

"What's in Andros?"

"I have a shop there. It's where I live," he replied. "I might have some books on the Incarti, and I don't trust leaving you here."

"Why not? I'm perfectly capable on my own." I scoffed, crossing my arms.

"Fine, lead them right to you with the smell of your blood and fear. See how I care." He shrugged and turned to walk away, folding his hands behind his back as he strode, leaving me to watch his bedazzled coat swish behind him.

"Wait!" I cried, cursing myself as I let panic slip into my voice. "They can smell fear?"

"And blood. Like sharks, except I don't know if sharks can smell fear. Though, they are much worse than sharks, but if you're perfectly capable, then I'll leave you to it. *Au revoir!*"

I took an adrenaline step forward, hand outstretched. "Then don't leave me here! What am I supposed to do?"

"You can be smart, for once, and realize the world is a lot worse place than you think it is. What fool declines an offer of help? Get some sense in your head. Or, you can continue being stupid and turn up dead before you even realize they've found you again. Your choice."

"Fine, I'll go with you, but what's in it for you? I wouldn't expect a wizard to go galivanting the world looking to free the people of their struggles."

He pretended to look offended. "You wound me. Of course that's what I do. I told you before, it's because I pity you."

"I'm not falling for that. Why are you really doing this?" I asked.

"I'm going to grind your bones and make bread with them," Alexei replied, smirking. "Or, I'll take your firstborn child and lock her up in a tower."

"You're despicable."

"The word you're looking for is charming." He flashed his teeth at me in a wide smile. "Don't worry, I'll throw you on a train right back to your precious Cyrene the second I figure this out. Are you ready?"

"You still didn't answer my question."

"We're going anyway. Are you ready?"

I failed to mention Cyrene didn't have a train station, I realized, but instead of telling him that, I nodded briefly, holding the best glare I could manage.

"Good." Alexei smiled.

The next thing I knew, he threw his hand up and crushed the crystal in his palm, sending shards raining down on the two of us. Alexei squeezed me to him tightly as a flash of light erupted from the crystal. I hid my face in his coat, clenching my teeth. For a moment, I felt like I was weightless, free falling. I muffled a scream in the wizard's coat, gripping onto him so tight, my knuckles turned white.

Then, it was over. I stumbled as my feet hit the ground again, but Alexei remained still as ever.

"Welcome to Andros," he said.

Slowly, I peeled my face from him, my eyes adjusting to find I was no longer in Lockdale. A breeze ruffled my hair, and I realized we were standing atop a balcony. Below us, the largest city I had ever seen stood tall, people and carriages filling the roads, trains whistling from a distance. It was colorful, each shop a different, vibrant hue, spanning miles and miles into the horizon. It smelled different than Cyrene, not wood and pine. Like Alexei, it smelled sweet, but a different sweet, a softer and more familiar sweet. I had never heard of a city called Andros, but as I stared at it, I realized that it felt strange to me. Foreign and expansive, but deep down, a feeling I couldn't quite place filled my being. I didn't know what it was, but it told me something.

For some reason, I felt I belonged there.

10

Though I wanted to gaze upon the city longer, Alexei turned from the railing and opened a giant glass door that led into his house. It was dark when we entered, but as we walked past the walls, bright lights lit up, casting a colorful glow that illuminated the hall. I glanced around in search of the source of light and realized the walls were embedded with hundreds of gems and jewels. Glowing gems and jewels, glittering and glistening, beautiful and strange, but Alexei stalked right past them, so fast I couldn't get a good look.

In the corner of my eye, I spotted a door, the only door on the upper floor. Alexei pushed past it, practically shoving me along, and led me to a winding staircase. As the two of us made our way down slowly, I wondered why the sudden increase of speed. I swallowed my anticipation as we stepped down the last step.

The lower floor was made from wood instead of bedazzled walls, but the wood still glistened with a fine polish, unlike my home in Cyrene. It was large, two huge windows letting light pour inside, shelves upon shelves filled with multi-colored bottles of all sizes lined up against the walls. A cluttered desk held books, paint, screws of all kinds, and papers. I tried to ignore my curiosity, but all I wanted to do was pluck those books right from Alexei's desk and allow myself to drown in words.

With one foot, Alexei dragged a chair out and set me down. "Let me find the bandages. I know they're around here somewhere." He rummaged through the drawers of the desk haphazardly, throwing the contents inside to the ground without much care. He groaned as he checked a drawer he had already searched, the gears in his eyes spinning rapidly.

"They're over here," a voice, small and airy, called.

I whipped my head up, unaware there was someone else in the room with us. However, as I scanned the room, I found nobody was. I glanced around in confusion, a spark of fear in my stomach, but I couldn't find the source of the voice.

Alexei pushed in the drawers with a sigh and crossed the room, over to one of the shelves. He extended his hand out with a smile.

"Thank you, Vince," the wizard said, and when he turned back toward me, I found he held a roll of bandages in his hand.

Puzzled, I craned my neck in an attempt to find where he had obtained the roll and caught a flash of movement. Something definitely was there.

"Don't look so scared." Alexei laughed as he knelt before me. "It's just Vince. He's my helper. You can come out, Vince."

I watched the shelf apprehensively and nearly jumped when the bottles began moving, separating to make space. A little figure squeezed out from in between the bottles and vials. I bit back a gasp. A little man wearing a professionally tailored suit and a black top hat hopped from the shelf and approached the two of us. His hair, black like a raven's feathers, swished at his neck, his skin like that of marble, and his eyes as blue as lapis lazuli. However, as he grew closer, I realized his hair really *was* made from raven feathers, his skin of marble, and his eyes of lapis lazuli.

I gawked as he stopped in front of me, grinning to reveal a set of literal pearl teeth. He bowed dramatically, even removing his hat. When he straightened himself up, he flicked his wrist and the hat flipped back onto his head. I marveled at the little man. He was like something straight out of a fairy tale.

"Vince, at your service," he said.

My face broke out in a grin that I had no chance of fighting. "Very nice to meet you, Vince. I'm Ivory."

"A lovely name. Did you know I used to be made from ivory? But then I broke and now I'm all marble, see?" He rolled up his sleeve to reveal his marble skin. "Alexei said he would make me a new outfit, one with a cape. I've always wanted a cape. Oh, I should ask for a cane, too!"

"Vince, I need a washcloth and some cool water. Would you mind getting them for me?" Alexei asked quickly before the little man could fit in another sentence.

"I'm on it! I'll get the alcohol too!" he called as he ran into a door on the opposite side of the room.

"I didn't say alcohol!" Alexei shook his head and turned to me with a sheepish grin. "He's a really good assistant, but he tends to be quite the chatterbox."

"What is he?" I asked, failing to keep the awe from my voice.

"Well, technically, he's a doll, but I found most of them don't like being called that. I made him. I made all of them," Alexei answered, a slight smile tugging at his lips.

"There's more of them?" I questioned.

"Yeah, somewhere hidden around here. They're quite shy, but they'll come around soon enough. I'm sure they'd all love to meet you."

"Really? Me?"

"Well, yeah, of course. They like stories, and I'm sure you have plenty to give." Alexei shrugged.

My brief excitement disappeared. I frowned, fumbling with my tattered skirt. I would've been more than happy to meet them all, but with a sinking disappointment, I realized I didn't have any stories. Nothing had really happened to me in my sixteen years of living. Unless they wanted to hear how I passed the days trapped behind locks, but I doubted anyone wanted to hear that.

"What, did I say something wrong? You don't have to meet them if you don't want to," Alexei said, noticing my sudden silence.

"Oh, no, no, it's not that." I sighed, shaking my head slightly, my eyes glued to my lap. "I don't have any stories to tell."

"What do you mean?"

I glanced up to find Alexei staring at me, his eyes as intense as a wildfire. An overwhelming desire to tell him *something*, just a small piece of explanation, washed over me, so strong I couldn't fight it. With hesitation, I parted my lips and sucked in a small breath, the words on my tongue.

"I didn't know if you wanted the blue towel or the pink one, so I grabbed both, I hope that's ok." Vince's voice seemed to come out of nowhere, and suddenly, he was standing right behind Alexei.

I clasped my lips tightly shut. What was I thinking, telling a wizard my life story? And for what? Pity? A wizard didn't need to know anything about me.

I was already crawling with nerves knowing the fact he knew my name and my home.

"That's fine, thank you," Alexei said, a very subtle twinge of irritation in his voice that I would've never been able to catch had it not been the same tone Layton often took with me.

Vince smiled and nodded. Beaming, he climbed up the handles of the drawers and sat on the edge of the desk, facing me. I eyed him wearily, finding myself no longer wanting to talk at all. I didn't trust myself with words.

"Where did you come from?" he asked, swinging his legs like a child.

"Cyrene."

"Where's that?"

"By Lockdale."

"Where's that?"

"Vince," Alexei huffed, "she's in a lot of pain right now. She can talk to you later."

For only a brief second, he was quiet. "Why, what happened? Did someone hurt her? Was it Embrasia? Does she not have papers?"

"I'm *not* a wizard," I burst out, clenching my fists. "I'm a human. Human! Is it that hard to understand?"

The two stared at me with identical wide eyes, silent. Their eyes caused my anger to flicker out, and I realized what I had said. Before I could fit in anything else, Vince and Alexei locked gazes, and the little man hurriedly stammered out an excuse and disappeared back behind the shelves.

"I—I'm sorry," I whispered, my hands trembling as I uncurled them. "I didn't mean to yell."

"No, no, you already told me you don't like wizards. I can understand if it makes you mad when you're mistaken for one," Alexei said. "I think your foot is twisted. It'll take a lot longer to heal if it is, and that wound might get infected if it's open for much longer. I hope I won't have to stitch you back up."

I swallowed nervously. "You know how to do that?"

"Of course. It's just like sewing," he answered shortly, and I felt my stomach lurch. "If you don't mind me asking, what *did* happen?"

I sighed. "I lost my shoes in a ditch. I fell through the floor. That Incarti attacked me and . . . tried suffocating me."

Alexei's eyebrows flew up. "So that's why there's blood on your face."

I reached up in an attempt to wipe it away, but it had already dried like plaster on my skin. Sitting felt so much better than standing, but the fiery pain didn't go away in my feet. It was more pain than I had ever experienced, but a small part of me was thankful for it. The pain left a memory other than my room, sparked a fire in me.

It showed me I had *lived*. And I wanted more of it.

"Here," Alexei said, snapping me from my thoughts and kneeling in front of me.

He doused a cloth in the bowl Vince had brought, wringing it out carefully, and slowly brought it to my face. So close, I could hear the rhythm of his breath, smell the scent of sweetness radiating off of him. I avoided his eyes, glancing around the room, but I could feel him studying me. I struggled to sit still under his gaze, Dad's voice echoing in my head.

No one is allowed to see you.

But Alexei was seeing me. Every inch of my face, in fact. I wondered how I looked to him, blood on my face and irritated eyes from crying so much, silver hair in tangles, one foot twisted the opposite way, skin ripped open by bloody splinters.

A sudden heat rose to my cheeks. I didn't want him to see me like that. He was the first person to not know me as the witch hidden in the house on the outskirts of the village. He had never heard the rumors of me. He didn't even know the rule I had lived under for most of my life. What did I look like to him? Who was I to him?

When Alexei pulled the cloth away, my face clean of blood and glowing pink from the scrubbing, he carried a strange look deep in his emerald eyes, a look I couldn't quite distinguish. I searched for clues in his face, but his expression remained unreadable as ever. He soaked the cloth back into the water, asking me to remove my sock.

As I peeled away the remainder of the sock, I winced in pain, feeling the sharp edges of the splinters embedded into the cloth dig into my skin.

"Wait, let me just cut it off. That'll be a lot easier." He stood and retrieved a pair of sewing scissors from a drawer. He knelt down again and slipped the cold blade beneath my skin and the fabric.

With ease, he tore it away, prying it from the dried blood. Hidden underneath, a cut ran up my calf, red and gushing. I hid my eyes in my hand, the sight leaving my face pale and flushed. My stomach knotted tightly, as did my throat. I wasn't sure if I had ever seen anything so gruesome.

"You might need a few stitches, but it's not as bad as I thought, judging by the way you were walking earlier. This won't take long." He stepped back to the drawer, rummaged through a few of them, before pulling out a needle and thread.

My stomach dropped as I watched him pour alcohol over the needle and realized for the first time that he was being completely serious. He was going to stick a needle in my leg.

"Wait, wait," I sputtered as he returned to his spot in front of me.

"It'll only hurt for a little. It'll be a lot worse if we keep it open. I could pasteurize it instead if you'd prefer that?" With a cock of his eyebrow, he rose his fist and set it aflame, chuckling when I shook my head rapidly. "I thought so. Keep still now."

"Please, wait, wait, wait." I realized I was just stalling, but I couldn't help it, the words flowing out of me faster than I could control, my panic spiraling out of my grasp. My blood seemed to stop.

"The longer it's open, the higher chance you can die," Alexei mused, running the cloth over the wound to clean it, fighting my trembling hands as I tried to push his away.

"Are you sure there isn't anything else you can do? Something that doesn't require . . . needles?"

"What, you scared?" A smirk spread across his face.

I narrowed my eyes, scoffing as I realized seeing me panic caused him amusement. A flame of anger licked up my stomach, threatening to overfill my being. I curled my fists, biting the inside of my cheek for some other source of pain. But before I could spit something at him, he reached into his coat and pulled out a flask.

"This might help," he said, offering it to me.

"I don't drink."

"What do you do?"

"Not drink."

"Obviously."

Despite my wishes, a flare of amusement rose up in my chest, a smile threateningly tugging on my lips. I tried ushering the feeling away, but it didn't quite disappear. Like a dull knife, my panic felt subdued, still there, but not entirely. Not enough to cut, at least.

"You can do it now," I said, my voice surprisingly even.

"Are you sure?"

I nodded and bit my lip as I watched him thread the needle.

11

I pulled my head through the linen fabric of the blouse Alexei had left for me, my hair still dripping from when I bathed. After Alexei had sewn up my wound and cleaned it, he told me I could use the spare room downstairs. A spacious bathroom connected to the room, one with white tile and a bathtub as large as my bed at home. A large mirror hung on the wall, big enough to cover the door. And on the bed, a skirt and blouse waited for me.

As I straightened the skirt, a few sizes too big, I turned toward the mirror and allowed myself to take in my appearance. I didn't remember my eyes having bags under them, my skin glowing pink due to the steaming bath water. All I wanted to do was dive back into the tub, let the warmth sink into my skin, drown the pain. Perhaps if I stayed in long enough, the warmth would remain trapped in my body, and I would never feel the absence of heat again. Wishful thinking.

I forced my eyes away from the mirror, disgusted with myself. I had betrayed Layton and Dean, betrayed my father, betrayed myself. I had trusted a wizard, allowed him to take me to his home, accepted his clothes, accepted his help. A dull fire raged in the pit of my stomach, along with a thousand butterflies. The sensation left me nauseous.

He had seen my tears, my pain, yet he still didn't know anything about me, and I didn't know anything about him. I didn't trust him, but for some reason, I felt he trusted me. And I hated that. He had yet to insult me again, but I couldn't quite forget about his words back in Lockdale. It seemed he had completely forgotten about our exchange of insults. To him, they were mere bickering.

I limped to the door and exited, only to find Alexei in the room he had offered to me, unfolding a large comforter and throwing it over the bed. He whirled around as I walked out, and a small smile formed on his face. I fought back a frown.

"I hope this room's fine. I know it's a bit small," he said.

"It's fine."

It was two times bigger than my room at home.

"I just have supper finished. Can you make it to the dining room?"

"There's a dining room?"

"Well . . . where else would I eat?" Genuine confusion carried in his voice, and I had to remind myself that he had never seen Cyrene—small Cyrene with no anything.

"Nevermind. And yes, I can make it." I turned my nose up slightly, taking a few steps forward to show him.

He stared for a moment, opened his mouth as if to say something, but shut it quickly after. Together, we exited the room, with me limping behind him, and crossed the main room. I eyed the desk as we passed and found the bloodied needle still there. My stomach lurched violently.

That's why he brought me here. He's probably going to mix my blood in some potion and sell it to whoever wants to use its unnatural power. Now that he has what he wants, what is he going to do with me? Surely, he was messing with me when he said he was going to grind my bones . . . right?

He led me into what I figured was the dining room, a large area much bigger than the kitchen back at home. The table was long, spreading almost all the way across the room, already set with plates and silverware and glasses filled with red wine. A scarlet tablecloth rested upon it. A chandelier hung above it, and in the corner of the room stood an ancient grandfather clock.

I wondered why he would need such a large table when nobody else lived in the house. Perhaps he frequently had many guests? *Or I'm not the first one to fall into his trap.*

I tried shaking the thought out of my head. Aside from the occasional insult, he had treated me fairly well. I still didn't know *why*, but I intended to find out as quickly as possible. If not, then leave as quick as possible.

"Go ahead and have a seat," Alexei said, and with a snap of his fingers, a door on the other side of the room flung open. Trays of food flew through, landing gracefully on the table.

My mouth dropped in awe, but Alexei merely sat in the chair opposite of me on the other side of the table, his face blank as ever. When he glanced up at me, however, a look of confusion crossed his features.

"What?" He cocked his head to one side.

A nervous laugh escaped my lips. "What? What do you mean *what*? You just made the food fly from out of nowhere!"

He blinked as if he couldn't believe my words. "You really have never met a wizard."

"Well, I've met one," I said, allowing myself to take a seat. The velvet cushion sank beneath my weight. The chairs at home were all just wood.

"Really? In Cyrene?" He picked up his glass, swirling the red wine inside.

"Yes, he's the only wizard in Cyrene," I answered, shifting uncomfortably in my seat. Talk of Peyton Payne always riled me up in one way or another, and talking about him to another wizard helped in no way.

"Hmm, who? Perhaps I know him." He brought the glass to his lips and took a sip.

"Peyton Payne."

At once, he spat out the wine, choking, his eyes the size of the plates sitting in front of us. Quickly, he tore his napkin from his lap and muffled his coughs. I watched in surprise. No way did he actually know Payne.

"No wonder you hate wizards so much! He's a cheat! He'll do anything to keep you coming to him!" Alexei shouted.

"You—you know him? How?" I stuttered, shocked by his outburst.

In a mere second, the anger on Alexei's face disappeared. He cleared his throat and returned his napkin to his lap. It was as if someone had turned a switch in his head.

"Let's just say he cheated me out of a deal, and I haven't been able to find him ever since. But thanks to you, I know exactly where he is. I knew you'd prove to be useful." He said the words so casually, I didn't know if I ought to have been offended or simply ignored it. Those words were words that should've sparked another argument.

But I was too interested in what Alexei had said about Payne. *He's a cheat! He'll do anything to keep you coming to him!* Even give me a false diagnosis? Claim he couldn't help me?

"Can Payne actually do magic?" I asked, and even I heard the desperation in my voice.

"Last I remember, he was better with potions," Alexei replied.

What was the difference between magic and potions? Could one of them be the key to filling the unbeating hole in my chest? Could he have done something about it long ago? Did he ever truly know what was wrong with me?

A blind panic filled my body. All I wanted to do was head straight home to tell Layton and Dean about this new piece of information. Maybe if we threatened him with the thought of Alexei, he would speak the truth.

"Don't tell me you've wasted your time with him." Alexei groaned at the sight of my blanched face.

"My whole life," I whispered, and dropped my head in my hands. "My whole life."

Silence passed between the two of us as we both soaked up these words. Alexei seemed as shocked as I was, and when I glanced up, I thought I saw pity, true pity in his eyes. I didn't know if that made me feel better or worse.

I inhaled a shaky breath. "I have to get home."

I heard a breath almost as shaky as mine.

"I'll check for train tickets, but you can't leave now. You can barely walk and the Incarti have your scent. You're safer here."

"So?" I snapped. Why did it matter to him if I wanted to get in harm's way?

"So? You'd be dead before you even got home. Be smart, won't you?"

Anger lashed at my stomach, replacing my previous dread. One second he was kind, and the next he was cruel. What was his problem? Why did he have to act so difficult?

"It isn't your job to monitor my safety! How do I know you're not just like him?" I shouted and pointed an accusing finger in his direction.

"Believe what you want, but I'm not the one coning you out of your money." He glared, resting a hand to his chest. "Why do you need to be back so urgently? Someone dying?" His voice was full of ridicule that sent my blood rushing.

Me! Looking like this, living like this! I wanted to scream, but instead, I made a show of pushing my plate away and standing.

"Thanks for everything, but I can handle the rest on my own," I said, and strode out of the dining room, forcing myself to walk straight.

Alexei followed after me. "If you die, don't expect any grievances from me!"

"Wasn't counting on it anyway!" I called back.

Though just as I reached for the doorknob, a knock resounded from the other side. I recoiled back instantly, stumbling away as Alexei rushed past me. He looked through the small eyehole on the door and sucked in a breath.

"Who is it?" I asked nervously.

"Lockdale police."

I gasped. They were there for me. It only took so long for Layton and Dean to go to the authorities. As fast as I could, I scrambled underneath the staircase. Alexei turned and shot me a strange look, but before he could say anything, the police knocked again, louder.

Alexei opened the door to reveal two officers standing on his doorstep. They wore the standard Lockdale colors, deep blue and black, along with plastered frowns.

"How may I help you, officers?" Alexei asked in a tone so innocent, I couldn't believe it was coming from his mouth.

"Good evening, Mister Pen. We've been alerted that a sixteen-year-old girl from Cyrene went missing just a day ago. Her name is Ivory Morrow. There were signs of struggle at her last known residence, so we are led to believe she was kidnapped. If you have seen anything suspicious or might know any information concerning her whereabouts, a reward of ten thousand gold pieces will be cashed out."

The speech felt so monotone, I could tell it wasn't the first time he had said it. No telling how many houses he had given my name, age, and home. And ten thousand gold pieces? Since when did we have that kind of money? Unless there was even more Layton and Dean didn't tell me.

"Ivory Morrow, you say?"

For a brief moment, I nearly forgot how to breathe.

"I'm sorry, I haven't heard of her, but I'll keep an eye out."

"Thank you, Mister Pen. Good day." With that, the two officers tipped their hats and moved onto the next door. Alexei closed his door and whirled around to greet me, his hands on his hips.

"Now, you owe me," he said. "I could do a lot with ten thousand gold pieces."

"We don't have ten thousand gold pieces!" I exclaimed as I crawled out from under the staircase.

"You didn't tell me you were kidnapped." He quirked an eyebrow.

"I wasn't!" I shouted, throwing my hands up in exasperation. "But of course, they would think I was."

"Who are they?" Alexei asked.

"None of your business," I spat.

"Oh, officers!"

"Ok, ok, just shut up!" I glared as he laughed. "*They* are the ones I'm running away from in the first place. It's their fault I ended up in that house at Lockdale. It's their fault I ran away."

"How exciting. I thought you were just stupid, but now I get it. You're a runaway."

"Am not! I'm planning on going back . . . someday."

But now that Alexei had said it, I found myself liking the word. Ivory the Runaway. Deep down, I felt they deserved this. This was my ultimate punishment for what they had done, and I was not going back until they were groveling for my forgiveness. Finally, I was the one in charge.

"Well, whatever the matter, you can't leave now. Lockdale officers are swarming the streets. You'd get caught in a matter of seconds," Alexei sneered. "How rich are you?"

"I don't have one penny to my name, so stop smiling like that," I snapped.

Alexei was right though. If I wanted this game to go on longer, I wouldn't be able to leave his shop. The thought sent my stomach twisting. We could barely go for ten minutes without fighting.

"Well, looks like you're stuck here," Alexei said, a stupid, smug grin spread across his face. "And something tells me you haven't eaten in a while, so how about we get back to supper, shall we?"

12

"Try not to move too much or else the stitches might snap and I'll have to redo them, and frankly, I don't think you'd ever let me do that again," Alexei said as I walked through the door to the guest room.

I turned to glare at him, heat rising in my face. "No, I'd rather collect that ten thousand for myself than let you anywhere near me with a needle again."

"What are you talking about? It was a great bonding moment." Alexei smirked, crossing his arms. "You, me, some blood. What else could we need?"

"Make sure to warn me when you want to have another 'bonding moment'," I said, using my fingers to quote his words. "I'll know when to start packing."

"You'd never leave when the food here is so good. You were practically drooling over dessert. It's like you've never had an eclair before."

"Says the one who ate four of them!"

"What, are you jealous?"

I resisted a chuckle. "I hate you."

"I hate you, too." A bright smile flashed on his face. "Now, goodnight, Snowflake. Hope you're haunted by your dreams."

"If they have your face in them, then I'm sure they will." I smirked as the smile on his face dropped and shut the door before he could fit in another word.

"Good one," he called through the door, chuckling. "Night!"

I listened as his footsteps faded away, as did the sound of his snickering. I didn't realize I had been smiling until I crawled into bed, finding my cheeks aching. I rubbed my cheeks, willing myself to stay strong with an indifferent frown, but it was nearly impossible. During dinner, the angry tension between us slowly faded as our jabs became more and more humorous. I didn't know how, but Alexei felt more like a brother than my own brothers ever had. Siblings were supposed to insult each other, not lock each other in a house for most of their lives and tell them their mother was dead. No, only my brothers did that.

Beside the bed, a curtain hung, concealing a glass windowpane behind it. Apprehensively, I peeled away the curtain to reveal the window, somehow surprised to find that it did not, in fact, have a chain on it. Just simple locks.

I inhaled a breath as I unclipped the locks, shoving the window open. Sounds filled the room, train whistles, distant chatter, shoes clicking against the cobblestone road. The city burst with light, casting a multicolored glow over my skin, and I almost had to squint to see it all. The smells of a thousand different restaurants filled my nose, along with a hint of salt. It was all so overwhelming, I found my blood rushing and my breath hitching. It was so big, massive, in fact.

Above the lights and towering buildings, a sky scattered with stars and a glowing crescent moon filled my vision. So many years I dreamt of the day I would be free to gaze upon the night's sky for however long I desired. So many days I dreamt of being somewhere big, different, with sights I had never seen before, sights that only belonged in my wildest dreams.

Perhaps my dream hadn't come true, but for just one night, I could pretend that it did. Just for one night, Andros would belong to me, and only me, and maybe that would be enough.

With a half-contented sigh, I wrapped a blanket around my shoulders and crawled closer to the windowsill, resting my head against the pane. For one night, I would have this.

For one night, the moon, stars, and the city was mine.

. . . .

I opened my eyes to find myself trapped in the darkness. The city had grown quiet, the lights dimmed, and the smells had gone faint. Only the salty breeze and the sky remained in what was once a booming city. I never thought Andros would ever go to sleep.

I rubbed my eyes and sat up, stretching my leg out slightly. The pain was like a never-ending beat of wings, waves going in and out, needles and blades dancing in my blood. But I found my exhaustion almost greater.

With a yawn, I struggled to close the window and lock it back up. I threw the curtain back over the glass, moving to return to the center of the huge bed.

But that's when I heard the voices.

I froze, holding my breath. They were faint, so faint I wondered if they were even there. I squinted through the darkness to find my door cracked open, though I distinctly remembered closing it on Alexei's face.

Perhaps the wind pushed it open. Yeah, like that's likely.

I ignored the pulsing agony in my calf as I slipped out of bed, cautiously approaching the door. The closer I got, the clearer the voices grew.

"The police are already looking for her." Alexei's voice. "She claims she doesn't have ten thousand gold pieces."

"Do you believe her?" A woman's voice. Elegant, dark.

"It doesn't matter whether or not I believe her. The fact that she came from somewhere expensive is what worries me." A sigh. "She said she lives in Cyrene, but there's no way a girl who looks like that lives there."

"Embrasia?"

"Perhaps. I still can't believe she's not a wizard."

"What makes you think she isn't a witch?"

"If she were a witch, she would've healed herself long ago."

"Speaking of which," the woman's voice grew sharp, "why haven't you healed her? I know you're no witch, but you could've handled a twisted foot."

A pause. I leaned in closer, yet not quite daring to look through.

"She said she doesn't like wizards. She would never let me use magic on her." His voice was different, softer.

The woman seemed to notice. "That's never stopped you before."

"She's stubborn."

"So, like you?"

"I am not stubborn!" His voice rose, but he quickly quieted himself.

Another pause. I tried sinking back into the shadows, clutching a hand over my lips in an attempt to muffle my heavy breathing. I knew I shouldn't have been listening, but no matter how much I tried, I couldn't move.

"You *want* her to stay, don't you? You could've taken her heart long ago, yet she's still here. What are you going to do with her? Keep her like some sort of pet?"

"Of course not!" He sucked in a breath as he quieted himself once more. "I can't take her heart if she's from Embrasia, now can I? The second I let her go, she'll run straight to those blasted Magicians and they'll be swarming my door. *Again.*"

"You should've thought of that before you told her your real name. What happened to being Pen?"

"It just slipped, I couldn't help it. We can't do anything about it now. I don't have any of that Forget-Me-Not potion left anyway."

"So, what are you going to do? Her leg will heal sooner or later, and she'll start to grow suspicious. She already hates you."

"She was kidding."

"Was she? She's almost as heartless as you."

If I hadn't been so scared, I would've laughed. I squeezed my hand tighter against my lips, feeling my chest tighten with lack of air as I peered forward, just enough so I could see the two.

Alexei was still fully clothed, a flask clutched in his hand. I hadn't even realized he had been drinking the whole time. The woman, however, I found wasn't a woman. She was a doll. One of the diamond dolls, with amber hair, eyes of onyx, literal diamond skin, and a cerulean dress hemmed with gold. She stood atop the desk, her arms folded tightly across her chest. She was taller than Vince and somehow seemed older. More mature. More human.

"I suggest you take her heart before she realizes anything," the doll said.

"Then what? I just told you I can't let her escape."

Escape. I was trapped all along. I went from one prison to the next. A different type of pain washed over me, a pain that had nothing to do with my leg. How could I have been so stupid to believe I was really free? Maybe I was never meant to have freedom.

The doll parted her pristine rose lips. "The dead don't talk."

A gasp slipped past my lips before I could stop it, and their heads whipped around toward me. My eyes met with Alexei's, locked. I pulled away, but I knew I was too late. He had already seen me. He knew.

I slammed the door shut and fumbled with the lock until it clicked. His boots slammed against the wood, then his fists against the door. Now that I knew his true motive, there really was nothing to stop him from killing me.

"Ivory—"

"Leave me alone!" I cried, scrambling as far away from the door as I could. "You wicked wizard!"

I tumbled over to the window, tearing the curtain aside. Behind me, I could hear the door jiggling. Drawing in gasps of air, I struggled with the locks. Just as they clicked open, so did the door.

Alexei burst in and crossed the room in a matter of seconds. I whirled around, and even though I was no match against him, I lifted my fists. With a deep breath, I threw a punch, basically throwing my whole body at him. He caught my fist with terrifying ease, tightened his grip, and pulled my arms around my back.

With adrenaline coursing through my veins, I struggled against his grasp, wrenching my body left and right, kicking my feet as he hauled me in the air.

"Help!" I screamed as loud as my voice could possibly go. "Someone, help! Help—"

He threw a hand over my mouth, which gave me a perfect opportunity. I bore down on his skin, sinking my teeth into his hand so hard, the taste of blood stained my tongue. He cried out and instantly dropped me. I crumpled to the floor with a yelp of surprise, but before I could return to my feet, he had me back in his grasp, his bloody hand over my mouth.

"Stop struggling! Let me explain! I'm not going to kill you!" he shouted as he wrestled to keep me restrained.

I screamed against his fingers, attempting to smash his feet. *It's another trick! He's going to kill me!*

"Ivory, listen! I'm not going to kill you, just listen to me for one second!"

I ignored him just as my stitches snapped, sending blood pouring down my calf. For once, I could barely feel the pain and the absence felt strange.

"Fine, don't. Maybe this'll be more persuasive!" He pulled his hand from my mouth, but before I could scream, his fist burst aflame. The heat instantly stilled me as I felt it against my skin, drawing sweat. I clasped my eyes shut.

"Please," I whispered, "don't kill me, I swear I was telling the truth, and— and I don't know anything about any Magicians."

"Alright, alright, I'm only going to ask you once. Where are you from?" Alexei asked, his fist threateningly close.

"I told you, I'm from Cyrene! I ran away, I swear, I've never even been to Embrasia. I—I've never been anywhere but Cyrene!" I sputtered.

"How do I know you're not lying?" He brought his fist closer, so close I felt my hair begin to singe.

"It was Payne! He said I manifested a magic deformity, and—and my brothers were so scared, they locked me inside! I escaped!" I spat out so quick, I wasn't sure if my words were even discernible.

I couldn't believe I was telling him everything, but nothing stopped the words from falling out of my mouth.

His grip loosened on me, his fist doused. My skin prickled as the warmth disappeared. He said nothing, the silence filled with my ragged breaths. I waited anxiously for his reply and even dared to pry my eyes open. His eyes were distant, a glaze coating over his irises.

"Fine, I'll let you go, but you can't run away, ok?"

I nodded rapidly. He sighed and lost his grasp on me. The second I was free, I immediately scrambled to the other side of the room, as far away as I could, rubbing my wrists. I felt like a mouse cornered by a cat.

"I'll make you a deal. I'll let you go with a ticket to wherever you want, but first I need your heart," he said.

Of course what Dulce said about wizards was true. What did he even want with a heart anyway?

"And if I don't give it up?" I asked, chest heaving, glaring.

He hesitated, and for once seemed to be at a loss for words. "Then, I'll . . . make you and abandon you somewhere with your eyes burned out." But even as he said it, he didn't sound too confident.

"Sure, I'll give it to you." Through my fear, I couldn't help but smile. "But you'll have to give me one first."

"What?"

"You'll have to give me one first," I repeated.

He grumbled, a flash of anger crossing his face. "What do you mean?"

"I told you. Payne said I have a deformation. In my chest. Specifically, where my heart *should* be," I answered, relishing the look on Alexei's face as he realized the meaning behind my words.

"You mean you're—"

"Heartless."

13

"So, ever since you were born, you haven't had a heart?" Alexei asked dubiously.

I shifted in the chair, the same chair he had sewn my leg, but this time, he merely dropped a black liquid over the wound. My skin curled in on itself until flesh began to regrow. The strange sensation sent shivers up my back, my skin sizzling and cracking. It burned like fire, yet somehow better than the needle.

"Never." I nodded, scrubbing the blood from my healed wound. If only he had done that the first time. Finally, I had a true reason not to trust him. A true reason to hate him.

"How are you alive then?"

"You think I know?" I snapped.

He frowned and pulled away, corking the bottle of black liquid, and turned to return it to the shelf. I stretched out my leg before standing, testing my weight on it until I was sure it was fully healed.

"What did you say about your brothers?" He swirled around and found my eyes.

I glared before I looked away. "None of your business. I would've never told you that had I known you weren't really going to kill me. You know, you set a very good example for wizards."

"I'll keep that in mind." He stepped toward me and grunted as I instantly took three steps back. "Where are your parents? Why don't you just go somewhere easier to live?"

"You could say my parents left for the market and we're still expecting them back," I answered with a sarcastic tone and wide, over-exaggerated grin.

"Oh." His features softened, causing my anger to rise. "Both of them?"

"Stop looking at me like that. It's not like they loved me anyway, though I really wouldn't know what that would feel like, now would I?" I crossed my arms. "As for moving, I don't think we could even afford a box in Andros. I really have no idea where these ten thousand gold pieces are coming from."

"So, you've really never left your house?"

I hesitated. I mean, I had, but I already felt foolish enough, and I didn't care to tell him about my secret expeditions.

"Locks sort of got in my way." I stepped around the chair, trying to subtly cross the room without getting closer to him. "But, seeing as I'm of no use to you and I can walk, I'd say this is goodbye."

"Wait a minute, you can't leave!" he exclaimed, holding his hand out as if to stop me.

"Why not? You want my eyes? My hair? 'Cause you can have them," I said, crossing my arms.

"No, it's the middle of the night. I don't know if the trains are even at the station during this time, and you don't know how to get back." A smug smirk tugged at his lips.

I cursed in my head, repeating a word Layton definitely would never let me use, a faint blush rising to my cheeks. Now that he knew I didn't know my way anywhere, he had a real reason to keep me there.

"And what are you going to do about the Incarti? If you think Payne can help you, then you better start digging your grave now," Alexei said, copying me by folding his arms.

I uncrossed my arms and glared. "Might as well kill me now if you think I'm falling for that again. I'd rather be awake to see how I die."

"If I wanted you dead, I wouldn't have helped you in the first place." He shook his head and turned toward the staircase, pinching the bridge of his nose. "Sleep, don't sleep, I don't care as long as you don't touch anything, but I'm going to bed. We'll sort this out in the morning."

"Fine," I called as he disappeared up the staircase.

Left in the dark silence, I glanced at the door. I could've easily left, and I knew I really wanted to, but deep down, I knew that wasn't the smartest choice. *Be rational.*

I sighed as I pulled out the desk chair and plopped down, rubbing my arms. I wanted nothing more than to return to the huge room, fall in bed, and drift off, leaving my problems for tomorrow, but I couldn't bring myself to trust Alexei enough. He could've been setting up another trick, lure me into a false sense of security, before . . .

I didn't really know what he would do, I just knew it wouldn't be good. I wanted to be alert, prepared for when he decided to strike. I didn't intend to be at his mercy again. I wanted him to be at mine.

. . . .

"Were you here all night?"

I jerked up. I hadn't even heard Alexei come down the stairs, much less walk right behind me. I scrambled from the chair, glad that my leg didn't slow me down anymore, and plastered myself against the wall on the other side of the room. I wiped my eyes as he stared at me. His hair fell unbrushed around his neck, his feet bare.

"I gave you a room for a reason," he continued, his eyebrow arched. "Why are your eyes red?"

I wiped them again, which by then, I had rubbed them so much, they had begun to hurt. Alexei sighed and took a step toward me. I cowered back.

"I already told you I'm not going to hurt you. You caught me at a bad time yesterday, I would've told her I'm not going to kill you. She's just like that," he said as he approached. "She's just jealous."

"Of what?" I scoffed. Never in my life did I think anyone would actually be jealous of me. What was there to be jealous of?

"She's an attention grabber. Whenever the attention isn't on her . . ."

"She tells you to kill people?"

"No." He huffed. "What I'm trying to say is I don't kill people."

I narrowed my eyes at him. "How do I know you're not lying?"

"I guess you'll just have to trust me." He sighed, exasperated.

"I'd trust the Incarti before I'd ever even think about trusting you," I spat. "Now, can I go home? Or would you like to keep me here longer?"

"Let me look for that book. Then, you'll be free to run back to your prison all you want."

I nearly gasped, wincing at his words. "At least there's no wizards there."

He huffed and turned, rummaging through the shelves and cabinets. I exhaled an angry breath as I watched, but soon Alexei had opened every drawer and riled through every shelf, coming empty-handed.

"You know, maybe if you cleaned around here, you'd be able to find it," I said smugly.

"You're not helping."

"Oh, I'm sorry. Perhaps I'll just threaten to kill someone while I'm waiting, as you do."

"Can you shut up for one minute?"

"Not until I'm out of this stupid shop."

He whirled around just to glare at me, but as he locked eyes with mine, I saw his irises radiating a bright green light. I clasped my mouth shut and stepped back, the smirk on my face dropping instantly. His face fell as he saw my expression, then he quickly wiped his eyes. When he pulled his hand away, his eyes were back to normal.

He turned his back on me, muttering to himself in his strange language as he returned to his search. The lack of insults being exchanged seemed to tear through the atmosphere.

What was that? His eyes just glowed! Do all wizards have glowing eyes?

I watched as he grew more and more agitated, disregarding each book with a fling of the wrist, sending them flying. My eyebrows knitted together the longer this went on. Pity squirmed its way into my thoughts. I coughed when he crossed the room for the third time, straight to the other shelves he had already searched. A dull headache knocked at my head.

"You know, it's fine," I said, taking a step toward him. I was tired of watching him scramble around, and though I couldn't admit it, I felt a little bad for him. "I'll just tell Payne about it. If not, my brothers will apparently pay ten thousand gold pieces for someone else to figure it out."

I tried offering him an awkward smile as he sighed in defeat. He hauled himself to his feet, yawning and stretching.

"Fine, if you want to leave so bad, be my guest." He crossed the room and yanked a coat from one of the coat hangers. He pulled out a fist full of gold pieces and dropped them in my hand.

I stared down at the pieces in my hand, shocked, the most money I had ever held. And he just handed them over like it was nothing. What, was he made of the stuff?

"What's wrong now?" he groaned.

I glanced up at him, for once, without a glare. "Nothing, just . . . thank you, I guess. For, uh, for this, and not killing me."

"Any decent wizard would do it." He shrugged.

"And—and I'm sorry for, well, I guess all of this."

"Oh." He dropped his sour expression, his features relaxing. "I'm sorry, too, then. Maybe if we meet again, I'll be nicer."

We both chuckled quietly, and if I could tell right, a little awkwardly. His words echoed in my head. *If we meet again.* How bad would it be if we happened to cross paths again? Maybe sometime in the distant future, I could see myself returning to the city of colors and lights. Perhaps I could convince Layton and Dean to look into it if we really did have that ten thousand gold pieces.

"I guess this is goodbye, then," I said.

"Actually, here." He plucked the coat, a simple black tailcoat, off the rack and handed it to me. "The sun's not up yet, and it can get really chilly. Plus, it might help against the people trying to turn you in for that reward. Wouldn't want you getting snatched by another wizard."

Laughs escaped our lips and filled the air, the previous tension slightly relieved. Why couldn't it always be so light and nice between the two of us? How could it be that the first person I met out of the village I couldn't even get along with? I slipped on the coat, naturally a bit too big, which would be good to hide my face. Our eyes met, but our lips remained unmoving.

After what seemed to be ages, Alexei cleared his throat. I snapped out of the daze his eyes sent me into.

"Well, goodbye." He held out his hand. "I hope you make it back home."

I do, too.

"Thanks." I accepted his outstretched hand.

But as I turned toward the door, the lights flickered and went out with a hiss. Behind me, a strangled cry flew out of Alexei's lips as he shot backward, thrown into the shelves of potions and books, sending them all crashing down on him.

A cold gust of breath tickled the back of my neck. Without needing to turn, I could see the glowing red of the Incarti's eyes.

14

I felt the air escape my lungs before the pain. My body collided with the wall, thrown against the stone with a familiar force that sent blood gushing from my nose. The pain seemed to overwhelm my fear, for all that filled my senses was a sort of twisted giddiness, as though I felt ready for the monster's next attack. Sweet, sweet adrenaline.

This time, I ignored the steady flow of blood, dodging the Incarti's grabbing hands as it reached out and pursued me. With a cry, I lunged at it, surprised to find flesh somewhere underneath the darkness of the creature. The two of us crashed to the ground, though just as it had done at the Lockdale house, it vanished as I hit the floor.

I flopped over on my back to see it peering over me, its eyes beady. It stretched its arm out for my neck, faster than the blink of an eye, and its ebony, scorching fingers wrapped around my throat.

"Leave her alone!" Alexei's voice resounded from the other side of the room, and suddenly, a blast of heat washed over me.

The Incarti released an ear-splitting scream, its hand unclasping. I scrambled out from underneath it and fought to jump up to my feet. His hands blazing, Alexei threw balls of fire through the air, hitting the Incarti one by one, causing them to evaporate from sight with a deadly shriek.

"You almost just blasted me!" I cried as I hauled the chair from the ground, using it to defend myself from my oncoming attackers.

"A simple thank you would suffice!" He sliced through three at a time with a jet of fire. "Please don't destroy that chair!"

I launched the chair at the Incarti, and it split into various pieces. "Oops, sorry! I totally didn't mean to do that!"

I heard him groan from the other side of the room, but I couldn't tell if it was because of me or the five Incarti trying to ambush him. I stumbled through the darkness, feeling for something I could use to defend myself.

Just as the glint of Alexei's sewing scissors caught my eye, something curled around my ankle and yanked, sending me crashing to the ground. The red-eyed Incarti dragged me from the desk, lifted me from the floor, and slammed me back down. My breath knocked from my lips as it repeated the attack.

Up, down, up, down, *up, down*. Blood. Darkness.

My vision faded in and out until only the glint of its eyes kept me grounded to consciousness. The blood from my nose ran down the sides of my face, dripping onto Alexei's nice, polished floor. The screams of the Incarti rang in my ears. My chest felt like it was going to burst any second as I struggled to force air into my lungs.

"Ale—!" Slam.

A scream roared through the shop, not from the Incarti, but from Alexei. All at once, fire erupted from the other side of the room, so quick the Incarti didn't even have time to cry out.

The red-eyed Incarti dropped me and disappeared, then the heat fell upon me. The shrieks had stopped, only to be replaced by the popping of fire. I gasped, drawing in breath after breath as though they might be my last. Smoke filled my mouth, but it felt better than my previous state, so I gladly sucked it in.

"Ivory!" Alexei crossed the floor in a matter of seconds, yanking me up by my arms. "The shop's coming down, we have to go!"

I blinked rapidly, but the tears in my eyes wouldn't allow me to see clearly anyway. He tried getting me to move, but no matter how hard I tried, my body wouldn't respond to me and dropped right back down. With a grunt of frustration, he had my arm wrapped around his shoulder, and together, we burst from the shop.

The blast of fresh air felt like being reborn. My chest heaved, uncontrolled, panicked. As Alexei's grip loosened, I fell to the cobblestone. I crumpled up as much as I could, hiding my eyes in my arms, tears of pain streaming down my face. I couldn't get enough air. I was still suffocating.

"Hey, hey, breathe!" Alexei exclaimed, crouching down and shaking me vigorously. "I didn't just burn my shop for you to die anyway."

A pressing thought occurred to me through my struggle for air. "The dolls," I choked out, fighting to regain enough balance to sit up. My head felt ready to split.

"They're fine. Nothing can destroy diamonds," he assured me. "They know what to do."

I nodded, a slight relief filling my chest. The moment's panic subsided, my lungs full of fresh air. I lifted my head toward the shop, watching the sunset-like flames swallow the beautiful walls in the dim morning. All of Alexei's belongings were in there, I realized with a sinking guilt. Everything he had, gone.

And it was all my fault.

"I'm sorry," I cried. "I'll get you that ten thousand, I promise."

"What are you talking about?" he asked and offered out a hand.

With blurry eyes, I accepted it, allowing him to haul me to my feet. "Your house, your shop, it's all gone. This never would've happened if I—"

"Hold on, you think this is your fault?"

With a sniff, I nodded, and another wave of tears washed over me. My bottom lip trembled, and before I could stop it, another wail escaped my lips.

"Hey, hey, this isn't your fault." A laugh fell from his lips. "The Incarti have been following me for ages. Believe me, this is not the first time that has happened."

"Really?"

"Of course. Now, wipe your eyes. I think I know where we need to go," he replied with a smile as he fished into his pocket and pulled out a red handkerchief, which he offered to me.

"The train station?"

"No, no, when I said we have to get out of here, I really meant get out of here. They have our scent. There's only one place we'll be able to lose them," he said matter-of-factly.

"Where?" I asked, wiping my eyes.

"The Adeleigh Wood."

My stomach dropped, and all at once, a barrage of memories came bursting into my head. I remembered Dean first, telling a six-year-old me about the famous and treacherous Adeleigh Wood. He had used it as a tactic to scare me to sleep.

"You know what the Adeleigh monsters do to little girls who don't sleep?" he had asked in a low voice.

I shook my head, but instead of the usual curiosity that filled my mind before Dean told a story, fear dripped in. I clutched my blanket to my body, though the warmth did not reach me.

"They grab your toes and drag you from your bed, and do you know what they do next?" His voice rose theatrically, and he slipped from my bed, holding up his arms and curling his fingers like claws. "They eat you!"

With a scream, I dove under the covers, trembling like a mouse. Dean's booming laughter filled my ears as he left my room, taking the lantern with him, leaving me in darkness. I remembered crying until Layton came bursting in with the lantern and allowed me to wrap my arms around him. His fingers stroked through my hair as he whispered through the night, reassuring me that I was safe.

But I didn't believe him.

I grew up with a lantern lit every night, even when Layton constantly told me Dean's story was a lie. It wasn't until I grew a little older did I realize the true horrors behind the Adeleigh Wood.

I wasn't supposed to know, I technically shouldn't have even been stealing the daily paper from Layton's room in the first place, but the raging Embrasia War had finally simmered, and I wanted all there was to know.

I recalled skipping over most of it in search of the wizards, but the mention of the Wood caught my eye, and I couldn't help but read what it had to say. The paragraph described the monsters of the Wood, the fey, sirens, goblins, banshees, and countless other horrors I had barely heard of. It listed the names of the children taken by the fairy queen, the number of men drowned by the sirens. It seemed we had lost almost as many citizens from the Adeleigh Wood than to the wizards.

The article had planted a permanent seed of fear in my head for the rest of my years. And now, Alexei wanted me to go there.

"We can't!" I exclaimed, snapping back to reality. "What about the monsters?"

"Monsters?" Alexei shot me a strange look.

I nodded. "The banshees and sirens and—"

"Woah, woah, slow down. How do you know all of that?" he asked, holding out his hands as if to steady me. "I thought you said you've never left Cyrene."

"I read it, after the war."

"Straight from Embrasia?" His eyebrow rose and he crossed his arms. He gave me a look that seemed degrading.

"Of course," I responded.

"No wonder." He sighed, a frown taking over his lips. "First lesson in the real world, don't believe what you read in the paper. It's all twisted to make the king look good."

"So, you're saying that hundreds of people didn't die in the Adeleigh Wood?" I clasped my hands on my hips.

"No, they did." He shushed me just as I opened my mouth. "But why do you think they did?"

"I don't know, they're monsters!"

"Oh, so, like me?"

"No! You're human!" I realized my mistake a second late.

"You see? I'm not human, but that doesn't make me a monster. Maybe the real monsters are the ones that claim to be human. The ones with the human faces."

I wavered for a second. "That's . . . absurd."

"What I'm trying to say," he groaned, "is that maybe there are two sides to every story."

When I shot him a confused look, he grunted and swatted the air as if swatting an invisible fly. "You know what, never mind. We better go before the Incarti shows up again."

He started walking, noticeably fast-paced, away from his burning home. He didn't bother to give it one last look, didn't bother to say goodbye, didn't bother to show any remorse for what was once his house. It left me wondering if perhaps his shop had never truly been home to him. If it wasn't, then what was? Where did he belong?

"Are you coming?" he called over his shoulder, though he didn't stop walking.

I glanced up at the house, then to Alexei. I knew it was a bad idea, the worst idea I ever had. Even worse than leaving Cyrene. Even worse than following Alexei to Andros.

Because this time, I wasn't just following him. I was trusting him.

I spared one last look to the house, offering a silent apology before I sprinted to catch up with Alexei. I trailed behind him without a sound, ignoring the smug look he cast me.

For just outside the colorful cobblestone of Andros, the Adeleigh Wood loomed, waiting to swallow whomever foolish enough to cross its trees.

15

"Are we almost there?" I asked for the fifth time, running my hands up and down my arms.

"Would you stop asking me that?" Alexei grumbled, nearly stomping into the mud, his voice laced with irritation.

"I'm just wondering. We've been walking forever." I stuck my nose up, shuffling my feet. Though a dull, everlasting fear remained lodged in my chest ever since we entered the Adeleigh Wood, I tried talking it away. Unfortunately, Alexei seemed very tired of my nonsensical chit-chat.

"It's literally been twenty minutes."

With a sigh, my shoulders dropped. The sun still hid beyond the trees, letting the glow of the fading moon guide our way, however, Alexei seemed to know exactly where we were going. I willed myself to keep quiet, but my lips tingled uncomfortably as if they yearned to move. I never was much of a talker, albeit, I never really had anyone to talk to, unless the characters of my books counted. Or, perhaps it was just my nerves causing my mouth to run.

The trees moaned and creaked, the leaves whispering. Nothing seemed still, like the whole forest was alive, with a beating heart and everything. The life of the Wood almost brought envy to my head.

It had taken Alexei approximately five minutes just to convince me to follow him in, and once he had finally given me enough courage, I took three steps in and nearly tripped over a tree root. The moments that followed were full of me jumping at the slightest sound. When I heard an owl coo, I nearly hightailed it back out, but Alexei grabbed my arm tight and hauled me back beside him.

The more I walked, the more my panic dispersed, though it never fully disappeared. I expected a ghoul to jump out at us any second, or at least a fairy. But our path remained clear of any creature, save the occasional snail or worm.

And that's when I started talking.

I started out with very small conversation, questions about Andros. What was the weather like? (Sunny in the summer, snowy in the winter.) Why were the houses so colorful? (I don't know, the old king wanted it that way.) Does Andros have a library? (Of course.) Then, I asked the first, "Are we almost there?"

In the beginning, he answered my questions patiently, but once I started repeating myself, he grew steadily annoyed. Deep down, I think I had done it on purpose, just to get on his nerves. But soon, I genuinely wondered when we would arrive at our location, wherever that would be.

"Whe—"

"Please, I'm trying to concentrate. We'll get there when we get there!" Alexei burst out, tugging on his hair.

"Concentrate? What do you mean?" I questioned.

"I mean," he turned, his face twisted in anger, his hair simmering and sparking, "I'm trying to find the way!"

I took a step back, eyes widened, and lifted my hand to point at him. "Your hair is on fire."

"Aaargh!" His magenta locks burst into flame, lighting the shadows of the forest. "How would you like it if I started asking you a bunch of questions, huh? Why are your brothers so afraid of you? Why did your parents leave? How is it living without a heart?"

I watched as he continued on, sputtering out questions I hadn't had the strength to face, shocked. I soaked up his words, though every time I tried answering, my mind ran blank. After a couple of minutes, the flames began to die down and Alexei's spew of words dwindled until the two of us were staring at each other in silence.

"I'm sorry," I finally whispered. "I, uh, I've just never had anyone to talk to, and—and I was scared."

Through the dim light cast by the moon, I could see his face drop, all his anger gone, replaced by . . . pity? Sadness? I couldn't tell, but I could recognize it. It was the same expression Dulce wore before I left him standing on the bridge of Cyrene.

"No," he cleared his throat, "I shouldn't have lost my temper. I'm sorry. What were you going to ask?"

"I was just wondering," I shook the thought of Dulce from my head, "where are we going?"

"I haven't told you yet?"

I shook my head. "No."

"Oh." A red blush crept to his cheeks. "I thought I did, sorry about that. Well, I have a house somewhere around here." He straightened up, his jaw set like stone.

"A house? In here? Is that even legal?" My eyebrows shot up.

"I've done the nixies a couple of favors and they let me share their land with them," Alexei answered.

"Nixies?"

"Amphibian people who live in ponds. Very lovely voices."

A second of silence passed between us as we continued on. With a little bit of thinking, I finally realized the true cause of his agitation.

"We're lost, aren't we?"

"No, I know exactly where we are!" he exclaimed, his blush deepening.

"Are you sure? Because I think we've passed that rock twice already."

"What? Are you serious?" he cried, and gripped onto his hair, giving it a sharp tug.

"No, but now I know that you don't know where we are," I replied, struggling to keep back a sly smile.

"That was mean." The panic displayed on his face slipped away. "And, I'm not lost. I just haven't been here for so long. It'll all come back to me."

"So that's what you were trying to concentrate on," I mused. "Well, any ideas?"

He sighed. "I know it's a lot deeper in. With the pace we're moving at now, it might take us the whole day to get there."

I frowned, my jaw nearly dropping. With an exaggerated groan, I threw my head back. Beside me, Alexei released a small laugh.

"Oh, don't worry, it won't be that bad. I'll answer all the questions you want," he coaxed.

"Really?"

"Sure." He smiled, flashing his white teeth.

I smiled back, but it faded quickly. The question that had been bothering me ever since we left Andros rose up in my head. "Why are you still helping me? You could've left me behind, but you didn't."

There was a pause.

"Starting with the easy questions, aren't you?"

I glared. He chuckled and scratched the back of his head, glancing up at the sky. The dwindling stars twinkled faintly. He released a long sigh. I didn't understand why this was such a hard question.

"Well, it's only once in every three blue moons that you come across a girl born with no heart," he said. "And I think I'd feel bad if you ended up dead somewhere."

Curiosity and pity. That was all that drove him. Somewhere deep down, a twinge of a tight feeling surfaced. Disappointment? No, it couldn't have been.

"And, I guess I want to meet you."

"You have met me," I said, puzzled.

"No, I've met a girl who's scared of me. I want to see who you really are. With or without a heart."

I glanced up at him, my eyebrows furrowed together. But why? What was the point of knowing me? What was the point of knowing anyone? Who was to say I even knew who I was?

"Who are you?" I asked after a brief pause.

He laughed. "I'll tell you when I know."

The weight of something much heavier pressured the tension between us. The conversation felt heavy upon my chest, almost pulling me down by it, tainting. Perhaps I wasn't meant to talk so much. Maybe talking wasn't as great as I thought it would be. Why did it hurt so much?

"Do you like to sing?" Alexei asked suddenly, his voice a bit more chipper than in the previous moment.

"No," I responded, a flare of amusement rising up in my chest. "Do you?"

"Sure, I like to, but I'd cause a mob if I actually tried doing it in public," he answered.

We chuckled together, and the tight feeling disappeared almost as quickly as it had come.

"Do you like sweets?" I inquired.

"Can't live without them!" he responded, his eyes shimmering. "Have you ever had chocolate crêpes and ice cream? Literally better than living."

I laughed and decided against telling him Layton didn't really allow me to eat sugar. Instead, I opted to listen to him. He named possibly every pastry in existence, and I think even made up one or two, his eyes sparkling with a shine I thought only possible for children's eyes.

Perhaps the wizard Alexei wasn't as bad as I had thought. I mean, how bad could I think of him after listening to him list ice cream flavors for an hour? He wasn't human, sure, but how human was I?

In a world like mine, how human was anyone?

. . . .

"Please, you've been talking about cinnamon bagels for forever now. You're making me hungry!"

"No, no, but when they're stuffed with vanilla creme, oh, and glazed!" Alexei exclaimed, practically jumping up and down like a child.

It seemed the mere talk of sugar sent the wizard in a sugar rush. Now, it was me trying to get *him* to stop talking. Our trail went on for hours, the sun had already come up, and gone back down, and the stars were just starting to shine again.

Although we had taken many, many breaks throughout the day, my feet were still tainted with a pain almost worse than when I had twisted it. The ache sank into my muscles, my bones. My chest began to heave, and I could barely lift my feet from the ground. Sweat trickled down the side of my face, but the incoming night's chill caused it to run cold, resulting in chattering teeth and visible breath. I felt frail, like a walking skeleton holding more burden than it could handle. Three times, I had seriously considered begging the fey to go ahead and take me.

And Alexei's constant chatter did not help.

"Alexei," I interrupted him, drawing in a deep breath through my nose, "are we almost there?" Even my voice sounded frail.

"Not much longer now," he replied, turning to face me with a smile, but it faded quickly. "Hey, are you ok? You aren't looking too good."

"As long as we're near, I'm fine," I responded, clutching onto the black tailcoat tighter, bringing it up to my chin and blowing air into it.

"Your lips are blue." He stopped, and I nearly ran into him. He extended his hand out to my face, his fingers flickering with flames.

Like a comforting furnace, his fire reached my skin, causing it to go all tingly. I met his eyes, deep and bright, gazing right into mine. A flush rose to my cheeks, but I wasn't sure if it was just from the cold. I snapped my head the other way and pushed his hand away.

"You don't have to do that," I said, and pushed past him, hiding my trembling hands in my coat.

"I'm just trying to help. Haven't you ever been taught to accept help when you need it?" he asked, but it sounded more like an insult.

"Haven't you ever been taught not to talk to strangers?"

"Well, when the stranger is being choked by Incarti, there isn't much time for introductions."

Usually, I would bite back with something, but my depleting energy didn't allow me to. Instead, I huffed as loud as I could and continued walking. I heard a sigh from Alexei, but that was all.

We ventured on, though to me, it felt more like fighting against a deadly wind, blowing against my body and keeping me from moving. My feet stumbled from underneath me. It nearly took all I had to correct myself.

This was all Layton and Dean's fault. Shutting me in for most my life caused my muscles to be weak. I didn't think I had ever walked so much in one day, and the pain was unlike anything, even the stitches Alexei had sewn into my leg. It was a type of burn, a heat, much like Alexei's scorching flames, deep, deep in my skin.

My legs trembled, my head bobbled, though I tried keeping it upright, focused on the path ahead of me. My feet couldn't seem to stay straight. I bumped into Alexei, nearly treading over his feet.

"Woah," he said and caught my arms, his hands like a midsummer's day. "We can take another break if you want."

I pulled away from his strong grasp, though I wished to stay. I wished he would wrap his arms around me, his skin radiating with a heat no other can produce, like my own personal blanket. One that never stopped talking about cake. But I knew that was out of the question and scolded myself silently for such a thought. Those thoughts were not allowed in my head.

"I can make it," I insisted. "Let's just keep going."

"You know, there's no harm in stopping."

It took all my willpower to ignore him, to continue going when my whole body screamed at me to stop. He caught up with me and stuck right by my side.

So close, the heat steaming off of him soaked into my skin, slightly thawing my ear and cheek.

Go closer to him.

No.

Do it, you idiot.

I'm fine.

Shut up.

Luckily for me, I didn't need to move any closer, for Alexei had already closed the small gap between us, his arm thrown around my shoulder. I couldn't help but lean in, my eyelids drooping. I knew, I *knew*, I shouldn't have, but I couldn't stop myself. And I also couldn't help the thoughts of bliss that slithered in like a snake.

"There it is!" He tore his arm away, taking all the heat for himself. He burst into a run, grabbing my hand and dragging me along with him.

Grinding my teeth with each step, the pain was easier to ignore now that we had arrived at our destination. The house wasn't as big as the shop, but still bigger than my house in Cyrene, with a wood interior and two floors, shingles decorated with vine. The faint sound of water falling echoed in my ears. A pond was nearby.

Alexei grabbed the padlock chained to the door and punched in the code. The door flung open with a flourished kick from Alexei's foot, revealing a dark living room containing many doors.

The two of us walked through the threshold, and Alexei lit his hands aflame, illuminating the interior.

"I know there are some lanterns around here," he mumbled and headed straight for one of the doors. He returned a moment later holding three lit lanterns.

I studied my surroundings, the smell of wood launching me to my memories, back to Cyrene, with the chained doors, locked windows. I needed air, but the scent in the house wasn't what I wanted.

I'm not chained in. I can get out. There's a door right there. The windows have no locks. I can get out. There are ways out.

A red circular rug laid across the floor, an empty desk stood on one side of the room, and a couch on the other, along with a coat rack and hat stand.

It was quite barren compared to Alexei's shop, but it felt more familiar to me.

Standing in the house, I asked myself: did I want to go home? I had to, right? I couldn't just leave forever. Or, could I? It would be less of a burden if I stayed away, but then again, why did my brothers send police after me? And, where would I even go?

Anywhere, a voice told me. *I could go anywhere. Do anything. Meet anyone.* My gaze found Alexei.

He perked up, and I quickly averted my eyes.

"You can take your coat and shoes off. Go ahead and take that couch, I'll get some blankets and pillows," he said, peeling off his own coat and throwing it on the rack.

"What about you? Where are you going to sleep?" I asked, carefully slipping off my pair of black slippers.

"Don't worry, there's another couch upstairs." He kicked his boots off. "I'm starving. There's some canned soup around here somewhere. I can heat some up."

I nodded blankly as he opened another door, this one concealing a staircase, and disappeared up the steps. I toyed with the hem of the coat, but I didn't take it off. My freezing blood wouldn't allow it.

I nearly collapsed on the couch, the cushions caving in under my weight. Five bones must've popped as I stretched, yawning, but I ignored the sound, releasing a long sigh of content.

I curled up in the tightest ball I could manage, finally letting my eyes drop completely, my body going limp. Though my head pounded with thoughts, I was too tired to listen to them, and the pain in my feet remained there, but my exertion pushed the thought of the ache away.

My mind, unnaturally quiet, drifted. And I was gone with it.

16

The chink of a door handle brought me back. My eyes fluttered open, though all that greeted me was darkness. I blinked until my vision adjusted and nearly jumped when I heard another sound.

Footsteps. Someone was here. Entering.

No, that's impossible. Alexei had a lock. Though one part of me wasn't certain. Fear sprouted in my head like a plant, growing ever higher.

Slowly, I lifted my head from the couch, noticing for the first time the blanket laying across my body. Without questioning it, I shoved the blanket from my legs, directing my gaze on the door. It creaked open, and the room filled with wind. Goosebumps prickled on my skin, but I ignored the chill.

Because it wasn't someone coming in. It was someone leaving. And the swish of a coat signified who it was.

"Alexei?" I whispered, leaning forward. My voice rose an octave. "Where are you going? Alexei!"

But he didn't seem to hear me, for he continued forward, not looking back or even acknowledging I had said something. My eyebrows knitted together in confusion as I swung my legs over the side of the couch. A familiar pain fatigued my feet, but I didn't give it any mind. Alexei's behavior caused a slight panic in my chest.

Is he leaving me? But I thought he said . . .

He vanished into the night, not bothering to close the door behind him. I crossed the room, stepping on the balls of my feet in an attempt to lighten the burning ache, and slipped out the front door in pursuit of the wizard.

The grass scratched my feet as I walked, and the moans of the gnarled trees drowned out my fuzzy thoughts. I squinted through the dark veil of the night, but Alexei's silhouette in the distance was all that remained of him.

Where could he possibly be going? He must've had plans to come back, right? He said he would help me. He said . . .

A tight feeling wrapped around my throat, calling a glassy sheen over my eyes.

But that's when I heard it.

Voices, multiple voices, singing with a harmony so beautiful, I had to pause. A mix of highs, like cricket chips, and lows, like a rushing waterfall filled the air, rising and falling like the gentle breath of a baby.

The song pulled my feet forward, and for once, the pain had gone, as if it had never lodged into my muscles in the first place. My lips tasted sugar and salt, my body finding warmth. The trees danced in the wind, all seeming to lean in the same direction. The very same direction I was going.

Where is it coming from?

The drop of water entered my ears. I swirled my head and found, not too far away, a pond of ocean green stretched along the trees. With each step, the song grew, a rising crescendo that filled my ears to the brim with an overwhelming sweetness. My ears rang with the harmony, slipping into my head, causing my blood to rush faster and faster.

My feet moved on their own, without needing instruction, driving me right toward the pond. A figure of magenta just barely caught my eye, but I ignored it. It wasn't what I was looking for, after all.

I neared the edge of the pond, and there, in the center of the infinite green, the water began to ripple and part, revealing a trio of men. They rose from the water, their lips forming the song that had so sweetly lodged into my ears, so sweetly led me to them.

Their skin radiated with a pearl-like glow, almost as bright as the moon, more captivating than the moon ever was. Long blond locks trailed down their shoulders, dripping, and robes of silk flowed down their refined bodies. Their lips were perfect, pink, and ever moving. Delicate like flowers, they moved across the pond, toward me. Their eyes, a vibrant glowing blue, shimmering like the stars themselves, burned in my own.

It took me a minute to realize that they were looking at me. Nothing else. All their attention, their gazes, those dazzling tanzanite eyes, on me. I couldn't help but take another step forward.

"Ivory," they spoke as one, their lips parting at the same time, "Ivory."

My chest tightened with the sound of my name. Hearing it come from their voices, the name sounded more like a rhyme itself. For once, I liked being called. For once, I wanted to listen.

"We know what you desire, Ivory," they sang. "We've known. We've waited. And now, you're finally here."

A cold melancholy filled my soul. I couldn't believe I had forced them to wait. How long were they waiting? How long had they wanted me to come to them? The thought of leaving them without me struck irresistibly painful.

"I'm sorry," I choked out, "but, I'm here! I'm here! What do you want me to do?"

Smiles blossomed on their faces, so serene I felt guilty just looking at them. With deliberate slowness, they extended their arms out, hands outstretched.

"Come closer."

My chest swelled, my eyes glued to their outstretched hands. Only a few steps away, just barely in the pond. Only the brim of my dress would get wet.

But I can't ruin this dress. It isn't even mine.

I blinked, and suddenly, all the pain came rushing back. I hadn't realized how hard my body shivered, my skin red with cold, my breath coming out in short bursts. The sounds of the Adeleigh Wood filled my ears once more, the cries of the birds, the groans of the trees, the shrieking of the wind. All so loud. How could I have not heard the noise before?

In the corner of my eye, I glimpsed a figure peering over the edge of the pond, teetering over the water's surface. A flash of magenta cut through the night. Even with my mind muddled, his name surfaced in my head.

I clasped my eyes tightly closed, forcing myself to focus. *How did I get here? Last I remember, I was following Alexei. What happened? Why can't I remember?*

"Just one more step, and we'll grant your heart's desire." The song was more of a hiss, a command full of dark magic.

My senses rushed back, so overwhelming, I nearly lost my footing, my mind a spiraling mess. The air tasted too sweet, almost enough to clog my throat, the night chilling my body. How long had I allowed the cold to seep into my skin?

I glanced back to the men, extravagant in their shimmering skin and watery robes, their jaws a little too refined, their voices a little too melodious, their eyes a little too bright. How had I not known before? It was obvious they weren't human.

My eyes returned to Alexei and for the first time, I noticed something else in the water. Heads of gold, hands of silver, reaching up for his face. Rose lips forming a stream of song that ran too beautiful.

I thought he wouldn't let them near, he would draw away, but to my surprise, he didn't. Shock coursed through me as I watched him lean into their touch, his eyes half-open in a dream-like state. His body was relaxed, his expression soft and yearning.

Yearning for their touch.

Sirens.

Of course.

"Alexei," I whispered, my voice like a breath of fresh air compared to the melody of the sirens. "They're sirens. Don't listen."

But he paid me no heed, instead slipping a ridiculous smile on his cheeks that nearly brought a blush creeping to my face just to condole for catching him looking so stupid.

The male sirens drew closer to the edge of the pond, just behind the moss, their voices going soft and soothing. I felt it slip in my ears and lodge into my brain, but I urged it out. I was done listening.

I sprinted from their gazes, throwing my hands on Alexei's shoulders, shaking him violently. His brilliant emerald eyes held a glossy glaze over them, muting the color. Fear had so smoothly etched itself into my brain, making my stomach twist in knots, but the sensation consoled me more than ever. I needed fear. It was my only lifeline.

"Alexei!" I cried, letting panic overrule my actions. "Snap out of it!"

I glimpsed the female sirens and watched as their faces morphed into something horrendous, their jaws jutting out, their noses sinking in, their skin becoming watery and green. They bared their fangs at me, emitting a high shrill.

I stumbled back, clasping my hands over my ringing ears. I heard a chuckle from Alexei as they swiped their pointed, webbed fingers along his cheek. *I'm going to kill him!*

I clasped onto the hem of Alexei's coat just as the sirens wrapped their fingers around his jaw, bringing him closer and closer to the water's surface. He pitched forward, his lips sinking through the water. I groaned as I caught all of his weight, hauling his face back up. His hair dripped with the pond water, soaking his clothes.

"Alexei!" I shouted desperately, my voice echoing through the trees, but he didn't give me any mind, continuing to reach for the sirens.

Their hands trailed up his arms, their skeletal bodies dragging him closer. I grunted with exertion, gasping for breath, but Alexei's weight and strength were too much for me.

His face dipped down toward the sirens, his lips capturing one of theirs just as they sank down together. I slipped forward, but held tight, digging my heels in the mud. No matter what, I wouldn't let go, even if that meant he dragged me down with him. My life was no better than his, after all. Perhaps someone would actually miss him when he was gone.

But then his body jerked, and a muffled scream rose up from the water. He thrashed against their hands, and if he had been alone, he never would've been able to break free. I wrapped my arms under his and scuffled my feet, my whole body leaning backward. My hair brushed the mud.

But it wasn't enough. Both of us were still slipping, only slowing now. I was making him drown slower.

With a scream, I grasped his chest from behind, and using all the energy I had left, I twisted my body. His face tore from the water's surface, his chest heaving. Water spewed from his lips.

I wrenched the two of us away, but as I pulled my hands from Alexei, my foot found a dip in the mud. I felt myself slip, and a wet hand clasped around my ankle, nails sinking into my skin, drawing blood. They yanked, and with a shriek, I plunged into the dark depths below.

The cold bit my skin like fangs, a hundred hands weighing my body down. I struggled against them, but they were strong, much stronger than me, and I had used up the last of my energy pulling Alexei free.

I sank lower and lower, the water dimming darker and darker until I couldn't discern between a hand or a brush of moss. My lungs burned like fire, embers and coals sitting at the bottom of my ribcage, jostling around in my stomach. My body felt full of sand and rocks, weighing me down even faster. I was going to burst. I needed air. My thoughts dwindled.

I couldn't help but think of Alexei. His sweet scent mixed with whiskey. His tan skin, deep accented voice.

Somewhere muddled in my mind, I thought I heard him, calling. Calling. Calling. I couldn't hold my breath much longer.

"Ivory! Ivory! Ivory!"

A splash.
I sucked in, and water filled my mouth.

17

All was dark and quiet.

Something pressed against my chest, over and over and over, harder, harder, harder, creating agonizing bursts. A heaviness seeped into my body, weighing me down. I sank and kept sinking until my back hit something hard. My skin tickled.

A blast of air filled my mouth, followed by a surge of pain. I jerked up in an instant, water erupting from my lips, sound bursting in my ears. A ragged breath heaved next to me, filling my ears. I gasped in short hollow breaths, air like a sharp knife to my lungs.

The darkness faded slowly until I faced a forest of gnarled trees and dying grass. I dug my fingers into the crisp grass underneath me, scratching my skin. Blinking rapidly, I turned my head toward the sound of breath.

Lying next to me, Alexei sprawled out, his chest rising and falling almost as quick as mine. He had lost his coat and his hair stuck to his face in wisps. Seeing him in such disarray knotted my stomach even more.

I coughed up the last of the freezing water, then realized I had been retching more than breathing. My body trembled violently, both from the cold and the vomiting.

"Alexei." His name was a gasp on my lips.

He whipped his head over and scrambled to my side. "I thought you were dead," he whispered, and suddenly, he had tucked me in his chest, swaying back and forth. "You weren't breathing. This is my fault. I couldn't tell—"

His voice broke, his tears mixing with the pond water in my hair. If I hadn't been breathing, there truly was no way to tell if I was alive. Searching for a heartbeat would only be in vain. I crumpled in his embrace, shaking.

How close had I been? How many more seconds until it was too late?

I breathed in his name until the ringing in my ears subsided. I couldn't tell how long we stayed there, but it wasn't long enough. Nobody had ever hugged me for so long. Nobody had ever cried for me. He pulled away first. I didn't think I would've ever pulled away.

"We have to leave. It's not safe here," he whispered in my ear, glancing toward the pond.

I lifted my head from his chest and found his eyes. "Where?"

"I don't know. Can you walk?" He plucked his fuchsia coat from the grass, hanging it over his arm.

The last thing I wanted to do was walk, but I nodded anyway and allowed him to help me up to my feet. My knees buckled from underneath me, but Alexei held my arm tight. The pain from the previous day of walking burned in the soles of my feet, but it was a good pain.

A reassuring pain. Pain that told me I was still alive.

Alexei led me back to the house, pushing the swinging door open. He lit the lanterns once again, his face grim, tear stained. I stood, shivering, watching. The constant fear that coursed through my blood sickened my stomach. Or, perhaps my stomach felt like knots because I hadn't eaten all day and just finished retching up the remainder of Alexei's supper.

That supper had only been one day ago, but it felt like years. I couldn't remember the taste of what we had eaten. I couldn't recall the warmth of his shop. All I remembered was fear.

He thrust a leather bag over his shoulder, and with a nod, gestured to the door. "Are you ready?"

He seemed to always ask that and every time, I never was, yet every time, I still responded the same way. I nodded. We slipped on our shoes, rung out our hair, and approached the door.

The two of us set out into the dark expanse of the Wood once again. The second I had entered, I expected the monsters, the fangs, the dark creatures. The chance of never making it out. But I still went in anyway, because Alexei was with me. He was still with me, but that didn't stop the sirens.

"What happened?" His voice was a mere whisper, a fraction of its usual confident tone.

I avoided his burning gaze. "I . . . I saw you leaving."

"Leaving?"

"Yes. I called out to you, but you didn't hear me. I got up and followed you, but then—" My voice broke off with a crack. Just thinking about the song, so beautiful, so seductive, so *ugly,* sent my head reeling. I inhaled a deep breath. "Then, I heard the singing. It led me to the pond, and you were there, and they were there."

"The sirens." He shivered next to me, hugging his body. "I thought the nixies were in the pond. I had no clue *they* would be there."

"It doesn't matter anymore," I said, noticing the guilty tone in his voice. "They couldn't bewitch me anyway."

Alexei glanced down at me. "Ivory . . ."

"Stop," I snapped. "You don't have to feel sorry for me."

"I don't." He sighed, a glint shining in his eyes. "I feel sorry for me. What a burden a heart is."

I let his words pass, trying hard to keep them from sinking into my system, but they had already taken place in my head. He was right, of course. If I hadn't been heartless, both of us wouldn't have made it out of there. Albeit, if I were normal, I would've never met Alexei anyway.

Or would I? Even if I possessed a heart, lived a normal life, was there any possibility that our paths crossed? If I were normal, would I have been attacked by the Incarti? Seen Andros?

I shook the thought from my head. No point in it being there. I wasn't normal. I never was, and I would never be.

"So, you didn't fall under their spell?" Alexei asked, pulling me from my thoughts.

"Well," I hesitated, "I'm not sure. I heard it, and suddenly, I felt warm and light. I couldn't hear anything but their voices, I couldn't think for myself. I only wanted to find where it was coming from."

"Yeah, I felt the same," the wizard said, nodding slowly as if lost in the memory of the spell. "And I tasted sugar on my lips. They were calling for me, saying that they had been waiting for me."

"'*And now, you're finally here*.'"

"What?"

"Hm? Oh, I'm sorry. It's just . . . what they said. The sirens."

Alexei's eyes widened. He stepped in front of me and grabbed my shoulders tight. For the first time since we had started the conversation, I locked eyes with him.

"You *did* fall under their spell!" he exclaimed.

"Maybe for like, a second," I pushed past him, continuing forward, "but I snapped out of it. Just in time, too. Oh, and before I forget, how much do you weigh? You almost pulled me right in!"

"Ivory, be serious! Don't you know what this means?"

I shook my head. I didn't want to hear him say it. It was a lie. False hope. But he said it anyway, his eyes shining with the hope I wished I could possess.

"You can love! You must have—"

"No, I don't! I can't! I have no pulse, Alexei! I've never loved anything or anyone. Not even the only people who protected me my whole life," I cut him off, slicing my arm through the air as if to silence him.

"You mean your brothers? They locked you up your whole life! How can you expect yourself to love them?" he countered, attempting to catch my eyes again, but I didn't let myself be swayed by his emerald irises.

"They're my family!" I shouted, swatting him away. "They protected me! They loved me! And I couldn't do the same."

"Ivory, listen to me—"

"No! I'm not letting you plant false hope in my head! I'm not normal, I never was normal, and I never will be! Let's just leave it at that!"

There was a pause before he replied. "Fine. Just know that sometimes, family doesn't always run on love." He spoke as though he had experience.

"What do you mean?" I asked, forcing my anger to burn out.

"It's," he sniffed, wavered, then pushed past me, his jaw set hard, "it's personal. Let's just keep moving and forget about it all, like you want."

I watched him walk, his coat swinging with each step. His shoulders were squared and tense, his fists clenched in tight balls. A mist of angry smoke rose up from his body.

I could feel his anger radiating from steps away. And after we had just saved each other's lives, too. Would we ever stop fighting? We were past insulting each other, we had shared questions and answers, and we both risked our lives just to see the other alive. We weren't strangers anymore.

"I—I'm sorry. Really, I am," I said softly, mostly to myself, my eyes glued to the grass beneath me. I couldn't stand to look at him with my cheeks so warm. "I've just wished, and hoped, and tried, but I can't. I just . . . can't."

Surprisingly, he was quiet. I clasped my lips shut, dread sinking into my stomach. My ruined black slippers sliding through the dirt path, drops of pond water falling from my hair, we continued on. The wind flew through my ears like a scream, seeming to tear my skin. The brilliant light Alexei cast faded from the corners of my vision, leaving darkness seeping into my eyes. The eternal green of the forest became more like a murky brown without Alexei's light. So dim, the light . . . gone.

My head flew up to find he was no longer in front of me.

He was gone.

I whirled around, my eyes darting. My throat tightened, a swell of pain rising in my chest. Panic instantly shot through my body, but I knew it wasn't the sirens this time. I had gone too far. He had finally grown sick of my arguing. I should've seen it earlier—why would he stay around if all I did was fight with him? Yet, I couldn't help the burn of tears scorching my eyes. What was I supposed to do now that he had left me alone?

"Alexei?" I whispered through the night, but I knew no answer would reply. Still, his name felt good on my tongue, almost like another apology. "Alexei! Alexei!"

Irresistible tears poured down my cheeks as I repeated his name over and over, like that would somehow bring him back. But he wasn't going to come back. And I was alone in the Wood. My legs wouldn't move; they only trembled in the vast darkness Alexei left me in.

But in the absence of Alexei, another voice jumped out at me.

"Mortal." It was high and shrill, calling out like a melody of hummingbird wings.

I jumped, scanning my surroundings, but without the light of Alexei, I could barely see in front of my eyes. The voice seemed to come out of nowhere, but I knew I hadn't imagined it. I could feel the weight of eyes on my every movement. I hastily scrubbed the tears from my cheeks, fear planting itself deep in my stomach. It wasn't the sirens this time. But if it wasn't them, then who? I was almost too scared to ask.

"Who are you?" I meant for it to sound demanding, but it came out more like a gasp. "Where are you?"

Like bells, laughter erupted from the trees. "We're everywhere. Our eyes are the leaves, the bark, the mushrooms. We are the wind, the snow, the light. We are eternal, and you are nothing. What are you doing in our domain, mortal?"

"I'm . . ." *What am I doing here? I only followed Alexei.* "I'm trying to find my way home."

"Home? You mortals have no home. You plunder, scour your whole lives without finding the place you belong, only leaving a trail of destruction in your path."

I took a frightened step back, but a tree root caught my foot and I toppled over. The voices burst out in another fit of booming laughter and giggles.

"Do you know what we do to mortals who trespass on our world?"

Dean's voice echoed in my ears. *Do you know what the Adeleigh monsters do to little girls when they don't go to sleep? They eat you!*

I trembled as I faced the sky of black, the mocking voices resounding from above. Dean had been right all along.

I crumpled up, giving up on holding my body upright. My muscles failed, my bones useless, my mind a blank slate. I couldn't tell if years or seconds were passing, shadows of the unknown filling me to the brim, entangling in my hair, clasping my hands, seeping into my skin, soaking into my thoughts. It was almost like the night was swallowing me. Or embracing me. I couldn't tell which one.

But then a face filled my vision, one so painfully familiar, curly brown hair, deep skin, and dark eyes. He held a bleeding animal over his shoulders, the poor creature's blood dripping down his brown cloak. He stared at me as if he wanted to tell me something.

"Dean," I mumbled. *Help me.* "Dean."

"Ivory!" From far away, my name slipped into my ear. It was like mist, barely there, yet so visible. I knew that voice.

Suddenly, a pair of inhumanly warm hands grabbed my shoulders tight. I found my lips and screamed, thrashing against the grasp while the laughter boomed in my ears. I imagined their teeth, fangs in crooked rows sinking into my flesh, their throats, their stomachs, where I would burn.

"Ivory!" Again, the calling echoed, slightly stronger this time. "Don't listen! Open your eyes!"

But my eyes are open.

"We'll take her to the queen. Midsummer's night grows near, and a sacrifice of mortal blood must be made." The shrill voices were distant now, not as roaring. They almost sounded childlike, and I was merely a part of an immature game.

"Ivory, open your eyes now!"

A flash poured into my vision and a thousand tiny hands replaced the darkness. Sounds seeped into my ears, distant screaming and thundering footsteps. I groggily pried open my eyelids and realized I was moving, though my legs were lying limp, completely still. My whole body remained unmoving, although the trees flew past me in a blur of green.

"She's awake."

Snickers.

"Maybe that wizard will chase us down until he drops dead."

Chuckles.

"Perhaps we'll bring back her skeleton for him."

Laughs.

I rolled my head to one side, face to face with the eyes of a freakishly thin and pale creature. Its face slanted in so narrow, its jawline appeared to be shaped like a perfect v. Its eyes glowed pure black, popping out against the white skin that belonged to the creature.

When we locked eyes, a crack-like smile spread across its face, revealing a set of both pointed and squared teeth. A scream caught in my throat as it licked its wrinkly lips. I tried pulling away, but my body remained stuck. My muscles locked up, tense and strained, protesting when I attempted pulling free. The creatures' small hands were of large numbers, and my paralyzed body was no match against them.

My head tilted back, bobbing forward and backward. My eyes flicked around, finding the moon dangling in the night. It shone with a red tint, crimson vapor pouring into the clouds.

I must be hallucinating! This can't be real!

The distant beat of footsteps dragged my gaze away from the bloody moon and, with my head hanging back, I saw something far off in the trees, darting toward me. I squinted, watching as the figure grew clearer and clearer.

It was a man. Coat. Blazing hair. Alexei.

A rush buzzed through my body like lightning striking through my muscles and I jerked up, struggling against the hands. Their shrill laughter resounded in my ears, but I only let it fuel my adrenaline.

"Let go of me, you cursed creatures!" I exclaimed, kicking and twisting.

A blast of flame flew past us, just barely licking my cheek. Their joyous laughter transformed into ear-piercing shrieks and their grip loosened. With one last twist, I plummeted to the ground below, landing straight on my back, my breath forced out of my lungs with the impact. I choked as I struggled to suck air back in.

"Ivory!" Alexei cried, and in the blink of an eye, he was by my side.

"The moon." I heaved, my chest rising and falling rapidly. "What's happening?"

"I should've known it was Midsummer's Eve." He shook his head and propped my head up. "Are you ok? What did they do?"

"Who were they? *What* were they? What's Midsummer's Eve? Why's the moon—"

"They're fey. I'll explain the rest to you later, but we have to run. They're not going to stay away forever," Alexei replied, hauling me up to my feet. "Turn your jacket inside out."

"Why?"

"Just do it!" he shouted, and before I could fit in anything else, he had burst into a sprint.

I followed after him and for the first time noticed how different he looked since he had abandoned me just minutes previous. He wore his coat inside out, which looked utterly ridiculous, and his stubbled chin made him appear even more like a mad man. Since when did he have stubble?

I struggled to run and rearrange my coat at the same time, slowing down as I shoved my arms back into the sleeves. Alexei reached back and grabbed my hand, pulling me forward. His panic only caused mine to thrive. His hand glowed with insane heat, almost enough to burn my skin, but he wouldn't let go. And I wasn't sure if I wanted him to.

"Where are we going?" I asked through heaving gasps. "What happened?"

"Rowan!" Without warning, he dived under a bramble, taking me with him. He crawled under and lodged the two of us in the hut of a large rowan tree, pushing me in the furthest until my back pressed against the wood.

"What are you—"

He hushed me, pressing his hand against my lips. A few silent seconds passed before a barrage of those little voices filled the air above us.

"Where did they go?"

"We can't lose the mortal!"

"The queen will have our heads!"

The soprano voices faded away slowly. Alexei relaxed slightly, pulling his hand away. Clasped in his other hand, a dagger of silver glinted in the dimness. His eyes swam with relief as he locked his gaze with mine.

"We'll be safe as long as we stay in here. The fairy folk hates rowan. Are you ok?" he asked.

"I'm fine, just please, tell me what's happening," I whispered, though all I wanted to do was shout.

"What do you remember?"

"I . . . ," I trailed off, thinking.

My memory was hazy, a vast field of mist and broken faces, shattered voices. Only Dean's voice was clear, his warning of the Adeleigh Wood. If only I had listened to him. If only I had never left Cyrene.

"I remember the darkness," I said.

"Before that," Alexei urged.

"I don't—" I gasped as memories came rushing back. Andros. Incarti. Sirens. The *sirens*. "The sirens. We were running away from them, and then, you—you were gone!"

"No, Ivory, I wasn't." His face dropped into a grim expression.

"What do you mean? You were right in front of me, then you weren't. I couldn't find you, I thought you had—"

"No, I never left. It was you who disappeared," he interrupted. "You ran off, shouting for me. I tried catching up with you, but you just disappeared. I should've been more careful, tried harder. I should've known." He dipped his head.

I racked my brain, trying to recall what he described, but all I saw was the empty forest, the blank spot Alexei should've been.

"I thought I lost you again." His voice broke off, but he continued. "I was so scared. The days passed—"

"Wait, days?" I cut in, holding up a hand. "What do you mean days?"

He paused, his eyes shimmering. "Ivory . . . *when* do you last remember?"

"What do you mean? It's been like, five minutes since you were gone," I replied.

"No," he sucked in a breath and caught my hand in his, "it's been three days."

18

His words echoed in my head like a mocking tune. *It's been three days*. No, it wasn't possible. I had just lost him in the forest minutes ago.

"No, no," I shook my head, "that's not possible. It's not."

"You were with the entourage of the fey. Time is obscured in their presence. Minutes can be days, days can be years. I'm just glad I found you before it was too late," Alexei explained.

My stomach dropped. "Too late for what? Where were they taking me? What were they going to do with me?" I tightened my grasp on Alexei's hand.

"Are you sure you want to know?" His eyebrows rose with a frown.

I swallowed the sickening fear rising up in my throat. "Yes. Tell me."

He nodded grimly before speaking, squeezing my hand briefly. "The faerie queen upholds a tradition every Midsummer's Eve. They bring a human to their realm, treat them with the finest food, drinks, games. But by the time the blood moon is full in the sky, they . . . sacrifice them."

I clasped my hand over my mouth, fear shaking my body. If Alexei hadn't found me, I would've been sacrificed like a lamb, tricked into playing games and drinking myself silly.

"W—what do we do now?" I asked, shaking as I pulled my hand from my lips, urging myself to forget Alexei's answer.

"I'm not sure yet," he responded, his voice slow and raspy. "I haven't been able to think for the past three days. I thought you were gone, and it would've been all my fault."

He squeezed my hand again, tighter, so tight I wouldn't have been able to pull away if I wanted to. I didn't. I allowed his smoldering skin heat mine, his touch like the brush of feathers compared to the fey. I couldn't help the thought of his identity slip into my mind. He was a wizard, a disgusting, evil, terrible wizard.

No. I forced the thought out. He saved my life more than once, he spent three days chasing after me. He was a wizard, yes, but that didn't mean evil swam in his heart. Dad was wrong all along.

"Are you sure you're ok?" Alexei asked, throwing me from my inner battle of thoughts.

I found his eyes and nodded, attempting to offer a small smile. A grin broke out on his face before he thrust his arms around me, pressing my body against his. His sweet aroma filled my nose, sending my blood rushing faster than a waterfall. He swayed back and forth, gave one last tight squeeze, then let go. His eyes burned in mine, my reflection shimmering in his pupils.

We sat in silence, lost in each other's gaze as if we had put each other in some type of spell. After a while, I felt myself shift uncomfortably, searching for something to say. What was I supposed to say? There was only one thing I could think of.

"Thank you."

His smile grew and he reached out, placing his hand on the top of my head. "Anything for my knight in shining armor."

A tint of pink dusted over my cheeks, but it went away as he ruffled his fingers through my hair, a laugh escaping his lips.

"Hey," I giggled, "stop that! You're messing up my hair."

"Believe me, I'm doing you a favor." His laughs mixed with mine. After the top of my hair stuck up in tufts did he finally withdraw his hand. "There, much better."

With a chuckle, I shoved him lightly. He swayed and toppled over purposefully, clutching onto his chest with a flare of dramatics. We laughed once more, but as I tried to reach out and ruffle his locks, he caught my hand mid-air, a dangerous smile dancing on his lips.

"Not the hair."

I burst out in a fit of laughter, his desperate desire to keep his hair intact sending a flare of amusement up my chest that scared away the fear that had taken root. Perhaps that was why it looked perfect even after so many days in the forest. The smirk that spread across his face uplifted my mood even more, but I knew our jokes would only last so long. We couldn't remain in the tree forever. How were we possibly going to escape the Adeleigh Wood? Where would we even go? I doubted Alexei owned another safe house, though I wasn't sure how surprised I would be if he truly did.

As if reading my thoughts, a crack cut through the air from outside the tree. The two of us froze, our lips tightly clamped shut. Fear burst in the pit of my stomach, all of the previous joy drained away. Alexei apprehensively pressed a finger to his lips as he drew his silver dagger, but instead of taking it with him, he pressed the hilt in my hand. With one last nod, he crawled out, gesturing to me to stay put. I watched him anxiously as he disappeared from the tree, my hands shaking around the hilt.

I sat in the dark silence, the seconds ticking away like hours, desperately trying to keep my increasingly ragged breaths quiet. I couldn't stand seeing the way out so close, yet so far away. Was the air thinning? I forced myself to breathe, hiding my eyes in my hands.

Relax, he's fine. He'll come back, and I'll get out. I'm not trapped. I'm not trapped.

Was he coming back? I pried my eyes open. How long had passed since he left? Surely not that long.

I eyed the exit nervously, fiddling with the dagger. I knew Alexei had told me to stay, but I needed to know what was out there. What if he needed help? What if the fey caught him?

What am I going to do about it? There's nothing I can do to help. I'm not a wizard. I'm barely even human. If anything, I'd create more of a distraction. More of a burden.

I sank back against the bark, a storm brewing in my mind. What if I was wrong? What if he really did need me? He did call me his knight, after all.

I crawled over to the opening of the tree, glancing up through the brambles. His figure was nowhere to be seen, causing my panic to rise ever higher. Only a trace of his voice could be heard. I waited, nerves biting at me, my body inching closer and closer to the opening.

His deep, husky voice fell into the tree. "It's alright! You can come out!"

With a relieved sigh, I scrambled up the dirt, fighting past the bramble, and burst into the vast expanse of the Wood, chest rising and falling rhythmically. The breeze chilled the sweat that had formed on my forehead, but I didn't care, as long as I was no longer alone in the tree.

"I know where to go, just follow me," Alexei said, traces of panic laced in his voice. "I gave us enough time, the edge of Adeleigh is only over those bushes!"

"What did you do?" I asked as I stalked behind the wizard, struggling to keep up with his brisk pace. "Wait, you're going too fast! Slow down!"

"Hurry, before it's too late." He flicked his eyes back at me briefly, motioning me to follow him.

"Wait!" I cried. "Shouldn't we go back to where it's safe?"

"We'll make it! We're almost there!"

I struggled to keep up with him, but as I kept my eyes glued to his back, I didn't see the tree root curling out from the ground. My foot caught and I crashed to the dirt. Alexei gasped and practically flew by my side, hauling me up. Fear prickled at my skin as he stared at me with pleading eyes. He opened his mouth to say something, but his words were cut off.

"Ivory!" an overly familiar voice called from the trees. Alexei's voice.

Alexei tumbled from the bramble, or rather, another Alexei. I gasped, scrambling away from the first Alexei, dagger held high. The second Alexei's eyes widened as he gazed upon his identical counterpart. The first one did the same.

"It's the fey!" the first Alexei cried, pointing at the second. "Get behind me! Hurry!"

"No, don't listen! I'm the real one!" the second Alexei exclaimed, his voice painfully uncanny to the other one.

I flicked my eyes back and forth, comparing the two, searching for a clue to signify the real one, but they were exactly the same, down to the slight crook in their noses, pierced ears, olive complexion, slanted eyes.

"Give me a sign!" I shouted as I backed away further and further, my hands trembling around the silver hilt. "I can't tell who is who!"

The two glanced at each other, then back at me. Even the curve of their lips was identical.

"You saved me, remember? From the sirens! That was me!" the second Alexei cried, flinging his arms out.

"He's lying! You saved *me* from the sirens! I remember you saving me! Their song tasted like sugar! We both tasted it!"

I paused, offering a look at the second Alexei, whose face fell by the words of the first. I turned the dagger toward him, inching back in the direction of the first.

"No, he's not me!" the second shrieked, his eyes swimming with effort. Something seemed to click in his features, and he found my eyes. "Remember dinner? I ate four eclairs!"

With a gasp, I spun on my heels, pointing the dagger at the first. The fey would never know a detail like that . . . right? Fey couldn't read memories, right? I recalled the passage about the Adeleigh Wood. Did it say anything about fey? I couldn't remember.

"Wait." The first held up his hand, the same one I'd been holding not too long ago. "He's getting in your mind! It's a trick, you must trust me! I know it's hard for you to trust someone like me, but I can't lose you again!"

My breath caught in my throat, the dagger wavering in my hand. My eyes darted between the two once more, studying each and every little movement. This was getting me nowhere. I needed something to convince me entirely. I couldn't be wrong.

"Alright, whoever answers this right gets to live," I announced, my voice shaking. I paused, hoping this would work. "What's my brother's name?"

The second Alexei's face dropped, flushing white, as the first answered.

"Dean! You told me—"

"Funny," I interrupted, "I don't remember ever telling you their names."

I flung the dagger at the first Alexei with all the strength I could muster. Like a shooting star, it flew through the air and landed dead center in his throat. A shrill ear-bursting shriek poured from the creature's lips as Alexei's face melted off in a stream of smoke and flesh, a blackish liquid spurting from the wound.

I recoiled back and nearly fell into Alexei, the *real* Alexei's arms. He reached out and steadied me, his grasp tight and trembling. He folded me into his chest, away from the sight of the dying fey.

I did that. I killed it. Murdered it. I swallowed my tears down, feeling as though I had been the one struck by the dagger.

"Let's get out of here." He led me into a sprint.

As we passed the screaming fey, it reached out for me, just barely brushing its smoking, gray fingers against my black slippers, its broken voice crying out after us.

"We'll kill you! We'll kill you! You'll be dead by morning! Look what you've done to me!"

"Run, Ivory, just run," Alexei whispered, his lips quivering. "Don't look."

We darted through the trees together, the light of the blood moon illuminating our path with a glowing red vapor. I couldn't help the tears streaming down my face as the fey's voice echoed in the forest. A moment later, I realized it wasn't just one.

It was thousands.

"We'll kill you, you cursed creatures! You foul girl! You inhuman girl! Atone for your sins!"

I nearly dropped due to my buckling knees, but Alexei held tight. My chest heaved up and down rapidly, but air refused to enter my lungs. Fear choked me, snaked around my throat and pulled into a noose. The lack of air encouraged me to stop, allow them to kill me, but the thought of death kept me running.

A thousand lights filled the sky and I knew right away that they weren't stars. They plummeted down, striking me and Alexei, pinching, biting, scratching our skin. Alexei let go of me and burst into flame with a pained groan, the fire weak and flickering. Warm blood slipped down my cheek, but I did nothing to wipe it away.

I deserved it, like I deserved their death. But I was still too scared to commit, like the coward I was. The fey were right. I truly was an inhuman girl.

We truly were cursed creatures.

19

Alexei

The sun peeked up from behind the trees, spilling light into the Adeleigh Wood. I had encountered that sunrise for the past three days, but my eyes were never on the scene. They were searching, searching, searching. And even when I found the one I was looking for, I still couldn't take my eyes away to gaze upon the sun greeting the world.

Ivory clung to my coat, her head bobbing as she tried to keep her eyes open. Blood crusted across her cheeks, stained her hair, seeped through her clothes. My coat, my favorite coat, was painted with her blood as I pressed her to me.

So much blood. Not enough of it was mine.

Fatigue plagued my muscles, exertion weighing me down, forcing me to move slow and sluggish. My heart pounded against my chest, screaming at me to go faster, but I couldn't comply. All I could do was take one step, then another, and another.

"We're almost there, Knight," I said for the third time. I felt she knew I was lying by now, but I couldn't help but try to comfort her. It was my fault she was here anyway.

If only I hadn't left her alone in that tree. If only I had known it was Midsummer's Eve. If only I never convinced her to go through the Adeleigh Wood with me in the first place. If only I hadn't been so selfish as to try to steal her heart.

It was all my fault. If she died, it would be another life on my hands. More blood. I couldn't imagine telling her insane brothers she died because of me. My heartbeat accelerated just thinking about it.

No, she will live. This time. This time.

I glanced down at her, grasping her cold hand in mine, attempting to feel for a pulse, but sensed none. I knew her skin was always cold, but that still didn't stop me from wanting to warm her, however, the fire in my soul flickered, smothered by each painful passing moment. Nerves crawled into my head like pesky spiders, spinning their webs across my thoughts. How was I supposed to help her if I couldn't even conjure a simple flame?

Her eyes dropped, her knees buckling. I gasped as she collapsed to her knees, her head hanging limply.

"Ivory," I said, wrapping her slack arm around my shoulder and rising back up to my feet, continuing forward. "We're almost there."

She hummed, her feet just barely grazing the dirt as we limped. I supported most of her weight. I liked the sound of her voice, telling me she was still alive. I feared if she closed her eyes, she wouldn't open them again, and I would have no way to tell if life still coursed through her veins. She was strong, I reminded myself. Much stronger than I thought. *She will get through this, and I will heal her as soon as I find a potion shop. She'll live. She'll live.*

I repeated the mantra to myself in my head as fear edged into my heart. I urged doubt from my thoughts. Doubt only slowed me down. I had only just met her, but something about her struck the chords deep in my heart. I had met plenty of heartless girls, but none quite like her. She reminded me of someone . . . someone I had lost a long time ago. Perhaps that was why I was so keen on keeping her alive. I really wasn't sure why else.

The bushes began thinning out, growing sparse and dying, but seeing the dead leaves only troubled me more. Nothing could stop the Adeleigh Wood from growing. At least, that was what the nixies had told me so long ago.

I pushed past the bushes to find a clearing. Light poured in through the cracks of leaves, warming my skin. My heart skipped a beat as I realized what it meant.

"We're out! Ivory, I found a clearing!" I exclaimed, fighting past my exertion as the two us burst through the bushes.

We faced a vast garden of large cherry blossoms painted pink and red, the petals falling like rain, showering the ground. Just beyond the trees, a castle of crystal stood tall, glinting in the new coming rays of the sun. I couldn't believe my eyes, though mostly because my vision had been fading in and out with each blink. It was the Embrasian castle.

"Ivory, I think we're in Embrasia." I couldn't help but let a smile creep onto my face, even though I knew I didn't have papers for the kingdom.

The dungeon was better than the Adeleigh Wood, however.

But Ivory didn't respond. I glanced down at her to find her eyes fully closed, her eyelashes resting upon the bags underneath them. Her chest rose and fell so softly, I could barely tell if it was moving at all. I realized that I had been holding her entire weight.

"Snowflake." I shook her gently, fighting to keep my voice in control. "Ivory, open your eyes. We made it. We're in Embrasia."

She remained silent and still. My breath hitched as I attempted to continue forward, but even though she was light, her weight was still a little too much for my trembling legs. The two of us plummeted to the grass, her body hitting the ground with a dreadful thud. The whole world spun in dark, fast circles.

"Hey, Knight." I reached out for her, but my vision filled with black spots as I crawled. "We're here. Please, wake up. Please."

I need to get up. I need to open my eyes. She'll die if I don't. I need to get up. I need to—

The rest of my thought drifted off, along with me.

20

A strange fuzz buried into my fingertips and toes. The sensation unnerved me like a snake slithering through my skin. I curled my fingers in, pressing my nails into my palm. The pain barely scared the fuzziness away.

Along with the strange fuzz, my body seemed to be full of sand, weighing me down against a soft surface. I fought to lift myself but to no avail. Frustrated heat rose to my cheeks.

"When do you think she'll wake up?" A distant voice crawled into my ear.

"It's hard to say. We did the best we could do, considering the circumstances. Right now, the best thing for her is rest."

"But she's been *resting* for two days now. Almost three!"

"I am aware, Mister Alexei, but you must understand, she is not as—" the man speaking hesitated— "sturdy as you. She's lucky to still be alive."

The two men quieted. The silence soaked into my senses and I realized the voices weren't just in my head. I fought to crack open my eyes, my whole body numb with pain, groaning slightly as I stirred awake.

"Ivory." A silvery warm voice etched its way into my ears. A familiar hand slipped into mine, and only then did the fuzzy numbness run away.

My eyes flew open by the sound of the voice, and standing above me, his emerald irises locked onto my blue ones, Alexei hovered. I squeezed his hand

and a grin spread across his cheeks. The room fell in darkness, but I could still see him clear as day, as though he were the sun.

"Oh, thank the gods and goddesses above," he sighed, kneeling to match my level, "I thought you were dead for real this time."

A smile broke out on my face despite the fatigue that seeped into my bones.

"You wish," I rasped, my throat like sandpaper.

He chuckled quietly, but a man's voice cut through his laughter. It was the same one he had just been previously talking to.

"Miss Morrow?" The man approached. "How are you feeling? Dizzy?"

I propped myself up on my elbows and blinked a couple of times. The man was tall, his skin white and pasty, his head of gray hair thinning, wrinkles forming around the corners of his eyes and lips. He wore a white coat, though the hem displayed diamonds, and a pin featuring purple and white was pinned to his lapel. A pure silver stethoscope hung around his neck.

I recognized the colors almost immediately. Embrasian colors.

"N—no, I'm ok," I stuttered out, trying hard to keep awe from my words.

"That's good." He smiled lightly and glanced down at the clipboard in his hands, rifling through the pages for a moment. "What about numb?"

"Oh, I . . . guess?" I replied, shooting Alexei a confused look. Where were we? Who was this man?

"Don't worry, that's normal," the man said. "Well, it appears you are all in order. I recommend a lot of rest, fluids, and food if you can keep it down."

I nodded, my mouth slightly hung agape. He nodded to Alexei.

"I'll leave you be, then."

Alexei nodded and they stiffly shook hands. The man pulled open a set of large marble doors. Light poured in for a brief second, then was gone as the man shut the doors behind him. The second he left, I turned to Alexei.

I could only manage one word. "What?"

"I know, I know, this is all weird. I woke up four days ago, here. I don't know how," he explained.

"Is this really . . ." I didn't need to finish my sentence.

He nodded grimly. "Yes. This is really the Embrasian castle."

"Why? How?" I swallowed my shock.

"I don't know, but they seemed pretty keen on making sure you're alive."

My hand flew to my chest. "Do they know?"

He paused, frowning. "Yes. I'm sorry, I had to tell them. They kept insisting to me that you were dead, but I knew they were wrong. They took you away, I thought they were going to dump your body somewhere, but then you started breathing and next thing I know, they were doing all these spells on you."

"What about you?" I asked.

"I'm fine, Ivory. They healed me, too," he replied, and I felt a wave of relief crash over me.

"So," I wavered, sitting up properly, "what now?"

He sighed. "I'm not sure. I have no clue what they're going to do with us. They know I don't have papers for Embrasia, they know about your . . . condition, but they really haven't said anything troubling. Yet."

"Maybe they'll just kick us out," I offered with a hopeful shrug.

"We won't kick you out."

Alexei and I gasped, whirling our heads toward the direction of the voice. Through the darkness, a young man stepped out of the shadows, his silver boots clicking against the floor. His caramel hair swished around his ears with each step, his skin burnt tan by too many hours in the sun. The lining of his green vest glittered gold, his white undershirt full of ruffles and buttons, his pants a dark green. A silver sword hung by his side, clanking against his thigh as he stepped toward us.

His face displayed a serious demeanor, though rounded like a small child's. His golden eyes shimmered with boredom as if he knew he had better places to be. I didn't understand how he had gotten in without either of us knowing. Was he there the whole time?

"I'm glad you're awake," he said as he approached. His voice bounced like a fluffy cloud, though drowned out by indifference.

"Who are you?" Alexei asked, but it sounded a lot more like a demand, as he stepped in front of me.

"Well, aren't you a little ray of sunshine," the man said, narrowing his eyes at Alexei. "I just want some explanation."

"You and me both," Alexei retorted with a sting of poison hidden deep in his tone.

The young man ignored him. "I just want to know who attacked you."

"Why?" Alexei narrowed his eyes.

"I'm not talking to you." He reached out and shoved Alexei over, catching my gaze in his. "You. Who attacked you?"

I glanced at Alexei, watching as he seethed with angry flames. I found his eyes and shook my head subtly. Somehow, I knew the man wasn't going to hurt either of us, and we didn't need to become criminals just because a man was rude. Alexei glared, though backed down slightly.

"Who's asking?" I quirked an eyebrow.

"I asked first."

"And I asked second. So what?" Out of the corner of my eye, I saw a smirk run across Alexei's face.

The man released a frustrated sigh. "If you're lucky, you won't know who I am. Just tell me, who stole your heart? Was it the Highwayman?"

"Who's the Highwayman?" I questioned, ignoring the fact he had assumed the reason of my heartlessness. And assumed wrong, for that matter.

"You're not answering my question!"

Alexei snickered, not trying very hard to hide it. "Well, maybe because you're asking the wrong question."

"Look, I'm just trying to help, I—"

A sharp knock against the door cut off the rest of his sentence. He gasped, whirling around to face the door.

"Don't tell him I was here," the young man whispered, before disappearing into the shadows at the back of the room.

The door opened and another man walked in. He wore a uniform displaying purple and white, the Embrasian colors, his black hair tied in a ponytail that trailed down his back. He looked to be around the same age as Layton, or perhaps a little older.

"Greetings, Mister Alexei and Miss Morrow, I am the king's personal squire. If you are well enough, the king has requested your presence at dinner tonight in the Blush Rose," the man said.

Alexei and I glanced at each other in shock. What could the king possibly want with us? I turned my head back to the squire to find his eyes scanning the room. Almost like he was looking for something. Or someone.

He took a step toward the rude young man's hiding place, and I couldn't stop myself from intervening, fearful he would discover the hidden man.

"We, uh, we accept his request," I spat out quickly, ignoring the strange look Alexei threw my way.

The squire paused in his tracks and returned his attention to the two of us. "Very well. I'm sure the king will be delighted."

With a bow to us, he whirled around and strode from the room. I released a breath I hadn't realized I had been holding, a breath for the rude young man.

"Alright, so what did you want to know?" I asked, slipping from the bed. "Hello?"

Silence greeted us. Alexei huffed, unimpressed, and peeled back a set of crimson curtains from the wall. Light spilled in, illuminating each and every crevice of the huge room, but the man was no longer there.

He was gone.

"Where did he go?" I asked aloud softly.

"Well, he's gone now, so good riddance," Alexei said with a deep intake of breath. "Are you sure you want to have dinner with the king?"

His words sent my stomach plummeting. I had tried to save the man when he wasn't even there in the first place. Anger teased at my emotions, but my dread overruled it. I couldn't meet the king! I had barely even met anyone in my whole life, let alone anyone as important as the king of Embrasia. But I had already accepted his dinner offer.

"It'll be fine." I nodded hesitantly.

"If you say so." Alexei shrugged uncertainty. "But I hope you don't plan on meeting him looking like that."

Only then did I realize Alexei wasn't wearing his usual attire, instead an agate blue coat with a silver trim, laced and ruffled white undershirt, black pants, and even blacker heeled boots. Diamonds hung from his ears and decorated his fingers. His hair was pulled into a bun, not one strand out of line, held by a golden pin. I could barely tear my eyes away, unsure if I had ever seen anyone so . . . I didn't know the right word to use, but I knew one thing.

He looked like royalty himself.

I glanced down at myself to find my torn and bloody black coat and green dress replaced by a white nightgown that hung down to my ankles.

"I know, I know, I woke up wearing something different too," Alexei said as he saw my distressed expression.

"This is weird," I groaned.

"I know," Alexei repeated, and strolled over to the marble cabinet pressed up against the wall.

He flung the doors open to reveal multiple dresses and shoes, all of different shapes, colors, and sizes, bigger and grander than any other dresses I had ever seen. The mere sight of them hugging each other sent my mind reeling even more.

"Here." He pulled out a long crimson dress and threw it in my arms. "Put that on. Dinner starts at six every evening. We don't have much time."

"But—"

"I'll be waiting outside."

I watched as he exited quickly, leaving me alone in a room much too big. I sighed and drew the curtains before hastily throwing off the nightgown and slipping into the dress.

There was no other word than *expensive* to describe it. The sleeves ended in lace and ruffles, the collar hemmed with red rubies. It hugged my waist a little tighter than I preferred and bunched out, just about long enough to graze the floor. Black buttons ran down the top, and a black ribbon tied around the middle. No doubt made from the finest silk. With every little movement, gems clicked together like the chimes of a bird.

I stepped in front of a vanity, gazing into the mirror, and my reflection almost frightened me. I looked like some sort of princess, a princess on the verge of vomiting, but a princess, nonetheless. I couldn't help but wonder what Layton and Dean would say if they saw me. Me, who only owned dresses of simple, banal colors.

I grabbed a brush and pulled my tangles out, tying a black ribbon through my snowy locks. With one last deep breath, I pinched my cheek in an attempt to get some color flowing into it, before joining Alexei out in the hall.

When I first stepped out, Alexei didn't seem to recognize me. He stared with wide eyes, his jaw slightly hung agape.

"What?" I asked. "Should I put on a different one?"

"No, no." He cleared his throat. "You look . . . fine. It's fine. Let's just go."

He set off, averting his gaze and still clearing his throat. I ignored his strange behavior, studying the crystal interior of the castle, shimmering and glittering in the light like drops of moontears.

"You know where we're going?" I asked.

"Of course," he responded. "Right around here."

We rounded a corner and a long hallway greeted us, a large set of double doors standing at the end, beneath carved words that read *Blush Rose*. A pair of men wearing the same Embrasian uniform stood attentive by the doors. As we approached, they bowed and pressed the door open silently. I tried offering a nod of thanks, but they seemed keen on keeping their eyes on the glittering floor.

Inside the Blush Rose, a table spanning across the whole room stood, a velvet tablecloth pressed down upon it. The room was huge, marble pillars reaching up to the ceiling. Uniformed men stood along the walls, unmoving, backs straight, though as Alexei led me to the table, I felt their eyes burning in the back of my head. Anxiety crept into my mind like a pesky, but unshakable, worm.

One of the men approached, pulling out a chair for both me and Alexei. Again, I nodded thanks, and again, it went unacknowledged. We sat, the matching velvet cushion like a pillow. I shot Alexei an uneasy glance, thankful that he caught it. He reached over and grabbed my hand, giving it a tight squeeze before letting go. The action somehow calmed my nerves.

On the other side of the room, a second pair of doors opened and two more uniformed men entered, pinning the doors to the walls.

"Introducing, the king of Embrasia, King Cathair!" one of them declared.

I swallowed my nerves as a towering man walked through, a large golden jeweled crown balanced perfectly on the top of his head of graying hair, his long purple cape swishing behind him. A short beard fell just below his jutting chin, his eyes a striking hazel. A scar ran up his square face, starting just below his left eye and ending above his lip. The small smile on his face contradicted his intimidating appearance.

"And, the prince of Embrasia, Prince Sasha!"

Another man walked in, not nearly as tall as his father, and barely as intimidating. His face was rounded like a child's, and his golden eyes shone with a familiar boredom. A silver crown rested upon his caramel hair.

I couldn't believe my eyes. It was the rude young man from earlier. And he was glaring at us as if to say, *"Don't utter a word."*

21

I couldn't rip my eyes away from the man, no, the *prince*. Standing in the colors of Embrasia instead of the dull greens he had previously been wearing, he appeared much more princely, yet I still couldn't believe it. After years of reading fairy tales full of handsome, valiant princes, I always imagined the prince of my own country just as so. Never in my wildest dreams did I imagine the prince to break into my room and demand answers to questions that weren't even correct. For a brief moment, I wondered if my eyes were merely playing tricks on me, the exhaustion of the past catching up with me.

But there was no mistaking it. Prince Sasha and the rude young man were one and the same.

Too caught up in my thoughts, I barely noticed Alexei stand. A second late, I scrambled to my feet, nearly knocking over my chair in the process, and copied Alexei's deep, elaborate bow. Only after I dropped in a bow did I remember I was supposed to curtsy. Heat sprung to my cheeks as I sent a silent prayer to the first god I could think of.

"I welcome you, Wizard Alexei and Miss Morrow, to my humble kingdom," King Cathair declared in a booming voice. His accent was so deep, I had to strain to understand his words. "I'm delighted you could be present this evening."

Alexei straightened, and a second later, I copied him once more. A smile that didn't quite reach his eyes slipped onto his face and when he spoke, he didn't sound as he usually did.

"Thank you, Your Majesty. We are honored to stand before you."

As his smile grew brighter, I urged my hands to stop shaking, my knees to stop buckling, but of course, my body paid no heed to my wants. I only trembled more, afraid I would collapse if I remained standing any longer.

Fortunately, with warm permission from the king, we sat, the two royalty halfway across the table. I forced myself to breathe, not too shallow, yet not too deep.

Don't mess this up, there's a lot of people looking at you right now. Gee, that was helpful. Shut up, shut up.

Before an awkward silence had the chance to creep in, King Cathair dove into conversation, his lips parting the second I sat down. Alexei perked up as the man spoke, his eyes trained intently on the king. Underneath the table, his fingers twirled around his napkin nervously. I wasn't sure if I had ever seen him so anxious.

"I was so relieved when I learned both of you fared well. I can't imagine what caused such damage, but please, if you would humor me," King Cathair said, and something more than mere curiosity gleamed in his eyes, but I couldn't quite tell what that something more was.

"Well, we were trying to cut through the Adeleigh Wood, Your Majesty. I hadn't realized Midsummer's Eve was so close, and," Alexei hesitated for a brief moment, "we ran into some complications with the fairy folk. And the sirens."

The king's eyes widened. "My, my, those wretched creatures. I thought I had taken care of them, but it appears they just won't be stopped. How did you ever escape?"

"We, uh," again, he wavered, searching for the right way to describe our Adeleigh expedition, "we mostly just ran for it. We hid in the rowan trees for a little while. I think we just barely managed to run through them."

For the first time since the conversation started, Prince Sasha spoke up. "You nearly lost your lives in doing so. You didn't happen to *run* by anything other than fairies and sirens?" His tone ran mocking.

"Oh, hush, Sasha," King Cathair scolded, then turned right back toward us with sharp attention. "Where did you come from? Were the trains not in order? Were you in a rush to get here?"

The king's questions struck strange to me, a little too forward, a little too lacking in formality, as if the three of us had been long-time childhood friends catching up after years of being apart. Nothing like how I imagined the king of Embrasia to be.

"No, no, no rush, but, well, you see, it's a bit of a complicated story, Your Majesty," Alexei replied. He glanced in my direction as if to signify my same thoughts ran through his head as well.

"By all means, I've got time!" the king thundered, laughing.

Alexei and I shot each other a quick, puzzled look, but before he could open his mouth, the doors flung open and a barrage of purple and white wearing men flew through, balancing at least a hundred silver trays on their shoulders. In seconds, they had set everything down and before I could even process what was going on, a bowl of soup sat in front of me and a napkin laid across my lap. My glass was filled high with white wine, and when I glanced at Alexei, I found he was already in the process of gulping down every last drop.

My hands continued trembling as we were welcomed to eat, my silver spoon clicking against the interior of the glittering bowl. I ate very little in fear anything I consumed would just come right back up, but out of respect (and slight fear), I swallowed down as much as I could. The fact that the food tasted like food of the gods didn't help at all.

"So, what is this complicated story you speak of?" King Cathair asked just after the third course was served, consisting of marinated elk drowning in a sauce of truffles and livers.

"Oh," Alexei uttered, seeming to be lost in the luxurious plates of poultry and fish, "yes, well, this all started because of excessive attacks by the hands of the Incarti. They relentlessly sought after us and the only way to shake them off was to burn down my own shop and flee into the Adeleigh Wood."

"How terrible." The king shook his head. "You say you own a shop?"

"Yes, Your Majesty, in Andros. A small business I gathered from the dust of the previous owners," Alexei replied, and by his tone, I knew his words were painted with lies. His unwavering ability to lie both unnerved me and reassured me.

"I didn't think Incarti attacked randomly," Prince Sasha piped up, his gaze narrowed in a suspicious glare.

But if anyone else thought this was suspicious, they didn't say so, for his remark went unacknowledged. Well, except for me, who caught his words clearly. Our eyes locked and his glare sharpened as if it were my fault nobody listened. I resisted the urge to glare back, just to see what he would do. But the more rational side of my brain advised me against it, and I drew my eyes back to the extravagant king.

"So, you lived in Andros?" King Cathair questioned, mercilessly tearing a lobster apart with his hands.

I gulped as Alexei answered for me.

"No, actually, only I lived in Andros. Ivory lived in Cyrene."

Lived. Was it really just that? Did I no longer live there? Did I ever really? If I didn't live in Cyrene, then where? For some reason, my eyes found Alexei.

"Ah, Cyrene, what a lovely little village," King Cathair mused. "And this whole time I've been assuming you two lived together."

"Cathair!" Prince Sasha exclaimed as both Alexei and I glowed with a red tint.

I glanced at the wizard to find his eyes were already set on me and we both tore our gazes away quicker than a bullet. I heard a clunk of silver against silver as Alexei dropped his fork.

"Ah, I speak too much, my apologies, dear friends." The king chuckled, not looking one bit sorry as he turned to me. "Mister Alexei must've paced the whole castle three times in the time you were recovering. Is there an expected proposal arriving shortly?"

"Please, stop," Prince Sasha groaned, his ears a little pink as he hid his eyes in his hands. "You're making this worse."

The king only laughed louder. "I jest, I jest. I'm done teasing, please excuse my twisted humor."

Alexei cleared his throat, the fire in his cheeks blaring bright red, but mine felt even worse, as if my whole face burned like a piece of firewood simmering a little too long, embers and ash beginning to fly. I wasn't sure if I had ever been so embarrassed in my life. How could it possibly appear we were married when I had loathed every part of the blasted wizard just days ago?

"I do love a good joke," Alexei said, fighting to snicker along with the king.

"Ah, and I love a man who can enjoy a joke!" King Cathair boomed in response, but just as quickly as he had burst out laughing, his face shifted into one of serious demeanor. "Although there is a time and place, I'm afraid I must steal the moment away. I still have a few questions I would like to be satisfied with."

"Of course." Alexei nodded just as the prince opened his mouth in protest. Again, only I seemed to catch his desire to add something in the conversation.

"The second I saw you, I recognized you, dear Alexei, and I knew you were to be welcomed like an honored guest. After all, your mother talked so much about you, I didn't think I would ever be able to miss the son she so fondly spoke of," King Cathair said.

Alexei froze, all color draining from his face. The sight sent my stomach dropping faster than a falling raindrop. His hands paused in mid-air, his fork clattering against his plate as it slipped from his grasp once again.

"I—I'm sorry, did you say," he swallowed roughly, "my mother?"

"Yes, of course. We used to dine in this very room together."

Alexei's face contorted with both confusion and pain. I frowned as I fought to catch his eyes, but his gaze remained trained on the king. I wanted to reach over and grab his trembling hands, as he would've done for me, but I couldn't bring myself to it, especially after King Cathair had thought we were a pair. I kept my puzzlement hidden, silently wondering what was so special about his mother.

"You two . . . know each other?" His voice shook just enough to notice.

The king's face fell, a frown taking over his lips. "My dear Alexei, did anyone ever tell you?"

When Alexei didn't reply, he continued. "Your mother, Scarlett, died just a year before the war ended. She joined my army amid the war and worked her way up to General. She's buried in the royal cemetery. I've been awaiting the day I could do this."

He snapped his fingers and a servant rushed forward, a box of gold laying on a crimson cushion resting in his arms. The king stood, instructing Alexei to do the same. He ignored my sharp look as he approached the king, who was in the process of opening the small box. His gloved hands daintily pulled out a gold medal with purple and white silken strands protruding from the bottom. He turned to Alexei, medal in hand.

"In honor of the best of my generals, I award this medal of honor to her son." He pinned the medal to Alexei's blue coat, then stepped back and saluted.

Through his amazement and confusion, Alexei saluted back, bowing before the two returned to their seats. I barely eyed the glimmering piece of gold upon my companion's lapel, instead focused on his face. A deep sorrow and traces of reminiscence plagued his expression. But it also seemed he had no clue what the king was talking about. I couldn't look away.

"Thank you," he ran a hand through his hair, "but I never knew my mom was here. We didn't know where she went."

"We?"

"My brothers and I," Alexei replied dismissively, as if it wasn't important, but it was the first time I had heard anything about siblings. "She . . . she knew how to fight?"

"Yes, and quite well, if I may say. To be honest, I'm not that surprised you were able to survive your nights in the Adeleigh Wood. With the amount of power she held, it's no wonder her son would be just as strong," King Cathair answered.

I wasn't sure if I just imagined it, but I sensed a hint of excitement in his tone. Something felt . . . wrong about the whole situation, different from the poison of lies and deception, but with hints of something similar. Something I couldn't quite put my finger on. Though just as my eyes narrowed by the king's words, Prince Sasha's golden eyes found mine, his frown of disdain growing, and I finally realized he wasn't frowning because he didn't like me. He was trying to warn me.

"Alexei," I whispered, ignoring the sirens blaring in my head, and reached out to grab his hand.

He jumped at my touch, and for the first time in my life, I was glad my skin was as cold as a winter snowstorm. His head whirled around to meet mine and his somber state melted away in an instant. I stared at him with pleading eyes, praying he would catch my message. With a subtle nod, it seemed he did.

But before either of us could say anything else, the king had begun talking again. This time, not to Alexei, but addressing me.

"My dear Ivory, I have seen the price on your head," he said, almost casually, even. "I can't imagine what a girl like you would be doing in a lovely, but *little* village like Cyrene."

I faced him, a sickening feeling rising up in my stomach. I could sense the words on his tongue, but I didn't want to hear them. Out of everyone in the world, it just had to be the king of Embrasia that knew of my heartlessness.

"I've never met a girl like you, and neither has my Magicians. They were baffled by your state of living, and they'd like to know more, see what they can do. But if you don't mind, might you tell me what it is keeping you breathing?" King Cathair continued.

Yes, I would very much mind, thank you very much. But nobody said no to the king.

"Of course, Your Majesty. The town wizard spent many years searching for an answer, but he never found one. He said I was born with a magical deformation, possibly caused by," I hesitated, swallowing roughly, "a sickness that killed my mother."

"Oh, how dreadful," the king moaned, shaking his head slowly, his eyes swimming with emotion. I couldn't tell if the show he displayed was fake and tried insisting to myself I was only imagining things. I could barely believe I had just lied to the king of Embrasia.

Alexei's burning gaze scorched my face, but I willed myself not to look at him. I didn't need to look as suspicious as I felt. I hoped my shaking hands weren't too noticeable.

"Does this *deformation*," he said the word like it held a mighty curse, "affect you in any way?"

"Cathair," the prince hissed, sending an icy glare at his father, who promptly ignored it.

I paused before I answered, the words on my tongue foreign and wrong. "Yes, my emotions are . . . altered because of it."

"Altered, you say?" He leaned forward eagerly, his eyes glistening with that same subtle excitement I had seen previously, but this time, Alexei seemed to catch it as well and squeezed my hand, almost with as much warning as the prince's golden eyes.

"Would you leave the poor girl alone? You've already tormented her long enough!" Prince Sasha snapped suddenly, his fists shaking with rage.

"If you're going to be difficult, you can excuse yourself, Sasha," King Cathair responded calmly. The prince crossed his arms and leaned back in his chair. But not one more word left his lips.

Alexei and I watched this exchange in confusion, leaving me wondering if this was what every dinner with the royal family consisted of. Annoyed glares, frowns of disdain, and ignorance toward each other. For a moment, I wondered if that was what it looked like every night at our dinner table in Cyrene between me and my brothers, but I wanted to think we were a little more civil. I wasn't sure if that made me feel better or worse.

"You were saying?" King Cathair shot a smile in my direction, of which I responded with a wavering crack of my lips, barely enough to show teeth.

"Uh, altered as in . . . I can't process specific emotions like normal people can," I continued, my eyes trained on anything but the prince.

"Interesting." The smile on his face quirked. "Well, my Magicians have offered to speak with you. They think they might know what to do, assuming you'd want them to."

Alexei and I perked up, my blood seeming to halt. Was he saying they knew how to fix me, and they would, just like that? It was impossible, too good to be true, but the unwavering confidence in the king's face said otherwise. I couldn't help but let a nervous laugh escape my lips.

"You—you mean they can give me a heart? Make me normal?" I asked in disbelief.

Layton's words echoed in my head. *You aren't normal. You never were normal, and you never will be!* But was this my chance, after so long dreaming of gaining the ability to love? How would they react if I returned home with a heartbeat of my own? I couldn't fathom it.

"Why, of course. I'll ring them right after dinner, if you'd like," King Cathair responded with a slight laugh to his words, as if this were the obvious solution and I should've beseeched him years ago.

My jaw nearly dropped, but through my shock, I thought I might've felt the corners of my lips twitch. Maybe I really was just imagining things earlier. Besides, what could the prince possibly be trying to warn me about?

"Yes, thank you, thank you, Your Majesty," I sputtered out.

My thoughts struggled to process. They were going to give me a heart. Love. Everything I ever wanted. I imagined returning home to Cyrene, telling Layton and Dean, explaining everything. We'd embrace each other like we used to, like a real family, and I would never be trapped inside ever again. *Because by this time tomorrow, I'll finally know what a heartbeat feels like.*

"I'm glad I could be of help." King Cathair's smile widened and he lifted his goblet of wine in a toast. Alexei and I followed suit. "Anything to repay my debt to Alexei Kementari."

I gasped, and the glass slipped from my hand, crashing against the table and splattering the two of us in white wine.

Did he just say . . . Kementari? As in, Gethan *Kementari?*

22

"Ivory!" Alexei cried, jumping up from his seat. "Are you ok? What is it?"

No, it couldn't be. He couldn't be. It must be a coincidence. Some people have the same last name, perhaps this one is a common one among wizards. They couldn't possibly be related.

But I didn't believe myself. He might've shared blood with the same man that tore apart my family.

"Get her some water, she looks like she's about to faint!" Prince Sasha barked, but it sounded distant, as if he were speaking through water.

Alexei's hand found my shoulder. One part of me wanted to leave it there, the other part wanted to dig my nails into his flesh until his blood soaked the crimson sleeve of my gown. Instead of doing either of those things, I shot up from the chair, dusting my hands rapidly against my skirt.

"I'm so sorry! Really, I am!" I cried. "I think the shock was a little too much for me. I can repay you for—"

"Nonsense, it is my fault." King Cathair motioned for some servants, and they came running. They cleared and replaced my glass in a matter of seconds, wiped down the table, and rushed away just as quickly as they had come. "I should have thought of the weight of my words."

Alexei stepped forward, a pointed look painted on his face, but I wouldn't look at him. Couldn't look at him. Even when he grabbed my hands and helped me back to my seat. Even when he kept his hands in mine, holding them tight in a way I might've thought reassuring.

"I—I'm sorry," I whispered, unsure if anyone even heard it, my face flushed white as snow, my stomach tying in terribly tight knots. I was insanely relieved I hadn't eaten much.

I glanced up to catch a glimpse of the king pulling out a golden pocket watch, his eyes widening as he read the time.

"I'm terribly sorry I must leave you now, but I'm afraid I have somewhere urgent to be. Please, stay as long as you wish and feel free to ask any of my staff for assistance. I wish health be upon you." The king stood in a rush, quickly marching out of the expansive Blush Rose, trailed by a quartet of guards.

The door slammed shut behind him, the crash echoing in my ears, leaving me alone with the prince of Embrasia and Alexei *Kementari*. I couldn't help but wish to be back in the presence of the sirens instead.

"Ivory, what's wrong?" Alexei leaned over and asked. "Are you dizzy? Maybe we never should've accepted this dinner request. You should've said something if you weren't feeling right."

"Didn't the doctor recommend rest? Perhaps she should return to her room," Prince Sasha said. "I'll escort you."

When Alexei opened his mouth to protest, the golden-eyed prince cut him off with a glare.

"Really, I insist." His voice was hard as stone.

So, I allowed them to assist me to my feet, Alexei's hand steadying me, and the three of us exited the Blush Rose, abandoning mountains of food piled high on silver and golden platters, returning to the never-ending crystal tunnels of the castle. As I walked, I felt myself sway slightly, and I knew it wasn't just from the shock. I really was exhausted. My head pounded, my stomach twisted, my skin grew clammy, and my body felt heavy as stones. So much so, I debated whether or not my buckling legs would even be able to carry me to my room. I prayed I wouldn't collapse in the arms of a wizard and the prince of my country.

It took a thousand years, but we eventually arrived back at my room of dazzling crystal windows and mirrors. As we walked through the threshold, Prince Sasha locked the door behind us and drew the curtains. He clicked on a couple hanging lanterns, then dropped down on the side of my bed.

"You're smarter than I thought. Most people wouldn't have the guts to pretend to get sick in front of Cathair," he said, crossing his arms.

"What are you talking about?" Alexei demanded as I slipped from his warm touch.

"You were pretending . . . weren't you?" he asked, pointing his gaze at me.

In response, my knees buckled from underneath me, sending me stumbling to regain my balance. Luckily, Alexei caught my arm before I hit the ground and directed me to the bed, where Prince Sasha immediately made room. My head spun, both of nausea and shock. Two types of shock.

I clutched my aching head in my hands, drawing in deep breaths. My dress clung to my skin with both wine and sweat.

"Should we get the doctor?" Alexei asked, turning toward the door.

But Prince Sasha caught his sleeve quick. "No. I need to talk to you while we still have privacy."

Alexei swiped his hand away. "What, you want to ask us more ludicrous questions?"

"Alexei," I scolded. Even if he was a strange prince, that didn't make him any less of a prince.

"Alright, I'll give you that one. I wasn't aware she was born like that, I thought—" He cut himself off, a veil of guilt cascading over his face.

"A wizard stole it?" Alexei growled.

"No," insisted Prince Sasha, "not a wizard. I thought it was the same person who attacked you in the Wood."

"That Highwayman?" I asked, remembering what he had said the first time we met.

"You know who he is?"

"Never heard of him."

"Neither have I," Alexei added.

The prince let out a frustrated groan. "You said it was the fey that attacked you. Did you encounter anyone else?"

"Other than the sirens, no," Alexei answered. "Why? You need a damsel in distress to save?"

"You're absurd," the prince snarled, crossing his arms in a childlike manner. "This is none of your business."

"Then why are you asking us questions about it?"

"Let me guess, you've never been to Embrasia before," Prince Sasha said in reply.

"Well, no, but—"

"Then it doesn't concern you. Just collect your medals of honor and hearts, and leave before it's too late."

"I would, but it sounds to me you need assistance. Is there any way a wizard could help?" Alexei asked stubbornly.

There he goes again, offering help to people who never asked for it, never wanted it. That doesn't make him a Kementari . . . right? It just makes him annoying. Or perhaps that's all the Kementaris do.

"You should focus on helping your girlfriend before a kingdom that's not even yours." Prince Sasha gestured to me.

"She's not my—ok, ok, whatever. I'll have you know I live under the laws of this kingdom, so it is my business. What is this Highwayman you keep talking about?"

I blinked away my nausea as Prince Sasha sighed, glaring at us uncertainly. I couldn't be distracted by Alexei; there were more pressing matters. I would address his identity later, considering he would even indulge me in on the truth.

"Cathair is trying to ignore it," the prince started, "but this kingdom is in trouble. Deep, deep trouble."

"Really? After so many years at war, no one would ever guess," Alexei said, sarcasm dripping in his words like an over-frosted cake.

Prince Sasha glared, but continued anyway. "That's the problem. Nobody *would* ever guess. And you won't realize it until it's too late."

"Too late?" I asked.

"Think of it this way. One second, you're rich as, well, as me, and then the next thing you know, your money is gone, your valuables, belongings, treasures, and your heart." He flinched as I shot him a look. "Oh, sorry. And nobody can figure out how such a robbery was committed, so as you're squawking over yourself, the bank next door goes through the exact same thing." He took a long breath as Alexei and I stared at him blankly.

"And then, they come flocking the castle, and you know what Cathair says? He says, "nothing to worry about", but there's everything to worry about! I think maybe if he simply set one foot outside, he'd see just how insane the streets are! I mean, nobody trusts each other, people can't trust the banks, the non-magic blame the wizards and the wizards blame the king!"

He collapsed against the wall, breathing deep, his lips moving as if he still had more to say. I sat, shocked that a prince would blurt out all the nation's secrets like that. He definitely wasn't how I imagined princes when I read all of those books. No, Prince Sasha, behind the glowering golden eyes, was more of a child than a prince. A very immature, naive child, but at least he had intentions of fixing his kingdom.

"And where does this Highwayman fellow fit in?" Alexei inquired, though only after a brief moment of shocked silence.

"It's the only lead I have. For weeks, I've been arranging hunts for whoever is responsible for this. I've caught quite a few of them, but no matter what we do, they won't talk. However, there are reports of whispers and gossip, someone called the Highwayman. Or something. A gang, an organization, maybe?" Prince Sasha replied. He had set to pacing, fumbling with the hilt of his silver sword.

"These men you caught, are they wizards?" Alexei asked lightly. I sensed a slight twinge of anticipation in his voice as I watched him pull on his collar.

"So far, no. If they were, they would've used magic to escape or defend themselves long ago."

Alexei's tense shoulders dropped slightly, a sigh taking over his whole body. One part of me wanted to be relieved with him too. I tried to ignore that part.

"I thought I was onto something the other day, some man with strange glowing hands. I chased him up to the edge of Adeleigh, and that's when I stumbled across the two of you lying bloody unconscious," Prince Sasha explained.

"Wait." I held out a hand and stood, my previous dizziness fading away. "*You* found us?"

The prince's hand flew to his mouth. "That's a secret! If Cathair knows I snuck out, I'll never see the light of day!"

"You mean you haven't told him about all of this? It's evidence that you can use to persuade him," Alexei insisted with eyebrows quirked.

"I can have all the evidence in the world and he still won't do anything about it," Prince Sasha responded knowingly.

I winced at the prince's words, feeling them hit hard. It reminded me a little too much of Layton and Dean, how I knew Dean had seen that Incarti, yet he still denied it. Why? Why had he denied it? Prince Sasha's childishness didn't come from the spoilt life of a prince; it was from the never-ending ignorance from his father. I was just as immature as he was.

"Well, what are you going to do about it now?" I questioned, all weariness gone.

"The only thing I can do is follow my last lead," he answered, defeat hidden somewhere deep in his voice. No wonder he told us the whole situation. There wasn't much else he could do.

"You mean the Adeleigh Wood?"

"Well, what else am I supposed to do? Not too long before riots take to the streets, and Embrasia doesn't need that. Not after a nine-year war," Prince Sasha replied, flinging his hands out in exasperation, before burying his face in them.

Alexei and I found each other's eyes, pity shining in both. The prince couldn't have been much older than Alexei, possibly even younger, with an ignorant father that refused to listen to a word he said. Even when it was for the good of the country. No wonder he acted so cruelly toward the king.

"So, as a thank you, or to repay our debt," Alexei smiled in a way that caught everyone's attention, "how can we help, Your Majesty?"

Prince Sasha slowly pulled his hands away from his face, the corners of his lips twitching slightly, a minuscule shine of hope glimmering in his eyes.

"First, call me Sasha." His smile blossomed. "I've always wanted to say that."

But before Sasha could fit in one more word, a knock at the door resounded and he instantly shrank back, taking a few steps backward. Alexei shot the two of us a look before he slowly approached the door, opening it as though a snake waited on the other side, fangs on display.

But standing on the opposite side of the door was not a snake, instead, a pair of fairly human-looking people. Though they were different genders, they wore the same exact thing, a purple robe with white embroidery stitched into designs. The man was rather short and stubby, his cheeks glowing natural red, black hair swept back by gel that twisted and curled at his neckline, wide eyes of eccentric green and blue. The woman, on the other hand, stood tall and slim, her skin a light bronze, her features refined sharply, and her dark hair trailed down her back in braids. Her dark eyes held a gentleness that calmed my nerves upon first glance.

"Good evening, Wizard Kementari!" the man practically shouted, his voice almost as booming as King Cathair's had been. I tried refraining from wincing at the reminder of the surname. "We are looking for the good lady Morrow!"

"And . . . you are?" Alexei covered the entrance, blocking their view.

"Ha, silly me! We are the royal Magicians," the man answered and dropped into a brief, dramatic bow. "We heard a certain heartless girl is in need of help."

Sasha locked eyes with me and shook his head. I furrowed my eyebrows and mouthed to him, asking why. But before he could attempt to answer, the man's thundering voice cut him off.

"My prince, what are you doing in there?"

"I'm just . . . showing them around," Sasha responded weakly, his face flushing white.

The two Magicians stepped past Alexei and entered. I watched them apprehensively, but nothing quite threatening to them stuck out to me. They were wizards, yes, but legal ones. Ones that worked for the country, fought in the war.

"Your Majesty, there are servants for that, as you know," the man said with a slight quirk of a smile. "I'm not certain your father would approve, to speak—"

"I know, I just wanted to," he hesitated, his eyes swimming, "escort them personally, as a welcoming gesture. They've never even been to Embrasia."

"Really?" The man's eyes grew wide as though really shocked. "Well, by all means, tour away, but I'm afraid we must borrow the Morrow." He chuckled but was the only one to do so.

Suddenly, all eyes were on me. My mind reeled as the Magicians drew closer. What was I to say? If they could really fix me, then why not allow them to do so? But what about Sasha's warning? What could the prince have possibly meant?

"Come with us, dear, and you'll be falling in love in no time." The man winked with a smile, extending his hand out to me.

I glanced at Alexei for an answer, but he seemed just as confused as I was. I wanted to talk it over with him, as though a heart was something one held a meeting over, but the decision was so huge. It would change my whole life, not only my life, but my thoughts along with it. The decision would make me into a different person.

I hadn't realized it before, but the thought of gaining what I had wished for my whole life terrified me.

But before I could express any of these thoughts, the royal Magician had me by the arm and was leading me out, away from Alexei and Sasha, and toward a different life.

A normal life.

23

"My name is Marble Thistle," the man said as we disappeared from Alexei and Sasha's view, leaving them alone with an excuse that they were touring the castle. "And this is my colleague, Crystal Lerk. I know, she talks a lot."

I chuckled politely as Crystal smiled.

"You're scaring her, Mar," she said with a shake of her head and stooped down to whisper in my ear. "Don't worry, you'll get used to his eccentricity."

I smiled, only because I wasn't sure what else to do. Though Crystal's soft voice proved soothing, I still couldn't rid myself of an uneasy feeling in the pit of my stomach. Once they gave me a heart, would I know love right away? Would it hurt? What if I didn't like it?

"It's a good thing we found you at such a young age. If it's true you manifested a magical deformity, then who knows if it'll continue manifesting? And I don't even know what would happen to you if it did." Marble nudged my shoulder. "But we won't let that happen."

Again, all I could do was smile. With the rate of words he spewed out, fitting in a sentence was almost an impossible task.

"We've seen a lot of people who had sold their hearts away, but I've yet to hear of never being born with one to begin with. You must have a lot of magic bubbling inside you, am I right? Uncontrolled explosions or unintentional gusts of wind? Rain? Lightning!"

I took a step back and nearly crashed into Crystal. "Um, no, actually. I don't have magic. Never have."

"Seriously?" Marble cried. "That's . . . strange. I assumed you would at least possess a little, if not more than anyone has ever seen before."

"Am I supposed to?" I lifted my eyebrows.

'Well," he cleared his throat, "with the amount of magic it would take to replace a heart, I'd think you'd be full of untamed magic, uncontrollable and unpredictable, but you say you've never used any?"

I shook my head. "I suppose not that I know of. Nothing's ever exploded around me before."

Marble hummed, a deep look in his eyes. I could see the thoughts running through his head. Dubious. Interested. Excited. Hungry. I felt like a toy a little kid received for their birthday but was told they weren't allowed to play with until later. I resisted the urge to shiver.

"Perhaps more subtle magic?" Crystal asked with a shrug. "Any small, weird things that's happened to you?"

I paused, thinking. I spent most of my hours alone in a small house snuggled up with books, dreaming of the moon. In those hours, it seemed like nothing in the real world happened, however, in the realm of my imagination, with stories of princes and kings, heroes and villains playing out in my head, magic seemed possible. Magic seemed everywhere.

But not the same magic Marble and Crystal had in mind.

"I don't think so," I replied.

"Well, no matter, we'll get to the bottom of this in no time," Marble declared with the uplifting of a finger.

If you say so. I reminded myself to keep hope remained somewhere in my head, though it proved a little difficult. With so many years dreaming of this day, I could barely believe it was real. But it was. So why did my thoughts keep running back to Alexei?

I wished he were with me, with his confident demeanor, his full of purpose strides, blissful grin, and warm hand that always seemed to know when to find mine. His presence calmed my blood, like the mention of a peaceful winter night. The smell of old books. The feel of paper against skin. The steam of hot apple cider on my chin.

Safe.

Though with him, I had never been in so much danger before. The Incarti, sirens, and fey. How could I possibly feel safe with him?

"Ah, here we are!" Marble announced. "The Mandrake's Asphodelus!"

Standing in front of us, a massive archway with the words *Mandrake's Asphodelus* carved into the top towered high, surrounded by flowers and vines swirling down the pillars. The doors were huge, made from silver, with large handles hanging from each door.

I marveled at the miraculous entrance, mouth hanging open, eyes slightly squinted due to the excessive shine it cast, like a moonbeam hitting a well of diamonds.

"This is where all the magic happens." Marble stopped to chuckle at himself. "Right this way, in we go!"

The two Magicians led me through the heavy silver doors and into what seemed to be a coliseum of white. Twisted marble pillars stretched to the painted ceiling, and a thousand carved archways led into different hallways bathed in darkness. Intricate patterns and symbols were carved into the walls, floors, and even over the painted ceiling. I felt like I had stepped into a beehive—a crystal, sparkling beehive.

As we walked through, countless other Magicians turned their heads, their eyes following our every movement. Some smiled, tipping their heads, and others just stared with a curiosity I could relate to. They all wore the same robes, purple and white. I wasn't sure if I had seen the Embrasian colors so many times in my life.

So many eyes threw anticipation at me, leaving my skin all prickly and my blood rushing even faster. *Well, I guess it's safe to say Dad's rule has gone down the drain.* But at that moment, I didn't want to be seen. I just wanted to be back with Alexei and Sasha, conversing over a way to rescue Embrasia from this Highwayman fiend.

Crystal, Marble and I passed under an archway and into a deep corridor. As we walked, invisible lanterns on the walls lit up, illuminating our way through the maze of arches. I had never seen anything so beautiful, mysterious, huge. Overwhelming. Even more overwhelming than the king himself.

Compared to the carvings and endless halls, I felt like a piece of coal among rare diamonds. Ugly, disregarded, while everything that surrounded me shimmered like the stars of the eternal galaxy up above. They had a purpose to spread beauty and wealth, while mine was only to burn and simmer, and leave an unwanted stain on the flesh of the ones who got their hands on me. A stain that took a lot to wash away.

Is that how Alexei sees me? When he's a diamond in the rough, and I'm the rough in the diamond? A scuff that makes you have to throw away the whole diamond?

"Here we are!" Marble's excessive voice tore me from my storm of thoughts.

I snapped back to reality to see we had passed into a room just as white and sparkling as all the others, a table of silver standing in the middle, along with a stand of sharp tools that seemed unnerving at first glance. Nooks full of potions and vials filled the walls. It was all symmetrical to each other, perfectly straight, perfectly placed, not one thing in disarray. In fact, it was so perfect, it was daunting.

Too perfect.

As I took nervous glances around the room, Marble and Crystal pulled on a pair of white gloves. They separated, Marble running disinfectant over the sharp tools, while Crystal combed through the shelves upon shelves of vials until she plucked a rather small clear one from the top shelf.

"Go ahead and sit, dear," Marble said, patting the silver table, still one very sharp scalpel in his hand.

I timidly complied, hopping up clumsily. I folded my hands in my lap as I watched Crystal wrap a stethoscope around her neck.

She approached me with a bashful smile. "You don't mind, do you?"

I shook my head and she plugged her ears with the device, pressing the cool bell against my chest, instructing me to take long, deep breaths. I did as she said, though couldn't help but feel a little foolish doing so. After a few seconds of silence, she pulled away and tore the stethoscope from her neck.

"That's one empty chest," she confirmed.

"Interesting," Marble responded, swirling the vial with the clear liquid.

"Good interesting?" I asked nervously, trying hard to refrain from eyeing the vial suspiciously.

They both chuckled, sending a flush of heat to my cheeks. My fingers trembled slightly as I forced myself to calm down. They weren't going to hurt me. They were going to help me. Give me a heart. I exhaled a subtle breath, wishing I had Alexei by my side, his warm hand clutched in mine. But instead, strangers surrounded me in a place so foreign and unknown, I felt I would have had better luck navigating a muddled dream.

"Well, nothing about missing a heart is good, but it seems you've been managing pretty well." Marble stopped to chuckle. "That reminds me, I was meaning to ask your age."

"Oh." I blinked. "I just turned sixteen, like last week."

"Splendid, splendid," he whispered, nodding. "And your full name, please."

I glimpsed Crystal scribbling down my answer on a clipboard in the corner of my eye. "Ivory Minerva Morrow."

"Prone to sickness?"

"Um, sometimes?"

"Good, good. Siblings?"

"T—two older brothers."

"Magic?"

"No."

"Parents?"

"Does this really have anything to do with my manifestation?" I asked instead of answering, a slight note of irritation dripping in my voice.

The two Magicians blinked at me blankly, a look passing between the two of them. It was almost as if nobody had ever refused to answer them before, and they didn't know what to do about it. I resisted the urge to huff indignantly.

"Well, your parents could," Marble responded. "If they possessed magic, it could have led to—"

"No, they didn't have magic," I interrupted shortly. "I've never seen magic, used, or have been associated with it my whole life."

Marble hummed. "Well, that sure does clear some things up. More or less."

"Do you know what the cause is? Do magical deformations just happen spontaneously?" I inquired abruptly. I was tired of all the questions, I just wanted an answer, and to know what they were planning on doing with me.

"Well, no. Magic usually doesn't happen spontaneously. That's what makes you so special," Marble replied with a grin.

I nearly cringed. I did not fancy being called "special". I felt like a child being fondled over by an overprotective parent.

"But don't you worry. We'll find out exactly what we need to know." His smile faltered a little. "But first, we must have your permission."

"Permission? Nothing's going to . . . go wrong, right?" My anxiety rose to new heights. Color drained from my face.

"Of course not! Nothing ever goes wrong," he answered, "but it's just a . . . new procedure the king has set in motion. Just for extra safety. You will be as safe as you can possibly be as long as you allow us to do exactly what we need to do."

"There's no need to worry, Miss Ivory." Crystal placed a gloved hand on my shoulder. "You will be perfectly safe."

"And besides, you won't be awake for most of it anyway."

Crystal nudged Marble hard upon seeing the look on my face.

"What do you mean I won't be awake?" I exclaimed, scooting backward slightly.

"Oh, darling, there isn't any reason to look so scared. He just meant that we need to anesthetize you in order to find out what we need to know to deliver a heart. We need to know exactly what's in your chest, and we can't do that without . . . ," Crystal trailed off, searching for words, but Marble finished her sentence before she could.

"Without opening up your chest cavity."

"You mean you're going to cut me open?" My face flushed white, fear tightly grabbing ahold of my veins. An urge to run, and run as fast and as far away as I could, slipped into my mind, nearly impossible to ignore.

"Calm down, darling, you won't feel any of it. It'll be just like falling asleep and waking up from a really long nap," Marble insisted serenely. "And when you wake, you'll have yourself a beating heart with the capability to love. We just need your permission first."

With wide eyes, I gazed at them, my thoughts racing. I couldn't possibly allow these strangers to tear into my chest and dig through my insides like I was some science project! But what other choice did I have? This was my chance, possibly my only chance, to gain a heart. Could I really pass it up just out of fear? What would Alexei say? What would Alexei do?

"And there's no other way?" I asked.

"Unfortunately, no. We would perform it instead if there was one, but with a situation like this, I'm afraid this is the only option," Crystal answered, taking my hand in hers like how a mother might. "There's nothing to worry about, we'll take good care of you. We just need a signature."

They handed me the clipboard, a line for my name mocking me at the bottom. I sighed, long and hard. There really was no other option. If I wanted to be normal, repay my brothers for everything they had done for me, I needed to sign. If I ever wanted to know the sweet release of love, I needed to sign.

I picked up the pen and signed my name with one shaky flourish. The two Magicians smiled and snatched the clipboard away. My skin felt numb with fear as they scrambled around the room gracefully, plucking countless tools and vials from out of nowhere, so fast my eyes could barely catch all of it.

I watched as Crystal poured about half of the clear liquid into a mini glass. She handed it to me, and I accepted it gingerly.

"This will help you go to sleep. Right after you drink it, lay back. Make sure to drink it all," she explained.

I glanced down at the liquid. "And none of this will hurt?"

"No, dear, the next time you open your eyes will be when we're all finished. And you'll have everything you ever wanted."

Everything I ever wanted. Why did Alexei's twinkling laugh come to mind?

I took a deep breath, failing to force courage into my system. I clasped my eyes shut and threw my head back, downing the liquid in one gulp.

Right as the clear liquid slipped down my throat, an overwhelming exhaustion took hold on my whole body and mind. My once swimming thoughts blurred like ripples of water, and keeping myself sitting upright demanded all of my ephemeral strength.

Crystal's grasp on me tightened as she helped me lay back gently. Despite my efforts to keep my eyes open, my vision went blurry and unfocused. The last thing I saw was Marble and Crystal's faces peering over me as if I were lying in a coffin underground.

Then I slipped into the darkness that called me so desperately.

· · · ·

The shadows embraced me in a familiar way that seeped into my cold skin, sinking its deep claws into my body and shaking me until my senses returned in a rush that sent my thoughts reeling. My nose prickled with a strong metallic tang and my skin burned like fire had harvested a home in my blood, boiling and blistering my skin. It was pure agony, but despite my efforts, I couldn't open my eyes.

Trapped in a sea of black, I willed myself to move, to scream, but my body refused to listen to me. I released countless shrieks, but only I heard them, for my lips remained unmoving.

"I don't think this is going to work, Marble." A voice crawled into my song of panic. I listened desperately, searching for release from the pain. "If we go on any longer, we might lose her."

"Look, she's still breathing, and breathing quite steadily. We can't stop after searching so long for something like this."

"She's only sixteen."

"We've lost younger. You seem to have forgotten that she signed the contract. Now stop your blubbering and hand me that hook."

Another sharp jab shot pain through my body and I screamed again, but I was still the only one able to hear it. I begged my body to move, my lips to twitch, my hand to spasm, anything to tell them I was awake. Anything to tell them I could feel everything they were doing.

"Maybe we should try something else, this is getting us nowhere. Perhaps Dust," Marble said.

I nearly replaced my screams with cries of joy. Healing Dust was exactly what I needed. Maybe it would even snap my body out of its paralyzed state.

"Fire Dust, do you think?"

No, healing! I need healing! What in the name of the goddesses would Fire Dust do?

"Exactly. That should soften this up enough for us to get through."

I waited anxiously, keeping a melody of cries playing in my head, hoping if I kept trying, they would eventually slip past my lips. I heard the clink of glass, the pop of a bottle, simply praying that whatever they were about to do would wake me up. Or at least, I wanted to believe that it wouldn't hurt.

But of course, I was wrong.

24

Alexei

The prince's long strides carried the two of us through the winding corridors and halls of the crystal castle. His brisk pace was almost difficult to keep up with, and it left no time to study the mysteries that surrounded me. Of course, I had never been to a palace before, and of course, I knew the Embrasian palace was probably the worst one to be in, considering it was technically illegal for me to even be there, but I still couldn't help but marvel at the impossible twists and turns. If I didn't know any better, I would've guessed the walls were built from magic.

"We mustn't dwindle too long in one place. If anyone catches us . . . ," Sasha trailed off, leaving my imagination to do the rest.

"Aren't you allowed to dwindle in your own home?" I asked with the quirk of an eyebrow.

"Not without the eyes of a hundred guards," he replied with an impatient sigh. "And I really should be spending my time reading and sitting through lessons and all the other boring princely things I'm supposed to be at."

"You sure make the job sound glamorous."

"Yeah, I just love not having one second to myself. It's so worth the custom-made silken clothes and seven-course dinner."

"No need to brag now."

The two of us shared a laugh. He nudged my shoulder, the touch strange and foreign to me. I nearly pulled away, but forced myself to stay by his side. He had a thing for physical contact, whether it be just a pat on the back or a nudge on the shoulder. It was almost like he had no clue what to do with his hands when they weren't wrapped around the hilt of his sword. I even caught him twirling his hair a couple of times.

"There must be some perks to being a wizard, right? I mean, you can call fire out of nowhere. Can you fly?"

I couldn't stop the laugh rising up in my throat. "I'm a wizard, not a bird. Though, I have levitated a few times, but that's not the point."

We continued on, our conversation light and fluffy, but I knew the real reason behind Sasha's words. He was trying to distract me. I wasn't aware of how disheveled I looked when those Magicians took Ivory away, but apparently, I had been hiding it worse than I thought. The prince rambled about mindless things, while my head played situations over and over. Situations that led Ivory to the grave.

I didn't want to admit it, but I was dying to ask Sasha about the Magicians. I had to assume they knew what they were doing, they were the royal wizards specifically chosen by the king, who fought alongside them during the war. They must've known every healing spell in the book. Then why did I feel so uneasy?

Their smiles, their unwavering, in-step strides, their perfect robes. Perfect. Was it possible they were too perfect? I couldn't help but find mistrust for them, no matter the fact they could grant what Ivory wanted.

And I think, somewhere deep down, a pit of shame welled up in my stomach. She had saved my life, and I had saved hers. We hated each other just days ago, but now . . . it was different. Fate brought her to a wizard, but I couldn't even help her with the one thing she truly wanted. And now she was all alone with wizards she had never met before, allowing them to tamper with her.

Just thinking about it brought a shiver running up my back. I wanted to be by her side, watching every little thing the Magicians did. Not only to reassure her, but to reassure myself.

"How long has it been?" I asked, cutting off whatever Sasha had been rambling about.

He didn't have to ask what I was talking about. "Not that long."

I bit my bottom lip. "I don't like this."

"Neither do I."

"What do you mean?" I questioned. I didn't realize my voice rose an octave.

Sasha avoided my eyes as he answered. "I tried to warn her, I really did, but the Magicians, well, they can be reckless at times. Especially around things they've never seen before."

"Ivory is not a *thing*!" I exclaimed. "What do you mean reckless? What are they doing to her?"

"I don't know. Non-Magicians aren't allowed in the Mandrake," Sasha responded. "I don't know much about them, but sometimes . . . people go in and never come back out."

My heart dropped, my face flushing white. Flames flicked off the tips of my hair in tendrils.

"We have to go to her!" I shouted.

"I told you, we aren't allowed in!" Sasha grabbed my shoulder, and it took all my willpower not to scorch his flesh.

"Are you telling me she might die if she stays there? And I'm not *allowed* in?"

"What I'm saying is the Magicians might not have the solution Ivory is looking for. Besides, I think only wizards can get in."

"You mean the entrance is enchanted?"

"Possibly?" He shrugged uncertainty.

I groaned and set to pacing, my strides two times faster than our previous pace. *Great, this is just great! I knew it! I knew I never should have let her out of my sight! Why do bad things happen every time we're separated?*

"Look, I'm sure there's nothing to worry about. They would never be reckless with an honored guest of the king," Sasha said. "They would be risking execution themselves, and I know they aren't stupid enough to dabble with magic they don't know of."

My heartbeat slowed, but it wasn't enough. I wanted to be certain. I wanted to hear Ivory herself say there was nothing to be worried about, but unfortunately, she was on the other side of some enchanted door. Blast this stupid country.

"We'll make our way to Mandrake and ask for her. They wouldn't deny their prince." Sasha pulled me into another hallway.

This time it was him who struggled to keep up with my pace. Though I couldn't force myself to trust him, I found his willingness to help me softened my cold attitude toward him. I couldn't imagine the boy being king, but maybe, just maybe, he could be an ally.

"So, how long have you two known each other?" he asked, I figured just to break the silence between us.

"We met last week," I answered shortly.

Sasha released something that might've been a cross between a gasp and a laugh. "Seriously?"

"Yes, why?"

"You seem like you've known each other your whole life. I mean, have you seen the way she looks at you?" Sasha replied.

"What do you mean?"

This time, he outright just laughed and refused to answer my question, no matter how hard I pushed. I tried ignoring the irritation clawing at the back of my head, but with little avail.

"Alright fine, if you're not going to tell me, then answer me this. Why do you call your father by his name?" I interrupted his laughter, and he immediately sobered.

"If you had a father that ignored your every request, you wouldn't care to call him father. That's a tile a man earns," Sasha responded, and said it with a twinge of poison too, like he didn't think I would understand.

But to his surprise, I nodded. I could understand, after all. "What about your mother?"

The prince frowned, shaking his head. "She died when I was young. I think that's why Cathair acts as he does, but he should know no Magician can bring the dead back. Sometimes I still catch him looking at her portrait and I see a faint flicker of his old self. He still hasn't let go."

"Have you?"

Sasha shook his head. I frowned, and not just from sympathy. I didn't want to admit it, but the fact that my own mother had been dead for years didn't sit well in my stomach. I never even knew I had to let go of her. She had been gone for so long, her departure mysterious, so I wasn't sure just how much I wanted to grieve for her. I thought one day, I would find her again and we'd be the family we used to be. Even though I knew she was dead, I still couldn't force the wish from my head.

What good were wishes if they were impossible to reach? It was like trying to swim to the bottom of a never-ending ocean, desperate and running out of air, but nothing to get in your way. Nothing but the hole that keeps growing deeper and deeper, until you find yourself lost in a trench far away from everything you once knew. And you had already gone so far, wasted so much pain, how could you possibly turn back? Was it even possible to turn back? And if it was, at what cost?

But I couldn't fall into that never-ending ocean now. Ivory needed me.

"So, what are you going to do about this Highwayman?" I asked, mostly just to change the subject.

"I'm going to go after him, of course," Sasha answered matter-of-factly.

"Running headfirst into a fight you didn't start is what gets you killed," I said.

"What do you suggest I do, then?"

"Well, first," I began, "you need a plan. I think I can help you there."

When I glanced at him with a smirk, I found he was smiling at me, too. I nearly faltered by the sight. I had forgotten the last time I had seen a smile like that directed toward me. It was one of pure trust.

Great, I thought, *I have to trust him now, don't I?* But somehow, the thought didn't seem as bad as I assumed it would be. In fact, it was a little . . . relieving.

We ventured through the castle, avoiding the eyes of the guards, slipping through secret passageways and doors to remain out of sight. Sasha seemed to know more about the secrets of the castle than his own father. It was a relatable trait.

I ran through countless plans, of which Sasha tweaked, adding information about what he knew about the streets of Embrasia. I explained everything I knew about the Adeleigh Wood, yet expressed a newfound dislike for it that I hadn't shown Ivory the day we first entered. I recounted the story of our days in the Wood with more detail, of which sent Sasha's golden eyes wide with both fear and excitement. To think danger would bring pleasure to a prince.

The distraction wasn't enough to calm my nerves, but it gave me something other than Ivory to think about. But just as she slipped from my thoughts, the plans pushing her out, was when the plump Magician with the slicked-back hair came running down the hall, his eyes wide, cheeks red, and face twisted in panic. My heart plummeted as he called my name.

"Wizard Alexei!" he shouted, gasping for breath, grabbing hold of my sleeve. "Something went wrong! We need you!"

I knew I should've never let her out of my sight.

25

Alexei

"What do you mean something went wrong?" I demanded as the Magician led me through the languorous halls of the palace, the crystals and diamonds mockingly shimmering as we flew past.

The sound of Sasha's quiet footsteps behind me planted a thought of relief in the mess that was my brain. At least if I had the prince with me, I wasn't just a wizard. With him, I was a wizard in favor of the kid who held charge over them and eventually, over the whole country.

"We—we tried using Dust on her, but she—she, oh, you'll just have to see!" he cried in response, picking up his pace excessively.

We skidded to a halt upon nearing a massive silver door, an archway reading *Mandrake's Asphodelus* hovering above it, decorated with plants and intricate carvings dancing down the pillars.

The Magician shoved the door open with such ease that signified that the doors were indeed magic. As the three of us burst through the entrance, the overwhelmingly sweet aroma of magic filled my nose, so much as to call flames flickering at my fingertips. I clenched my fists in an attempt to douse the flames, but with the amount of magic in the Mandrake, it was nearly impossible to keep my own magic at bay.

The inside of the Mandrake consisted of hundreds of separate entryways leading to unknown rooms, everything glowing with a white shine. So much shine, I wrestled to keep my eyes completely open.

We shot through one of the entrances and resurfaced in a spacious room decorated with shelves of potions. A mass of Magicians crowded around a table in the center of the room, scrambling with panic. Through the crowd, I spotted a pale hand hanging limply over the edge.

Ivory.

A gasp caught in my throat as I dove into the crowd, shoving my way through. Once they saw it was me, they immediately made room, standing aside and locking eyes on every movement of mine. The sight that greeted me sent my pounding heart spinning.

It was her, but not the Ivory I knew.

Her hair fell in dark curls down the table, her skin emitting an unnatural red glow that contradicted all the white surrounding her. Her eyes were flung open wide, her icy blue irises shining with a chocolate sheen that swirled in them. Her mouth hung open in a silent scream, steam rolling from her lips in smoky tendrils. Her whole body shook with uncontrolled spasms, her face twisted in pure agony.

Without thinking, I plucked her limp body from the table, bringing her head of dark hair to my lap. Panic pounded in my heart, but I tried to keep it at bay.

"Ivory." My voice trembled. "Can you hear me? Ivory?"

She gave no response. I pressed my hand into hers, shoving my fingers against her pressure points. Nothing.

But just before I pulled away, her body jerked upward, her head rising for a mere second and falling back down. I pushed down on her pressure points again, harder, and received the same reaction.

"What did you do?" I shouted to the Magicians behind me.

"We thought it would—" a woman with long dark braids started.

"*What* did you *do?*"

"Fire Dust," the woman answered. "We injected it into her system."

Injected! What kind of wizards are these people?

I let Ivory go gently, taking a small step back. It was a stretch, but I might've had an idea. My father had taught me how to command fire. Everything he taught me had never failed me. Fire was supposed to answer to me, and if it was fire coursing through Ivory's blood, only I could draw it out.

I held my hands over her twitching body, and with a deep intake of breath, pressed my palms to her arms. Her overheated skin jumped at the contact. I sensed a thousand dancing flames in her veins, fighting to take control, fighting to spread and destroy, as fire tended to do.

I pushed a surge of power into her flesh, cringing as the raging fire in her squirmed under my touch. I bit my lip roughly as I released another surge, magic seeping out of my fingertips and heat rushing back in.

I pulled the unnatural heat from her blood, grinding my teeth as a red vapor rose from her body. Her head jerked one way, a gasp escaping her lips. I forced the red vapor into my body, the rush of heat like an over intake of sugar. I swallowed the flames down my throat, a burst of energy briefly locking in my bones, before evaporating into nothing.

Behind me, the Magicians burst into applause, but the sound pounded somewhere far away. My vision blurred and my body swayed left and right. I clutched the side of the table for support, the heart inside my chest screaming for more fire. More heat. I gasped for breath, my chest heaving rapidly.

Get a grip, I urged myself, but I also couldn't help but realize I had never cast a spell like that. I didn't even know a spell like that existed, and I wasn't very sure what I did, but whatever it was, it left my body trembling from exertion. My magic was depleting, and depleting fast.

"Alexei." Sasha's voice came from somewhere distant. "Are you ok?"

I blinked before I turned toward him. Sound rushed back into my ears, my momentary exhaustion fading away. I ignored the empty chill the spell left in my heart.

"I'm fine," I insisted, and my eyes found Ivory.

The girl I came to know was back, her hair shining silver, her skin pale and painted with freckles. Her eyes were barely open, but the crystal blue shine caught my gaze anyway. Her chest smoothly rose up and down. It took me a minute to realize her lips were moving.

I leaned forward, hoping to catch what words her lips formed, but they were quiet and raspy.

"It's ok, Ivory," I whispered. "You're ok now."

She drew a breath in, her words shaking. "I . . . I'm awake. I'm awake. I'm awake."

I slipped my hand in hers, but she jerked away. Even though her skin had lost its unnatural heat, it still felt warmer than her usual temperature. Her usual temperature brought shivers down my spine and goosebumps prickling on my arms with just one touch. But now, she felt . . . almost normal. Not good.

"I think she has a fever," I said to the Magicians. "Bring me a cold towel."

At first, they just stared blankly at me, but as Sasha stepped forward, they scrambled to comply. The prince took my side, his face unreadable, but his fists trembled, and his jaw was clenched tightly.

The woman with the braids handed me a damp towel and I pressed it over Ivory's forehead. I swept back her sweaty hair, almost sighing in relief when she didn't flinch at my touch. An urge to peck her skin with a kiss washed over me, like how Mom used to do to me when I had fevers, but I couldn't bring myself to do it.

"Layton," she whispered before I had the chance to pull away.

"It's me, Ivory," I responded.

Her eyes cracked open. "Alexei. I'm awake. I'm . . . aw—"

Before she could finish her sentence, her head sank back, her eyes closed. I waited for them to open, but they remained clasped down. Panic washed over me.

"Ivory? Ivory!"

"It's alright." The Magician with the black hair pulled me away. "She's just sleeping, and I reckon she'll be sleeping for quite a while."

I tore myself from his grasp, fighting to keep a glare from my eyes. "And who's fault is that? What kind of wizard injects Dust into someone? Who do you think you are?"

"Alexei." Sasha reached out, his fingers just barely brushing my shoulder.

I forced my anger to simmer. I knew scorching the royal Magicians of Embrasia would not sit well with the king. Or Ivory.

"We'll move her back to her room. She'll be more comfortable there," the Magician said. The corners of his lips pitched downwards, his eyes holding some type of demented disappointment.

"What?" Sasha asked, noticing his sorrowful tone. "Will she be ok? Tell me she'll be fine!"

"Yes, of course, Your Majesty, it's just," the Magician faltered, "she's still . . . heartless."

"That doesn't matter," I spat. "You could've killed her. If it wasn't for me, she'd be dead." I pointed an accusing finger in their direction.

"Alexei, you're on fire," Sasha muttered.

I glanced down at my hands to find yellow and orange had taken refuge in my fingers. I shook the flames away, irritated. This wasn't the time to lose my temper, even though all I wanted to do was burn the oblivious Magicians to a crisp along with the annoying shine of the kingdom. Seriously, who decided to build an entire castle out of crystal? Now that was just a bad design job.

"We should go. It's almost sundown." Sasha tugged on my sleeve, glancing around nervously as if afraid his father would walk through the entrance at any moment.

I clenched my jaw and faced the prince. If we wanted our plan to catch the Highwayman to work, we needed to get out of there, and fast, but the thought of leaving Ivory behind planted panic in the pit of my stomach. I couldn't possibly leave her alone with those crazy wizards, and I had a feeling she would need me once she woke up.

I'll be back before she wakes us. She'll never even know I was gone.

I stole one last glance behind me, her skin blotchy with red, her eyes tightly closed, as though she were afraid to open them. She looked small and vulnerable, like a mouse being overlooked by a snake.

My heart throbbed as I followed Sasha out of the Mandrake, the image of her unmoving body burned in my head. I tried to tell myself she was fine, but I had a hard time believing it. Without me, I couldn't picture her being safe anywhere. She wasn't even safe in her own home, having lived behind locks set by her ignorant brothers. How could I possibly let her return to Cyrene when I knew I might never see her again? When I knew she might never see the wonders of life?

She deserved to see, to know. To hear and taste and feel. To love.

To live.

But without me, she never would be able to.

As Sasha and I escaped the prying eyes of the Magicians, narrowly missed the watch of the guards, and slipped into Sasha's room, I made myself a promise. I made Ivory a promise.

I would show her the world how she deserved to see it.

"Ready?" Sasha asked as he handed me a long silver sword, sheathing his own.

I nodded. But before I could show her anything, I needed to rid Embrasia of this thief of hearts.

26

"It's me, Ivory." Alexei's voice echoed in the static of my mind in a never-ending loop, over and over.

Over time it faded, grew closer, and faded again, always just out of my reach, always hidden behind a veil of darkness, and when I tried reaching out, my hand would disappear in the ebony, along with his voice.

I thought I would be trapped forever in a world of black with the familiar voice of Alexei somewhere far off, impossible to reach. I wondered if he reached for me, too. Or had he abandoned me long ago? Like how my mother and father did. His all too familiar accent pulled me through my thoughts, so familiar I was sure I had heard it before, sometime a long, long time ago.

I jerked awake, his name on my dry lips. My head ached like a hammer pounded against my forehead, and suddenly, I couldn't remember what I had thought so familiar.

I blinked a couple of times, digging my nails into the mattress beneath me. *No table. No Magicians. Was it all a dream?*

"Alexei?" I called out hoarsely.

Silence answered. I took a deep breath and a stab of pain shot through my chest. I cried out and grasped my blouse. It hurt to breathe, like air consisted of daggers, but I couldn't keep holding my breath forever. I sucked in short, shallow gasps of air, only enough to keep the tightness in my chest loose.

"Layton?" I choked out, tears prickling in my eyes. "Dean? Layton?"

No response came. I pushed through the pain and forced myself upright, the blanket falling into my lap. Sweat coated my skin like a layer of snow, calling goosebumps all over, leaving me shivering.

I shoved the comforters away and blindly made my way through the darkness, determined to find out where I was. It all couldn't have been a dream. Alexei was real. The Adeleigh Wood was real. The Embrasian palace, Sasha, the Magicians. It couldn't have all been a dream.

Yet, I still couldn't help but be afraid Layton would walk through the door at any moment.

My hand found a doorknob. My doorknob? I couldn't tell, but with a release of breath, it opened with the easiest turn of my wrist. No locks. No creaks.

The light of distant fire spilled into the room as I peered out, squinting. A crystal hallway greeted me. I swallowed roughly, relief washing over me, a smile tugging on my lips despite the odds. I knew it hadn't all been a dream.

I stepped into the hall to see two guards standing by my door, crystal armor and long spears in hand. They turned their heads just as I spotted them and as they realized it was me, they stepped in front of the door, blocking my exit.

"Wizard Alexei requested you stay here until he returns," one said in a voice rough as nails.

"Oh," I breathed. "Where is he?"

"He has gotten in contact with your brothers and the wizard Peyton Payne. He wished to notify them."

"He went to Cyrene!" I exclaimed, my eyebrows shooting up.

"You mustn't worry yourself, Miss Morrow. He should be back in a few hours."

"We advise you rest more," the other guard added.

I stared up at them in disbelief, my mouth slightly hung open. "What about the prince?"

They glanced at each other through the corners of their eyes, so subtly, I nearly missed it.

"What about him?"

"May I speak with him?" I asked, failing to keep hesitation from my voice. I knew I would be able to trust the prince, but I wasn't sure the guards would allow the two of us to meet again. At least, not without them breathing down our necks.

"I'm afraid not, Miss Morrow. It's the middle of the night, he had retired to bed long ago."

I frowned. I knew I should've trusted their words, but something told me against it. I had trusted the Magicians, after all, and look where that got me. I shivered just thinking about it.

"You'll be reunited with Wizard Alexei in the morning and you'll be free to speak with the prince tomorrow." The guard leaned over me and pushed my door open all the way. "We were told you need to rest."

I clasped my lips shut, exhaling a long breath through my nose. I knew I couldn't fight them, so I stepped back into the dark room, watching as their large hands pulled my door closed, leaving me alone in the silence of the night with a stomach that twisted into knots.

I couldn't bring myself to find the bed again, where my sweat had soaked the sheets. The last thing I wanted to do was fall back to sleep, where I wouldn't be able to control my thoughts or move my body. I was done being the one without control.

I bit my bottom lip, pacing my pain away as a storm rolled into my head. The guards had said Alexei went to Cyrene, but that wasn't possible. Alexei didn't have papers to Cyrene. And he knew my situation with my brothers. He wouldn't tell them where I was, right? No, he could've easily just turned me over to the police if he wanted me back with them. And there was no way he would ever go running to Payne. We both shared a hatred for the wizard that not one of us would ask for Payne's help. Not even if we were dying.

Then, where, if he wasn't at Cyrene, was he? I weighed my options, searching for the answer that made the most sense. A trip to Cyrene wasn't plausible, but where would be?

The Highwayman.

No. He wouldn't.

Ah, what am I kidding? Knowing Alexei, he's probably in the middle of negotiating terms of peace with the Highwayman right this second.

I crossed the room and tore the curtains from the glass walls, revealing a half-moon shining in the sky, blanketing the trees of Adeleigh with scattered light. A shiver crawled up my back as I studied the all too familiar forest and the spot where Prince Sasha had found us lying half dead.

Without meaning to, I pictured Alexei's body in the same place, mangled with rowan, and hair dripping with the pond water of the dead. I shook my head, blinking the image away, but it wouldn't quite disappear. Alexei needed me, like the first time we entered the Wood.

And I was going to find him.

I stumbled over to the wardrobe, rummaging through the extravagant dresses of diamonds and gems, slightly disturbed that once again, I was not wearing what I had been the last time I had been awake. Instead, a thin nightgown of lace covered my pale skin, doing nothing whatsoever to warm my prickling flesh. I pulled out a coat of fur, bedazzled with diamonds, but the best to wear in the midst of the cold night. A pair of slippers caught my eye, but I thought against it. Now wasn't the time for slippers.

Instead, I found a pair of heeled, black boots. I shoved my bare feet in the boots and slipped my arms through the inside-out sleeves of the coat. I snuggled up in the fur, burying my cold nose in the warmth of the fluff.

I returned to the windows, and with as much caution as I could manage, I pried the locks free, pushing the pane open. The wind caught the glass, sending it flying from my grasp and swinging haphazardly. I gasped and jumped to catch it, leaning out of the window to steady it.

The wind screamed in my ears, taking hold of my hair and throwing it every which way. With a shaky breath, I glimpsed down and the sight sent my stomach tumbling.

It was a good twenty feet drop, but it felt more like one hundred. Jumping from the top window in my bathroom was one thing, sliding down the side of a castle was another. Could I really do this? And for a wizard I just previously hated?

He would do it for me. And he would do it jumping headfirst, hands blazing.

I sucked in the cool air, shivering as it filled my lungs to the brim. The air had scared away my headache, but brought a chill unlike my usual cold seeping into my skin. I tightened the coat, then swung my legs over the glass sill.

My feet slipped a little on the crystal of the palace as I set them down, sending my blood rushing like a current. With one last deep intake of breath, I released the sill slowly, cautiously making my way across the inclining roof of the palace, inching one small step at a time.

Don't look down. Don't look down. Don't look down.

I kept my hands clutched to the crystal tiles of the roof, my breath growing more and more labored with each passing second. Not from exertion, but from panic.

By the time I had reached the edge of the roof, a sloped pillar standing underneath my feet, my chest heaved uncontrollably, leaving me hyperventilating almost as loud as the wind. Grinding my teeth, I glanced down at the pillar and nearly lost my balance, the ground so far down seeming to be getting smaller. I forced my eyes shut, pressing my body against the castle, fear coursing through my veins faster than my blood. My legs trembled from underneath me, quivering like leaves in the autumn breeze. I urged my eyes open and shakily knelt in front of the marble pillar. The carvings were deep enough for me to grasp onto, but that still didn't confirm I wouldn't fall to my death.

I shook my head and Alexei's emerald eyes flashed in my mind, his deep laugh, foreign accent. He needed me. Who knew if the fey had already made a meal of him? And the Embrasians were no help, whatsoever. No way was I going to trust any of them, save the exception of Sasha. I had to do this alone. Just as I had gone through life. Alone.

I turned my back against the wind and crouched down, carefully finding an indention in the carvings to place my feet. I curled my fingers around the marble, and with a quick prayer, let go of the edge.

My weight immediately came down on my weak legs, dragging me down the slanted pillar. I yelped in surprise, digging my fingers in the carvings until I could find the strength to hold my own weight. My fingers almost instantly turned red with both the pressure and the cold.

It was tedious and painful, but with enough time and focus, I managed to scramble my way down, one foot at a time. When my feet hit the grass, I nearly collapsed due to my buckling knees. It took everything in me to refrain from kissing the ground. Instead, I ran from the palace and to the edge of Adeleigh, the trees looming ominously, casting a blanket of shadows. The rustling of the leaves filled my ears like a melody.

I bit back my fear and sprinted past the trees, back into the treacherous Adeleigh Wood. My feet carried me like a rolling wave, each step growing more sturdier than the last, as if the deeper I went, the more my confidence grew. Adrenaline pumped in my veins, urging me faster. I couldn't help but comply, and it wasn't until I had lost sight of the castle behind me did I realize I was smiling.

I tried wiping the grin from my face, but nothing could bring me to do it. I wasn't entirely sure the purpose of my bliss, but I blamed it on my success in escaping the Embrasian castle. I felt like a character in one of my fairy tales, like a valiant prince myself. No, not a prince. A knight.

Pride bubbled up in my chest, overflowing and overwhelming my senses. I tugged my hair from inside my coat, letting it fly in the wind that tickled my neck so. I knew my chest was empty, but that didn't stop me from feeling . . . alive.

Alive. Invincible. Valiant. *Alone.* So very alone.

A frown tugged at my lips as I slowed to a walk, taking in my surroundings. If Alexei were with me, I would know exactly where I was. He would know exactly where we were. But instead, I alone faced the endless trail of whispering trees with only my thoughts to occupy me.

A slight twinge of anticipation crept into the back of my mind as I ventured further. Questions I had tried keeping out banged on my conscience, begging to be heard.

What if I didn't find him? What if the fey recognized me? What if the guards at the castle realize I was gone? What if, what if, what if? Too many what-ifs.

I huffed, a breath of warm air circling around my lips, shaking my head as if it would shake all of the bad thoughts from it.

Calm down, Ivory. Everything will be fine; I'll find him, and we'll leave this gods-awful place. No need to fret.

I took a deep breath, urging myself to believe my own thoughts, slowing once more to a casual walk, my chest heaving slightly. Despite the harsh, biting wind, a thin layer of perspiration coated my forehead. I reached up and wiped the beads of sweat with the back of my hand.

I continued silently, convinced the whispers were getting louder, growing closer, but when my fear forced me to stop, I would realize it was just the trees. Nonetheless, the foul fear drove me switching between a walk and a panic-induced sprint. I tried catching when I lost my thoughts a little too much, using tactics I had picked up over the years to calm myself.

Count to ten. Take three deep, twenty-second breaths. Pace. Search for something.

My eyes found the sky, navigating the stars and studying the moon. It lit up the sky like a pool of light, the stars like fireflies. Guilt plagued my mind the longer I stared, as though the moon didn't belong to me. As though I were breaking another rule just by watching it drift through the night ever so slowly. As though I were intruding on something deep and personal that only concerned the moon and the stars.

"That doesn't stop you from shining," I murmured to the moon, trying to dig my way into the deep conversation the moon and the stars shared.

"You should've seen the blood moon. Now that was a sight."

I screamed and jumped at least four feet in the air. When I regained my balance, I scanned my surroundings, searching for the source of the voice. Was it a fairy? The Incarti?

"Ha, sorry," the voice said from behind me. "I thought you saw me."

I whirled around to face a boy just a few, noticeable inches shorter than me, with long, curly hair the shade of the bark of the trees and skin of burnt umber. A brown vest covered his chest, but as for his legs . . .

"You . . . you're a satyr," I stuttered out in disbelief, eyes wide.

He glanced down at his hairy goat legs and cloven hooves. "And I can see you're not blind."

"No, I've just," I paused, hesitating, "never seen a satyr before."

"Well, then today's your lucky day because you are gazing upon the best-looking satyr of Adeleigh." He struck a pose, puckering his lips.

I let loose a very nervous chuckle, perhaps to be polite, perhaps because I had no clue what else to do. He dropped his pose with a smile and sauntered right up to me, circling me like a hungry vulture.

"So, what brings a wizard like you to Adeleigh at this time of night? Escaping that wicked king?" the satyr asked, his eyes flicking up and down.

"I—I'm not a wizard." I corrected him, glad to have the oversized coat covering every inch of my body. "And . . . well, yes, in a way, I am escaping the king."

"Ah, so now he's got the humans fleeing too. What a shame. I heard the town of Embrasia is beautiful to behold. Too bad none of us will ever get to see it." He sighed, shrugging. "No matter. My name is Furn."

I wavered before replying. "I'm Pen."

No way was I trusting this boy of the Adeleigh with my name, no matter how nice he appeared to be. The sirens seemed to be gods at first impression, and I had already made the mistake of allowing them to carry me away with their spell of sweetness and love.

"Pen, huh? You mortals have such strange names. I ran into some guy the other day named Yavanna."

Yavanna? Why did that sound so familiar?

"And he with some other boy, some Bay or Nikoli or whatever. Seriously, awful names. They were marching around with these stupid silver swords, you see."

I swallowed a gasp. If I knew anything, I knew Prince Sasha carried a silver sword on his belt.

"Where did they go?" I exclaimed, taking a desperate step toward the satyr.

Furn laughed at my sudden reaction. "What, you've planned a date you gotta get to?"

"No!" I shouted, ignoring the heat that rose up to my cheeks. "I've just been looking for them."

"Really? I think you can do much better."

"Yes, yes, now, please, tell me where they are!"

"Ok." He smiled and held his hand out toward me. "But first, you must give me something in return."

I frowned. What did I have to give? Nothing on me I actually owned, and I didn't quite fancy the idea of giving away the palace's property. But, I would, if that was what it took to find Alexei.

I pulled a ribbon from the nightgown underneath my coat and held it out. "How about this ribbon?"

Surprisingly, Furn's dark eyes lit up, like a child's on a holiday, and he swiped the small piece of white cloth from my hand.

"Now, please, tell me where they are."

"Fine, I suppose this is good enough," Furn muttered, tying the ribbon around his wrist, where I noticed countless other shimmering things. He examined his new addition to his collection for a moment or two, smiling in content. "So, what did you want again?"

"My friends, those men, where did you see them go?" I asked, failing to hide my annoyance.

"Oh, right." He snickered. "They're probably dead. The Highwayman must've done away with them by now."

"The Highwayman?" I inquired, shock caught in my words. "You saw the Highwayman? What happened? Where did he take them? Who is the Highwayman?"

"Oh, some guy . . . ," Furn trailed off, holding out his hand once more. "You know, that diamond sure looks sparkly."

I scoffed as I glanced down at my coat, adorned with diamonds. I ripped one off and slapped it into his hand. He grinned, bringing it close to his eyes.

"He's a mortal, like you, but with the amount of hearts he's stolen, I'd say he's stronger than any wizard," Furn explained. "And there are rumors. Rumors that say he would do anything for the right price. I've heard he hoards gold like a dragon. What I would do to see that collection."

I subconsciously reached up and pressed my hand against my unbeating chest. If I had a heartbeat, I would've been able to feel it pounding against my palm, like a frantic bird trying to escape. A least, that's how books described it.

"Where can I find him?" I demanded.

"Who?"

"The Highwayman!"

"Hush, Pen! You don't know who could be lurking in the shadows." Furn pressed a finger to my cold lips.

I grumbled angrily as I pushed him away. "Tell me where he is! Please!"

"By now, you should know I don't work that way," he sneered, turning his back on me and crossing his arms.

"Fine, here!" I thrust the coat into his arms, leaving my own bare, unveiled to the biting wind. The sudden lack of cloth left me feeling more vulnerable than ever.

"Now we're talking!" Furn exclaimed, shoving his furry arms through the bedazzled sleeves. He took a few moments to ogle at himself.

"Now tell me!" I shouted, stomping my foot as I threw my hands out in exasperation.

The satyr smiled widely. "There's a weeping tree somewhere down this path. It's the only willow in Adeleigh. That's the Highwayman's secret base. That's where you'll find him."

I lifted my head, gazing into the sea of trees surrounding me. All of them looked so similar. Gnarled. Ominous. Looming. Of course, the Highwayman's secret base was one of them.

"Don't worry, you'll know it when you see it." Furn shrugged. "But are you sure you want to?"

"Of course I'm sure," I replied, but my voice betrayed me.

"If you insist. It was nice knowing you. I wish you weren't going to die tonight, I think we could've been friends."

Yeah, like that's likely.

"Ok, well, take good care of that coat," I said, pointing to it as I circled around him. "Goodbye."

"Goodbye. Maybe if I'm lucky, I'll find your bones!" Furn called after me as I sped down the path.

Maybe if I'm lucky, I'll never see you again.

27

My adrenaline rush had long disappeared, replaced by a sticky apprehension that sank into the corners of my mind. It sent me jumping every time a leaf rustled or a twig snapped. The wind sang my fear, screaming through the night like a ghost. Furn's words echoed in my head.

Maybe if I'm lucky, I'll find your bones!

He couldn't have been serious, right? He must've been messing with me, trying to get me to stay with him, probably so he could loot even more valuables from me. I rubbed my arms, cursing the satyr's name with all the words Layton had never let me use. I wasn't going to let myself be swayed by the words of the annoying boy. I wouldn't give him the satisfaction of scaring me.

But what if he's right? What if Alexei and Sasha really are dead? And what if I'm walking to my own demise?

I swallowed the bile rising up in my throat, listening to the moans of the Wood. So sorrowful, like they knew something terrible was just about to unwind. I shuddered, directing my eyes forward, reminding myself to keep focus. I only needed to spot the one willow tree. Then I'd be back with Alexei and things would go back to normal.

Well, as normal as it got with Alexei.

I carried on quietly, fear wafting behind me, always there, but only just enough that I could barely sense its malicious fangs. My growing dread, mixed with the cold that tore into my flesh, steadily chased my anxiety away. But it wasn't enough. I would've gladly taken on a snowstorm had I possessed the courage to face it. All I needed was courage. But where would I find it after so many years protected by locks? I never needed bravery in my life, and my fear seemed to know this.

Just as the thought of turning back entered my mind, a looming willow seemed to emerge from the darkness, draping vines falling like rain from the massive tree. It must've been the biggest tree I had ever seen, large enough to need five or more people just to wrap around the trunk. I tilted my head back, squinting, trying to find where the tree came to a stop, but it seemed to keep going into the night, high as a tower.

This has to be it, I thought as I timidly approached the colossal tree. *But, then, where is Alexei? Sasha? The Highwayman?*

I glanced around, but I was still as alone as I had been before I saw the willow. With delicate feet, I circled the trunk, using my arm to push away the vines in my way, but I saw nothing other than a regular willow tree.

I returned to the front of the tree, wavering as I reached out and touched the bark. I pressed hard, but nothing happened.

I cleared my throat, nervously glancing around. "Hello? Anyone here?"

I received no answer. The vines flew in the wind, entangling me in their grasp. I pulled away, shielding my face to prevent getting smacked over and over. I backed away a couple of large steps, and the vines settled.

"That's weird," I muttered to myself.

Cautiously, I jumped a few steps toward the tree, and again, the vines lashed out at me. I returned just beyond the tree's reach, gazing at it quizzically. It was almost like it was alive.

No, not alive. Enchanted.

"Excuse me?" a weak voice called out.

I jumped and trapped a scream in my throat. At first, I was convinced it was the tree that had spoken, but when I turned, I found a small, old man standing behind me. He held a long cane in one hand, running it through the grass. His eyes stared blankly into mine, and I noticed the color slightly muted. Whatever color there was, it swirled in his irises in a strange circular pattern. The old man blinked, and the swirling stopped.

"Is there someone there? I could've sworn I heard something," the man said.

I opened my mouth to reply, my rushing blood calming down a bit. It was just a blind old man. Or was it? How did I not hear him? I hesitated before I committed to speaking.

"Are you fey?" I asked.

"Me?" The man laughed. "Nay, I'm just a blind fellow."

Something about his voice struck familiar to me. I couldn't quite put my finger on it, but I swore I had heard the same broken Embrasian accent before. And something about his eyes. Had I seen those eyes before?

"Have I . . . met you before?" I questioned.

He pulled on his collar. "Me? No, no, I'm not from here. I was just admiring this tree."

I shot him a confused look. How could he admire it when he couldn't see it?

"Such a polite tree," the man continued. "If you just ask it for what you want, it will give it to you."

I turned to the tree, watching its vines sway in the wind. "You mean it's a magic tree? How do you know?"

The man didn't answer me. I glanced over my shoulder to find he was gone. Vanished. I tried ignoring my confusion, but I couldn't help but feel that he wasn't just a blind old man. And for the life of me, I swore I had met him before.

It doesn't matter. What matters now is Sasha and Alexei. Just forget about it.

I stole one last glance to search, but the man truly had disappeared. So, I turned to the tree once more. The man said to just ask it. It couldn't possibly be that easy, right?

I cleared my throat, my cheeks burning as I inhaled a long breath.

This is foolish. Yes, but it might work.

"Um, hello, tree," I started, offering a shaky smile, "I'm looking for the Highwayman. I don't suppose you know where he is?"

At first, the tree did nothing, as trees were supposed to do, but with a gust of wind, the vines shot out in my direction. I shrieked, though before I could run, my arms had been entangled, the vines dragging me forward. I struggled against them, but they were stronger than any man. Stronger than any wizard.

"Wait!" I cried as the dirt beneath my feet began to tremble. With a crack, it split. "Wait, please don't—"

But before I could finish my cry, the vines shoved me in the gaping hole. I teetered off the edge before plummeting through the darkness, the wind shrieking in my ears. My body came in contact with a rough surface of gravel and dirt, but with the force I had been pushed, it was impossible to get up to my feet on time. I tumbled down, down, down until I hit solid ground with a hard thud, knocking the breath from my lips.

I gasped, choking on the musty air, blinking the tears from my eyes as I recollected my thoughts. Out of everything I had endured during the last couple of weeks, that definitely was the most unexpected. Sirens? Sure. Fairies and kings? Why not? But a tree that threw me into a secret base underground? Never saw that one coming.

I groaned as I fought to my feet, brushing off my once white nightgown. Now dirt spread across the front and it stuck to my bloody knees like glue. My skin had torn open from the fall, leaving it a bloodied, blistering mess from my knees down to my ankles. It burned, but the pain wasn't any different than what I had previously endured. In fact, after so long trapped in the darkness under the potion the Magicians had given me, the pain in the dim of the underground base felt reassuring.

I turned toward where the light seemed to be coming from. My first few steps were difficult, but soon I grew accustomed to the burning sensation and traveled through the tight tunnel with barely a limp. Not bad for falling down a deep hole.

I didn't get very far, however, before a voice resounded through the tunnel, bouncing off the walls. I jumped, trapping a scream in my throat.

"Hey! What are you doing here?" It was a man's voice, one of exceptional rasp, like he had grown up on a diet of cigars.

I whirled around to see two men running toward me, torches in hand. One stood incredibly tall, and the other rather short, both wearing outfits of leather. I noted knives hanging from their belts. Their faces were covered in grime, hiding young features.

They must have great fashion sense. Should I run? I feel like I should run.

But before I had the chance to take off, they had their knives pointed at me threateningly. I couldn't think of anything else to do except throw my hands up in surrender. So much for being brave.

"I—I'm looking for someone," I sputtered out quickly, stumbling backward.

"How did you get here?" the tall man demanded.

I hesitated. "He told me to come."

"Who?"

"The Highwayman," I responded with as much confidence I could muster. "I have . . . business with him."

No, no! He *has business with* me*! Ah, why am I so stupid?*

The men exchanged glances as though they didn't believe me, but if that were true, they didn't show it any further. They slid their knives back into their belts.

The short one gestured forward. "This way then, but if you're lying," he grabbed my arm tightly, digging his fingers into my flesh, "we'll kill you and leave your body for the crows."

I gulped down a ball of fear that rose up in my throat. The men practically shoved me through the tunnel, kicking the backs of my heels as we walked. I kept my whimpers trapped in my throat. I wouldn't give them the satisfaction of knowing they were really getting to me. So, I held my head high, displaying an indifferent face, like I wasn't worried at all. Perhaps if I pretended long enough, I would start to believe it.

It didn't take long for the distant dim to grow brighter and brighter. We stepped into a large underground cave, the walls lined with torches, the ground littered with tents and huts and men. It was huge, spanning at least a mile long.

As the two men and I passed by, the crowd turned, stopping what they had been doing just to see the new arrival. I tried keeping my eyes away, but curiosity got the better of me and I couldn't help but take a peek.

They were like straight out of a fairy tale, the evil cast of thieves and murderers ready to steal someone's watch or something like that. Scars and malicious snickers. Sharpening blades. Cocking pistols. Typical stuff. Shivers ran up my back, my pounding blood telling me to make a run for it, scream, do something. Like my captors, they were surprisingly young, easy to mistake as a delinquent gathering of teenagers.

Eventually, we neared a tent noticeably larger than all of the others, flecks of gold shimmering in the cloth. A giant totem pole stuck up in the dirt, guarding the tent, and two men were tied by their hands, held by the towering wood.

I caught a gasp. It was Alexei and Sasha. They were both missing their silken coats, shoes, and weapons. Their faces were stained with both mud and swelling bruises, blood long dried on their skin. Alexei's eye was swollen and purple, and the prince's hands displayed open cuts that soaked his bounds with blood. My face flushed at the sight, my stomach rolling violently.

But at least they were still alive.

"Keep moving," the man behind me growled, shoving me with a quick thrust that sent me stumbling to regain my balance.

A ripple of laughter burst from behind me and when I stole a glance over my shoulder, I found a crowd had accumulated, watching me with a curious hunger. Their laughter sent Alexei and Sasha stirring. They shot their heads in my direction, and at the same time, their jaws dropped upon seeing me.

I resisted the urge to shoot them a glare, jumping as a man burst from the gold tent. He wore Alexei's shoes on his feet, though a few noticeable inches taller than him, and displayed a narrow face with a jaw that looked strong enough to bite through stone. His eyes were a muddy brown, and the sides of his head were neatly shaved, leaving gelled hair falling down his forehead. He was young, older than Alexei by probably a good few years, but still too young to be running a whole regiment of criminals.

I noticed the way he fumbled with a few gold coins in his hand, throwing them in the air absentmindedly. And yet, he never let one drop to the floor.

I swallowed roughly. There he was. The Highwayman, decked out with gold watches and silver pieces sewn into his lapel.

"What's going on?" he shouted, and the laughter immediately ceased. His voice was tough as nails, though traces of youth could be found, if one listened close enough. His eyes found mine.

"This girl says she's got business with you, boss," the man behind me said, shoving me forward once more.

The Highwayman smiled, approaching me with a hungry look in his eyes. I resisted the urge to step away as he grew closer, watching as his eyes flicked up and down, no doubt taking in my strange appearance.

"And what could a little girl such as yourself be wanting with a man like me?" he asked softly, pulling out a golden dagger from his belt, twirling it in his hands.

I tore my eyes from the shimmering dagger and found his brown ones. "I'm here for them." I pointed to Alexei and Sasha.

Again, the crowd erupted with laughter, along with the Highwayman. I found Alexei's eyes, wide with panic, but still open. As long as they stayed open. He shook his head frantically at me, but all I could do was ignore it.

"Do you know who I am?" He bent his legs to reach my eye level, using the side of the dagger to direct my chin toward his face. Up close, I saw his eyes were bloodshot.

"You're the Highwayman," I answered, hiding my trembling hands behind my back.

His smile grew as he nodded, withdrawing his dagger. "Yes, that is one of my names. Who told you?"

I forced myself to keep my eyes on him. "Nobody did. I found out myself."

"You did, did you?" He chuckled. "And I suppose you just happened to stumble across the heaviest secured base in the country?"

"I wouldn't exactly say an enchanted tree is the heaviest secured base. All you have to do is ask."

For a second, the whole underground went silent. The Highwayman stared at me blankly, until a giggle from Sasha seemed to shake them out of it. I fought back a smile myself, but found it was already too late. He had already seen my grin.

"So, who are you? The best Magician of Embrasia? A war spy?" The Highwayman glared, showing off his dagger once more. "I want the truth, or you get a lovely scar."

"The truth." I gulped. *Well, if he wants the truth, might as well give it to him.* "Sure. Well, you see, I'm actually the top wanted in Embrasia. A reward of ten thousand gold pieces for my safe return. Ask for the missing girl and any police can tell you my description."

"A runaway, huh? And what is your business with the prince of Embrasia? Last I heard, missing girls don't make friends with princes."

Oh, if only you knew.

"Look, how about we make a deal?" I asked. "You release both of them, and I'll let you turn me in for that reward. Ten thousand on the line."

"What if I keep you and the prince and hold the both of you for ransom? Why should I settle for ten thousand if I can get one hundred thousand?" The Highwayman sneered, pointing his dagger at my neck.

"Sure, you could, but—" I threw my hands out, knocking the dagger from his grasp and clutched it in mine.

For a moment, he gazed at me with wide eyes. My bluff was farfetched, I knew, but something told me he valued money more than his reputation. It was the only thing I had to go on. The crowd began to stir, but with an uplifting of the Highwayman's hand, they paused.

"You think you can fight me? Go ahead and try," he said with an easy grin, holding his arms out.

I only had a second to form a plan, and the first plan that popped into my head was what I went with. I held the dagger against my own neck. His grin dropped.

"No!" Alexei screamed.

"You wouldn't." The Highwayman narrowed his eyes, but I could see his clenched fists quiver slightly, twitching to reach for the silver embedded in his lapel.

"Yes, she will!" Sasha cried. "She's crazy!"

"So, what will it be?" I asked. "You in the mood for losing a free ten thousand? They won't pay you for a dead girl and last I heard, the kingdom doesn't pay ransoms."

As he hesitated, I pressed a little pressure, just enough to get beads of blood dripping. A stinging pain spread across my throat. I clenched my jaw, maintaining unwavering eye contact. *What if he doesn't go for it? Oh, why am I so stupid? Stupid! Stupid!*

"Alright, alright," the Highwayman blurted, much to my surprise and relief. "The prince and the wizard go, but you stay."

"That's the deal." I nodded, withdrawing the dagger. I glanced down at the blade, glimpsing the deep blood that had stained it.

I backed away from the Highwayman, running to Alexei and Sasha's side, using the bloodied dagger to saw through their ropes.

"What do you think you're doing?" Alexei hissed.

"Saving you." I glared back.

"You don't have to do this. If you think for one second that I'm going to leave you here with him, then you really have gone mad," he whispered frantically. "The second I get loose, jump behind me. I'm blasting us out of here."

"You can't fight hundreds of men at a time. The Highwayman is powerful. He'll blast you before you even ignite a spark."

"I'm *not* leaving you here."

"You're gonna have to."

"Augh, why do you have to be so . . . so . . . heartless?" Alexei spat.

Sasha took a breath through clenched teeth, wincing. "Now that was cold."

I cut away the last of their binds and scrambled as the three of us climbed to our feet. Alexei's fist simmered, ash flying from his fingers, but before he had the chance to spark a flame, the two of them were grabbed and restrained by a couple of the Highwayman's men, knives pressed against their throats.

Then, they had me in their grasp, too. Forcing my arms behind my back, they pinned them together tightly, their rough hands scratching my skin like claws.

"Just in case you get any ideas," the Highwayman murmured in my ear, smirking menacingly as he drew a pistol from his belt. He aimed it right at Sasha's chest.

"No! You said you'd let them go!" I cried, struggling against the arms of the monstrous men.

"Oh, I will, but first I'll take the wizard's heart and kill the prince. Then I'll let them go," the Highwayman replied simply. He threw me a look. "You should really know who you're gambling with before you start the game."

"Wait!" I shrieked as he cocked the pistol. "I'll give you anything! More money! Identification papers! Anything!"

"Not good enough," the Highwayman sang, directing his aim.

With panic surging through my veins, I realized I had been played. He had played me just as I had tried playing him. Well, if that was the type of game he wanted.

"I heard you collect hearts!" I swallowed roughly, displaying a fake countenance of hesitation. "You can have mine, just please don't kill him! My heart and the money."

His smirk widened, growing on his face like a deep crack, and he shoved the pistol back into his belt. I wanted to release the breath I had been holding, but he didn't give me enough time.

"Can you perform memory spells?" he asked, and upon seeing my confusion added, "Only a wizard of high ranking can perform such spells. So, can you cast memory spells?"

The men restraining me let go as the Highwayman motioned for me to join his side. I complied warily, my knees buckling. He wrapped a hand around my shoulder, leaning close to my face. He smelled of blood and liquor, with a little bit of death and unbrushed teeth for days. I resisted the urge to gag.

"Of course," I answered, the tremble in my voice a little too real.

"Then wipe the prince's memory of this whole experience. Then I'll let him go, safe and sound back to his dear old dad."

I lifted my face toward Alexei and Sasha, their eyes wide with fear. The men holding Sasha let go of him, shoving him in my direction. How was I possibly going to pull this off? Lying? Sure. But actually casting a spell? We were all as good as dead.

With a shaky breath, I took a small step forward, my head swimming. I took one more step, wondering how long I could possibly get away with stalling.

"Um." I cleared my throat. The men, and even the Highwayman, all leaned forward curiously. "Ok, uh, yeah. Just gotta—"

All of a sudden, Sasha released a gasp and pitched backward, before teetering forward and collapsing to the dirt. Just before he managed to hide his face in his arm, I caught a glimpse of his upturned lips.

Alexei blinked in puzzlement. His eyes clicked a fraction of a second later, and he quickly tore himself from the men's grasp, kneeling by Sasha's side, his face anguished. He threw an accusing finger at me. "No! How could you?"

I bit the smile from my cheeks, going along with the act. "I'm sorry, it was the only way!"

The men cackled as they tore Alexei from Sasha's side, dragging him from the crumpled prince. I struggled to keep a chuckle from escaping my lips as Alexei continued to thrash, dramatically shouting things like, "you'll never take me alive".

"How impressive," the Highwayman purred. All of a sudden, it was a lot easier holding back my laughter. "I don't think I've ever encountered a wizard strong enough to cast a memory spell."

I opened my mouth to correct him, then remembered the whole point of the game I played was that he believed I really was a wizard. So, I clasped it shut, watching him circle me with both fear and hatred. I wasn't sure which one was part of my act.

"Maybe I'll keep you around though. Heartless girls are a lot more entertaining than heartful girls." He shrugged.

I couldn't help but let my curiosity get the better of me. "And why's that?"

"Because," he chuckled, "it's like they know what they're missing, but however hard they try, they can never gain it back again. It's fun to watch the life pour from their eyes as if they really had died. Some girls actually begged me to kill them."

I gulped nervously, a tight feeling rising up in my throat.

"Now please don't move too much, this tends to get messy sometimes."

Before I could catch his next move, my body erupted in pain, a burning like no other, seeping through my bones, my muscles, my flesh like a scavenging fire. My ears rang, throwing out every other sound. I released the loudest shriek I could manage, my legs failing from underneath me. I collapsed headfirst into the mud, my hands pressed against my chest, where the agony had burst from.

Just as quickly as it had come, it disappeared, leaving nothing but an excruciating numbness in my body. I curled up, hugging myself as tightly as I could.

When I glanced up at the Highwayman, I found he held a small, glowing orb in his palm, a blue vapor rising from it like smoke. Sparks of white flew from the orb, and it wasn't until my vision cleared did I realize the sparks were not sparks at all, but snowflakes.

28

I searched for Alexei's eyes, but once I found them, I saw that they weren't on me. They were transfixed on the orb the Highwayman held. Even Sasha, who was supposed to be pretending to be unconscious, had lifted his head to see what had happened. Thing was, I didn't even know what had happened, but there was one thing I did know.

I felt lighter than before, almost like I could be washed away by the slightest of breezes. Or perhaps, ride the wind as I pleased. The numbness in my body sank into my bones, a chill taking over. I fought to my knees and wrapped my arms around myself.

The crowd of the Highwayman's men began to cheer a deafening chime, throwing their fists up and punching the air excitedly. For a brief moment, they seemed to forget all about Sasha and Alexei, lost in their triumph. Alexei seemed to notice too.

The wizard slipped away quickly, taking my side. He grasped my arms and hauled me up, his eyes unfocused and dazed. Clouded with fear.

"What happened?" I croaked, glancing between Alexei and the Highwayman.

"I think he stole it."

"Stole what? There was nothing there to begin with."

"I think you might want to rethink some things. We have to get it back and get out of here."

"Not so fast." The Highwayman stepped in front of the two of us, a maniacal smile spread across his cheeks. "I still have one more heart I need to reap."

"Reap this!" Alexei pushed me behind him, throwing a flaming punch at the Highwayman.

The Highwayman jerked backward, holding the glowing orb away from Alexei's reaching grasp. With a bursting laugh, he brought the orb to his lips, pressing his fingers into it tightly.

"No!" Alexei shouted, jumping to attack him again, but the criminal dodged with just as much ease as he did before.

The orb began sinking into the Highwayman's mouth, almost like it was made from liquid light, but as the snowflake sparks entered, he stopped short. He tugged the orb away, coughing violently.

I reached out for Alexei. "What's happening to him?"

Frost seemed to appear from out of nowhere, climbing up the Highwayman's arms, spreading as fast as a wildfire, seeping into his skin. He shrieked, stumbling backward. He clawed at his frosting skin, but as his fingertips came in contact with the ice, it spread with the touch. He cried out again. The ice continued spreading, closer and closer to his chest, to his lips.

"What did you do to me?" he screamed, thrusting a finger in my direction. He lunged for me, but Alexei yanked me from his grasp.

"Let it go!" Alexei shouted. "Let it go, you daft man!"

"No!" The Highwayman jerked left and right, but that didn't stop the frost from advancing up his body. He sucked in a short, panicked breath. "It's mine! It's mine!"

"Let go!" Alexei tried again, and this time when he jumped at the Highwayman, the criminal flung the orb from his fingertips.

I watched it soar through the air like a shooting star, wincing as it crashed to the dirt. The ice had ceased to spread on the Highwayman, slowing receding back toward his fingers. The man clutched his chest, gasping as he stumbled for balance.

"Ivory, grab it!"

I scrambled for the orb, gingery scooping it in my hands. The blue vapor bit my flesh with cold, but it was a good kind of cold. A familiar cold. I glanced down at it, and images surfaced in my head. My mother's face.

Gethan Kementari's book. My bow and arrows I had received for my fourth birthday. A child's face, his eyes of emerald green and hair of crimson fuchsia.

"You!" The Highwayman screamed, hurtling toward me with his hands glowing red.

I blinked the images from my mind, tumbling backward, tripping over my feet. I fell to my back and quickly tried to right myself. A surge of energy rushed through me as I grasped onto the orb tight, digging my fingernails into the delicious freeze. I clasped my eyes shut, waiting for the attack.

But it never came.

A hush fell over the crowd, so silent my ragged breaths sounded thunderous. I cracked open my eyes a sliver, just enough to see the orb had disappeared from my hands, and so had that terribly light feeling in my chest. My skin prickled with its usual cold, and I felt more like myself again. Like I had regained what I had lost.

"Ivory." A whisper dug into my ears.

I pried my eyes open completely and gasped as I saw what appeared before me. It was the Highwayman, frozen in mid-step, his hand stretched out for me, still emitting a fading glow under the coat of ice. I cried out in alarm, scrambling away. As I searched for Alexei and Sasha, I found myself gazing into the eyes of hundreds of frozen men, standing like statues in the underground base.

I opened my mouth to scream, but Alexei rushed forward, kneeling beside me.

"Don't scream," he whispered. "It's a weak spell. It'll break easily."

I whirled my head around to meet his eyes, my mouth still hanging open. Nothing escaped my lips, even though I wanted to ask a thousand questions. Scream a thousand times.

"Are you ok?" he asked, assisting me to my feet. "Your knees are bleeding. We should wrap those up."

"Alexei." His name was more of a gasp. "What . . . what did I do?"

"It doesn't matter right now—"

"Alexei!"

He winced as my voice echoed throughout the cave. Instead of answering, he led me near Sasha, who had climbed up to his feet warily, glancing around with eyes wide.

"This is . . ." He blinked a couple of times, turning in a full circle. "I actually don't know what this is, but, uh . . . good work, Ivory."

"Good work? Good work! I just—"

"You just rid the kingdom of the most dangerous gang in the history of Embrasia. So, yes, I'd say good work," Sasha replied, wiping his bloodstained face with his torn shirt.

"Ivory, are you ok? What did it feel like?" Alexei pulled me to him, his eyes searching my face.

"Look," I pushed him away, "I don't even know what happened, and right now, I don't really care, just please tell me you can reverse this."

"Reverse it? Why would we reverse it?" Sasha cut in.

"We can't just leave them like this!" I exclaimed, gesturing to the sea of frozen men.

"Why not?"

"It would be like killing them!"

"Good!"

"Alright!" Alexei shouted, stepping in between me and the prince. "Enough, you two. Ivory's right, Sasha. If we left them, it would make us just as bad as they are. They'll be fine in the dungeon, won't they?"

"Yes," Sasha grumbled regretfully, crossing his arms.

"This spell will wear off eventually, so we'll show the guards where this place is and have them arrested before it wears off. Problem solved," Alexei said simply.

Sasha grumbled again and disappeared into the golden tent with a huff. The ball of dread that had embedded into my stomach disintegrated slowly, relief flooding into me. I took a deep breath, willing myself to forget about what had happened. I told myself I'd lose a night of sleep over it later. I needed to focus on the task at hand.

Alexei turned toward me, his hand outstretched, words on his lips, but I stepped away, following after Sasha. Whatever he wanted to say, I didn't want to hear it. At least, not yet. Not while we were surrounded by frozen men and the prince of Embrasia was just around the corner. Whatever he wanted to say, I only wanted to know when it went back to being just the two of us.

I pushed past the flaps of the tent and found Sasha hauling huge bags filled to the brim over his shoulder. The tent was full of them, littering the ground like mere trash, but I knew what was inside. Embrasia's gold.

"We'll take these back to the castle and make sure everything is accounted for before we return them to the banks," Sasha said. He threw two of them in my arms and two in Alexei's. "Let's get out of here."

I glanced down at the heavy bags weighing down my arms, blinking blankly. For once in my life, someone was trusting me with something. Nobody had ever trusted me with anything. "I can carry some more. Let me help as much as I can."

The two stared at me blankly. A laugh slipped from Sasha's lips as he grabbed another bag.

"Of course, our knight in shining armor." Sasha lowered himself in a dramatic bow, handing me the bag.

I chuckled. "Next time I'll come riding a white stallion."

The three of us laughed, and the previous tension from before faded away. Sasha plucked a sword from the ground, and with further examination, I realized it was the same sword that hung from his belt when we first met.

"Alright men, let's march," Sasha declared in a voice that sounded a little too much like his father's.

Alexei and I smiled, but I could sense a tension between us, a different one from before. It was like he knew something I didn't, and he needed to tell me. I felt I could see the words hanging on his lips.

But I had to ignore the quick glances he cast me. I had to ignore them because I didn't know what I would do if he knew all I wanted was to catch his eyes too. And not just catch them, but keep them.

. . . .

"So, how did you two end up there?" I asked.

The night had grown colder since I had fallen into the underground base, leaving me shivering and glad the bags were so heavy as to leave my blood rushing with effort, warming up my body the slightest bit.

"We had a plan." Sasha sighed. "And then . . ."

"It was that obnoxious satyr's fault. If it weren't for him, we would've seen the trap," Alexei grumbled.

"Wait, you don't mean—"

"Hey, Pen! Yavanna! Bay-Nikoli-Whatever!"

The three of us stopped dead in our tracks, our faces flushing an identical white. *It can't be.*

But as we turned around, the sight of a satyr dressed in a coat of diamond fur greeted us. He sprinted to catch up, slapping his hand against Alexei's back, a grin painted across his face. He pitched forward, heaving like he had been running all night, using Alexei to support himself.

194

"Oh, gods, why?" Sasha mumbled under his breath.

"What do you want, Furn?" I asked, trying and failing to keep irritation from my voice.

"Well, I see you got your friends back. I'm glad you're not dead," he responded, flicking his dark, sweaty hair from his eyes.

"Gee, thanks. Is that it?"

"Of course not! I just thought you'd like to know the king is looking for you."

I paused as Sasha released an audible groan.

"I've been running into those annoying guards all night. "Where's the prince? Where's the Morrow? Where's the wizard?" They just never shut up," he explained, shoving a hoof in the dirt.

My mouth fell open in horror as I buried my face in my hands. Fear sank into my veins like a deadly poison, leaving me paralyzed in the cold night.

"Don't worry, Ivory," Sasha whispered to me as he caught a glimpse of my distressed face. "I won't let him do anything to you."

"Why would she be in trouble?" Furn asked, laying his hands on his hips.

"None of your business," Alexei spat, gripping my shoulder and leading me the other way.

"Wait, I won't tell anyone! Please, I'm so bored!" Furn exclaimed, running after us.

The three of us tried to ignore him, but as he kept pushing and pushing, I couldn't help but break under his voice and fixed gaze.

"I wasn't really supposed to leave the castle, but I left anyway." I sighed and glanced up at Alexei and Sasha. "At least you guys had an excuse."

"An excuse? What do you mean?" Alexei questioned, eyebrows furrowed.

"They told me you went to Cyrene. That is what you told them . . . right?"

The two clenched their teeth, shooting a look at each other. Not a good look.

"No, we kind of just . . . left. I suppose they told you that in an attempt to keep you from leaving," Sasha answered. "But I guess it didn't work."

"Are you serious?" I gaped. "I could've figured out that much myself. You seriously didn't have a cover? And left me there without even giving me a clue to where you really were?"

"You were still unconscious when we left!" Alexei cried. "We thought we'd be back before you woke, before anyone even realized we were gone."

His words did little to simmer my anger, but with a deep breath, I forced my rage down. It wasn't the time to be cross with them. Just next time, if they didn't even bother to tell when they decided to go on an adventure, I wouldn't come and save them.

"Yes, yes," Furn whispered, nodding. He seemed to have grabbed a notebook from out of nowhere, jotting down our conversation quickly.

"So, how did you get out?" Sasha quirked an eyebrow, shooting a look at me.

I avoided his gaze, stumbling on my words. "I just . . . did. It doesn't matter."

"No, no, no, it does matter. We told you what happened to us," Alexei said.

"Fine." I released a breath. "I climbed out the window."

Sasha burst out laughing as Alexei muffled a gasp. The prince patted me on the back, shaking his head playfully. And Alexei told him to stop encouraging my shenanigans.

"So, what did you do with the Highwayman?" Furn asked.

The three of us paused. The smile had wiped from Sasha's lips and suddenly Alexei and I looked opposite directions from each other.

"That bad?" Furn released a small giggle.

Sasha avoided my eyes, looking at anything but me. "We took care of it."

"Ah, I see." Furn nodded.

I thought he would push for more and keep asking for everything in full detail. However, before he got the chance to part his lips once more, his head jerked around. He halted abruptly, narrowing his eyes at the vast darkness.

"They've found you," he whispered, before disappearing into the shadows of the trees.

Just as we were about to question what he had meant, a barrage of voices burst from the Wood. The light of fire came rushing toward us in all directions, blocking off our every possible path of escape. We stumbled backward and crowded together, Sasha raising his sword high, Alexei baring flaming fists, and me protecting the bags of gold.

"We found them!" the voices cried, echoing through the trees.

A group of the Embrasian guards burst from the shadows of the trees, rushing toward us in a flurry of movement. A pair of hands clutched my arm and pulled me away with such force that I dropped the bags of gold I had been balancing. The person engulfed me in their arms, crying out in what seemed to be joy.

"We've been looking everywhere for you, dear girl!"

All the color drained from my face as I realized who had me in their grasp so tight. I pushed my head away, glancing up to see Marble's eccentric eyes. I resisted the urge to struggle, it wasn't the best time to make a scene, but the screams caught in my throat were fighting to be heard.

I squirmed from his uncomfortable embrace, trying to make it subtle that I desperately wanted to be as far away as possible from him. Just the smell of him, the shade of purple on white of his cloak, sent my stomach twisting and my head reeling. My fingers twitched a couple of times as I rapidly flexed and unflexed them, reminding myself that I was awake, that I could move and be heard.

That I was the one in control.

I searched for Alexei and Sasha among the crowd of guards in shining armor and watched as they were handed vials of what was definitely some type of potion. They downed the bottles and color instantly sprang to their faces, the swollen bruises deflating, purple eyes fading back to a natural tan.

"Oh, poor girl!" Marble exclaimed. His cries were dramatized, probably to convince everyone about his undying compassion toward me. "You must be freezing!"

He draped his cloak over me, which sent all of my muscles to lock up. I ground my teeth, resisting the urge to tear it from my shoulders and throw it into the bushes.

"The king requests an audience with you, Prince Sasha," a guard said, separating him from Alexei.

I took a few steps forward to join Alexei's side, but the hand of Marble grabbed the collar of my nightgown and he kept me planted an inch away from him. It was a restrain not noticeable just by the glance of an eye, but to me, it felt even worse than the grasp of the Highwayman's men. He placed a hand on the small of my back, leading me to the castle.

Alexei glanced over, catching the panic in my eyes, but before he could cut in, a guard grabbed his arm, not threateningly, but tight enough to send a subtle message. All he could do was give me a nod, which was better than nothing. I accepted his nod, trying to find reassurance.

But for once, I wasn't sure how he could get us out of this one.

29

I knew I hated when Layton and Dean did it, but I spent the remainder of the night pacing. And pacing. And pacing a little more.

The moment I had passed through my door back at the Embrasian castle, a click resounded through the darkness, a sound only audible if one really listened for it. But my whole life, I was accustomed to the click of a locked door, leaving me at the will of whoever held the key. And knowing it wasn't Layton that held the key to this door sent my anxiety storming my head like a typhoon.

The biting silence was almost worse than the click of the lock, clearing my head just enough for whatever horrible thought deciding to pass through. A prisoner to my own mind, I yearned for a different sound other than my own footsteps. I wanted Alexei's voice, his eyes, another nod, anything to reassure me like he tried in the Adeleigh Wood. Perhaps even the awkward conversation between one of the palace guards, just anything to distract me.

But all remained still and silent. And it would stay that way all through the night until a merciful guard unlocked my door.

At least, that's what I thought.

With a burst of sound, a figure appeared in the corner of my room, stumbling for balance and drawing breath in roughly. I gasped, scrambling to the other side of the room, but as the light of the lanterns cast upon figure, I realized it wasn't the Incarti, as I thought it would be.

It was Alexei. He was back in his recognizable magenta coat and brown pants, his hair grazing his shoulders, unrestrained by ribbon, emerald earrings dangling from his ears. In his arm, he held a banal blouse and skirt, light blue with black buttons. In his other hand, he held a long black ribbon. The one I wore when I first met him.

"Alexei," I whispered, approaching him with light feet, "how did you do that?"

He took a deep breath before answering. "I stole a spell from one of those Magicians. Teleportation spell. Oh, gods, those are hard!"

I held my arms out, leading him to my bed. He plopped down, his chest heaving. Sweat coated his forehead, but he still somehow looked better than ever. Back in his regular coat, he looked like himself again.

I waited until he caught his breath and offered him a cloth from the bathroom. He nodded thanks and wiped his forehead, before returning to his feet. He even wore his old black shoes from before.

"I brought you these." He held out the clothes. "I thought you'd be more comfortable."

"Thanks." I accepted them, running my hands through the normal cloth. No silk. No diamonds or jewels. Just regular old buttons. I couldn't resist hugging them close to my chest.

"We're leaving as soon as we can. I don't trust these people any further than I trust the Incarti," Alexei said. He paused and looked me up and down. "Are you ok? You look pale. Well, paler than usual."

"I'm—" I hesitated. Was I ok? I couldn't tell anymore. "Well, I can't say I've been better."

Alexei gazed down at me, even when I tore my eyes away, back down at the blouse, at the floor, at the window, anything but him. A sigh escaped his lips, and I wondered if he held the same thoughts as I did.

What thoughts did I hold? I kept pushing them out, keeping them at bay, forcing them from processing. But I knew I couldn't keep them away forever. I needed answers, though for once, I didn't want them.

"Look, I think we need to talk." He held out his hand, but I stepped from his reach.

I still couldn't meet his eyes. "I don't want to talk. Can't we just forget about it?"

"About what, Ivory? The Highwayman? The Magicians? Your little show at dinner?" Irritation laced in his voice like a knife, sharp and unforgiving.

I wanted to clutch my hands over my ears. Of course, he knew everything I had been trying to avoid. Of course, he just needed to know everything, probably so he could try to fix it, like he always did. Well, I didn't ask for his help. I never wanted it, and now I was stuck with him.

Why did I want to stay stuck? Like a fly trapped in a spider's web, not even strong enough to struggle against the sticky line. That was what I was. Not strong enough. At least with him, I felt like I was. I felt like I could do anything.

Except break from that web.

"You're a Kementari." I turned my back on him, wrapping my arms around myself shamefully, an incredibly tight feeling clutching my throat.

"What has that got to do with anything?" Alexei snapped.

I whirled around and finally forced myself to hold his furious gaze. "Your father. Is he Gethan Kementari?"

Alexei's expression of rage dropped as the words escaped my lips, his face flushing white. His eyebrows furrowed together as his eyes glared suspiciously at me.

"How do you know that?"

The tight sensation in my throat rose up, calling tears to my eyes, tears I couldn't resist, no matter how hard I tried. I didn't even try to wipe them away. For once, I welcomed them, because, for the first time since I found out the secret, I was finally able to cry about it.

"He abandoned your family when you were young, right?" I continued, losing my will to keep eye contact. I didn't want to see the confusion in his eyes.

"How do you know that?" he repeated, his voice a mix of anger and puzzlement.

"My brothers told me that my mother was dead," I said. I paused, mainly because I wasn't entirely sure how to finish the sentence. That was probably a piece of information he didn't need to know. So why did I tell him? "The day I ran away was the same day they told me she was alive. The day they told me *why* she left."

"What are you saying?" Alexei inquired. I could feel the apprehension in his tone, almost like he had already figured out what was next. But, like me, he didn't want to believe it.

"They told me she was dead because they didn't want me to know the truth. They didn't want me to know *who* she left us for. They knew I couldn't handle it." I stopped to chuckle at myself. If I were smart enough to not push for answers, where would I be? Still in Cyrene, carrying on with my worthless life? Doing nothing, reading stupid books that never amounted to anything? Waiting until it was my turn to die, still dreaming of the daunting moon?

The burn of tears scorched my throat. I knew I would have to face the truth someday, but I never expected it to be with someone who went through the same thing.

"Don't finish. I think I know where you're going with this." He held up a shaky hand, his voice quivering slightly.

I couldn't stop though. "I read the letters between them. She wanted to take me with her. She wanted me to live with *him* as if he were my father."

Alexei's outstretched hand dropped to his side, his face frozen. I didn't know why I was telling him everything, but I couldn't stop myself, the words flowing from my lips uncontrollably, matching the flow of my tears. My cheeks burned; my mind screamed at me to stop.

He's going to hate me. I can already see it in his face, he hates me. He should. Why don't I shut up then? Why am I telling him this?

"That house in Lockdale, it's where my family used to live. That's why I was there. I was looking for answers, something to explain everything to myself."

"And you found me instead," Alexei muttered. He paused. "Ivory, look at me."

"No. I don't blame you if you hate me, it's why I hated you, even before I knew you're a Kementari." I blinked a couple of tears from my eyes, sighing. "I can't accept your help anymore. I'll just go back to Cyrene and we can pretend this never happened."

"Look at me!" He grasped my shoulder and shook me roughly.

My head shot up to meet his eyes, wide and glistening with tears. A gasp caught in my throat. I never expected to see him cry so freely, so close that I thought I could feel the heat radiating from his fresh tears.

"I might be my father's son, but I am nothing like him. I've known for years what he did. Don't you think I've read the letters too? I told you I recognized your last name the first time we met." He withdrew his hand but had trapped my gaze in his, identical tears shining on our cheeks. "I knew he didn't love us. And I don't care anymore. I haven't cared for a long time."

I hesitated, swallowing roughly. "Then why are you crying?"

"I'm crying for you." He reached up and wiped his face harshly, leaving red smudges along his cheeks.

"Why?" I stepped away, and through my despair, a flicker of anger ignited. I didn't want his tears. If he was truly unbothered by all of this, I didn't want his pity.

"Don't you remember me?" he asked, a note of pain ringing in his voice like a funeral bell.

I ran the back of my hand over my eyes, my eyebrows stitched together in confusion and irritation. His eyes were full of a specific pain, a pain that only surfaced with real dread, like he had lost something important. But he hadn't. So why did he stare at me with such pain swimming in his eyes?

"What do you mean? We've never met before. I would've remembered."

"Don't you remember what love feels like?"

I cringed as the words left his lips. What was the purpose of taunting me? He already knew everything there was to know. Perhaps he really did hate me. Perhaps he wanted to see the same pain swimming in his eyes in mine as well.

"I've told you everything. I've never felt love, and I've never met anyone out of Cyrene!" I exclaimed, throwing a finger at him. "What are you trying to do? Mock me? You think this is a joke?"

"No! Ivory, listen to me, there is so much more to this than you think." He thrust his arm out toward me. "It's my fault you're like this. It's my fault you can't feel love. That's why I'm crying."

"What—what do you mean?" I asked, my voice dying out like a smothered flame.

Alexei paused, his chest heaving from all the sobbing and shouting. Our gazes were like fire and ice, so evenly matched, yet so destructive to each other. Too much of one would kill the other. But we were both willing to die under each other's hand, with both a surplus and lack of trust, an unusual dynamic, a twisted game of fate.

Because that was all this had been. Fate. Cruel, untimely fate.

"You don't remember anything before, do you?" Alexei took a wavering step forward, almost as if he were afraid of me. Or perhaps, afraid of how I would react.

"Before what?" I asked, exhausted tears staining my face. I thought I had all the answers, finally cracked the code, put all the puzzle pieces together, but then came along Alexei Kementari, a piece that just wouldn't fit anywhere. A piece that didn't seem to even belong in this puzzle, but somehow, he was still in the box. And he was the last piece I had left.

When he didn't answer, I pushed for a reply. "What do you mean it's your fault I can't feel love? What do you mean 'before'? Why do you think we've met before?"

He sighed. "You might want to sit for this."

I scoffed, but with a drop in my stomach, I couldn't help but comply. I tossed the clothes over the vanity and collapsed on the bed, for once annoyed by the way it sank under my weight. I never thought I would miss my hard mattress back in Cyrene.

"You told me the real reason you were at the Lockdale house, so I guess I should too, but I have to start at the beginning," Alexei said. He waited for me to nod in order to continue. "My father, Gethan, taught me and my brothers magic while we were growing up. Strong magic. Dark. Controversial. My mother never approved, but my brothers always wanted to learn more. They were eager to know everything, so he taught them everything. I preferred to sew and cook with my mother."

"You never told me you have brothers," I said before he could continue.

"Well, I'm telling you now. Can I keep going?"

"Wait. Tell me their names first."

Alexei sighed. "The oldest is Valentin, then Mercedes, and lastly Francois. Now can I go back to the story?"

I nodded.

"They grew to be so strong, there wasn't much more Gethan could teach them, and that's when he decided to leave for the heart of a faraway woman he had been receiving letters from for months. He didn't try to hide it very hard, and when we figured it out, my mother was so distraught—" His voice broke with a crack of pain. Reminiscence shone in his eyes like stars, but with a gulp, he continued. "My brothers were furious, and with such untrained magic boiling up inside them, it didn't take long for them to be overwhelmed by their own fury. They changed, their unbridled magic sinking into their hearts like a sickness. It's the consequence of being a wizard, the pressure of knowing your magic could always just swallow you whole and leave you to rot. It's what happened to them, and I couldn't do anything to stop it.

"Before my mother or I could stop them, they left in pursuit of the family that broke ours. My mother begged me not to go, to stay safe, but I was young, and I wanted to know what my brothers were going to do. I followed them all the way to Lockdale until they found the house. Through the

203

window, they saw a little girl with curly brown hair. She was asleep but clutched in her hands was a book written by my father. The sight sent my brothers outraged, and it was the final pull on their magic. They cast a spell, one that Gethan didn't even teach them because it was so dangerous, to kill the girl. Out of jealousy for our father's heart, they decided to take away hers."

"Wait." I had to stop him, the story too much for me to process in such a short amount of time. I couldn't believe it; I didn't want to believe it. My thoughts traveled back to the photograph I had found along with the letters. The photograph with the picture of the small girl who looked exactly like my mom.

Alexei's voice had become taunt and shaky. "The spell was meant to murder her right there in her bed, to heat up her little human heart until it imploded in flames, so she'd burn from the inside. Smoke would fill her lungs, ash would fill her veins, her blood would boil, and her heart would shrivel in the fire. All I could do was watch. The spell was flawless, and they left laughing. But I couldn't let you die."

I nearly gasped. When did the "her" become a "you"? All I could do was continue listening.

"I knew my magic wasn't nearly as strong as my brothers, but I had to do something. The only thing I could think of was to freeze the spell. It wouldn't be enough to reverse their curse, but I thought it would at least give you a few more days. Maybe then it would give you enough time to seek out a real wizard for help. I cast the spell, but I didn't know my brothers had been watching me the whole time. They attacked me, ran me out of town, and—" His voice cracked. He cleared his throat a couple of times, shifting uncomfortably— "and they got away with a piece of my heart."

"Your heart?" I gasped.

"A heart is a wizard's source of magic. It's why the Highwayman was stealing them. It's why I tried stealing yours. Losing a heart is almost like death to a wizard. Perhaps worse."

"Did you get it back?" I leaned forward anxiously.

"No." He reached up to his chest. "I've never been able to steal one. It hasn't affected my emotions, but with each passing day, I can feel it getting weaker and weaker. Like that teleportation spell. I used to be able to use those without even breaking a sweat."

I watched as he pulled his hand away, clenching it in a fist. So that was why he asked for my heart when we first met. A mournful smile broke on his lips.

"I still haven't told you what I was doing at the Lockdale house. Well, I lived on my own for as long as I could manage, and when I returned home, I found our house empty, my mother gone, my brothers gone. Then I went back to the house in Lockdale to find it abandoned too. I've been searching for my mother ever since and hiding from my brothers. And every once and awhile, I'll go back to that house in Lockdale, hoping to find out what happened to that little girl," Alexei explained. "But the years passed, and I never found her. I tracked down my father to find he had long dropped the woman he left us for and had moved on to the next. I traveled all around the country in order to keep my identity a secret. I built my diamond dolls for extra protection, changed my name countless times." He stopped suddenly and found my eyes.

My breath hitched as he reached out and folded his warm hands in mine. Though his words shook me, I couldn't help but shake even more just by the simple touch. My eyes burned again, my throat and chest tight. I didn't know if I could believe his words. If I believed them, then that would mean we really *had* met each other before. It meant that I lived in that Lockdale house. It meant the girl in the photograph really was me all along.

It meant I had a heart the whole time. Frozen. But still there.

"Ivory," his breath caught, his hands squeezing mine tighter, "please forgive me. I tried so hard to find you, to help you. I never thought you'd survive so long. I thought you had died long ago, but I still couldn't stop myself from going to that house, searching for you. I know my family has stolen so much from you, and I don't know if you could possibly forgive me, but—"

I cut him off as I leapt to embrace him. I wrapped my arms around his shoulders and squeezed tightly, staining his coat with my tears. My whole body shook with sobs, but for once, they were good sobs.

"Of course I forgive you. How could I not?"

He squeezed back, whispering, "Thank the gods."

I wasn't sure how long we stayed there, standing in the center of a room in the Embrasian palace, but it didn't seem long enough. When we pulled away, he laughed as he ran his thumbs along my cheeks, wiping away my cold tears. I chuckled and rubbed his cheeks free of his warm tears.

Alexei Kementari froze my heart. Alexei Kementari saved my life. Our lives were intertwined since the beginning, before that first insult was thrown. And fate had brought us back together.

I couldn't face the fact I had a heart my whole life. I couldn't face the fact that Layton and Dean kept me locked behind doors in order to protect me from the brothers of Alexei. All that mattered was that I was with Alexei and he was with me, and for once, it seemed we were safe from everything outside the doors, even though we both knew it wasn't true. But we could pretend.

"You should get cleaned up. Your knees are caked with blood," Alexei said, running his sleeves along his red-rimmed eyes one last time.

I sniffed as I nodded, grabbing the clothes he had brought for me before disappearing in the tiled bathroom. I ran the sink as I threw the stained nightgown off, glad to be rid of the bloodied silk. I rubbed my knees with a damp cloth until the dried blood had gone and slipped into the blouse and skirt. I tied the black ribbon into my hair, threw the nightgown in the trash, and joined Alexei in the dim room.

He greeted me with a smile that could light up the night. "There's the Ivory I remember. I guess royal life just doesn't suit us."

"You can say that again." I chuckled, crossing the floor with barely a limp that I prided myself on. I approached the glass windows and pulled back the curtain. Of course, they were bolted shut now.

"Gladly. I guess royal life just doesn't suit us," Alexei repeated. "Eh, we can deal with it tomorrow. I'm exhausted."

"The sun is about to rise," I whispered, mostly to myself.

The stars no longer danced in the sky, scared away by the rays of light spilling over the trees. The moon still hung low in the darkness, descending like a bird diving for its prey.

I sighed, resting my elbows on the windowpane. With everything said and done, I realized how fiercely my stomach ached for food, but my exhaustion canceled out any thought of eating. My eyes dropped like they were made of stone, gravity urging them down.

Behind me, Alexei yawned. I glanced over my shoulder to see him plop down on my ginormous bed, headfirst into the mattress. A smile that I couldn't resist tugged on my lips as I hoisted myself up on the windowsill and leaned against the glass, watching with eyes half-opened as the sun rose up over the horizon.

30

A bang at the door pulled me from my dreamless slumber. For a second, I thought it was Layton, but the fuzz left by sleep soon cleared and I remembered where I was with a start.

I jerked awake, falling from the window nook and landed face-first onto the floor. When I lifted my head, ignoring the pain, I saw Alexei was in the same situation, struggling to free himself from the grasp of blankets wrapped around his legs. I turned my head and nearly gasped, surprised and puzzled to find Sasha stirring on the floor just a few feet away from me, covered in blankets.

When did he get here?

His golden eyes snapped open as the knocking continued and he threw the blankets off, drool staining his chin. He stumbled sleepily over to the door. As he struggled to turn the knob, I wondered why he had decided to come sleep with us instead of on his own bed in his own room.

Sasha finally got the door open, leaning against it casually as he flashed a charming smile to the guard waiting outside. "Hey, Klein, my man, my favorite guard. What brings you here?"

The guard didn't miss a beat, unamused. "The king requests dinner in the Blush Rose with his son and guests. He's been waiting."

"Dinner? What time is it?" Sasha asked, running a hand through his disheveled caramel hair.

"Nearly seven in the evening, Your Majesty."

"Oh." The three of us winced. "We'll be there in five minutes."

Before Klein could fit in another word, Sasha slammed the door and the sound reverberated through the dim room, chasing away the last of my exhaustion. I shot up from the floor, dusting off my skirt and straightening my blouse as Alexei slipped from the bed, running his hands through his hair in an attempt to fix it. Sasha whirled around, facing us with wide eyes.

"Well, good morning to you, princey," Alexei said, his voice raspy.

Sasha laughed. "Good morning, fellow adventurers. You have drool on your chin."

Alexei bashfully wiped his chin with his sleeve, glaring with playful eyes. Sasha and I chuckled, our voices dangerously loud, but that didn't stop us.

"What are you doing here?" I asked Sasha, tilting my head. I cleared my throat in an attempt to get rid of my rasp.

His bubbly grin dropped as he clenched his fists in tight balls. "I . . . I just didn't want to be alone anymore. Cathair spent hours 'shaming' and 'disgracing me from the royal line' yesterday. I just wanted to be in the company of some normal people." He used his fingers to air-quote, rolling his eyes.

"Normal?" Alexei quirked an eyebrow, a smile playing on his lips. "Please, tell me what part of us is normal. Really, I'd like to know."

"Oh, shut up." Sasha snickered as I failed to hide my bursting grin.

Alexei released a throaty laugh. "No, sorry, you're right. We're as normal as can be. Just your average, everyday Embrasian. Following the laws, gods watch over the king." He saluted to Sasha.

This time, we all couldn't stop our laughter. The sound rang through the room like a bell, genuine and bursting. I wasn't sure if I had ever laughed so hard, and when we calmed, my cheeks ached from all the smiling, my chest heaving just from laughter.

Would I ever be able to laugh with Layton and Dean like that? Carefree, without holding back. To just let the moment flow, mention of work nowhere to be found. To just . . . *be*.

I barely remembered what it was like in that house in Cyrene, constant fear of my own brothers, constant fear of being blamed for something, of letting them down, breaking a rule, staring at a lock for a second too long. The permanent smell of wood seemed like a distant memory, the texture of rough meat lost to me. I could barely see the knowing looks of my brothers, like they always knew something I didn't.

And I guessed the whole time, they really knew too much.

How long had I been gone? My old life seemed so distant, it was difficult to call it back. Was it bad that I didn't miss it? Was it bad that I would choose Alexei and Sasha over Cyrene? Would I choose them over my own brothers? I didn't know.

"We should get this over with," Alexei said as the moment passed, thrusting me back to reality.

Sasha and I immediately sobered, our smiles long gone. We caught each other's eyes, an unspoken question hanging in the air, pressing a daunting pressure over the three of us.

Were we ever going to see each other again?

Somehow, I found solace in the prince. I wasn't sure how, but somehow, Sasha had become a friend. My first friend, other than Alexei. Together, we were a band of misfits. But apart? Apart we were just lonely children trying to find our way through the waves of life. If I didn't have Sasha or Alexei, then I didn't really have anything.

I silently shoved on a pair of simple black slippers before the three of us sluggishly made our way to the door. Sasha cast us one last look and opened the door to reveal a group of guards waiting outside. As we stepped out, they took our sides, stepping in between the three of us, cutting us off from each other. I tried to hold Alexei's gaze, but the guard walked too fast to let me. I trotted to keep up, still rubbing the sleep from my eyes.

With the brisk pace the guards set, it didn't take long to arrive at the Blush Rose. They shoved the doors open, bowing as we walked through. The action sent a spike of irritation shooting up my stomach, a spike from somewhere unknown. I swallowed down my annoyance, knowing very well it wasn't the time for such feelings.

King Cathair sat at the other side of the table, his hands neatly folded, his face displaying indifference. Sasha stalked forward without a sign of hesitation, followed by Alexei, but as I made a move, I couldn't ignore the apprehension rising up in my stomach. The king couldn't stop us from leaving . . . right?

Technically, he can do whatever he wants. That's the purpose of the whole "king" title.

I swallowed nervously as Alexei and I dipped in deep bows, our foreheads almost touching the crystal floor. I was grateful that Alexei committed to all the talking.

"Your Majesty, we apologize for our disturbance. We have decided it would be best for us to take our leave," Alexei announced. "We thank you for your hospitality and kindness."

I resisted the urge to gag, while Sasha didn't even try.

"You may stand, friends." King Cathair narrowed his eyes at his son as he sighed. "I suppose I should've expected this. With the amount of trouble Sasha gets in on his own, I shouldn't have been surprised when I heard he included both of you in one of his troublesome plans."

Sasha took the words with not even a wince, but something deep in his eyes darkened, the shine of a young man flickering out for a moment. But as I caught his eyes, the shine returned. I nodded reassurance to him, not really knowing what I was trying to say, but still wanting to say it anyway.

"You are welcome to stay for one last dinner, if you please," the king said smoothly, a smile fighting its way to his lips.

"Thank you, Your Majesty, but we have already stayed too long." Alexei and I took one last bow, just for extra politeness, before beginning to turn.

"Wait!" Sasha exclaimed. He turned toward his father, his expression set in stone. "I'm going with them."

King Cathair's apathetic face abruptly twisted into one of anger, his cheeks glowing with an angry red. He slammed his clenched fists against the table. "No, you are *not*. Sit down, Sasha."

"No!" Sasha shouted. "I'm not waiting around this blasted castle anymore! How can I possibly be ready to rule this country if I don't even know the streets?"

"Enough! I don't want to hear it!" King Cathair waved the guards over and threw a finger at me and Alexei. "Guards, get them out of here, now!"

Before I could process what was happening, the guards swarmed the two of us. One of them caught my arms, twisting them behind my back painfully, and shoved me across the Blush Rose.

"Ivory!" Alexei cried, running toward me, but with an ambush of multiple shining guards, they trapped him in a restraint as well, hauling the two of us from the dining room.

"Let them go!" Sasha sprinted after us, screaming at the guards, but they paid him no heed.

I went limp in order to ease the pain, but Alexei struggled against their grasp, growling under his breath. His fingers sparked once. Twice. Not too long before a flame ignited.

"Alexei," I called.

He caught my fixed eyes through his efforts, his eyebrows furrowing together when I shook my head. Sure, the king deserved to have his castle burned down, but we were already in enough trouble. Vandalism didn't need to be added to the list. I breathed out a sigh of relief as he seemed to catch my thoughts, cutting off the sparks as he closed his fist tightly.

As we passed through the castle, I almost couldn't help but be glad we were finally leaving, albeit I would have rathered we didn't have to be manhandled out, but I tried to look on the bright side of things.

They threw open the gates, shoving us to the crystal streets of the city of Embrasia. I threw my hands out in an attempt to break my fall, but I still ended up landing with a hard thud anyway. Then, they disappeared back into the castle without a second glance, cutting off the sound of Sasha's cries. The bustle of the city behind us filled my ears.

"Ivory," Alexei stumbled to his feet, holding his hand out for me, "are you ok? I think your knee is bleeding again."

I accepted his hand, letting out a gust of breath as he tugged me up to my feet. The breeze of the evening stung against my opened wound, but the pain wasn't anything I couldn't handle. I felt like I could face any pain as long as Alexei stood by my side.

"I'm fine," I said, brushing off my skirt. "Are you ok?"

"Well, that wasn't the worst way I've been kicked out, so I'd say I'm doing pretty good."

I knew it was probably the worst time, but I couldn't help but laugh. Not only laugh at Alexei, but laugh at the whole situation. Because, of course, that happened. Of course, we were literally thrown out of the Embrasian palace by the fury of the king. Of course, our friend, the prince, was still stuck in there. And of course, we had nowhere to go now.

"I was *this* close to burning the hands off those stupid guards." Alexei brought his thumb and index together, leaving no space in between.

"What would you do without me?" I shot a grin at him.

"Burn down the Embrasian castle, apparently." He shrugged. "We better get a move on. The sun is already going down."

"So much for sleeping all day," I grumbled as we began to walk away from the glimmering crystal castle. "Do you have any idea where we're going?"

"There must be an inn somewhere around here."

"But we don't have any money."

Alexei smirked as he fished through his jacket and pulled out a mini bag jangling with coins. I gasped, marveling as he dropped the bag in my hand. It must've weighed a couple of pounds, at least.

"Where did you get this?" I asked, awed.

"Sasha gave it to me. I guess he knew King Cathair would throw us out all along. Good thing he knows his father," he answered with a shrug, swiping the bag back and returning it to his coat.

Though the money gave us something to be glad about, the name of the prince left a sour note in the air. Never in my wildest dreams did I ever expect to befriend the prince of Embrasia, but lately, everything that was thrown my way seemed to be a dream. Some more nightmares than others. Knowing I was conscious, *living*, sent an awakening shock through my body.

This is all real. I'm in Embrasia. My friend is the prince. And for some unknown reason, my most trusted companion is a wizard, and not just any wizard, the wizard that froze my heart as a child.

I frowned despite the flash of excitement that came from my thoughts. I had always dreamed of going on an adventure, but after so long running, I wasn't sure how much longer I wanted this adventure to last. I ached for the presence of Sasha, his light, bubbly laugh and atmosphere that he cast. I knew what it was like trapped behind doors, the pressure of the locks, the disproving eyes, the feeling of the doors growing closer and closer, the walls shrinking, every corner—

"Ivory?" Alexei's voice hauled me from my panicked memories.

I had to take a breath before I could respond. "Yes? What is it?"

He took a moment flicking his eyes across my face, the corners of his lips tipping down slightly. In the corner of my eye, I glimpsed his hand twitch.

"Don't worry," he said. "Sasha will find a way out of there. We'll see him again."

Of course he knew what taunted my thoughts. How did he seem to read my mind like an open book? Was it the way my thoughts took over my expression, or was it something else?

I smiled weakly. "Thanks."

I wasn't exactly sure what I was thanking him for, but when I caught Alexei's eyes, he seemed to know.

. . . .

The scattered rays of light were diminishing faster and faster, stealing away the sun and inviting the darkness with open arms. The streets of the city had begun clearing, the chatter growing sparse. I recalled the city of Andros, how I thought it would never sleep, how the chatter, music, lights seemed to go on all through the night like a never-ending party. I guessed Embrasia was nothing like that. Embrasia retired much earlier, like an old man as opposed to the rambunctious child Andros was.

The dim lights left led Alexei and me through the city, like untrusting guides, able to flicker out at any moment and plunge the two of us in darkness. We moved quickly, despite our aching feet and fatigue. We both rued declining the king's last offer of dinner, the silence between us filled with the embarrassing rumble of our stomachs. I couldn't even remember the last thing I had tasted, and the craving for chocolate wafting after me didn't help either.

"How big is this bloody city?" Alexei exclaimed suddenly, throwing his hands up.

I cast him a look of sympathy. Just by watching him for the past hour, I could sense his anxiety rising steadier and steadier with each passing minute. His fingers twitched every once in a while, he had rearranged his hair four times, and buttoned and unbuttoned his coat five times. I even caught him sucking on a strand of his dark hair.

The fact that he couldn't navigate perfectly seemed to taunt him. I guessed I couldn't blame him. I mean, he spent most of his life avoiding his own brothers. His jumpiness seemed to come from his past of hiding for years, but we couldn't hide. We were in plain sight, walking among the crowd, and as the crowd slowly disappeared, his twitchiness increased, even though we had concealed ourselves behind the fabrics of stolen cloaks.

It was almost like he expected his brothers to jump out from behind a corner and attack him right then and there, like they were some type of monsters. But I couldn't think of them like that, remembering the rage and confusion I felt when I learned the truth about my mom. Even presently, it was still there, biting at the back of my brain.

Surely, his brothers still couldn't have been angry. Perhaps they had regained control over their magic. Perhaps guilt plagued them like a terrible sickness. Perhaps they had been searching for Alexei not to finish an act of revenge, but to apologize. Perhaps, if they were no longer under the influence of their crazed magic, they would be willing to reverse Alexei's spell. Willing to help me. They were strong enough, I knew.

But when I glanced up at Alexei, his face cast over by a shadow of anticipation, fear drowning in his eyes, I wasn't sure if he would ever give his brothers a chance. Seeing him so disheveled unnerved me, sending a different type of shiver running up my back. The only thing I thought to do was offer some type of distraction.

"So," I started unevenly, "Embrasia, huh? I expected it to be . . ."

"Please don't say bigger."

"No." I chuckled weakly. "Definitely not bigger. More . . . kingdom-y?"

"That's not a word." He cast me a sideways glance, his eyebrow perking up.

Eyebrow perks were good.

"It is now." I shot him a smile despite the pain biting at my feet.

A grin snaked its way to his lips and I inwardly rejoiced. Amusement swallowed the fear shining in his eyes, and the shadow of anxiety across his face ran away along with it. I thought I could've gazed upon his face forever, taken in the curve of his throat, his strong chin, and refined jawbone. The way his eyes glittered like literal emeralds when he smiled. Just the way his smile seemed so natural, like it belonged there.

"Ivory, look!"

I snapped out of my trance and whirled my head toward his outstretched finger. Only a few more blocks down the lane, a towering wooden inn overlooked the two of us.

"Yes!" he cheered, jumping up and punching the air.

I released a laugh along with him, and when we entered the nearly empty inn, we couldn't get rid of the relieved smiles on our cheeks. It was spacious inside, a furnace next to a couch warming the air. A couple of tables and chairs were strewn about and a small bar sat beside a staircase opposite from the check-in desk. It was empty, except for one man sleeping, his head slumped over the table, his hand loosely clasped around a shot glass. Paintings of the king hung on the walls and the sight caused my smile to falter.

"Hello, how can I help you?" An old man approached us with a warming grin, his hands folded into each other.

"Good evening." Alexei smiled brightly. "We would like a room, please."

"Of course." The man nodded and hurried to get us a key. He had to rummage through a few shelves and drawers until he found one.

As he told us our room number, he handed it to Alexei and didn't forget to remind us of the price of staying a night. We thanked him quickly, eager to hide in the privacy of a room after so long wandering the open streets. We climbed up the staircase to a hallway of doors, the wooden boards creaking beneath our feet. We found our room and Alexei unlocked the door, holding it wide open.

"After you, shining armor." He grinned, talking in a mocking tone as he impersonated the king's booming voice.

"Why, thank you, my good damsel." I chuckled and sauntered through.

The room was small, the floors creaky, and quite dusty. The smell of must filled my nose the second I walked in. It was pretty bare, save a rug, bed, and lone desk. The bathroom was small, the shower only big enough to step inside and stand. But we really didn't care.

"Thank the gods." Alexei released a puff of air as he collapsed onto the bed, using his feet to shove off his boots. "I've never been so happy to stand inside some sketchy inn ever in my life."

"I've never even stood inside a sketchy inn."

Alexei couldn't resist a chuckle, which he tried to hide. He sat up and pulled his coat from his arms, hanging it on a hanger clumsily nailed to the wall. I stepped out of my slippers and pulled out the wooden chair from the desk, plopping down with a sigh. I knew both of us were tired and didn't want to think about it, but I had to ask the question hanging over our heads.

"What do we do now?"

Alexei sighed, as if he had expected the question. "We'll figure something out."

"If you haven't noticed, we sort of need that 'something' figured out now," I said. "We can only be so lucky. Sooner or later . . ."

He shot me a look that cut me off. I wasn't exactly sure what would happen sooner or later. Alexei's heart would fail and leave him defenseless? The police would find me and drag me back to Cyrene? Some fortunate soul would recognize me and drag me to the police? Anything could happen, and I didn't like it. Nothing in my life before just *happened*.

"I'm tired, Ivory. Let's just leave it for the morning," Alexei said, and a twinge of an old familiar irritation rose up in his voice.

I could barely resist the urge to scoff. "You can't keep running. Sooner or later, you'll have to confront your brothers, and you know it. If you won't, then I will."

All I knew about Valentin, Mercedes, and Francois was that they were extremely powerful, they tried killing me as a child, and they were corrupted by magic a long time ago. I knew Alexei wouldn't tell me any more about them, even if I begged. But I still couldn't help but bring them up.

"Don't be stupid," Alexei spat. "They see you, they kill you. They see me, they kill me. It's a lose-lose situation."

"It's been years, Alexei. How do you know they're still," I faltered, searching for the correct word, "still . . . like that?"

He found my gaze, his own sharp like knives. "You don't know them. You haven't even met them, so don't try to pretend you have. They're crazy, and they wouldn't hesitate to kill us if they just had the chance. I'm not going to give them that chance."

"Alexei," I hated how pleading my voice sounded, "they might be the only way to make me normal."

He wavered for a brief second, his countenance of anger dropping, but it didn't stay gone for long. "I know you want your heart back, but they are not the answer."

"How can you possibly know that?"

"Ivory." His voice was firm and growing increasingly aggravated. "I'm telling you, finding them would be a death wish. Maybe not even death, they could find something much worse to do to you. They're worse than anything you've seen, worse than the Highwayman, the sirens, the fey."

"They're your family!"

"So?" This time, he didn't hesitate to shout, his anger flaring up along with a couple of flames. "All I've gained from my family is grief! All *you've* gained from yours is grief!"

I opened my mouth to retort something back, but a sharp knock at the door cut me off. We both instantly stood down, our anger evaporating like mist. We rushed to take each other's side. Alexei's hands flickered for good measure. He gestured for me to stay back while he slowly approached the door. With each step he took, my anticipation rose higher, and I wanted to be the one in danger's way instead of him.

He pressed his eye to the eyehole, and I watched in confusion as he murmured something in his foreign language like a hushed gasp. He stepped away and turned the knob.

Outside the door stood the prince himself, wearing the biggest grin on his face.

31

"Sasha?" Alexei and I cried in unison.

A giggle escaped his lips as he jumped into our room, throwing himself at us with his arms outstretched. He wrapped us in a tight hug, probably the tightest I had ever received, his laugh bouncing off the creaky wooden walls.

We all let go slowly, laughs dancing on our lips. Before he spoke, he made sure to lock the door behind him.

"Miss me?"

"Yeah, things were starting to get boring without you," I replied, chuckling, my cheeks aching from the sudden amount of smiling.

"How'd you get out?" Alexei asked, taking off the boy's cloak and throwing it on a hanger quickly.

Underneath his cloak, his white and purple vest was gone, replaced with the same green vest we had met him in. Except, he seemed to have torn the golden trim off, and the diamonds were missing too. His silver sword hung by his side, along with a sack of what seemed to be coins.

"I went through the catacombs. There's a secret passageway in the castle, and nobody goes down there due to all the ghosts," Sasha explained, his chest puffed up proudly.

"Then what took you so long?" Alexei sneered.

Sasha gasped dramatically, throwing his hand against his chest. The three of us laughed and the argument between me and Alexei seemed to be long forgotten.

"Does anyone know?" I asked.

"Nobody. I don't think I can trust anyone in the castle anymore," Sasha responded. "Cathair will just have to beg for us to come back."

We all burst out laughing once more, Sasha so hard that he toppled over. Yeah, like that would happen. The king would've rather send a thousand guards than ask for our return. It took a while, but we eventually calmed down, wiping the tears from our eyes and drawing in deep breaths.

"So, what's the plan?" Sasha asked, a smile lingering on his face.

The light atmosphere Sasha had brought us disappeared faster than the blink of an eye. Alexei and I mentally glared at each other, our argument continuing internally. I spoke quickly, before Alexei even had the chance to open his mouth.

"*I* am going to find the Kementaris."

"No, you're not."

"Yes, I am."

Alexei and I glared at each other, our fight caught in our throats, threatening to rise up again. Sasha glanced at the two of us, realization dawning over his features.

"Ooh, you're fighting." He giggled.

"Are not!" Alexei and I exclaimed.

Sasha paused, his eyes flicking between the two of us, before breaking out in laughter. I crossed my arms and turned my head away from the two men, huffing in annoyance. When I glimpsed at Alexei, I found his cheeks dusted with a rose tint. He cleared his throat and the color was gone, making me wonder if it really had been there in the first place.

"Care to explain?" Sasha questioned, failing at hiding his curiosity.

Alexei and I glanced at each other, almost as if asking for permission. At the same time, we shrugged.

"Alright, but if I'm going to tell this story again, I'm going to need a drink." Alexei sighed, already slipping on his coat and boots.

Sasha nodded, retightening his cloak as he followed Alexei to the door. "You coming?"

"No," I answered quickly, "I think I'll just stay here."

"Alright. We'll be back."

"Don't go anywhere." Sasha cast me a smirk.

I smiled, waving limply as they left. My smile dropped the second the door closed behind them. Though the presence of the prince offered a great respite to my storming thoughts, I still felt stressed as ever. The fact that I finally knew the answer to my problem, and I couldn't go ask for help, drove me crazy with a reckless feeling. I wanted to seek after them, find them, but I knew I could never leave Alexei and Sasha behind like that.

They aren't the cursed ones. You're the one with the frozen heart. Don't I deserve it by now?

I pushed the thoughts away angrily. Thinking like that was dangerous, thinking like that was what led to reckless and stupid decisions. Thinking that I deserved more than I had. The world owed me nothing, I knew, but I still found myself struggling to snuff out the flicker of hope that had begun to rise up in me.

I paced across the room, my head aching just from deciding the right or wrong choice. Why was it so hard to choose? Risk the wrath of angry wizards for the small chance they might return what I had yearned for my whole life or leave Alexei. Just thinking about abandoning him sent my stomach tumbling like a rock rolling down a hill. After everything we had gone through, after the days spent together, the tears shed together, the blood dripped together, how could I tear us apart?

But could I forget about gaining my heart back for him?

I pressed a hand against my chest silently, waiting, but it remained still as ever, as it always had. I wondered what it would be like to feel a little beat beneath my palm. How weak would it be? How strong?

The sound of knuckles against wood filled my ears, and I nearly jumped at the sound, reminding myself the danger had passed. Alexei and Sasha probably just forgot the key back in. I hurried to open the door and froze as the person waiting outside was revealed.

"Oh, Ivory, I missed you so much!" Marble exclaimed, pulling me into a tight hug.

I gasped and had to kick myself in order to refrain from kicking him, my whole body cringing at the Magician's touch, breathing hard from shock.

"What—what are you doing here?" I sputtered, stumbling back through the threshold.

He stepped inside, glancing around the room as he closed the door behind him as though in search of something. Or someone.

"The king has sent me to retrieve the three of you," he answered after a brief moment of silent searching, directing his eyes on me.

"Three?" I faked confusion, furrowing my eyebrows tightly, shooting him a strange look.

"Yes. You, Alexei and Sasha."

I shook my head slowly. "But, Marble, it's just me and Alexei here."

Marble's rosy face flushed white. I wanted to see more color drain from his face. I wanted to see that stupid grin wipe off his cheeks, his eyes to go dull from defeat. I wanted him out, never to show himself in front of me again.

"You mean . . . nobody *else* is with you?" His voice trembled, causing a slight flare of satisfaction to spike up in my chest.

"No," I shook my head, priding myself with the concern in both my eyes and tone, "why? Did something happen?"

Marble bit off a hanging fingernail, his eyes scanning the room as if Sasha would show up only if he looked hard enough. His gaze snapped back to mine quickly, and if I hadn't previously distrusted him, I wasn't sure if I would've caught his suspicious behavior.

"Nevermind." He swiped his hand through the air, shaking his head. "I'm here to bring you back to the castle, on the king's request."

I gulped, my face flushing almost as white as Marble's had as he stepped forward and grabbed my hands. My stomach lurched by the touch, and it took all of my willpower not to swipe my hands away. I hurried to find some sort of response.

"I . . . can't."

"What?"

"I can't. I'm not going back," I stated, hoping my voice sounded firmer than what I heard.

"Why not?" Marble questioned, his grip on my hands dropping. I tried not to let relief flood my expression as his hands returned to his sides.

Behind his mask of surprise, I caught a trace of anger. His eyes narrowed like slits, his nose flaring, and behind his back hid a clenched fist. If I hadn't been so shaken by his presence, I would've laughed.

"Alexei and I have someone really important to meet. They've been waiting for a long time and we can't waste any more time," I answered. *Technically, I'm not lying.*

"Are you certain you can't stay a little longer? King Cathair has desired for your return."

I held back a scoff. At least I had the decency to tell a somewhat truth.

"I'm sorry, Marble, I really am, but we'll return soon." *Yeah, right.* "Right now, we have to leave as soon as possible."

His mouth hung open, his eyes swimming in search of words, but before he could get anything out, I opened the door behind him, standing aside to allow him to pass through.

"I'm sorry." I let my voice break and even dared to avoid my gaze guiltily.

"Oh, it's all right, dear girl." He sighed with a forced smile, strolling out the door slowly, his eyes lingering. "We'll meet again, my dear Ivory."

I fought, wrestled, *struggled* for a smile as I nodded, watching him sorrowfully as he made his way out. The second he crossed the threshold, I tried not to slam the door, though I yearned to, instead closing it slowly. I waited until I was sure I had heard his footsteps disappear before turning the lock promptly.

That wretch! I glared at where Marble once stood, wiping my hands on my skirt, shivering just by the memory of his touch. Of him holding me down against that table, injecting that burning crystal into my blood. I remembered Crystal, her pleading voice to stop him, but he didn't listen.

The kingdom of Embrasia might've been the most beautiful in the world, but the beauty seemed to come at the cost of rotten hearts and twisted minds.

How did Marble get here without noticing Alexei and Sasha downstairs?

Just as I was slipping on my shoes to check downstairs, a sudden anxiety swelling in my stomach, the lock clicked the other way. The door opened, revealing Alexei and Sasha rushing in, slamming the door behind them.

"What is it?" I immediately asked, noticing the blatant panic on their faces.

"Police and the Embrasian guards. They know we're here," Alexei answered, out of breath.

I gasped. Were they here to send me back to Cyrene? Or to the palace?

"We have to get out of here," Sasha said.

"Wait!" I cried as they motioned me to the door. "Marble's here! He might be waiting for us!"

"Marble?" Alexei and Sasha exclaimed at the same time.

"Are we cornered?" Sasha asked, his voice rising an octave with panic.

For once, Alexei seemed at a loss for words, his eyes wide, fear drowning in them. His lack of answers seemed to set Sasha off, sending the prince hyperventilating and pacing. Though panic pounded in my chest, threatening to take over my thoughts, I couldn't help but recall how I felt in Cyrene. It seemed I was in the same situation, blocked off exits in every nook and cranny.

But I got out anyway. And I would now, too.

"Alright," I nearly had to shout to capture their attention, "calm down!"

Their gazes shot to mine, their mouths clasped tightly closed as if surprised by my loud tone. I let out a huff before I crossed the room, peeling the tattered curtains from the window. No matter where I went, it seemed I always ended up jumping out the nearest glass. At least this time I could push Alexei and Sasha before me.

"Are you crazy?" Sasha cried.

Yes. "You've got a better idea? 'Cause I'd love to hear it in the minute of freedom we have left."

That seemed to do it. The two rushed forward, practically tripping over themselves to join my side. I unlocked the window, tugged the frame up as much as it could go, welcoming the fresh breeze as it beckoned through my hair. It was only two stories high, the descent nothing like the one at the castle. Probably enough to break a bone if landed wrong, but I had yet to land wrong.

"Ready?" I asked.

Beyond the door, the sound of pounding footsteps echoed through the halls, thumping against each stair like a gunshot. I forced myself to swallow my fear.

"I'll go first," Alexei whispered breathlessly, gazing at the drop with a countenance of apprehension.

He took a deep breath as he climbed through, and with one last whispered prayer in his unknown language, he slid off. The sight of him plummeting through the air was enough to send my own stomach rolling as though I had been the one that jumped. He caught himself with his hands as he landed, stumbling for a few moments before righting himself properly. He turned to offer a smile and a thumbs up. I couldn't help but breathe out a sigh of relief.

The sight of Alexei's successful land seemed to soothe Sasha's nerves. His expression of fear switched to one of excitement.

"I'll go next. That way, I'll be able to catch you." With a smirk, he sent a wink my way, and before I could slap him, he had climbed through the window.

Just as he dropped, the door flew open behind me. I gasped, whirling around as the Embrasian guards stormed the room, led by the one and only Marble. They rushed toward me, seizing my arms painfully. I kicked and struggled, my panic drowned out by adrenaline, but I was no match against them.

Or was I? I escaped the Highwayman and his regime of criminals. How were these guards any different?

"I know they're here, Morrow. Where are they?" Marble approached, his eyes glaring, but his lips smirking. He looked like a madman. "Don't make me hurt you. I wouldn't want to use Fire Dust again, now would I?"

The remaining color of my already flushed face disappeared. Marble cackled, and I couldn't help but remember what he had said before his twisted experiment with me.

With the amount of magic it would take to replace a heart, I'd think you'd be full of untamed magic, uncontrollable and unpredictable. What if he had been right all along?

"You touch me, see what happens. Go on," I hissed.

Marble only laughed again. "Why should I be scared of a little, pathetic girl like you? A girl who can't even love?"

I smirked. "And that'll be your downfall."

Before he could fit in anything else, the guards holding me screamed out, dropping me from their grasp as a layer of frost climbed up their fingers. I darted to the window, where Alexei and Sasha were gazing up with fearful eyes.

"Ivory, watch out!" Alexei screamed.

I only had enough time to turn my head to see Marble wielding a glowing piece of crystal Fire Dust. He threw it in the air and with an ear-piercing bang, the room exploded with fiery hot mist. I screamed out in pain as the vapor seeped into my skin, my body already failing from underneath me.

I stumbled over to the window, but before I could catch the sweet release of the night air, a pair of hands grasped my arm tightly. I fought against Marble, fitting in a few kicks and punches, but as he trapped me between him and the window, my movement was limited. The scorching mist made my head pound, my vision spinning. The only thing that kept me fighting was the shriek of Alexei below.

I dug my fingers into Marble's skin, the two of us groaning out in agony as the other delivered magic so strong, the room became a mix of ice and fire. Soon, with the ice biting up his fingers, Marble tore himself from my grasp, releasing a cry of pain. I stumbled again, and when I hit the edge of the window, I didn't have enough energy to stop myself.

My body fell through and the wind filled my ears almost as loud as Alexei's screams as I plummeted from the second story of the burning inn.

32

Down. Down. Down.

I wasn't sure if I had fallen for minutes or for a mere half-second. Gods, I wasn't even sure if I had managed to stay conscious the whole way down, but the next thing I knew, I landed with barely a thud. I pried my eyes open as I swallowed the scream in my throat, rapidly drawing in shallow gasps of breath.

"I got you," Alexei whispered. "I got you."

We slowly made our way to the solid ground, Sasha gazing up at us with his jaw dropped. Alexei allowed me to slip from his grasp before he ushered us to run. I wanted to fall to my knees and kiss the ground, but I knew the guards weren't far away. Just because I had managed my way from Marble didn't mean we were safe. No, far from it, in fact.

So, I ran.

"You told me you couldn't fly!" Sasha exclaimed as we tore down the darkened streets.

"I can't!" Alexei replied.

"Then what was that?"

"I—I don't know!" Alexei sputtered. "If you haven't noticed, now is not a good time."

Sasha opened his mouth to retort something back, but seemed to think better of it as he realized Alexei was right. We barreled through the darkness like criminals ourselves, the veil of night our only friend. Distant voices echoed through the city, and when I glanced back, I found the lanterns clicking on.

"They're turning the lanterns back on!" I cried.

Alexei and Sasha glanced over their shoulders, their eyes widening as they saw what I meant. Though I wasn't sure how, we picked up our pace despite the exhaustion biting at our legs. Running was our only option, unless Alexei had an invisibility spell somewhere up his sleeve, but I seriously doubted it. Just thinking about the way he had caught me, literally, in mid-air sent my blood pulsing faster than ever before, his arms supporting all my weight like I was a feather, the way we drifted down like a peaceful leaf falling from a tree in autumn.

"This way," Sasha hissed and lunged into a dark alleyway.

We followed suit, pressing ourselves against the walls as light burst in the streets. We scooted further into the darkness while guards flew by, shouting and carrying blazing lanterns. Marble led them like the alpha of a pack, and I caught a glimpse of his hands, black with frostbite. I gasped at the sight of them and Alexei pulled me closer to him, hiding my eyes with his shaking hands.

Once they passed, Alexei slowly peeled his hands away as we finally allowed ourselves to breathe. We slumped back in relief, and my knees almost failed out from underneath me. We waited an extra minute just for precaution before we even thought about speaking again.

"Are they gone?" I whispered in the faintest breath.

"I think so," Sasha replied. "Is everyone alright? Ivory?"

"I'm fine." The pain from the Fire Dust had cooled from the drop and the running, but the panic was much worse than the pain had been. However much I tried sucking air into my lungs, I just couldn't get enough. My chest felt tight, too tight, like suffocation had grasped my airways with its foul hands.

"Are you sure? Did they hurt you? Let me see." Alexei held my face, inspecting it like how a doctor might, though I knew Alexei was the furthest from a doctor than anyone.

I wiggled from his hands, nearly collapsing into the wall behind me. Were they closing in? Were we going to be crushed? Was the air getting thinner? How was there enough space for the three of us?

I tried directing my fear on the task at hand. "I said I'm fine. We need a plan. We need to get out of here." I barely realized how fast the words spewed from my lips.

"It might be safer to stay here," Alexei said.

"No!" I cried, then clasped my hands to my lips quickly.

"Alright, alright." Sasha gripped my shoulder and the touch made my breath hitch. "I think I know someone who can help us."

"Who?"

"His name's Cecil. I met him a long time ago, when I got lost in the Square of Embrasia. He was the only one that recognized me as the prince, and he helped me back to my mother. He runs the trains now."

"Where's the train station?" Alexei asked.

The gleam of slight hope diminished in Sasha's eyes. "The other side of Embrasia."

Alexei buried his face in his hands. "There's no way we can make it there without being caught."

"No, not with all these guards running around," Sasha agreed. His facial expression switched, like an idea had struck him. "We could always go back to the Adeleigh Wood."

"No!" Alexei and I groaned, but the certainty shining on Sasha's face outmatched our grumbles.

It made the most sense. Adeleigh surrounded Embrasia in a wooded embrace, so close and so hidden. The guards and police would never think to look for us there, and even if they did, their cowardice would convince them against treading through the gnarled trees of oak. And, at least, we had one ally already waiting for us there.

The walls around us seemed to lean, tilt, shrink smaller, and grow bigger. Trapping us, winding forever. I wanted to stretch my arms out in an attempt to keep them in place, but there wasn't even enough room to do that. I was sure the air had been seeping out of the small corner ever since we had arrived. All at once, the wooden walls back in Cyrene flashed in my mind. Though I hated the thought of returning to the Adeleigh Wood, my desperate need to escape the alleyway stood much taller, overwhelming.

I just wanted to leave the grasp of the alley's dark corners, even if that meant trudging through the night with Furn.

"Alright, fine. Let's just go." I shoved past them. "And quickly, please."

. . . .

It didn't take long to find Furn, and it didn't take much to convince him to hide us away for the night. Just the promise to tell him everything that had happened, so I swore I would tell the previous evening's events, making sure to emphasize the secrecy of it all.

He happily chatted as he led us through the winding paths of trees, where we ended up in a burrow, covered by a hand-made door crafted from wooden planks and vines. It was actually almost impressive, but of course, I didn't tell the narcissistic satyr that. He was already full of himself enough.

But as we stepped inside, I couldn't stop my jaw from dropping. It was expansive, the walls of dirt embedded with countless shimmering trinkets. Stolen trinkets. I even saw the coat I had given him curled up neatly on the floor. It was a giant hole, yes, but a very nicely decorated giant hole, with glowing crystals of Dust illuminating the burrow. Sasha and Alexei seemed impressed too, but they had hidden the fact a lot swifter than I had.

"Here, let me get snacks. Oh, and wine. Then you can tell me everything!" Furn exclaimed excitedly. He rummaged around before pulling out a basket of a variety of berries along with a bottle of wine he had definitely stolen from the palace somehow. He ushered us to sit as he dropped them in front of the three of us, and plopped down, his eyes shimmering like a child waiting for a bedtime story.

So, just because I *had* promised, and he *had* fed us and let us hide out in his home, I started the tale of Silver Morrow, the liar and a cheater.

The story dragged on for almost two hours, two hours of weaving the days of my life, two hours of reminiscing as I popped grapes in my mouth, and when I had finally ended it, I had covered everything that had led up to hiding out in his very home on that very night. For once, it left Furn quiet. It left everyone in the burrow quiet. Even Alexei had stopped drinking.

"Ivory," Sasha whispered, his eyes holding a type of pain I couldn't distinguish.

If I hadn't been so tired, I would've snapped at him, snapped at all of them to stop looking at me like I was some lost kitten missing a leg. But, instead, I concluded the story with one last remark.

"Although all that's happened has seemed like a nightmare, I wouldn't want to live through any other dream. This is a nightmare I don't want to wake up from."

Without a conscious reason, my eyes found Alexei's, his pools of emerald drowning with emotion. But what emotion? Was I just too tired to discern it?

Or was it something truly foreign to me? I wanted to think I knew it, understood it. I wanted to think I could hold that much emotion in my own eyes.

Furn was the one to break the trance my story seemed to have cast, and I was grateful, for once, of his talkative nature.

"That's gotta be the best story I have ever heard. A bit unrealistic, but pretty good anyway." He shrugged, a smile tugging at his lips.

A grin broke out on my own lips despite myself. The grin and Furn's comment seemed to ease some tension I had created, and the two men managed a weak chuckle through their stupid emotional eyes. Furn cleared away our midnight meal and returned with silken curtains that he passed out as blankets.

I couldn't help but laugh as he handed me mine, a sudden realization dawning on me. Furn didn't want gossip, or jewels and gems. He wanted memories. He wanted companions. Friends. He, like I had been for countless years, was lonely. I sympathized with him, glad Sasha had suggested we go to him for the first time since we arrived. For years I had dreamed of a friend coming to my door, with it never happening. And now, I had just made it happen for Furn. I couldn't fight the pride and happiness rising up in my chest.

Alexei finished his golden goblet of wine before he hastily accepted the curtain. He had drunk more than he had been able to in the past week, but it still wasn't enough to mess with his state of mind. Nothing more than a little tipsy. The wine seemed to have calmed his nerves, his twitchiness long gone the moment he took the first sip.

All four of us found a spot to settle down, Furn babbling away about something or other, but I listened intently despite the exhaustion clawing at me like a savage monster. However, as time passed, his remarks grew quiet and sparse, until his voice faded off in a sigh of sleep.

I whispered a goodnight, tugging the curtain higher on my cold body, and smiled as two voices responded back to me.

"Goodnight, Knight."

"Goodnight," Alexei took a deep breath, as if searching for a better word, "Ivory."

Content on fruit and refreshing sips of wine, sleep tugging me to my dreams, I didn't have enough energy to access his hesitation. But, if I had, what would I have made out of the slight falter?

. . . .

Furn had supplied us with a breakfast of crackers and berries, chatting us awake throughout the morning. All three of us woke up feeling more tired than the night before, our eyes refusing to open, our bodies tethered to the ground, which somehow had grown to be the most comfortable 'bed' I had ever slept on. We could only mumble our replies to Furn. Only when the satyr nearly splashed a bucket of the freezing pond water over us did we burst fully awake, shoved down the breakfast, and engaged in his conversations.

I could tell he didn't want us to go, and the knowledge sent spikes of guilt impaling my stomach like knives. If only he could come along, but a satyr would attract much more attention than my silver hair. He seemed to be aware of this, but still escorted us from the burrow and to the edge of Adeleigh anyway, where the city had already woken long ago, the streets cluttered with nicely dressed people rushing from place to place. In the giant crowd, I almost expected nobody to recognize us through the bustle, but we weren't going to take any chances. Not after what happened the previous night.

"Here." Furn thrust the fur coat in my arms. "I thought you might need it. And, here." He handed Alexei and Sasha dark cloaks, looking a little sheepish. It was almost like he had never given anything away before.

"Thank you, Furn." I smiled, and an urge to reach out and hug him took over me, leaving me a little confused. Since when did I want to hug people? Especially satyrs?

"Just," he struggled with his words for a moment, "don't get yourself caught by that wicked king. Us outcasts have to stick together."

My smile only grew by being called an outcast. That had a very nice ring to it.

Sasha released a laugh. "I couldn't have said it better myself. Take care of yourself, Furn, and between you and me, keep doing what you're doing."

Furn's eyes lit up as he nodded at the prince. Only Sasha would give a satyr permission to steal his family's possessions.

"Well," Alexei flashed a charming smile, "it's been great, but we better get moving. I want to get out of this blasted city as quickly as possible."

"If you must." Furn sighed. "I guess this is goodbye then."

"Not goodbye," I said instantly. "Just . . . until we meet again."

Furn's downturned lips quirked up, the shine in his eyes like diamonds as he beamed. "You know, you're not so bad for a heartless girl."

The three of us couldn't resist a laugh. We bid our last farewells, though without exactly saying goodbye, before we slipped into the chaotic crowd, concealing our faces with the clothing Furn had given us.

We rushed through the city, weaving around countless people, countless carts and stands. I forced my eyes on the path ahead of me, but my curiosity banged to be let in. I bet whatever the sellers held in their carts was nothing like I had ever seen before, things only found in Embrasia, things I would never even dream of seeing in Cyrene. I wanted to drink in the sights like beautifully aged wine, but the consequence of getting drunk with my eyes proved too great. I couldn't allow myself to be distracted. I couldn't allow myself that first poisonous sip.

As we moved, nobody seemed to notice us flying through, but it was only a matter of time before someone caught sight of my terribly abnormal hair or recognized their precious prince. Constantly glancing over my shoulders, anticipation dug a home in my head. We took each step with paranoia, anxiety radiating off each other.

I wasn't sure how long we had traveled through the city before a whistle resounded in the distance, offering a slight flicker of hope to the three of us.

"We're almost there," Sasha whispered from under his cloak. "Just right up here."

I flicked my eyes up to see smoke billowing from a train, the whistle blowing once more. It was almost enough to scare away some of my fear. Almost enough to send a tug to my lips. I brushed a stray piece of hair from my face, tucking it tightly behind my ear, my other hand ensuring my hood remained over my head.

"Just past these shops," Sasha muttered, his voice laced with apprehension.

I swallowed roughly. Knowing Sasha was nervous didn't help at all. He and Alexei were supposed to be the ones that knew everything, that had the situation under control. But the more time I spent with them, the more I realized they weren't as strong as I had thought. All of us were so different, but we at least had one thing in common.

None of us knew what we were doing.

I took a subtle breath, expecting a regiment of guards to pop out of nowhere, ready to seize us. *Stop it. We're almost there. We'll make it.*

But of course, I was wrong.

"Ivory!" The voice came from somewhere far away, and as the cry filled my ears, I had a hard time recognizing it. "Ivory, wait! Ivory!"

"Where is that coming from?" Alexei hissed as he whirled around and scanned the crowd pushing past us.

Out of the corner of my eyes, I found a couple of pedestrians pause in their stead, whispering to each other as they directed their gazes toward the direction of the voice. Whoever it was calling me didn't seem to understand shouting the name of a ten thousand gold reward in the most crowded square of one of the biggest cities in the country was not a good idea.

I thought I would collapse just from panic. Well, either collapse or break out in an adrenaline-induced sprint. I couldn't decide which one to apply to myself. But, luckily for me, I didn't have enough time to choose because the source of the voice burst out from the crowd, showing himself to me.

I couldn't stop the gasp that escaped my lips. It was the boy I least expected to see. The boy I thought I would never see again.

Dulce.

I knew I should've ran. I knew I should've gotten out of his line of sight. I knew, but my body wouldn't allow me to move. I was frozen, breath caught in my throat, blood pulsing underneath my skin like a raging river, my lips slightly hung agape.

He rushed forward and didn't hesitate to grab my hands as though we had known each other our whole lives. As though he were someone I actually knew. As though he was actually someone to me.

"Ivory, I can't believe I found you!" he exclaimed, oblivious of how loud his voice sounded. "I've been looking everywhere!"

"D—Dulce," I choked out, my mind blank and fuzzy. I urged myself to do something. But what? Tear my hands away? Run? Listen to what he had to say? Introduce him?

"You know him?" Alexei asked dubiously.

"Yes, well, no. Sorta!" I responded. "Dulce, what are you doing here?"

His eyes flicked up at Alexei for a moment before he answered. "I'm here to bring you home. Your brothers sent me. Well, and I wanted to, of course."

My breath hitched. Just the reminder of Cyrene sent my stomach dropping even more than the sight of Dulce already had. I opened my mouth to reply, but nothing came out. *Speak, stupid! Say something! Anything!*

"Well, she isn't going with you." Alexei glared down at him, his eyes shooting daggers. "So, if you'd ever so kindly excuse us, we have somewhere to be."

"Wait a minute, who do you think you are?" Dulce shoved a finger in Alexei's face. He turned back to me, his hand grasping my shoulder tightly. "Don't tell me you've been with *him* this whole time."

Before I could even open my mouth to spit out a reply, Alexei swiped his arm through Dulce's, ripping the bakery boy's hand from my shoulder. The tips of his hair flicked with fire, his green eyes giving off a dim glow. Dulce stumbled back, his face twisted in horror.

"Wizard," he spat.

"Ivory, as much as I'd love to see Alexei explode, you might want to wrap this up," Sasha whispered, glancing around nervously.

I took a second to access our surroundings. People had begun to stare, their hushed conversation carrying over the crowd like the rolling of waves. They had stopped, and even had offered a little bit of space for the four of us as Dulce and Alexei's transaction went down. I had to do something before someone else stepped in. Before someone else decided to ruin our plans.

"Alright, alright." I stepped in between Alexei and Dulce, holding my hands out as if to hold them back. "Enough. Yes, I have been with him this whole time, Dulce."

"But—but he's a wizard!"

Say it louder, I don't think the person in the back heard you.

I hushed him as a spike of panic shot up in my chest. The crowd around us began to stir. Stirring was not good. I didn't like stirring. The whispers grew increasingly louder until I felt all I could hear was the hushed chatter of the crowd.

"Did he just say wizard?"

"Is that a girl under that coat?"

"What's all the shouting about?"

"Ivory." Sasha's voice was full of warning as he too seemed to catch the crowd's growing interest on us, lightly laying his hand on my shoulder.

"I'm working on it," I muttered back to him and whirled around to face Dulce and Alexei, who seemed to have been in the middle of a death stare off. "Would you two grow up? I'm not going anywhere I don't want to, got that?"

"But—"

"No buts," I snapped. "Look, Dulce, I appreciate all of . . . this, but I can't go back to Cyrene."

"What? Why not?" he demanded as Alexei released a not-so-subtle snicker from behind me.

"I'm not going back, ok?" I replied shortly.

Dulce's glare caught Alexei's eyes. "Does this have something to do with your heart?"

I took a wounded step back. Why had I told him about my heart? Why?

"She said no, so why don't you run back to your precious Cyrene?" Alexei cut in, heated anger radiating off of him like a vapor.

This time, Dulce just ignored him entirely. "Ivory, listen to me. You have to come back. It's not safe out here for a girl like you."

"A girl like me?" My eyebrows shot up and I couldn't resist crossing my arms. "What, you don't think I can handle myself? Is that what my brothers told you?"

"It's exactly what they told me! They said you'd be dead if you tried being on your own. And now I can see what they meant! Don't you know how dangerous wizards are? Where are you even going?"

I held up my hand to stop Alexei and Sasha from cutting in. Alexei's irritation with Dulce had only made the situation worse, and if the prince wouldn't be able to hold himself back, then we were as good as arrested. I needed to end the conversation, and end it fast before we attracted more attention than we already had. It was a miracle no officer or guard had checked to see what all the commotion was about. But I knew the miracle wouldn't last for long.

"I can't tell you where I'm going, but I can tell you one thing. I'm not going back. Not now. And not ever if I don't find what I'm looking for. Right now, I belong with them." I cast Alexei and Sasha a half-smile. "I can't say I'm sorry, Dulce."

He clasped his lips shut in surprise, his eyes swimming as he narrowed his gaze at the three of us. I wasn't sure if I could have convinced him I was fine on my own, but I knew I could convince him I was better off left to finish my quest. Out of anyone, he had to understand. He knew what it was like to feel trapped. He knew what it was like to dream of bigger things, dream of dangerous things, dream of crazy things. Dream of things impossible in Cyrene, our prison.

"So, you're really not going to come back with me?"

I didn't miss a beat. "No."

"And nothing I say can convince you?"

"No."

A look of pain crossed his features, but he didn't say anymore. He found my eyes one last time, gazing as if it would be his last. He sighed and shook his head sorrowfully.

"Then I guess I'll have to make you." Before any of us could stop him, he took a deep breath and cried out, "Guards!"

Without warning, a pack of guards rushed from the crowd, and a smile had cracked across his cheeks. I couldn't believe it. He set us up.

He tore the hood from my head, restraining me from Alexei and Sasha as the Embrasian guards seized them. All around, the pedestrians rushed to get out of the way, nearly tripping over themselves to give the regiment of Embrasians room. The crowd dispersed quickly, and with a little more shoving, they had completely gone, leaving us with no witnesses.

"Let go of me! Let go!" I screamed, flailing, but the boy was somehow stronger than me. Maybe he really was cut out to be a soldier like he wanted.

The guards had already apprehended Sasha's sword, pinning him to the cobblestone like a criminal, but they seemed to have a harder time catching Alexei, who had burst into flame altogether, magma sparks flying from the wizard. I watched as he fought against the guards, scorching their skin as they got too close. For a second, I thought he had the situation under control, like he always did.

For a second, I thought he was going to save us. But then, the Magicians showed up.

They came flying in with their cloaks of white and purple like a swarm of wasps, so quick I could barely keep up with them. As Alexei realized who they were, he paused mid-step, his face falling. He ever so slowly dropped his stance, and he even smothered his flames to a simmer. I shook my head as I realized what he was doing. He was giving up. How could he give up?

Run, Alexei. Run.

But he didn't run. He waited as they grew closer, his eyes taking in the band of Magicians. What was he doing? I wanted to scream as he lifted his hands in a faint surrender, catching the slight mischievous gleam in his eyes. I could recognize that gleam from miles away. He had a plan.

"You know, I'd love to stay and chat but—" He didn't finish his sentence, or rather, he was cut off by a loud bang as smoke erupted from his body. As the smoke swallowed us up, clogging our throats and burning our eyes, I thought I heard him laugh. Of course, he was laughing.

I slammed my foot against Dulce's, rejoicing at the sound of pain he released as I managed to tear myself from his grasp, plunging myself deeper into the smoke. I clasped one hand to my mouth, running in search of Alexei. I wanted to call out, scream for him, but I didn't want to lead anyone right to me. So, I barreled through the smoke silently, tears running down my face, coughs stuck in my throat.

"Ivory." Sasha's voice filled my ears as his hands wrapped around my arm. "Get out of here. Run!"

"Sasha!" I cried, holding his bleeding cheeks in my hands. His own guards' work. His own guards drew blood on their prince. What type of nightmare were we living through?

"Run!" he cried again. "It's not like they can hurt me anymore than this, but you and Alexei *have* to get out of here."

"I'm not leaving you here," I insisted, my resolve strong but my voice breaking. I ignored my biting fear, determined to get all three of us out. Determined to keep us together. Determined to escape as three.

But where was Alexei?

"Brave now, are we little Morrow?" A voice snaked into my ears like a sweet poison. My blood ran cold as I recognized it, unsure if I would ever rid myself of his voice ever again.

I whirled around as Marble lifted his hands and a gust of wind threw Sasha and me back, stumbling for balance. His wind cleared the smoke in a matter of seconds, and as I blinked the tears from my eyes, I finally caught sight of Alexei.

The wizard, with his hands tied behind his back, appeared utterly defeated as he spotted the two of us. I gasped as I realized his smoke show was only a distraction. He had meant to get caught. He had tried giving me and Sasha more time, and of course, it didn't work.

Beside me, a guard seized Sasha once more, catching him despite the prince's desperate and panic-induced punches and kicks. If only he still had his sword. If only I had realized Alexei's stupid plan earlier. What kind of guy sacrifices himself?

Marble sauntered forward, smirking as he dug his black frostbitten fingers into my arm, yanking me to the ground. Ravenous anger exploded in the pit of my stomach. I despised his smirk. His cloak. His eyes.

I despised him, and I wanted him to scream just as the Highwayman had as my frost seeped into his skin and spread across his body like a fast-moving plague. I wanted to watch all the color drain from his cheeks, his veins go blue, his chest frozen.

I wanted to destroy him. I knew I could've.

"Ivory!" Alexei shrieked from the guard's restrain.

No. That's not me. I don't kill.

I found Alexei's fear stained eyes. Had my own been glowing just a moment before?

"Marble, what is the meaning of this?" Sasha demanded. "Release us this instant or I'll have all of you thrown in the dungeon!"

"I'm afraid your father had made it clear that we are not to take orders from you, *Your Highness*." Marble's voice dripped with mocking sarcasm. He addressed the guards holding Sasha back. "Take him back to the castle, and *don't* let him escape this time."

Sasha's face flushed white. "No, you can't do this! I'm the prince! Let go of me! Let go!"

But they paid him no heed, shoving a cloth in his mouth with a burst of laughter. I watched in horror as they dragged him away, breathing heavily. Was that even legal? Cathair couldn't denounce Sasha, could he? Sasha was his only heir!

"You vile traitor!" Alexei called, thrashing violently, but I could see fatigue biting at him, his sparks diminishing faster and faster. "Let her go!"

Marble only laughed. He tugged me up by my hair, and without warning, shoved me to the ground. My head banged against the cobblestone, stars swimming in my vision, my breath knocked from my lips. I groaned as I pressed a hand to the back of my head, sucking in a breath as I felt something warm drip onto my fingers.

"Don't you worry, Kementari. We'll return her home safe and sound, where she'll stay," Marble jested. "In the meantime, I think I ought to have you arrested."

"You can't do that! I haven't done anything wrong!" Alexei exclaimed. "Run, Ivory! Run!"

I blinked the stars away, pulling myself up. I knew I needed to listen to him, I needed to run, but my head pounded so painfully, I wasn't sure how far I would make it.

A pair of hands I could only discern as Dulce's found me, holding my head up. He brushed my bloodied hair away, his eyebrows furrowed together. Was it guilt I saw? It was his fault we were in the situation in the first place! He had no right looking like that!

"Really?" Marble asked dramatically. "I think you have plenty of crimes on your hands. Attacking the palace guards, kidnapping this poor girl from her home in Cyrene, and oh dear, I think you might've given her a concussion!"

Marble swung his leg and kicked me in the face, sending me sprawling out of Dulce's arms, my head connecting with the hard road again, enough to splatter blood upon the stone.

My only instinct was to curl up as tight as I could, covering my face like a coward as pain exploded through my head. And yet, I couldn't stop myself from forcing my eyes to find Alexei again, wincing as he screamed my name. I wanted to answer, I wanted to hold his gaze, but I couldn't bring myself to move anymore. Instead, I clasped my eyes shut and focused on drawing air in. I just wanted it all to end, I wanted to be somewhere safe. I wanted to be home.

Why was it that my only home seemed to be Alexei?

"What's wrong with you?" Dulce cried as he scooped me up again. "You said nobody would get hurt!"

"I don't remember saying that." Marble's voice was distant, so distant I had to wonder if it even belonged to the Magician. "Give her this. It'll make all the pain go away."

Dulce shifted as he reached out for something and the sound of a cork popping filled my ears. Something cold was pressed against my lips.

"Ivory, don't drink it! Ivory, fight! Get up!"

A thick liquid poured down my throat, and I didn't have enough energy to choke on it. Suddenly, everything spun in rapid circles, my ears ringing. My whole body went numb and spineless, rendered useless by whatever had slipped through my lips. My head dipped backward as I struggled to pry my eyes open.

"Ivory! *Ivory!*"

I clung onto his voice, but soon the ringing drowned him out and I fell into darkness.

33

Get up. Get up. Get up.

An urgency tugged at my consciousness like a rope, pulling, hauling, screaming at me to do something. But what? What was it that I needed to do? What was it that caused my blood to rush with such anxiety? What was I supposed to do?

Breath. Open your eyes. Get up.

I sucked in a gust of air, recoiling as the strongest scent of musty wood filled my nose, along with the faintest hint of smoke. I knew the smell. I knew it all too well.

I jerked my eyes open, my chest rising and falling like the waves of a raging storm, short hollow gasps puffing from my lips. A wooden ceiling greeted me, a ceiling that I had spent hours upon hours gazing upon. An ache in the back of my head pounded against my thoughts painfully, and when I reached up to hold my forehead, my fingers brushed the unmistakable cotton of gauze.

I groaned, the blankets slipping from my bed as I struggled to sit up. I didn't want to believe it. I yearned to ignore the dreadful familiarity of it all, of the blankets and the wooden aroma, the hard mattress underneath me, the distasteful silence. There was only one place I knew of with such elements.

Cyrene.

What happened? Why can't I remember? I thought with rising panic. I knew I shouldn't have been there, I belonged somewhere else. With someone. I had something I needed to do. Someone I needed to . . .

Rescue?

The thought was ridiculous, but I couldn't rid myself of it. Why would I need to rescue someone? Who would I need to rescue? I couldn't possibly. I was just a girl. I was just Ivory.

A rapid-fire of flashes seared through the mind. Eyes of emerald, eyes of gold, eyes of terrifying eccentricity. A voice I swore I would never forget in my nightmares. The voice of a person I had wanted to kill. It all came rushing back to me so fast I could barely keep up with them, whirling around in my head like a dancing blizzard, names resurfacing. Marble. Alexei. Sasha. Dulce.

Alexei.

I slid from my bed, kicking off the blankets. I groaned out in pain as my head spun while I stumbled across my room. I threw myself at the doorknob, swinging the door open. I had to get back to them. I had to save them. They needed me.

I rammed into the wall of the hallway, my vision blurry as my head reeled with pain. Each step took more energy than the last, more pain, more focus, but I didn't care. All that mattered was getting back to Embrasia.

"Ivory!" Two voices tore through my panic-induced sprint. Voices I knew far too well. Voices I was not ready to face so soon.

I stopped, blinking rapidly as I turned to greet my brothers, wincing. Their dark eyes pierced into my own as they gazed at me. I expected to see anger, I expected for the shouting to begin, the locks, the degrading, the scolding. But none of that happened.

Instead, they rushed forward and wrapped me in their arms, so quick we all lost our balance and dropped to our knees. Next to me, Dean laughed, running his hand through my hair. On the other side of me, Layton shook violently, pulling me tighter as if scared I would disappear if he didn't. Just as their actions registered, so did my shock.

Why weren't they . . . mad? Furious, in fact? In a mere second, my shock transformed into confusion.

"Layton," I choked out, "Dean. You. . . . You're kind of suffocating me."

They pulled away with cries of apologies, wrapping their hands around my arms as they helped me up to my feet, so gentle, like they were afraid I would shatter with a grasp too tight. I dusted my skirt off, though the smell of smoke had permanently soaked the cloth. Suddenly, maintaining eye contact was a little more difficult than ever before. We all wanted to say something, I could tell, but the words seemed to be stuck on our tongues. Only when I cleared my throat did they snap out of it.

"Come to the kitchen," Layton said, putting a hand on my shoulder as he directed me down the hall. "You must be starving. We were told you haven't eaten in days."

As I followed after them, his words registered slowly, the mention of food both the best and worst thing to hear. I didn't want to admit it, but I was starving, and not even the sick dread in the pit of my stomach could chase away my biting hunger.

"Wait, who?" I asked, my voice pathetically weak.

"Who what?" Layton cast me a look.

"Who told you?" But before he could answer, a more pressing question surfaced. "How did I get here?"

We stepped into the kitchen and I nearly had to do a double-take. Sitting at the table, at *my* table, was Dulce. All of a sudden, the pieces clicked together.

"You," I whispered, anger swallowing my previous fatigue as I watched him rise from the chair he had been so comfortably sitting in, turning to face me.

"Dulce brought you back. After he told us you left, he tried catching up with you," Layton explained.

"You ok, Ivory?" Dean asked as my face flushed white.

I tore myself from their loose clutches, throwing a finger at Dulce, allowing my anger to overwhelm me for a moment. "You told them! You ratted us out, you rat! You maggot! You—you—"

"Ivory!" my brothers exclaimed. Dean rushed forward and held me back, but his grip was loose as ever.

"You wretch! You traitor!" I ripped from Dean's hands, practically lunging at Dulce.

The boy's eyes grew wide as he jumped behind the chair, using it like some sort of shield. The fear in his eyes brought satisfaction rising up in my chest, but it wasn't enough. He knew what I could do. He knew he should very well be afraid of me. And yet he dared to show his face to me again, in my own house.

Before I could get my hands on him, Layton and Dean had me apprehended once more, and they seemed to understand that they needed to hold on tight if they wanted me to stay in one place, but that did nothing to stop me from fighting. I flailed, throwing kicks in the air, shooting insult after insult. However, whatever strength I had gained while with Alexei, theirs outmatched mine severely.

"Stop it, Ivory!" Dean shouted.

"Calm down, please!" Layton added pleadingly. I almost wanted to listen, but I reminded myself they didn't know what Dulce had cost me. What he had cost me, Alexei, and Sasha.

"It's alright," Dulce said with a calm wave of a hand. "She's just still under a spell. She'll snap out of it."

"Spell?" I spat. My chest heaved rapidly, and my head pounded with agonizing pulses, but I was determined to hold myself strongly. "What are you talking about?"

"Ivory, hun," Layton grabbed my shoulders, nearly forcing me down in a chair, "please, calm down and we'll explain everything to you."

My eyebrows furrowed together. Shouldn't I be the one that had to explain? What in the name of the goddesses above did they need to explain to me? And since when did Layton call me *hun*?

But through my puzzlement, I begrudgingly settled in my chair. "Alright, fine, *explain* this to me." I couldn't keep the sarcasm from my voice no matter how hard I tried.

My brothers exchanged a look, one of their famous looks that obviously said they knew more than me. But, for once, I knew I was the one more knowledgeable.

Layton shifted uncomfortably as he began. "I know you might not believe us right now, but that's ok." He took a troubled breath. "Something very bad happened to you while you were gone."

So, is he referring to the Incarti or the sirens? Perhaps the fey, or maybe the Highwayman? The king booting me out of his palace? Having my head kicked to the curb? He's gonna really have to narrow this down.

"Alright." I took an impatient breath. "So, are you going somewhere with this? Or can I go back to what I was doing?" I shot Dulce a hateful glare and nearly smirked as he tensed up.

"Hun," he said again, and I had to stop myself from cringing, "you don't understand. For the past two weeks, you've been under a wizard's spell."

My face fell. What was he talking about? More importantly, who was he talking about? Layton bit his bottom lip, a flash of pain striking his features.

"Oh, I can't," he cried and burst into tears.

"Get ahold of yourself!" Dean shouted, shaking our older brother.

The sight sent a wave of unease rolling into my stomach. Layton never cried. The last time I had caught him crying was . . . I couldn't even remember. He was supposed to be the mature one between the three of us, the strong one, the one always in control.

"A spell," I repeated faintly. "What about a spell?"

"Ivory," Dean continued as Layton shook his tears away, "you were kidnapped. Two weeks ago. It was a wizard, and he put you under a spell to follow him. He's responsible for those stitches in the back of your head. Do you remember any of this?"

I shot Dulce another glare, but the boy gave nothing away. "I see."

"You—you do?" Layton questioned hopefully.

"Uh-huh." I nodded, then pointed to Dulce. "Alright, now tell them the truth, Dulce."

"What are you talking about? That is the truth," he insisted, but he wasn't fooling me. I could barely believe he was fooling Layton and Dean.

"You know it's not," I snapped. "You were there. You saw the whole thing."

"I saw you brainwashed by that barbarian, if that's what you mean," he shot back with just as much disdain I had used.

I jumped to my feet in an instant, nearly knocking my chair to the floor, my face scrunched up. "Alexei is *not* a barbarian!"

"Ivory, please." Layton reached for me, but I pulled away.

"He's lying! You must listen to me, he's working for the Magicians!" I shouted desperately. "I know you haven't trusted me with anything, but please trust me with this!"

For a second, Dean's face flashed, and I thought I had gotten to him, but Layton cut in before he could say anything.

"You're under a spell. Nothing you think happened really happened. That wizard was dangerous, like all of those nasty wizards. He didn't even have papers for Embrasia."

I found Dulce's eyes, despising how afraid I looked, how desperate, how pleading, but I couldn't hold back anymore. "Tell them, Dulce. Please, I know you're just telling them what Marble told you to tell them. *He's* the one that did this to me. We should be trying to get him arrested."

But Dulce only shook his head. "You've got it mixed up. Marble is the one who saved you from that barbarian in the first place, the one who realized you were under a spell, the one who stitched your head and bandaged it."

"You're lying! You're lying and you know it!" I cried, shoving an accusing finger at him.

"Don't worry, Ivory," Layton interrupted. "Payne said the spell would wear off. Soon, you'll realize the truth."

"Payne?" I exclaimed, my stomach dropping. Of course, they had gotten Payne involved. Oh, who was I kidding? Payne was probably working under Marble as well. "Payne's been here?"

"Of course he has, and he should be back any minute," Layton answered.

Fear hit me like a powerful wave. I had to get out before Payne arrived. I had to get out before anything happened to Alexei. I had to get out.

With one last deep breath, I darted for the door, my hands trembling as I pulled on the knob, but it didn't budge. I whirled around to face my brothers, who hadn't moved an inch. In fact, they appeared strangely unbothered by my escape attempt.

"Let me out," I demanded. "Give me the key."

"The key won't help you. Payne enchanted every exit so you can't leave again. That door isn't locked," Layton responded.

I checked the door, and just as he said, it wasn't locked. I clasped my mouth shut in surprise. This wasn't just locks anymore. I really was trapped this time. More trapped than I had ever been.

Layton's face fell as he seemed to notice my misery, his expression going soft. He slowly approached me with an outstretched hand. Before he could touch me, however, I slapped it away and shoved past him, giving Dulce one last glare before I scrambled back to my room. I slammed the door shut behind me and locked it for good measure, even though I knew they had a key to every door in the house.

I flew to the window in my bathroom, my breathing growing increasingly labored as I pulled and tugged, but whatever I threw at it, or however hard I pulled, it wouldn't budge. With hot tears welling up in my eyes, I whirled around, facing a newly installed mirror. I scoured for a plan, just as Alexei would do, but I couldn't get one clear thought through my head.

I needed help, I knew that much, but Alexei was the only one with the power to help, and unfortunately for me, he was probably sitting in a cold and dingy dungeon all the way in Embrasia. Just thinking about it sent a shiver up my spine.

I ached for his presence, the way he always seemed to know what to do even if he really had no clue, his light strides, his unflawed hair, his reassuring smile, as if he knew things were going to turn out right in the end.

I took a shaky breath, pressing my forehead to the mirror, the cold tingle it sent down my back refreshing. I wouldn't be able to escape without him. Now, more than ever, I needed him.

"Oh, Alexei," I whispered, "if only you were here."

I pulled away slowly, cringing at the sight of my reflection. My cheeks had sunken in and dark circles had taken root underneath my watery eyes. The bandages wrapped around my head only reminded me of Marble. I wanted to tear them off, destroy them, but my willpower to fight was diminishing faster than a dying flame.

I had to be strong. But for what? Escaping was impossible, thanks to my own brothers, Dulce and Marble's lies weaving into their heads like deadly spider silk. And if I couldn't even manage to escape my own house, how was I going to make it all the way to Embrasia and save both Alexei and Sasha?

Face it. It's impossible. I lost. This adventure is over. But why couldn't I accept that?

I took one last gaze in the mirror, but something gave me pause. I narrowed my eyes, taking a step forward, but I was seeing correctly. My reflection rippled. I blinked, rubbing my eyes, but it only did it again. And again. And again.

The ripples grew until I couldn't even see my reflection anymore, a dark image slowly appearing from what used to be me. It slowly formed into what seemed to be a small, dark room. No, not a room. A cell. And leaning against the grimy wall, Alexei was there, chewing on his hair.

"Alexei!" I gasped, leaning toward the mirror in surprise.

His head perked up, whirling side to side. It was almost like he had heard me . . .

"Ivory?" he whispered, his face twisted in confusion. "Is that you?"

I sucked in a breath, and before I knew it, a smile had spread across my face. "Yes, yes, it is me! I—I think I cast a spell through my mirror! Are you ok?" I rambled, peering forward.

"I'm fine. Where are you?" he asked, standing as a grin of his own cracked on his lips.

"Cyrene." I nearly choked on the name. "My brothers won't let me leave."

He raised an eyebrow. "The girl who escaped the Embrasian palace can't escape her own house?"

"They got Payne to enchant every exit, genius. There's no way I can leave this time," I explained, glaring.

"Oh." His face fell for a second, but his natural confidence returned as he shrugged. "Well, if you're good enough to cast this spell, I'm sure you can break the enchantment."

"How?"

"Dunno, but I bet you can figure it out."

"Gee, thanks, that's a lot of help," I grumbled.

"Sorry." He dropped his gaze. "Are you alright? What's that on your head?"

"Bandages," I answered, and as I saw his face flush white, I quickly added, "but, I'm fine. It barely hurts."

He groaned, running his hands through his hair, his voice breaking as he spoke. "Ivory, I'm so sorry. I should've tried harder. This is all my fault."

"No, it's not," I snapped, failing to hide my irritation. "It's Dulce's fault. Or mine, technically, but now is not the time for the blame game. I need to find a way to get to Embrasia."

"No!" he cried. "I don't want you anywhere near here. After what happened with Marble, I want you the furthest away you could possibly be from here."

A pang hit my chest full force, painful and overwhelming. I recoiled back as if something had really hit me. How could he say such a thing after how I had proven myself so many times? After the sirens and the fey, and the Highwayman? It was me that saved him from those obstacles.

It was me with the magic writhing in my heart. And it was him with the failing heart.

The edges of the mirror blurred with my angered thoughts.

"Wait, I didn't mean it that way!" Alexei exclaimed. "I just don't want you to get hurt. I can't . . ."

"You can't what?" I fumed.

"I can't see you get hurt again. I just can't." He buried his head in his trembling hands as his voice broke off, his hair tumbling from behind his ears.

I wanted to reach out and tuck those strands of hair back, lift his face up and cup his cheeks, feel the warmth he radiated, smell his sweet aroma. Just be with him. But a sheet of glass was in my way.

"Sometimes, the pain is worth the reward," I said. "I'd rather die a hundred times with you than stay safe without you."

He pulled his face up, the tears shining in his eyes falling down his cheeks. It hurt not being able to wipe them away.

"We're in this together. We die together," Alexei smiled, "we thrive together."

"And we also apparently get chased by the fey together too, but we don't talk about that."

Despite our terrible situation, we laughed, without holding back. His laugh rang like a melody and hearing it again sent a flicker of hope returning to me. I would do anything to hear it every day. I watched as he wiped his tears away with a grin.

With as much confidence as I could muster, I said, "I'll find a way back to you. I'll get you out of there. I'll get myself out of here."

Alexei nodded. "Of course you will. After all, what is a knight in shining armor without a damsel in distress? Or, in this case, wizard in distress."

I chuckled, reaching up and laying my hand on the mirror. I didn't want to admit it, but somewhere deep down, I was secretly attempting to see if I could just reach through and pull Alexei out. To my dismay, the mirror didn't budge.

"Just," he released a deep breath, "don't get hurt. Please, be careful."

"I will. I promise I will," I assured him.

From beyond my door, the sound of footsteps echoed from the living room, and a muffled voice found its way to my ears. My stomach dropped.

"Someone's here, I think it's Payne," I whispered. "I should go."

Alexei nodded. "I'll be here. Be careful. Don't drink anything he gives you."

I gave a nod as Alexei's image began to ripple, and suddenly, a thousand more things popped into my head that I wanted to tell him. I held onto his image, trying to implant the sway of his hair and the light of his eyes into my head.

"And, Ivory?" His voice was distant.

"Yes?"

"I . . ." A word formed on his lips, but at the last second, he clasped his mouth shut. Before he disappeared, I heard one last thing. ". . . miss you."

Then he was gone, and my own blue eyes gazed back at me.

"I miss you, too."

34

I cracked my door open without a second thought, poking my face out just enough to hear the conversation carrying from the living room. I hadn't heard Peyton Payne's voice in years, but I recognized it immediately. The slow rasp that made him sound like a madman. Deep like a grave, crisp like any other Embrasian. It was a voice one didn't just forget. And I had caught him in the middle of a sentence.

"You say she's been with the Kementari?"

"Yes," Dulce's voice answered quickly. "I found her trailing behind him in the middle of the Embrasian Square."

Payne clicked his tongue. "It's a wonder she's still alive. That Kementari is as bad as wizards get."

"You've met him?" Layton asked, his voice dripping with apprehension.

"Yes, but this isn't about me. A spell cast by a Kementari could be dangerous, strong, ruthless."

"What are you saying?"

"She could be under a spell of dark magic."

As my brothers sucked in a gasp, I clenched my fist tight enough to puncture my palm, tearing down on the sides of my cheeks to keep from shouting out. Before, I might've been able to convince them, maybe Dean, but now with Payne's consensus, they would never believe me. They didn't know how much of a cheat Payne was like how Alexei and I knew. Anger bubbled up in my stomach, almost impossible to swallow down, but I fought against it to keep my temper in check. I didn't need to do something stupid.

"Can you do anything?" Layton's voice was tainted with desperation, and that was all that Payne needed. Just a little reckless desperation. "She's not herself. She's never been so . . . so . . . blatant. She hasn't listened to one thing we've said, and she doesn't even seem to realize how hard it was for us to get her back. She used to be so calm and quiet before any of this happened."

A different type of pain hit my chest. I was . . . blatant? What did that even mean? Of course I couldn't be calm anymore, they should've expected that a long time ago. A girl with no heart couldn't possibly be expected to stay quiet forever, couldn't possibly be expected to remain without that one thing missing. Especially when that one missing thing was so close.

Of course I was different from before I had left. Because now, I had answers. I had hope. Purpose. And I wasn't going to let it go.

"I understand your concern, and there is one thing that I think can do the trick, if you're willing," Payne reconciled.

Don't be willing. Don't be willing. Whatever it is, it's not good. Don't trust him.

"Anything to get the old Ivory back," Layton replied, and for the first time since I had returned, his voice carried his usual strength.

My stomach dropped and I nearly lost my footing as if his words had really struck me. I regained my balance, grasping onto the side of my door so tight, my knuckles flushed pale. I forced myself back to the conversation despite the temptation to pull away and cover my ears, to pretend I hadn't heard, to pretend he had never said that.

"Take this. It'll give you back the Ivory you remember. The Ivory from two weeks ago." A note of something malicious hid behind his rasp of a voice.

"What is it?" Dean asked.

"Just a little potion," Payne said softly. "Each drop she drinks, a day she will forget. The number of drops to the number of days she's been gone, and she won't remember any of this. She'll be just like before."

With a violent lurch of my stomach, I pressed a hand against my mouth to keep from gasping. My anger dissolved into mist, replaced by a biting fear that sank into my senses. They wouldn't. They couldn't! I knew they didn't have enough cruelty in their hearts to commit to it.

Then why have they not declined?

"Layton, we'd have to trick her into drinking it. We can't," Dean insisted, his voice quivering.

A spike of hope shot up in me. I knew I could count on Dean. I knew he would never let Payne give them such a thing.

"Well, what do you want to do?" Layton snapped. "She's probably clawing at the doors to run back to that wizard *rat*, and she's not afraid to do whatever it takes. You heard her, she thinks the royal Magicians are out to get her."

"But it seems so . . . ," Dean trailed off, as if totally aware of how crazy it was.

So . . . what? Convince them, Dean. Refuse! Tell Layton to kick Payne out. And Dulce while you're at it. Just finish your sentence!

But he didn't. Instead, he sighed and said no more.

"We'll take it."

"Very well." I could practically taste the evil smirk in Payne's voice.

I listened to the transaction, to Layton offering way too many gold pieces, and Payne accepting them without a second thought, to their goodbyes, and to the front door shut closed.

"She'll come out for dinner sooner or later. We'll give it to her then." Layton sighed, and I could hear his fingertips clicking against the glass of the potion.

"Will she remember me?" Dulce asked suddenly.

A heavy silence descending on the three. Only when Layton awkwardly cleared his throat did he answer.

"No, but you can meet her again. Make a better impression. I'm sure she'll be happy."

I frowned, not only because of my brother's terrible plan, but because, though I didn't want to admit it, I would've been delighted to meet such a boy as Dulce before I left. The idea of meeting someone that knew I wasn't some illegal witch or a foolish girl with a run-in with a wizard sounded quite appealing to me, even after spending all the time away. The idea of meeting someone new. The idea of spreading my imagination from one dreamer to another.

Maybe the old Ivory isn't entirely gone after all. I despised the thought. The old Ivory was a coward, a helpless little nobody. An arrogant and narrow-minded girl. Nothing like a knight in shining armor.

Dulce held no place in my thoughts. He was nothing, nothing to me and nothing to my frozen heart, yet I still wanted to remember him. I wanted to remember my burning hatred for him. The way he betrayed me in Embrasia, gotten in the way of my freedom. I wanted to remember my hatred for *all* of them. My brothers. Dulce. Payne. King Cathair. Marble. Cyrene.

I stumbled away from the door, pacing across my room as I muttered angrily. I had to remind myself to keep my fury at bay, to keep it from controlling my actions, to keep me from my own recklessness, but it was growing increasingly difficult. Just one shout, just one punch, just one . . .

No.

I took a deep breath, forcing composure upon myself. I couldn't allow myself to be swallowed in my own flaring wrath like a flame swallowed by wind. If they wanted a calm and quiet sister, then I would give it to them.

I waited impatiently for a knock upon my door, running plans over and over in my head, but none of them seemed good enough to really work. I even tried calling the frost I had used to attack Marble with, however, no matter how hard I tried, my fingers remained frostless as ever, not even a whisper of ice to slice the silence. How had I done it? I recalled the cries of pain of everyone that had been touched by my magic. The Highwayman, that idiot. Marble, that despicable traitor. And even the Embrasian guards, who were way too far over their heads.

It took an eternity, the smell of fresh meat and newly baked bread wafting to my room, torturing my already rumbling stomach, but eventually, a knock resounded from behind my door.

Yes, my dear fiend of a brother?

"Ivory?" It was Dean's voice, and suddenly my glare dropped. I had always been terrible at staying mad at Dean. "Dinner's ready, if—if you want."

I hesitated as I reached out for the doorknob. Alexei had warned me not to drink anything they gave me, but did that include food too? I didn't know how long I had been unconscious, but the last meal I remembered was Furn's wine and plucked berries. Sure, it was good, but it didn't compare to sizzling meat and fresh bread. Just thinking about it brought drool to my lips.

But I could feel Dean behind the door, silently pleading I stayed inside, silent pleading for more time. Well, if they were going to be cruel, then so would I.

I wiped all traces of hunger from my face as I stepped out, greeting Dean with an indifferent glance. He stared down at me nervously while I strode right past him. I found the table already set, Layton just finishing setting down platters of meat and vegetables and bread. I glared at Dulce as I sat, who sat right across from me. The dinner was nothing like that of the palace, but the simplicity of it all made me want to indulge like never before.

As I settled, ignoring the heavy stares of the others, I caught a whiff of something other than the food. Something else entirely. I subtly leaned toward where it came from, shocked to find my nose leading me to Dad's untouched chair. But what I smelled wasn't the residue of cigars. Wasn't the heavy and everlasting scent of rum. It was something familiarly sweet, and I knew of only one thing that shared the same aroma.

Magic.

35

I thought I had been thrust right back to the castle, to the Mandrake, as I writhed under Marble's hungry smirk, the agony of fire burning my skin, coursing through my blood like a lethal snake. The needles shoved into my flesh, injecting that scorching Dust. I saw the white walls as they closed in on me, shrinking smaller and smaller, the air seeping from my lungs. And lastly, I saw the darkness that I had been trapped in for so long.

The sharp scent of spice filled my nose and I flew back to Cyrene, swaying slightly in my chair as I struggled to hold back the warm liquid that had risen up in my throat.

"Sparkling apple cider, your favorite," Layton said, snapping me out of my nightmares entirely as he placed a tall glass in front of my plate.

My hands twitched to reach out for it and down the contents as quickly as I could, allow the potion to erase my memories of Marble, but even though I yearned to do it, my arms wouldn't lift themselves from my lap. They remained unmoving, as if reminding me of everything else. Alexei and Sasha. Andros. The moon bathed in crimson, the sight equally terrifying and beautiful. I couldn't throw all of those memories away. I couldn't let Alexei down.

So, I swallowed the sickness and fear, casually wiping my sweaty hands on my skirt underneath the table, watching as Dean and Layton sat down.

"What is *he* still doing here?" I gave a nod to gesture at Dulce, glaring.

The boy didn't have enough guts to glare back, as I had been challenging him to do so. He only glanced up from his food, a slight and barely noticeable look of irritation crossing his features.

"Ivory, you shouldn't say that," Layton scolded, and I almost felt like I had gotten the old Layton to break through, with his scolds and jabs.

I dared to eye Dad's chair again despite the swinging reel it gave me and noticed an empty plate sitting in front of it. Why did it reek of magic? Where had the scent come from?

I gestured to the lone plate. "Why's that plate there?"

Just as the question left my lips, a knock at the front door startled me. I hoped nobody had caught my flinch, but it seemed they had all turned their attention to the door. A smile spread across Layton's face, sending an uneasy sensation squirming in my stomach. I almost didn't want to know who stood behind the door.

Layton slipped from his chair, heading to answer the door. "There's someone that would like to meet you, Ivory."

My older brother disappeared from the kitchen, leaving me with an anxiety far greater than before. Layton never invited people inside, not while I was there. Not while people could see me with my pale white skin and abnormal silver hair. Just the thought of another citizen of Cyrene casting their eyes on me sent my stomach rolling.

Their distant chatter grew louder as Layton returned with a stranger at his side. A tall and muscular stranger, with a wide chest and square shoulders, face set, and jaw that seemed harder than rock. The way he held himself made me think of a puppet, like his body didn't really belong to him and he had yet to grow accustomed to it.

He wore a dark collared shirt and a pair of black pants, a golden watch hanging from his pocket. His hair, like his clothes, was a dark shade and even his shoes matched. I found his eyes, expecting them to be just as black, but the sight that greeted me was not what I thought I would see.

Swirls of emerald. Just like Alexei's.

I struggled to keep my jaw closed as the man locked his gaze with me. A knowing glint flared in his eyes as if he could see straight through me. As if he could see the truth. He blinked and the swirling in his eyes stopped.

"Ivory, this is Aven Calvo."

I nodded absentmindedly, not trusting myself to speak. My hands trembled underneath the table. It couldn't possibly be Alexei . . . could it? Or was I just seeing things?

Layton led Aven to Dad's chair and as he passed me by, the sweetest scent flew over me like a dove. My breath hitched.

"So, Ivory." Aven's voice rang loud and deep—a strange slurred Embrasian accent—and as his words passed through my ears, I was sure I had heard his voice before. "I've been told of your little "adventure" and I'm here to help relieve some stress from your experiences."

I snapped out of my trance. Of course it wasn't Alexei. How could I have thought something so hopeful and foolish? Anger boiled up in the pit of my stomach, but I showed no sign of it on my face. Apparently, the potion wasn't enough. No, what my brothers decided I needed was a psychiatrist.

I nodded again, distrusting my words for an entirely different reason. I had to control myself, my temper, my unbridled rage. It would be the only way to get through dinner.

As the others dove into the meal, I quietly picked at my food, daydreaming of eating it, but not daring to let even a bite slip past my lips. If they were as cruel as to agree to the potion, then who knew where they sneaked it in. Perhaps my meat had been glazed with it. Or my drink downed with it. I tapped my foot against the floor over and over just for something to occupy myself with.

Dean was the first to finish and did it in a record time of five minutes, the fastest I had ever seen him consume a whole plate, and in the time it took him to finish eating, I rearranged my plate at least ten times. Out of the corner of my eye, I caught glimpses of Layton growing increasingly impatient and restless. Dulce shared the same twitchiness.

It was Layton that cracked first, and only about six or seven minutes into dinner. "You haven't taken one bite, Ivory. Would you at least drink something?"

"You can't expect her to want to eat, Mr. Morrow. It may take some time," Aven said before I had the chance to open my mouth.

"Of course." Layton swallowed, nodding with a twinge of nerves.

The stranger then turned to me. "Now, Ms. Ivory, I'd like to have a nice, long conversation about the previous two weeks. I believe a certain Magician has told me some of it, but I'd like to hear it from you."

"Marble?" I nearly winced just by having the name on my lips.

The corners of his mouth twitched upward. "Yes, but he told me some questionable things. I can't possibly believe you jumped from the window of the castle, now can I?"

Well, at least Marble told him one truth.

"I didn't exactly jump, more like . . . slid."

"You did *what?*" Layton and Dean shouted in perfect unison that probably could've made me laugh had I been in a different situation.

"There were guards at the door!" I cried. "How else was I supposed to get out?"

Before they could respond, however, Aven held up a gloved hand. "Now, now, please. Ivory, if you wouldn't mind, I'll move on to my next point. Tell me about your relationship with Alexei."

"The Kementari," Dulce growled from the other side of the table. I resisted the urge to stick my tongue out at him.

I opened my mouth to answer, but suddenly, my mind went blank. How was I supposed to describe us when I didn't even know? I hated him just a week ago, convinced he was out to kill me. Then I saved his life from the sirens, we escaped the Adeleigh Wood together, and everything was different. After so many close calls, we both didn't want to actually find the other dead. And all of a sudden, I trusted him more than anyone else in my life. How was I supposed to describe that?

"You seem very close with him," Aven continued.

I tried to ignore the disapproving stares of the others. "Yeah, I guess I do. We got really close."

"And how do you know if he's genuine?"

Ah, here we go. The whole "it's a spell" talk. Just end me already.

"You wouldn't believe me if I told you anyway, so how about we save some time, hm?" I snapped, shooting a glare.

Layton opened his mouth, but before he could get anything out, Aven again held up his hand and passed a look to my older brother. A look that seemed to say he knew exactly what he was doing.

How much is Layton paying this guy?

"I suppose I should just get to the point. Do you remember Alexei casting a spell around the time you first met?" Aven said.

I hated the way he said Alexei's name, almost like he knew him himself. Like he had been there the whole time with us, in the conversations, the fights, the escapes.

"Sure," I answered impatiently, "he cast a lot of spells."

"Really?" Aven's eyes slightly widened as he perked up. I wondered if it was really surprise or just mockery.

I narrowed my eyes at him with slight confusion. I wanted to think he was mocking me, but it really didn't seem so. But if he truly was surprised, why would he care? I considered if he had, in fact, met Alexei before. How would that make any sense? If he knew Alexei, wouldn't he be offering to help me?

Perhaps he had been trying to help. Perhaps the conversation held a subtle message behind it.

I chose my words carefully as I spoke again. "Wizards' magic is tied to their hearts, right?"

Aven nearly choked on his drink and I relished in seeing him so disoriented, but the reaction also sent another wave of puzzlement my way. It seemed he had realized I had caught on, if there really was something to catch in the first place.

"Did he tell you that?" Aven asked as he quickly composed himself.

I didn't know why, but I hesitated. The idea of giving away our conversations created an uneasy feeling in my stomach. I felt as though I was telling everyone everything, and I knew Alexei wouldn't want me revealing anything about him.

So, instead of answering, I reached out and grabbed my cup, swirling the contents inside. The sugar and spice wafted from the rim, filling my nose, and if I hadn't been paying attention, I wouldn't have noticed the flash of shock over Aven's features. Or the icy glare Dean shot Layton. Tension rose in the room as I stayed silent.

"Did he tell you anything about potions?" Aven inquired, his voice wobbling slightly. I caught him glance down at the drink in my hand. It was almost as though he was trying to . . . warn me.

I pulled the glass to my lips just to get a reaction, the overly sweet and thick scent of magic elevating from the cup. Of course Layton put the potion in my favorite drink. I watched as everyone seemed to lean forward. Aven's hand twitched, but as I locked my gaze with his, his tense stance relaxed, a knowing glint returning to his eyes as if to dare me to take a sip. He knew I was messing with him.

"Heartless as ever, I see," he muttered under his breath, so quiet only I could hear.

His words caused something deep inside me to snap like an old thread. I jumped to my feet and dunked the contents of my glass over Aven's head, watching as he calmly covered his mouth with his sleeve.

"Alright, that's enough!" Dean shouted, and before anything else could happen, I fled back to my room, my hands trembling.

Oh, what had I done?

Just as I reached for the lock, Dean burst in and I expected more yelling, more scolding, more angry and confused demands, but as he closed the door behind him, I was shocked to see a hint of a smile dancing along his lips. He reached out and pulled me into a quick but tight embrace. I begged myself to feel something, anything, for him, but all I wanted to do was ask if Aven was thirsty for more.

"You know you can always tell me everything, right?" Dean whispered.

My breath hitched as I pulled away and nodded, though I really didn't know. I pretended I knew, however, telling myself that maybe if I pretended to understand, I would someday not have to pretend anymore.

"Have you met that man before?" he asked, his eyes narrowed as he glanced back in the direction of the kitchen.

I wavered. "Does this mean you believe me?"

I—I don't know," Dean stuttered, "but I want to."

I resisted the smile tugging on my lips as a surge of triumph rose up in my chest. I knew I could count on Dean.

"I think Aven's a wizard," I explained, speaking in a low, hushed voice. "And he knows about Alexei, somehow. I think they've met before or something."

"A wizard?" Dean repeated faintly.

I nodded. "I just hope he's not a Magician."

"Would that be bad?"

"Very."

"Oh."

A knock at the door interrupted us. It opened to reveal Aven, his face wiped clean but his hair dripping and his shirt soaked. Dean took a subtle step in front of me.

"Please, give me a moment with her. I can clearly see she's traumatized," he said smoothly.

But Dean didn't move, although his knees did begin shaking. Layton appeared at the door and ushered Dean out, who tried to explain, but his words seemed to be stuck in his throat thanks to his fear. He cast me a look as he hesitantly followed Layton out, and I tried offering my bravest face. If I could escape the Highwayman, then I could deal with whoever Aven truly was.

As Dean and Layton disappeared down the hall, Aven eased the door closed and caught my eye. I kept my guard up, sirens of panic blaring in my head.

When he spoke, a different voice escaped his lips, a light voice with a deep accent. "Very funny, Ivory. I didn't expect you to be so humorous."

His change of voice startled me, but I didn't let it be known. I took a hesitant step back, looking him up and down.

"Who are you?" I demanded, hoping my voice sounded stronger than what I heard.

"I'm Francois." He held out a hand, but when I didn't shake it, he awkwardly let it fall to his side. "Look, I know you have no reason to trust me, but I'm here to help you."

As his name passed through my ears, I couldn't help but recall the names of Alexei's older brothers. Valentin. Mercedes. Francois. Surely, this Francois couldn't have been . . .

"So you're not working with Marble?" I asked dubiously as I shot him a suspicious look.

"Of course not!" Francois exclaimed. "I saw what he did back in the Embrasian Square."

"You were there? Why didn't you, oh, I don't know, help?"

"I would've, but I don't think Alexei would've been very happy to see me," he replied.

"Well, if you didn't notice, he was in the middle of getting arrested, so I don't think he would've minded a little help," I shot back.

"You don't understand, he really hates me. He would rather be arrested than see me again." He clenched his fist, directing his gaze to the floor with a pained expression.

I faltered before I opened my mouth again, taking in his green eyes and accented voice, his magic that felt a little too familiar, his knowledge that no normal wizard would just know. His name repeated over and over in my head. There was something he wasn't telling me, a very key factor.

"Who are you really?"

"Do you remember the man that helped you find G.K.'s book at the library?" Francois asked in response.

My eyebrows knitted together as confusion washed over me. It seemed like forever ago, but I did remember it. That was the day I first met Dulce, the day I found my mother's letter. What did that have to do with anything? How did he even know about that?

"And," he continued, "do you remember the blind man that helped you in the Adeleigh Wood?"

Suddenly, I recalled why his voice seemed so familiar to me. I had heard it before. Twice.

"You mean—"

"Yes. That was me, both times," he interrupted quickly. "I tried stepping in whenever I could, but I couldn't let Alexei see me. If he knew I've been helping you this whole time . . ."

"Why?" I pushed past my shock. I should've seen it earlier, after all. It was obvious that both the man in the library and the blind man weren't human. I should've realized their identical accents way sooner. "What does Alexei have against you?"

Francois winced as he spoke. "I don't suppose Alexei told you about . . . his older brothers?"

I gasped. Without thinking, I grabbed the closest thing to use as a weapon, which just so happened to be a book. He put his hands up, his eyes growing wide, but I wasn't buying it. He was acting. He had to be.

"Get out of my house!" I cried as I threw the book in my hand. I reached for another one, and soon I had books flying at Francois at top speed, crashing against the other side of the room as he dodged them without much effort.

"Wait, please! I'm here to help! I promise!" he exclaimed, then let out a yelp of surprise as a book rammed into his face full force.

All at once, his expression shifted. His eyes glowed bright green and the book I had just released from my hand stopped in mid-air. It fell to the ground with a thud, and when I glanced back up at Francois, he again had his hands up in surrender. I paused, shocked, recalling what Alexei had said about his brothers.

They see you, you're dead. They won't hesitate to kill you if they just had the chance.

Then why did Francois seem so . . . innocuous? He already had plenty of chances, plenty of opportunities to kill me, but he hadn't put one scratch on me. Yet, his magic held so much power. I could smell it from all the way across the room. Not to mention, he had already helped me twice before. I had met him way before I ever even knew of the Kementaris.

"Just let me explain myself. Look, I'll stay all the way over here." He scrambled back and pressed himself to the wall on the other side of the room, nearly tripping over the books that now littered the floor.

I glared at him suspiciously, but my curiosity got the better of me. Alexei's warnings blared in my head, but I couldn't listen. Countless questions piled up in my head, questions that I knew he had the answers to. There were so many. Which one did I possibly start with?

"Fine," I finally said.

His tense shoulders relaxed, a relieved smile spreading across his face. He slowly lowered his hands. I resisted the urge to grab another book.

"Thank you."

"For what?" I put my hands on my hips.

"For trusting me. I know you probably haven't heard very good things about me from Alexei, and I know that I made a very awful first impression, but I promise I can help," he replied with a growing smile.

I wanted to tell him that I didn't trust him one bit, and I never would, but instead, I asked, "So you can get Alexei out of prison?"

"Well, not me, but I can help you do it."

"Why can't your brothers do it then, if you can't?" I questioned with little patience.

Francois' smile dropped instantly. "Well, I didn't really want to bring them up, but they're still . . ."

"Crazy?"

"No, well, yes." He shook his head. "I've been using the term magic-controlled."

"So, you're saying your brothers still want me dead? Seriously? How many years has it been?" My voice filled with anger, but somewhere deep down, a flare of fear sparked.

Was this all a trick? A cruel act to lure me into a false sense of security? Perhaps they were trying to get me to lead them right to Alexei. Perhaps they really were as evil as Alexei had described them.

But when I stared at Francois, his light green eyes, airy voice, awkward mannerisms, I couldn't see him as the monster Alexei had described. In fact, I saw a desperate and scared young man.

"So, they don't know you're here, do they?" I dropped my glare, my voice a little lighter.

"No." He frowned. "And they can't know. I can't stay for much longer, so please listen."

"Wait." I held up a hand. "What would they do if they found you out? You're family."

"That doesn't matter to them. If they were lost enough to try to kill you as a child and rip Alexei's heart out, then they're lost enough to do the same to me."

"So, you've just been pretending all these years?"

"I have to," he replied as he ran his hand through his hair. "But I'm hoping I won't have to for much longer. I have a plan."

"Ok, but what does this have to do with me?" I asked.

"You want your heart back, don't you?"

"Of course."

"Well, the only way to break the spell is through an act of pure love. The stronger the act, the more guarantee it'll break," Francois answered, and even dared to use a simple tone, like it was the obvious reply. "And I think I've got the perfect act."

Pure love? How was I supposed to perform an act of pure love if I wasn't even capable of feeling it in the first place? What even was an act of pure love? Yet, through my angry confusion, hope that I had never felt before sparked into a roaring flame. The one thing I had been searching for my whole life, the one question, the one desire, and now I finally knew how to obtain it. My hands were already reached out for it, my fingers just barely brushing it. All I had to do was grab it. Whatever this act was, I would do it without a second thought.

"Alright, tell me."

"I think you need to help my brothers, Valentin and Mercedes, break from the hatred in their hearts. I think you need to make amends."

36

"Make amends? You're the ones who tried to kill me in the first place!" I exclaimed, throwing my hands out.

"I know, I know, but that's why I think it'll work." Francois' eyes sparkled as he spoke. "And then you'll have your heart back and I'll have my brothers back. It's a win-win situation."

"Not if they kill me first!" I cried.

"Don't worry, I've got that covered too." With a wink, he conjured a flame, morphing it into the shape of a heart. "I'll teach you how to control your magic. You're a lot more powerful than you think."

I resisted the urge to roll my eyes. "Sure."

He grasped the flame and held it out. I watched as the fire folded in on itself until the fake heart was nothing but ash, trying to hide my obvious awe.

"This is more or less what your heart looks like right now, except, you know, icy. All the magic is blocked, but with just a little pressure," he dug his fingers into the ash and suddenly it erupted into flames, "you can unlock its full potential. The magic you've used already is just a fraction of what you can really do."

I gazed into the dancing fire, transfixed, his words bringing both excitement and fear. I didn't want to admit it, but the idea of allowing the rest of the magic billowed up inside me free made me want to pretend I never had magic in the first place. I mean, I wasn't *supposed* to even have it. Humans didn't have magic, and yet I was cursed with it. Just the small amount I had used over the previous week frightened me.

But if mastering my magic meant regaining my heart and giving Alexei his family back, then so be it.

"Alright, so how do I unblock my magic or whatever?" I asked, crossing my arms.

"Well, usually magic takes years and years to perfect, but yours has been working ever since Alexei cast that spell. It has been growing, perfecting itself by keeping you alive. When you unblock it, it'll rush full force through your body. You'll have to remember to control yourself," Francois answered. "By doing this, you'll be as powerful as any wizard. Maybe more, I'm not sure."

"You're not sure?"

"What? This has never happened before. How am I supposed to know exactly what's going to happen?"

I scowled, though only to hide the fear that had blossomed in my chest like a thorny rose, the sharp needles digging into the sides of my stomach mercilessly. I feared if I coughed, a rose petal would fly from my lips.

"Alright, so what do I do?" I shook my fearful thoughts to the back of my head as I spoke, urging myself to stay strong. Stay brave. Stay a knight.

"How well do you do under pressure?"

I shot him a suspicious glare. "Why?"

"I'm afraid the easiest way is through a flight or fight situation that sort of *must* be a fight situation," Francois responded, twisting his shirt around his finger nervously, as if anxious of my reply.

I recalled the Highwayman, the way my fear had seemed to take over, the way my thoughts had turned off, the way my body just released magic on instinct. And it was the same against the guards of Embrasia and Marble. With panic coursing through my veins more than my own blood, I had been able to call upon the ice trapped in my chest.

But now, without any threat actively trying to murder me, summoning that magic appeared impossible.

"And how am I going to do that?" I groaned, slumping my shoulders.

Francois frowned, his shoulders copying mine. "I . . . don't know. It has to be something quick, but enough to really get past your adrenaline."

"What if you tried, I don't know, attacking me?" The question felt foolish on my lips, and heat burned my cheeks.

Francois took a step back, running into the wall, shaking his head. "No, I can't. Not again." His face flushed pure white. His eyes seemed plagued by a distant memory, and I could guess what memory.

"Alright, alright, we'll do something else," I said quickly. With a swipe through my hair, I sighed. "Got any ideas?"

"You could . . . jump out the window?"

"Enchanted exits."

"Oh."

An awkward silence poured in between the two of us as we racked our brains for some panic-inducing act terrifying enough to force the magic out of me. Without actually killing me, of course.

"What if I tried picking a fight with my brothers?" I suggested uncertainty.

Francois shook his head, his fist pressed to his chin. "No, that's not good enough."

I huffed, mostly because I knew he was right. It was almost scary how similar he was to Alexei, not just the eyes of green and accented voice, but the way he so genuinely wanted to help. True, he kind of owed me after trying to kill me as a child, but the act was still something to take note of. I mean, he could've been just like his brothers, convinced killing me would somehow compensate for their father's decisions, but instead, he was risking his heart to help me. To help me when I didn't ask for it.

Just like Alexei.

The thought of Alexei sent a wave of sadness crashing over me like a raging storm. I saw his radiant smile, his magenta coat, his swinging hair, his glowing caramel skin. I yearned for the reassuring sound of his deep voice, telling me things were going to be ok. Just as he had done in the Adeleigh Wood. Just as he had done at the Embrasian castle when—

"I got it!" I cried, snapping my fingers.

"What?" Francois stumbled across the room, despite saying he would stay on the other side, but I didn't really care. A hopeful smile painted his cheeks.

"Isn't it obvious? Fire Dust! Why didn't I think of it sooner?"

Francois' smile dropped. "Fire Dust? You can't be serious."

"Why not?"

"Why not?" A flash of irritation crossed his features, along with a spark of shock. "Fire Dust is way too dangerous for your frozen heart!"

"I survived it once before," I countered as I crossed my arms, "I can do it again."

The little color Francois had regained instantly sank away as he stared at me with wide eyes, like I was absolutely insane. Maybe I was. But I didn't care. It was the quickest way, guaranteed to work, and I at least knew what to expect.

"You can't! It'll kill you. With so much direct magical heat, it'll rush right to your heart. It'll burn you from the inside. It'll create some type of . . . of . . ."

"Heartburn."

"You're crazy."

"I'm right."

Francois sighed, running his fingers through his hair. Like me, he seemed to have realized it was the best way. The only way, perhaps. His frown dipped even further, if that were possible, a shadow of fear darkening his face. I tried to ignore his expression, telling myself that I would survive it, telling myself that he wouldn't have to deal with my dead body.

"Alright, just a little bit," he said begrudgingly, and as I smiled, he quickly added, "but if it's too much, you must let me know."

I nodded, fighting to keep a smile from my lips. With one more sigh, he clasped his hands together. A spark flew from his fingers, and when he pulled his hands apart, a shining crystal hovered above his palm, casting a red glow over his skin. At the sight of it, my stomach dropped, my lips quivered, and my fingers twitched, but I forced myself to ignore my body's desperate warnings. I took a few steps toward Francois, feeling as though walking through thick mud.

"Are you sure you want to do this?" he asked.

No.

I nodded, pursing my lips together to keep from revealing my shaky breath, and held out my hand. The apparent apprehension painted on his face was almost enough to stop me, to think it through one more time, but with a flick up to his eyes, I saw Alexei. If Alexei would sacrifice himself to be arrested, then I would do whatever it took to free him.

I pushed away the flickering fear in my stomach as I accepted the crystal, puffing my chest out in an attempt to convince myself I was braver than what I thought. Heat radiated from the small crystal, enough to feel a slight burn on my palm. I gulped nervously.

Alexei would do it for me.

With that thought, I clasped my eyes shut and threw the crystal in my mouth, wincing as I felt it slip down my throat with more burn than the strongest alcohol. With more burn than fire, it seemed. I had been expecting the fire, the burn of flames and smoke billowing in my chest, suffocating, like what I had felt at the Mandrake.

But it was nothing like that. It was so much worse.

It wasn't even fire, no, it was like magma, magma running through my veins, and I could sense it bubbling under my skin, crawling to scour every inch of my body. It came so fast, like a thousand bullets, sending me stumbling back. My knees failed, but as the world turned upside down, a pair of hands grabbed my shoulders. I recoiled at the touch, wanting nothing more than purging any sense of feeling. Just his fingertips caused my prickling skin to contract, like it was on the verge of exploding.

"Hey, hey, hey." His voice was so distant, merely a whisper. "Don't you dare close your eyes. Don't you dare die."

What else am I supposed to do? Regret washed over me, and through the mess of my wild and disheveled thoughts, I realized he had been right. The Dust truly would kill me, and I knew I couldn't stop it. I couldn't fight it.

"You're stronger than this. You have magic like no other. You must use it! Only you can freeze the pain!"

But I didn't want to. All I wanted was for it to end, whether that meant letting it just kill me, I would've accepted death like an old friend. If it meant giving up my heart entirely, I would've done it. Just anything to stop the scorching agony from searching my veins.

Smoke rolled from my lips in black clouds, steamy tears falling down my cheeks. My whole body failed, lying limply in Francois' arms like an old, broken doll plunged in an incinerator. My bubbling skin took on a red hue, brighter than the crystal that I had swallowed. My chest seemed to have contracted on itself, my mouth hanging open as no air passed through my shriveling lungs. I dug my fingernails in my palms, drawing as much blood as I could, trying to free the hot magma running through my body. It felt as though I was being burned alive, on the inside and out. My vision began to fade, spots of darkness seeping into the corners of my eyes like the cloak of death. I wanted to jump in its arms, let it take all the pain away, but something past the excruciating, burning pain kept my eyes half open.

A memory. A memory of a boy with crimson-fuchsia hair speaking to me, telling me about his mother. His mother, who he had disobeyed to come to me—to save me. To save me from what?

From the same tormenting pain, I realized.

With his little hands hovering over me, his cheeks shining with tears of panic, a chill swept over my body, seeping into my skin like a kiss of ice. My chest, once trapped in a web of embers, overwhelmed by the screaming cold, allowed me to breathe again, hollow as the inside of a wide oak tree.

I remembered that feeling, that night. I remembered the way a chill swallowed my whole being, painting my hair, flushing my skin, sinking into my eyes. I remembered the way my suffering chest calmed, and calmed more than normal, so calm, it became still. I remembered it all.

And just like that, with the image of that little boy peering through my window embedded in my mind, the burning pain subsided, the kiss of ice overtaking it with a force so strong, Francois swiped his hands away. I fell to my knees, sucking in gasps of air as my vision returned to me steadily. A vapor of icy mist sucked the red glow away, dancing off my skin in snowflakes, leaving my flesh covered in a thin layer of snow. I blinked the rest of my dizziness away as I glanced up at Francois.

His eyes were wide as plates, his mouth hanging open in shock. He held his arms over his torso as he shivered. As we locked gazes, the corners of his lips twitched up. I couldn't help but let my own follow suit.

"You did it!" he beamed, rushing forward to help me to my feet.

I coughed, releasing a last few puffs of smoke as I allowed him to lead me to my desk, where I plopped down in my chair. I could see quite clearly the ice vapor leaving my body and the way Francois shivered around me, his skin prickling with goosebumps, but I felt not one whisper of cold. For once, I felt as though my body truly belonged to me. My chest, of course, still felt hollow and empty as ever, but a different power stirred deep inside my stomach. It was heavy, biting to be let out like a raging monster, but I kept it quiet. For now, at least.

"How do you feel?" Francois asked, offering me a handkerchief.

I accepted the cloth, wiping the chilled tears from my cheeks. "I feel . . . hungry. Not literally, well, yes literally, but in another way too. I . . . don't understand it."

Francois chuckled. "It's ok, that's quite normal. It's just your magic wanting to be released, but you have to control it. Untamed magic can be twice as dangerous."

I nodded, using my desk to support myself as I fought to my feet. I swayed slightly as I stood, off-centered, my eyes drooping heavily. Exhaustion seeped into my body, and both hunger for food and magic bit at my stomach, incredibly distracting. I wanted to fall into bed, allow myself the many lost hours of sleep and at the same time, I wanted to indulge in the biggest feast to behold, decked out with triple layer cakes, puddings, pies, cookies, sparkling cider, fruit, and any other sweet treat imaginable. I even found myself craving the champagne that Alexei had favored so much.

But I knew all of that would have to wait. I still had a mission left to do. I still had to evade my brothers. I still had Alexei and Sasha to save, all the way in Embrasia. Oh, gods, I still had to find a way to Embrasia.

"Thank you, Francois." I offered a weak and tired smile, trying to be considerate. "I'm sure Alexei will forgive you. I know I already do."

The wizard's triumphant beam flickered for a moment, his grin loosening. I thought I saw a shimmer in his eyes.

"What's wrong?" I asked. "Did I do something?"

"No, no." He chuckled, hastily wiping his eyes. "I just . . . I never thought you would forgive me. I never thought I could be forgiven for what I'd done." His voice broke at the end of his sentence, and he directed his glossy eyes to the floor.

"You can't live in the past. Look what you've just done now," I said with a growing smile. "Our pasts don't define us. Only our presents do. And that determines the future."

Through his trembling lips, a smile formed. "I can see why you and Alexei get along so well."

I bit my lip to keep in a laugh, remembering the first couple days we knew each other. Oh, it was a wonder we didn't kill each other.

"I'm glad I could help." His smile once again dipped into a frown. "But I'm afraid I need to leave you. I can't be gone for much longer, but we'll meet again soon, perhaps not in this body, however." He ended the sentence with a wink.

Wait, what?

But before I could question him, he had already stepped out the door. I rushed to follow, trailing behind him as we entered the living room, where Layton, Dean, and Dulce were waiting. They perked up as we appeared, their eyes searching anxiously. I fought to resist the smirk tugging on my lips, their gazes a little less terrifying than before. Now, I at least had access to the magic billowed up inside me. Now, I could at least defend myself.

"She's made amazing progress tonight, thanks to you, Mr. Morrow," Francois said in that deep and husky voice he had used for Aven, stepping forward and shaking Layton's hand. "I can assure you, she's in good hands."

"Thank you, thank you so much," Layton replied, shaking his hand vigorously.

As they bid their last goodbyes, I noticed Dean cross the room slowly, subtly taking my side. He leaned over, speaking in a hushed whisper.

"Evil wizard?"

"Good wizard." I could practically taste the lingering smile on my lips.

Francois turned, catching my eye, and I didn't miss the wink he sent my way before he gracefully exited the house. And just like that, he was gone, disappeared in the darkness of Cyrene. Layton closed the door, releasing a long sigh. For a second, I was afraid he would bring up dinner again, but to my ultimate surprise, when he turned to look at me, he wore a smile.

"I think that's enough for one day," he said.

Just those words triggered a yawn, a yawn almost impossible to fight, but I managed it with some struggling. I knew I was tired, but I needed to stay awake. I needed to get to Embrasia and sleeping would just set me back too many hours.

Desperate to steal away back to my room, I performed an overly dramatic yawn, throwing my arms over my head as I stretched.

"I'll see you tomorrow, then," I said with a not-so-fake sleepy smile, backpedaling to the hallway.

"Goodnight, Ivory," Layton called, his hopeful smile both infuriating and pitiful.

"Night," Dean added faintly.

I whirled around and disappeared back into my room, kicking the door closed behind me. Before I started anything, I lit a few extra candles, placing them on the edge of my bed stand. They were the closest I would get to stars.

Just as I was about to search for a bag or sack to carry some extra tools, I heard the sound of my door creaking open. I turned, expecting to see Francois making a surprise return, but instead, Dulce's grim face greeted me.

"Oh, it's you," I mumbled.

"What?"

"Nothing." I waved my hand through the air as if swatting an annoying fly. "What do you want?"

"I'm here to talk," he answered confidently, which only triggered my irritation toward him.

"About what? Marble slamming my face in the street or Alexei being accused of kidnapping me? Or perhaps you want to talk about the fact that you're denying these things when you were there to see them."

"Ivory—"

"You know I'm not under a spell. You know Marble is the true culprit. You know Alexei is innocent, and yet you still dare to show your face to me, wanting to *talk*," I cut him off, arms crossed against my chest, shooting a glare. "So, talk. What do you want?"

"You're different," he blurted out quickly.

I scoffed. "People change. It's human."

"But you don't know what being human feels like."

I took a wounded step back, shocked. I was just as human as he was. I was just as human as anyone. *Except, I can't feel love. Except, I have magic whirling inside me, crying to be let out.* I bit my lip as my face flushed white with the realization.

"Says the one despicable enough to betray me," I spat, pointing an accusing finger at him.

"I didn't betray you, I saved you. You should be thanking me," he countered, his voice trembling with anger.

"Thank you? Fine, I'll thank you. Thanks, Dulce, for letting my only friends be taken away from me. Thanks for watching Marble beat me to the stone. Thanks for bringing me back to this nightmare, where I'm literally trapped. Thanks for lying to my brothers, and thanks, once more, for letting them poison my drink. Was that enough thanks, or would you like some more?"

The color in his face disappeared. "You knew about the potion?"

"Of course I knew. I've been living with a wizard, try to keep up," I replied, rolling my eyes.

"So, what are you planning now, huh? Just never going to drink anything ever again?" Dulce questioned, venom dripping in his voice.

"Of course not. I'm—" I cut myself off. I couldn't tell him I had a plan to escape, though I desperately wanted to see the look on his face if I did, but I knew he would just run to Layton and they'd ring Payne for some other potion or enchantment. I did not need to put up with that.

"You're stuck here, Ivory."

That's what you think.

"And I take it you don't do well in confined spaces."

I paused, my stomach dropping. "What are you getting at?"

"I can get you out of here," he responded with a smirk.

"And why, might I ask, would you want to do that?" I crossed my arms again, tighter.

His smirk grew. "You know the king, right? In exchange for your freedom, you get me a spot in his army."

"You want to be part of his army?" I restated, not trying very hard to hide my disgust.

"What, you think I'm not good enough?"

"No, no, you'll fit right in with those traitors and liars," I replied swiftly.

Dulce's eyes widened and he pulled his arm back as if planning to strike me. All of the courage I had gained with Francois suddenly disappeared, and I winced, holding my hands over my face as I waited for the blow.

"You're pathetic," he hissed instead.

I cracked my eyes open to see him pulling away, hating myself for giving in to my fear, and hating Dulce for everything else. I would never be able to rescue Alexei if I winced at every mention of danger. What would he think if he saw the way I had cowered? I was the one who was supposed to save him. I could not be afraid anymore. Not of pain, not of death, not of anything.

So, I stood up straight and looked him in the eye, offering one warning. "Get out of my house."

"Or what?" He leaned forward, towering over me.

You asked for this.

If he wanted to test me, then he would have to face my wrath. I used the anger and that biting hunger in my stomach to fuel my actions as I lifted my hands in the air. The lights flickered and died out. A chill swept over the room, sending hair snapping across our faces. His loose shirt flapped in the wind, as did my skirt.

Dulce gasped, jumping with a whimper as he whirled around, searching for the source. All at once, his eyes fell on me.

"What are you doing?" he asked, his voice quivering.

I smirked, delighted to hear the terror that I caused, and shut my eyes tight. When I opened them, they glowed bright blue, an icy mist pouring from my skin. I heard him cry out in alarm, jumping for the door, but as his hands made contact with the knob, a bite of frost nipped at his fingers from the metal. He gasped and stumbled away, the wind knocking him, leaving him cowering in front of my feet.

"I—I'm sorry!" he exclaimed. "Please, stop!"

I halted everything. The wind died out in an instant, the lights slowly fading back on. I drew the frost from the doorknob as my eyes flickered back to normal.

"Who's pathetic now?" I snickered, peering over him.

"How d—did you do that?" he stuttered, his eyes wide as he crawled to his feet, backing away from me.

I frowned, stepping toward him as I answered. "You think you know so much, don't you? Well, you don't. You think a king like Cathair would be worth serving? You saw his Magicians. They're ruthless and cruel, the whole lot of them."

"No, no, they can't all be like that. I thought Embrasia was . . ."

"Perfect? Amazing? Beautiful? That's what I thought too before I met that blasted king."

He opened his mouth to say more, but nothing came out, his expression falling. All at once, his anger returned, hot and raging.

"You're lying! I don't care what you say, you witch!" he shouted, shoving a finger at me.

I glared, standing my ground. I thought I had been able to get to him. I thought . . . well, I guessed wrong. No matter.

"Fine, go to Embrasia, but I don't need your help." I shook my head, curling my fists. "Swear your allegiance to the king. Join the ranks. Spend your life fighting a cause the king is too lazy to address himself. Die in some ragtag assassination."

"You don't know what you're talking about."

"I know much more than you. Maybe if you used your head for once, you could see that."

"Enough!" he cried, his face red with anger, his fists trembling. "I'm not listening to you anymore. Just remember I offered to help."

With one last long scowl, he whirled around and barreled through the door, slamming it shut behind him. I stared at where he once stood, anger piling high in my stomach. My fingers twitched with frost. Ice stuck my feet to the wood, wind howled through my hair, and snow swirled around the small square I called a room, sending books flying, pages soaring everywhere.

I glanced down at my fingertips, my nails long with crystals of ice, snow dancing through my fingers. I released a long breath, clenched my fist, and the wind died. The books fell. The snow melted away and disappeared, the ice retracted back into my skin.

"And remember I tried to help, too."

37

I pulled Dean's oversized shirt over my head, tucking it into the pair of
trousers I had stolen from him as well, trousers that I used two belts to keep
tight. I tied the sleeves short, folding them up multiple times to keep them
from slipping. To complete the look, I shoved my feet in a pair of Dean's old
hunting boots, just about small enough to fit my feet.

When I glanced up at the mirror, I couldn't help but smile. Sure, it wasn't
any shining armor, but it felt like it. At least, a lot more than skirts and
diamond slippers. I flicked my long braid over my shoulder as I turned to
retrieve the rucksack I had found buried deep in the supply closet. But as I
lifted it, it weighed a little more than I remembered.

Confused, I set it down and zipped it open. Sitting on top of an extra
shirt, one of Dean's daggers, a roll of bandages, and a few extra candles with
matches, a small drawstring bag and a wrapped object sat, a note stuck to the
two items. I picked up the note, scanning it in puzzlement.

Thought you'd need this. Look in the side pocket. Good luck. -Aven Calvo

I couldn't resist the chuckle that rose up in my throat, tucking the note
away as I pulled out the small drawstring bag, opening it to reveal a few
pounds of gold coins. I gazed down in the bag, shocked. I had never expected

to see so many gold coins again, and they were all for me. I couldn't possibly accept them. I couldn't.

But I did.

I stuffed the bag back and plucked the other thing Francois had left me. I gingerly peeled the wrapping away to find cinnamon bread and a roll of sausage. I stared down at the food in disbelief, my mouth hanging open.

Thank the gods and goddesses above for Francois.

But before I could indulge, I checked the side pocket, tugging a cylinder canteen from my rucksack. I didn't hold myself back, throwing the cap off and chugging the contents inside. The sweet surprise of apple danced on my taste buds. I pulled the canteen away, my eyes practically shining. It was sparkling apple cider.

I tore a piece of bread off, sticking it in my mouth, before I shoved everything back, promising myself I would eat later. First, I needed to escape my own house.

I threw my rucksack over my shoulder, the extra weight feeling a little more comfortable, like I was truly ready now, and pulled my door open. Night had long descended, and the hallways had long been empty and silent, but I still couldn't help but fear Layton would make an appearance. At least I didn't have to worry about Dulce anymore.

Just as I figured, the halls were empty as ever. I stepped into the darkness, swiftly making my way to the living room. I could've gotten out by the window in my bathroom, but I knew it would take longer. Plus, I secretly wanted the satisfaction of walking out the front door.

I grabbed one of Dean's cloaks and swung it over my shoulders, fastening the hook carefully. I felt like some type of criminal with my face covered and dagger in my bag. The feeling was a bit more pleasurable than I would have liked to admit. I wasn't a knight anymore. I was a thief, stealing my freedom. Stealing the prince of Embrasia. Stealing Alexei.

I made my way to the door, glanced once behind my shoulder, and locked eyes with the knob. I took a deep breath, the scent of magic filling my nose. I concentrated on the angry hunger in the pit of my stomach, yearning to be let free. I pictured a pair of hands wrapping around the knob.

"*Open.*"

The lock clicked and the door fell open. I bit back a smile as the night's breeze filled my hood with its cold breath. All at once, I felt I could breathe myself. I felt normal again.

"Ivory."

I gasped, whirling to face the whispered voice. Dean greeted me, his face plagued by too many hours without sleep. He wore his pajamas, his feet bare, and as I studied him, I wagered I would've been able to outrun him. But he didn't try to stop me.

"Be careful," he muttered.

Relief washed over me like a wave crashing onto the shore. I didn't even realize a smile had formed on my lips. I nodded once, pulling the door a little wider.

"Are you coming back?" he asked quickly, taking a step forward.

I nodded. "Yes."

"Will you be long?"

"I don't know."

He released a breath of . . . defeat? Or was it relief? I couldn't tell. He looked so tired, so old. I wanted to reassure him, to give him a sense of security, but I wasn't sure if I was capable. Everything was my fault, after all. How could I possibly fix our relationship when I couldn't even fix myself?

I didn't know what else to say, so instead, I asked, "Will you keep Layton in control for me?"

"Of course," he replied. His voice came out as a rasp.

A frown tugged at my lips. I wanted to say something else, but what? What could I possibly say to make things better? I hated the tearing guilt in the pit of my stomach, but I knew I deserved it. I was just as bad as they were, I knew. We were blood, after all.

I ignored the guilt, the sadness tethering me in place, turning my back on my brother. My brother, who always took my side. My brother, who I could always count on. The night was calling me like a siren's song, beckoning me sweetly. I couldn't help but listen.

"I love you," Dean called after me. "I know you haven't heard those words in a long time, and I'm sorry."

I winced, tensing up in a pause. Pain, an actual hurt from a place unknown, flowed through my chest like a spreading poison. I glanced back, taking in his features one last time. For the first time ever, I thought I saw a trace of me there. Wide eyes. Soft chin. How had I never realized how much we looked alike?

"I'll love you when I can," I replied, and set off through the darkness, willing myself not to look back.

. . . .

The headlights of the train were my only source of light as I neared Lockdale. The food Francois had packed me supplied my body with enough energy to cross Cyrene in a matter of hours and the trek seemed a little easier than the first time I had done it. Daylight was still hours away, but I could feel the pressure of the sun waiting to rise, waiting to remind me that another day had passed. Another day of Alexei imprisoned as I ran free.

I picked up my pace, nearly trotting toward the train station, the giant train breathing with smoke in the night. I didn't know the trains ran so late, but I couldn't question it. As long as it would take me to Embrasia, I had no need for questions.

I rushed up to the ticket booth, where a man who seemed half asleep stood, his burly arms crossed over his wide chest as he nodded off. I approached timidly, hoping I wouldn't have to resort to waking the man.

"Um, hello," I sputtered nervously, fumbling with my rucksack to retrieve my bag of coins, "I'd like a ticket to Embrasia, please."

"Sorry, we're out," the man grumbled, barely casting me a glance through his half-open eyes.

I glanced over to the train, the lights blaring on, the doors wide open, yet nobody in sight. It seemed pretty empty to me.

"When will the next train be here then?" I asked, concealing the spark of irritation that had risen in my stomach.

"Dunno."

The spark flickered to a flame, billowing up in my chest. I swallowed, attempting to push it down. Going all ice magic on the man wouldn't be the best idea, though I was considering it. Francois' warning repeated in my head like a mantra.

Don't lose control. Don't lose control. Don't lose control.

I fished a handful of gold coins and dropped them on the ledge of the booth noisily. The chinking echoed, seeming louder than the train huffing right next to us.

"I need a ticket, *please.*"

The man suddenly appeared much more awake. He stared down at the coins with lights in his eyes as he swiped them from the table in his huge, meaty hands. I bit my lip to keep from scowling, clasping my hands behind my back as my fingertips began to prickle dangerously.

"Kurt!" a voice shouted from the train.

I turned my head to see a young blond man jumping from the train, jogging toward me. He was tall and skimpy, his clothes stained with coal, his hat lopsided. He quickly wiped his hands on his trousers before he extended a hand to me.

"You're Ivory, right? I've been expecting you," he said as we shook hands. "Sorry about ol' Kurt. He's not used to the night shift."

"Who's this?" the ticket man, or Kurt, asked as he gestured to me.

"A friend of mine," the boy replied with a smile. He turned to me. "Go ahead and get on. I'll have you in Embrasia by early morning."

I bit back my confusion and my questions, and hesitantly did as he said, stepping toward the open doors of the train. I walked through the billowing smoke, taking a moment to gawk at the mechanism of transportation. I had never seen a train so . . . sparkly.

It seemed to have been made from the same thing everything in Embrasia was made from. Crystals and jewels. It was huge, expansive and long, stretching from one side of the station to the other. It looked like it had no business stationed in boring old Lockdale, where the trains were of normal steel and iron. I blinked a couple of times just to make sure I was seeing right.

The blond boy caught up with me and offered out his arm to help me up the steps. I didn't need the help, but I decided to humor him anyway and accepted his arm. Inside, warm air blasted the two of us as we walked in, the hall of compartments wide and spacious, carpeted with velvet. It was empty, just as I had suspected. Where was everyone? I couldn't possibly have been the only one in need of the train.

The boy slid open a compartment, one that must've cost a fortune. It was capacious, with velvet cushioned seats on both sides, the window large and lined with gold. A pull-out table caught my eye.

"Is this good? You should be comfortable here," he said as he looked it up and down, his hands on his hips.

"Yes, it's fine. I mean, it's perfect." I wavered, the questions rising in me, questions that I could no longer hold back. "But how do you know me?"

"I got a letter a few days ago from some satyr." He stopped to fish something from his pocket, pulling out a crumpled-up paper. "It's from the prince. He told me about you, and he's asked me to take you to Embrasia. I've been waiting here ever since."

"Wait," I held up my hand, "are you Cecil?"

"Ah, so he does talk about me." He chuckled. "But yes, I am Cecil."

I couldn't resist the grin that crept on my lips. Finally, something good was happening! Of course Sasha would still have a way to be heard from beyond the castle. And now he got Furn in on it too? When did that happen? More importantly, how did that happen? I didn't really care, however, my spirits lifted by the familiar names of Sasha and Furn. It was good to be reminded of the people on my side.

"Oh, before I forget, I have one more thing for you," Cecil said, and reached into his vest, pulling out a letter with a golden seal.

I accepted the letter gratefully, hungry for the words of the prince. I opened it immediately, not caring Cecil was still there, careful not to tear anything. I unfolded the letter inside, smoothing it out. The handwriting was small and messy.

> Dear, Ivory
>
> I hope this letter finds you. Furn managed to get in contact with me. He apparently saw the whole debacle in the Square, so he's been sending letters out for me ever since then. I don't know much about Alexei though. It's impossible to get past the guards and Magicians. My friend, Cecil, should bring you to Embrasia, but I'm afraid that's the only thing I can do for you. I wish I could help more, but security is tight. It'll only take so much time before Furn is caught and my letters are intercepted. Until then, I'll be trying to work something else out, but right now, I can't do much. To be honest, I don't know how you'll get in, but I know you'll find a way. You are our knight in shining armor, after all. We're waiting for you.
>
> -Sasha

I scanned the letter twice more, making sure I wasn't missing anything, the sound of Sasha's voice filling my head with his heavy Embrasian accent. I yearned to hear it in real life, to have him beside me. At least he seemed alright, however. He'd be ready to escape when I arrived.

I purposely avoided the fact that Sasha had no way of getting me in and that I would have to find a way to rescue them all on my own.

"Thank you, Cecil, for everything." I shoved the letter in my pocket, glancing up at the boy sincerely.

"Anything for a friend of Sasha," he responded with a smile. "We should get to Embrasia by morning. If you need anything, just ask."

With that, he turned and exited the compartment, sliding the door shut behind him, leaving me to stew in my plans of rescue.

I rubbed my arms as I walked through the mist, my fingers gliding over the countless goosebumps painting my flesh. My legs moved, unwavering, through the town, past the tall shops and restaurants crowded behind the sidewalks.

I pulled on my cardigan as I neared a towering shop, a grin tugging at my lips. The walls were decorated with glittering diamonds that glowed through the vapor, the only source of light, strong and flawless.

The door opened to reveal Alexei, a coat of dazzling amethyst hanging from his shoulders loosely, his throat and fingers adorned with sparkling gems. Following behind him, Sasha walked out next, wearing a coat that obviously belonged to Alexei, decked out with glitter and color.

As Alexei found my eyes, warmth spread through my cold veins, a flush of heat rising to my cheeks. He smiled, wide and radiant, his teeth whiter than snow, and he held out his hand for me.

"What took you so long?" he asked as I accepted his hand, sending another flush of heat through my body.

"Oh, hush." I chuckled, straightening my flowing skirt.

The pair of them laughed, their voices ringing like bells in the quiet melody of the city around us. Sasha reached out just to ruffle my hair, and as three, we turned to the shop.

But when we stepped inside, it was pure black, and Sasha and Alexei were gone. I called for them with no reply, the spark of panic in my chest fanning to a flame. I whirled around, but instead of finding a door, I found a pair of big, red eyes gazing down at me.

. . . .

I woke with a start, jerking my eyes open as I shot up, my skin coated with a fine layer of cold sweat. My breath came out in short hollow bursts, almost louder than the train's wheels clacking as it ran down the rails.

I swallowed roughly, blinking away the glowing red eyes from my sight, shivering in the darkness of the compartment. Though no matter how many times I blinked, the eyes stayed in my vision, watching me, waiting, feeding my fear like wood to a fire. All of a sudden, my trembles weren't just from the cold.

"Hello?" I whispered, voice quaking. I yearned for a blanket to pull over my head, like how I did when I was a child, like it was enough to protect me from the imaginary monsters dwelling in the dark corners of my room.

Except I wasn't sure how imaginary this monster was.

A figure slid from the darkness, darker than the night itself, and the glowing red switched to bright green, casting a glow over my pale, flushed skin. It grew closer, its breathing labored slightly. Incarti.

I inhaled to scream, my fingertips dancing with uncontrollable snowflakes, but the Incarti sank back slightly, shrinking, its long arms held up.

"I'm sorry," the Incarti said quickly in a voice painfully familiar. "I didn't mean to scare you."

I swallowed my scream, letting loose a long, relieved breath. "Francois. Why'd you have to come like *that*?"

"I couldn't risk a physical body this time. This was the only way," he replied, and I noticed a note of fear in his voice.

"Ok, ok, I get it." I swung my legs over the seat, facing his glowing green eyes. "So, what are you doing here?"

"I'm here to ask you if you have a plan."

Just as the words left his lips, my cheeks heated up. Outside the window, a sky full of stars shone through the night, the train humming. I didn't realize I had fallen asleep. Oh, gods, I had fallen asleep while trying to form an escape plan!

I bit my bottom lip, wanting to hide my face in shame. How could I have possibly let myself sleep when a plan was so much more important?

"You don't, don't you?"

"I—"

"Don't worry. I have an idea."

"Really?"

"Don't sound so surprised." The Incarti, or rather, Francois crossed his arms, his eyes slanted like the slits of a snake.

"Sorry, I didn't mean—"

"I know, I know." He sighed. "I don't have much time, so we have to be quick."

I clasped my mouth shut, nodding eagerly. I knew Francois was my only chance of success. If he were caught. . . . I shivered just thinking about it. If his brothers were so ruthless to Alexei just for saving a child's life, I couldn't imagine what they would do to Francois.

"This is a talisman." He stopped to hold out his hands, and with a flash of light, a short piece of parchment appeared, hovering over his palms. "There's a spell written on it. A disguise spell. You can change all you want, but you can only use the spell once. If the disguise melts off, it's over."

With each word, his voice grew shakier, spewing from his lips faster and faster until I had to strain to keep up. I wished I hadn't fallen asleep, the fuzz of my dreams still clogging my clear thoughts.

"Wait until you're off the train and read it aloud."

A voice of the same accent as Alexei and Francois filled the compartment, echoing from somewhere far, far away.

"Fran? What are you doing?"

"Good luck," Francois whispered, shoving the talisman in my hands before he disappeared.

Shocked, I stood frozen, waiting anxiously for the voices to return, but the compartment remained silent. I had a feeling Francois was not coming back. I glimpsed down at the talisman in my hand, studying the thick, messy words scribbled over it in black ink. The paper radiated with sweet magic that sank into my fingers just by touching it.

I thought of Alexei, the way his hands were so warm, the way the scent of magic followed him everywhere. If I didn't get to him quickly, that scent would soon disappear, never to return again. I couldn't imagine his hands without the excessive heat, the way flames licked off his hair when he got angry. I wouldn't let his heart fail on him. I only had one shot at it. I had to succeed.

I didn't fall asleep again that night.

38

I slipped my hand in my pocket once more, the rough texture of the parchment a source of relief for me the closer we got to Embrasia. When the train eventually rolled to a creaking stop, I couldn't help but wish the ride carried on longer. I wanted more time to think, more time to plan, but with the break of the train sounding its stop, I knew I had run out of time.

I met Cecil at the exit, attempting to offer the best smile I could manage, but my thoughts plagued me to no end. I hoped he couldn't see the apparent stress on my face, the bags and wrinkles under my eyes telling a story of my previous couple nights.

He slid the doors open to reveal the place I never wanted to see again, the place of glittering structures and people of wealth roaming the excessive Square. It was packed, gentlemen with top hats and tailcoats chatting loudly, with their mustaches and golden watches, and the women, with their parasols, mushroom-like skirts, and pinned hair, tittering about like flocks of colorful birds.

"Well, this is your stop," Cecil said, smiling obliviously.

I pushed back my nerves. "Yes, uh, thank you. Thank you so much."

"Anything for Sasha," he replied with a tip of his cap.

I gave one last smile, which I really hoped was an actual smile, and stepped off the train. My grimy boots felt strange standing upon the dazzling roads of Embrasia, where most wore heeled, diamond shoes. Or something expensive like that.

"Goodbye." I nodded to Cecil, wishing I was back on the train.

"Goodbye." He nodded back, his smile widening. "Maybe we'll meet again. Perhaps we'll all have tea."

Before I could either agree or disagree, he had closed the door shut, and not long after, the whistle of the train sliced through the chatter of the station. I watched as the train woke up again, steam huffing from the crystal as it disappeared from sight. The moment it was gone, I felt a thousand times more vulnerable, and nearly panicked when I didn't feel the talisman in my pocket, just to realize I had put it in the other pocket.

I swallowed nervously as I pulled the paper out, feeling rather inconspicuous, but not one citizen cast me even the slightest glance. I figured it was the way my baggy clothes and cloak had swallowed me up, but knowing that nobody was looking at me sent the slightest hint of relief to my stomach. All my life, I thought people would stare, point, scream at the sight of me, but nobody was even looking. They were way too busy doing their own things.

Too busy to even notice the girl with silver hair whisper a spell in the midst of the Square. Too busy to notice the piece of paper in her hands crumble to ash. Too busy to notice her change entirely.

The first thing I realized after I whispered the spell, the talisman disintegrating in my hands, was my absence of cloak and baggy clothes. In the blink of an eye, my former clothes had been replaced with a dress almost identical to every other dress in the Square. Tight corset. Bows and ribbons. Flowing, velvet skirt. Oh, gods, heeled boots.

As I stepped into the crowd, a mess of black tangles tickling my neck, I noticed I had grown taller, not just because of the heeled boots, but physically taller. When I reached up to tug my new hair behind my ear, I found my skin an average peach, slightly sun kissed.

I struggled to resist gawking at myself, but it was a difficult feat. For as long as I could remember, I had yearned, dreamed, wished to look normal, for the same complexion, clothes, and hair as everyone else. But as I made my way through the bustling crowd, I couldn't help but miss my old look. I tried to find some fun in the change, stepping with an extra bounce just to get my hair to bounce along with me. After that, however, I couldn't find much to be happy about.

I walked briskly, nervously playing with my skirts as I struggled to maintain my balance on my new heeled boots. I wobbled and stumbled with every other step, my corset tight enough to cut off half of the air trying to pass through my lungs. I ignored my rather annoying new disguise, grateful that not one person even glanced my way. For once, I was just another one of the crowd. For once, I was just as normal as they were, with my normal, human life.

Though, I wasn't able to be just another one of the crowd for long. I neared the castle a lot quicker than I thought it would take, remembering the first time I had crossed through Embrasia. This time, however, I recognized every twist, every turn, every alleyway that could serve as a shortcut. My tread consisted of mostly shortcuts, across alleys, over and under bridges. I hated how familiar the sights were, how easily I could navigate through without the eyes of the unwanted.

I knew the police and guards on patrol couldn't recognize me, but that still didn't stop me from dodging from their line of sight. Almost all of them knew me, and knew me as the one who was kicked out of the castle, or the girl worth ten thousand gold pieces. I didn't even want to imagine what would happen if I were caught.

The gleam of the castle no longer amazed me, no longer appeared beautiful, only served as a reminder of the terrible days spent in Embrasia; only the source of a very annoying glint that forced me to squint. As I got closer, the shine grew brighter and brighter, and soon I was stepping upon the cherry blossom infested crystal path, crushing the petals beneath my feet.

A line of guards marched in front of the gate, their faces just as intimidating and expressionless as I remembered. Their crystal armor reflected off the light of the sun, sending rays of light through the sky. I had to shield my eyes just to look at them, wondering how I could possibly get past them. Normal girls didn't just saunter into the castle. Normal girls didn't even go near the castle.

But then something *not* blinding caught my eye. I quickly ran near despite my feet screaming in protest, pressing myself to the bark of a cherry blossom tree. I dared to take another look and couldn't stop the gasp that rose up in my throat.

Seized by four guards, a satyr wearing a thick coat struggled and screamed violently, letters falling from his clenched fists as the Embrasians rattled him harshly. I couldn't believe it. Furn!

Without thinking, my appearance changed again. I stood a lot taller than before, armor shielding my lean, flat chest, concealing sharp legs and arms. My hair receded back, neatly packed inside the helmet that appeared over my head. I glanced down at my slender hands, skin a few shades darker than before.

I was no longer just another girl in the crowd. No, now, I was an Embrasian guard. I couldn't stop my stomach from dropping as I tried to convince myself it was a good thing. With the disguise, I would at least be able to get into the castle. That didn't ensure I wouldn't get caught, in fact, it might've put me in even more danger than before, but I tried to ignore the odds stacking up against me, as well as the plan that had formed in my head.

But now that I had a plan, I couldn't turn a blind eye to it. It might've been insanely stupid and crazy, but it was a plan. And if it had any chance of working, then I had to go with it. For Sasha. For Furn. For Alexei.

Because now, I truly was their knight in shining armor.

I puffed my chest out confidently, though confidence was the last thing I possessed, and joined the four guards by the gate, keeping a straight face, even though I was terrified beyond compare. As they paused to look at me, I thought they had seen right through me, seen my disguise, seen my freckles and silver hair. Seen my lie.

But instead of dropping Furn to arrest me, they shoved their helmets up with a laugh.

"Look who we found crawling around in the cherry bushes," one said to me as he nudged my shoulder.

It was nearly impossible to hide my relief. I forced myself to keep calm and natural, laughing along with the others using a voice a few octaves lower than my usual one. Maybe I had picked up more from Francois than I first thought.

"Stupid creature." Another guard snickered as he shoved Furn, sending the boy stumbling for balance.

I nearly reached out to steady him, but caught myself at the last second, my fingers twitching. I had to force out a laugh as the others burst out in booming jests and mockeries, wincing while I watched them continue to shove and punch Furn like they were young children vandalizing their own toy. They threw him around a bit, tearing his coat from his body and discarding it. They spat at him when he tried to reach for it back.

When they punched him again, he went tumbling at me. I couldn't help but catch him, holding his bare arms steady. We locked gazes, identical fear shining in our eyes. I didn't know what to do, holding him steady with the other guards staring. I wanted to pull him away, wrap his coat back over his body, and apologize rapidly. But as their laughter slowly diminished, I knew I had to do something, and something fast. How could I hurt him though? How could I allow them to continue harassing him?

So, I tugged his arms behind his back quicker than he could keep up with, holding them securely, but not tight enough to hurt. He gasped out in surprise, and the laughing thankfully carried on.

"I'm thinking," I paused for dramatic effect, allowing my voice to take on a heavy Embrasian accent full of ridicule, "the dungeon? Since he wanted to be here so much."

Furn tensed the second I began speaking, his shoulders going completely stiff. He dared to glance back at me, his eyes wide, searching, confused. All that greeted him was the face of an Embrasian guard.

One of the guards slapped me on the back, creating a clang of metal ringing in my ears. "Maybe we'll put him with that new wizard. They can rot together."

This time, I didn't laugh, barely managing a chuckle. For a brief moment, I thought my skin flashed snow pale, but when I swallowed the panic that came from the guard's words, it returned to the shade my disguise had taken on. I let out a subtle breath of relief.

So that's what Francois meant when he said I can't lose the disguise.

I understood now, if I allowed my thoughts to take over my rational side of thinking, the disguise would pay. I bit my bottom lip nervously as I followed the others through the gates of the castle, the very same gates they had thrown me through not too long ago, feeling a little dizzy as I entered the palace of shine and shimmer. I couldn't allow myself to lose the disguise. If I lost it, I would lose everything. As long as I didn't run into any—

"You there!"

My blood stopped. . . . It couldn't be.

But when I obediently stopped with the others, the voice of bubbles and nightmares carried on. It killed me to face him, to see his eyes again, to hear his voice again. I gulped, focusing on keeping the spell intact.

"Magician Marble, we did as you said. We caught the satyr," a guard reported. "We were just about to deliver it to the dungeon."

"Did you get the letters?" Marble asked, a twinge of irritation hidden deep under his facade of light tones and optimistic voice.

"Letters?"

"This satyr was sending letters from the prince; we cannot let them be sent. Go get them and report back to me. I have a feeling the person he's trying to get in contact with won't stay away for long. We must keep the prince from any outside contact at all costs, got it?" Marble replied shortly, gesturing to Furn angrily as his face glowed red with anger, though his voice remained terrifyingly steady.

My fingers trembled as I held Furn's hands behind his back. My knees nearly buckled when Marble's gaze rested on me. A few strands of white hair tickled the back of my neck, but with a mental slap, they vanished.

"You." He pointed at me, his eyes holding a fake sparkle to them. "Get that satyr to the dungeon. The rest of you retrieve the letters."

The other guards rushed to comply, hurrying out the doors we had just walked through. Marble cast me one last glance that seemed more like a glare hidden by a smile, and whirled around, disappearing from the corridor. I couldn't resist the sigh of relief that bubbled up my chest when he was gone, but I forced myself to keep the insults that had piled up on my tongue back.

For once, I had something I could thank Marble for. He basically led me right to Alexei. He had just made my job a lot easier. And he had handed Furn over to me without a second thought. I couldn't believe my luck.

But I knew my luck never lasted long.

Furn and I navigated through the castle in an awkward silence, his steps wavering and slow. Bruises created by the guards decorated his body with purple and red. Blood dripped from his nose. He winced with each intake of breath.

I winced along with him. I wanted to lead him out, back to his burrow with excessive wines and sparkly trinkets or whatever else he wanted, guilt like a monster biting at my mind savagely. I wanted to steal some of that healing potion right off of Marble and let him drink as much as he needed. I wanted to let him watch guards get pounded to the dirt, spat on, ridiculed.

But what I wanted didn't matter. Not now, at least, when so many other people were counting on me.

It took a while longer than I wished, and with my anxiety running high, keeping the spell intact grew increasingly difficult, but I eventually stumbled upon the door to the dungeon, flanked by two stone-faced guards. Both Furn and I tensed as they directed their eyes on us.

I fought for courage, and with a mental apology to Furn, I shoved him forward lightly. "Marble's prisoner."

I swallowed roughly when they didn't move, but a second later, with deliberate slowness, they stepped aside to let me through.

"Here. Don't talk to the new wizard. He's known to be . . . persuasive." One of them dropped a ring of keys in my hand, of which I nearly lost between my fingers.

I nodded, bashfully gaining a grasp on the keys. If I hadn't been so scared, I would've laughed at the fact Alexei had already gained a reputation in the dungeon. I could've told anyone he was persuasive. It was the most annoying trait about him.

I made a show of pushing Furn once more, not hard enough to send him stumbling, but enough to convince the guards as I walked through the wide, heavy doors, stepping onto the top of a dark, stone staircase. The doors shut soundly behind us.

My nose twitched, a musty smell of mold and rot filling my nostrils. I held onto Furn tighter, ensuring he didn't fall down the steps as we made our descent. He stumbled a bit, but I held on tight, no longer pinning his arms behind his back, instead supporting his weight as much as he needed. I caught him each time he slipped, following the twisting staircase until we arrived at a dark hallway lined with cells.

I knew I hadn't yet freed Alexei, but a surge of triumph exploded in my chest, so strong I couldn't fight the grin creeping its way to my lips. I was so close, so very close.

However, as I began down the hall, I couldn't ignore the faces of the prisoners, tainting my burst of joy. Some of them looked young, my age young, their faces pale and gaunt to match with their frail bodies, their hair stringy and oily. Even the older ones looked just as weak, the women with black bags under their eyes, the men whose clothing appeared stained just as much as the floor beneath them, their beards growing out long and mangy.

It almost seemed like they were forgotten down there. And forgotten a long, long time ago.

The more I caught glances, the more their eyes caught me. And what eyes did these prisoners have. They were incredibly dull, unnaturally dull, like a sheen blocked the color, but behind that sheen, their eyes held hues I had never seen before in irises. Eyes of violet and burning orange, eyes of gray and rose. Mismatched colors swirling into each other. Eyes of crystal white, mirror cream.

In other words, eyes like mine.

As I moved past them, something seemed to flicker and they perked up, all of their attention on me, studying me with incredibility. I kept myself from shivering under their curious and heavy gazes, reminding myself of the whole reason I was there.

I continued on, my metal boots clanking against the stone audibly, mixing with the increasing whispers of the prisoners. I scanned each cell, my frown deepening with each new sight, and I thought Furn had grasped my hands for a second to stop me from trembling.

I would've never found him—I would've walked right past, missed his blazing hair, his ripped coat, and tanned skin, if he hadn't talked.

"Furn?"

All at once, I stopped and whirled to see *him*. My Alexei. But as we locked eyes, I realized he was glaring at me with all the hatred he could muster. My grip on Furn loosened. His hatred left my knees quaking, my breath hitching. Before I could stop it, silver strands of hair poured down my face. A type of pain hit me, the same pain I had felt in my brother's presence. The same pain I felt when Dulce betrayed me.

But then I remembered he couldn't see me, the real me, and ushered the hair away. The slip, however, took a toll on my energy, and I strained to keep the spell going. I needed to keep it if I wanted to get us out alive, but I wasn't sure how much longer I could've held it. If it happened again, I didn't know if I would've been able to fix it.

I sucked in a subtle breath as I studied him, standing up to the edge of his cell with his hands curled around the bars, his skin flushed pale and sickly. He had lost all of his diamonds, seeming bare without the bling, his hair hanging loosely down his neck, his clothes stained with grime. Like the other prisoners, his eyes held a glassy dullness over them, blocking the magnificent emerald glow they usually held.

"Alexei?" Furn whispered, squinting as he cocked his head. "You look awful."

"You're not looking much better." Alexei paused just to glare at me again, but the fire of hatred in his eyes was gone. Instead, he looked tired. Exhausted, even.

I bit my lip, both pained and amused. Of course, even after several draining days, his spunk remained flamboyant as ever. It was relieving to know and a sense of pride for him rose up in my chest. He was still as Alexei as ever.

I fumbled with the keys, holding Furn with one tight hand to ensure he didn't make a run for it, and shoved one into the lock of Alexei's cell. Furrowing my eyebrows as it didn't budge, I tried another key. When that one didn't work, and I had released a sigh of exasperation, a small chuckle rebounded from the cell.

My head shot up to see Alexei covering his mouth as his shoulders shook with laughter, failing to keep in his snickers. I scoffed, biting back the smile teasing at my lips. Of course, he hadn't changed one bit.

"Maybe try that one," Furn said, pointing to a rusty key dangling in between two large ones.

I hung my head, a cross between a sigh and a laugh escaping my throat. "You know, don't you?"

"You're not as inconspicuous as you think. Especially with that awful Embrasian accent." Furn shrugged, slipping from my clutches easily. I realized he could've escaped my grasp long ago; he had been playing me the whole way to the dungeon, like how I had tried playing him.

"Wait, you know him?" Alexei asked, his glare finally dropping as I rammed the key Furn had pointed to into the lock.

Furn and I shared a look, smirks playing at our lips like we were mischievous children. I couldn't stop myself from beaming.

"I sure do." Furn leaned casually against the moldy walls, his voice dancing with amusement.

"Who are you?" Alexei questioned, displaying a painfully confused face as he locked his dull eyes on me.

"Isn't it obvious?" I swung the cell door open with a dramatic flourish. "I'm your knight in shining armor."

A look of sweet realization dawned on his face and Furn burst out laughing at his expression. I flashed a smile, stepping aside as he dumbfoundedly stepped out of the cell.

"Ivory?" he whispered. "How?"

"I can explain later, but we still need to get Sasha out and this spell isn't—"

Before I could finish my sentence, Alexei flung forward, throwing his arms around me. I stumbled back, closing my eyes as his overwhelming sweet scent filled my nose, stronger than it was ever before, flowing like steam from a hot drink, curling around me in a tight embrace.

When I tugged my eyes open, I was no longer tall and muscular, my short hair taken over by long strands of silver. My borrowed baggy clothes had returned, my skin flushed pale once again, splattered with freckles.

The spell had melted off.

I pulled away from Alexei in an instant, holding my hands in front of my eyes, flipping them over, stepping around as I tried to remember what it was like being so short. Dread curled into my thoughts despite my triumph of finding Alexei.

"There you are," the wizard said, reaching out to take my white hands. His touch was almost enough to burn my skin, but the warmth supplied me with a familiar reassurance that forced my hands to stay in place.

"I'm sorry I took so long, I tried to—"

"Hey, hey, it's ok. You're here now, and that's all that matters," he interrupted quickly, squeezing my hands with a little more pressure that sent a crawling warmth up my skin.

I tried to fight off the smile bubbling up, but the longer his voice filled my ears, the more I lost the resolve to win the fight. I wanted to be back in his warm embrace, sink in his freedom as much as I could, but I knew time was fleeting. Sooner or later, everything would fall apart, like it always did. I was determined to make it out, for once, in one piece.

I slipped my hands from Alexei's, shivering as my natural cold seeped back into my flesh like a familiar greeting.

"You do know your eyes are glowing, right?" Furn stepped forward, gesturing to Alexei with a quirked eyebrow.

I glanced up, and surely enough, the dull sheen had disappeared from his pupils, leaving his green eyes shimmering like a jewel. He wiped them quickly, but it didn't do anything to dim the glow.

"I know, it's just my magic," Alexei answered, and for the first time, I noticed a slight gleam to his skin as well. "These cells are meant to suppress any power. It'll take a second for my magic to calm down now that I'm out."

I sucked in a breath, imagining what it felt like. I had only just gained full control of my magic, but the idea of it being blocked sent a shudder up my body, my eyes traveling warily to the opened cell. If I were caught, it would become mine. It would claim all of us.

"We need to get moving," I said. "What's the plan?"

"You mean you don't have one?"

"That disguise spell *was* my plan."

"Oh," the two said in unison, their shoulders slumping.

293

Our once blissful moment disappeared in an instant, squashed by my words like a bug under a boot. Alexei's skin and eyes continued to glow for a few more moments before the light succumbed to the darkness surrounding us.

"I got it!" Furn exclaimed, hitting a fist to his palm. "We can use Ivory as bait and make a run for it ourselves."

Alexei and I glared, backhanding him at the same time while he laughed. Obviously, we weren't amused.

"With this surge of magic, I might be able to conjure some type of disguise," Alexei said, ignoring Furn as the satyr doubled over with laughter. "I'm not sure how strong it'll be, or how long it'll last."

A crack of a snicker split through our conversation, a snicker that didn't belong to Furn. All at once, we whirled around in the direction of the voice, facing a cell of three prisoners on the other side of the hall. The three were men, their eyes of coral and black just as dull as all the others, but their faces shone with a type of mockery that sent my blood boiling.

"Are you . . . laughing at us?" I asked incredulously, my eyebrows shooting up.

"You must forgive me, but escaping is impossible. Even with those keys and your power, you won't stand a chance against the Magicians," one of them replied, a man with hair blond as the sun and a build that once might've been very muscular.

"Leave them alone," another voice called from the other side of the dungeon.

We all turned to see a man seeming only a little older than the other three leaning out of the bars that confined him, his hair a strange light rose, cascading down his shoulders in wispy strands. A scar ran down his narrow face, through one of his apricot-colored eyes in an angry slash.

"If you haven't noticed," the man said irritably, "they're more free than you are. If they managed this far, they might be able to do it."

"Don't give them false hope, Mackel," the blond prisoner snapped. "It'll just get them right back down here, or worse."

"Alright, alright, what is going on here?" Alexei cut in before the two could continue their back and forth banter. "We didn't ask for your opinions."

"Well, you might as well take it," the blond man responded with a shrug. "You might end up dead if you don't."

"You really shouldn't be saying that to the ones with the keys, Aleric," another prisoner piped up, this one a woman of olive skin and curly hair, her eyes a swirl of green and blue.

"They're children!" the blond, or Aleric, as the woman called him, cried. "I'm trying to do them a favor."

"Wait, wait." This time, it was I who cut in. "Do you all know each other?"

"Of course we do," the one called Mackle answered, swiping his pink hair from his scarred face. "We all fought alongside each other in the war, before we were thrown in here."

"You're all war criminals?" Alexei questioned.

A burst of laughter rippled throughout the dungeon and it seemed every prisoner had their eyes and ears on us intently, leaning in between the bars curiously. Their gazes felt incredibly heavy, pressuring each word that escaped my lips and every little movement I made.

Alexei, Furn, and I shot each other a confused look, looking for some type of explanation for the cause of their laughter, but we all appeared just as clueless as the other, wondering what the prisoners found so funny.

Aleric barked out a laugh. "War criminals? We're just as criminal as you!"

"But we're not criminals," Alexei insisted.

"Exactly."

Furn whirled around in puzzlement, scanning each face around us, before leaning inconspicuously toward me. "Do you have any idea what they're talking about?"

I waved him away before addressing the prisoners again. "What do you mean?"

"We all share the same crime," Aleric responded smoothly, gesturing to everyone with a flourish of his hand.

"And that would be?"

"We're all wizards stupid enough to tangle ourselves with the king."

Alexei and I glanced at each other through the corners of our eyes, apparent disturb expressed on our features. I decided to ignore the fact they had assumed I was a wizard, instead letting it slide without batting an eye. The title was starting to grow on me anyway.

"Stop messing with them and just tell them." The woman huffed, shaking her head exasperatingly.

"Fine, fine." Aleric sighed and motioned us forward with a finger.

I complied first, ignoring Alexei's hesitance as I stepped toward the blond wizard. A twinge of nerves banged against the back of my head, telling me I wouldn't like what I was about to hear, but I ignored that as well. Whatever the wizard wanted to say, I sensed it was something that changed the whole game. Something that twisted the game in the hands of the blasted king, a permanent checkmate against us.

A piece of information that might've had the power to finally give us the advantage we needed.

"I'm sure you've heard of King Cathair's infamous army, the army that pushed back the rebel wizards to Naxos and banished them there, right?" Aleric started and didn't continue until all three of us nodded. "Well, apparently, there is a very thin line between ally and rebel, as we all learned the hard way."

"You mean you're all—"

"The king's army? Yes, we are. Or, we were."

"I thought the wizards that fought in the war were made Magicians," Alexei countered, but his flushed face signified he believed every word that had passed through Aleric's lips. "Or sent home, with as many documentation papers they wanted."

"Have you ever met a wizard that fought on the king's side during the war?"

The rest of the color in Alexei's face vanished and he dropped his head in his shaking hands.

"But why? Why would he keep you all down here?" I asked.

"He'll be able to use us again if he calls for another war," Aleric replied simply without batting an eye.

"He can't do that!" I exclaimed.

"He can. We belong to him, by contract, ever since the first war. We drafted ourselves, or at least, most of us did. He's technically not breaking any of his own laws."

"But he has no right to keep you here! You should at least be able to live in Naxos!"

"Believe me, kid, if I had the chance, I would take it, but not one of us has escaped since the war ended." Aleric slumped back, but I saw something else in his dull eyes.

I saw fire. I saw passion. I saw a never-ending fight for freedom, wild and untamed, yearning to wreak havoc on everything that the king stood for. I shared the same driving motivation.

"Here's your chance." Before anyone could stop me, I shoved the key in the lock and pulled the door open.

"Ivory!" Alexei exclaimed.

I whirled around to face him, my tone sharp. "What? You want to leave them here? You want them to stay while we leave?"

A flash passed over his features, and I thought I saw a hint of a prideful smile play at his lips. Without a trace of hesitation, he spoke again, much firmer than before, the tremble in his voice gone and his eyes set like stone.

"Carry on, then."

A smile burst across my face and a sudden urge to pull Alexei into a hug washed over me, and I might've actually done it had so many others not been watching. I made a note to save that hug for later, perhaps when we weren't about to dive into an all-out battle against the kingdom of Embrasia. Instead, I turned to the sea of wizard prisoners, their strange eyes set on me, anticipation and excitement buzzing in the air.

"Who's ready to regain their freedom?" I inquired, holding up the keys for everyone to see.

A cry, loud and passionate, responded, ringing throughout the dark expanse of the dungeon like the thundering drums of war. A grin tugged at my lips and I stepped forward, toward the countless prisoners desperate for their long-awaited chance to take back their freedom. Not a trace of doubt held a place in my mind as I unlocked each and every cell, the dark dungeon soon illuminated by the glowing skin of the freed wizards as their blocked magic rushed back to them.

Eager to release the long-suppressed magic coursing through their veins, they followed me as I motioned to the winding stone staircase, Alexei and Furn taking my sides.

"Are you sure about this?" Alexei asked as the doors grew closer.

I caught his eyes, the words on my tongue hesitating. I couldn't answer him when I didn't even know the answer. How could I possibly have been sure of leading a wizard rebellion in the midst of the Embrasian castle?

I don't have to be sure anymore.

For once, I had nobody telling me what to do, nobody trapping me in their fearful and selfish grasp, away from the storms of the world. Away from seeing and hearing and feeling the painful and delicious kisses of life. I didn't have to be sure. I didn't need anyone to tell me what to do, or what not to do.

For once, I wasn't acting upon the wishes of others. For once, my feet moved with precision and purpose. My decision to spark this rebellion was mine, and only mine.

I flashed Alexei a confident smile. "Let's go take our lives back."

39

The roaring clash of battle surrounded me like an unwanted embrace, spilling into my ears like poison, screams like knives tearing through the air. My boots pounded against the crystal floor of the castle, echoes of hundreds of other footsteps rebounding off the glass walls. My strong and confident will had quickly faded, adrenaline and fear rising up in my chest instead, curling up my body like wild flames.

We burst from the dungeon in an entourage of untamed and unbridled magic, power bursting from our seams like rice pouring from a bag torn apart by one single split thread. Honestly, we had made it much further than I thought we would before we found ourselves facing the wrath of the Embrasian soldiers.

They came at us like wasps, quick and sharp, easy to strike down, but overwhelming in number. Seeming to materialize from thin air, their large numbers didn't take long to serve as a challenge. Eventually, we found ourselves in a repetition, a pattern of the wizards pushing past, followed by another surge of soldiers to shove us right back, only for us to break through once more.

Chaos ran through the corridors, snaking in and out of every hallway, and soon it became the main motivation of both fighting sides. Even I felt myself fall victim to the discord of swords and magical blasts, my mind like static as I raced past as many guards I could, numbing their senses with a single touch.

With so much flowing magic filling the atmosphere, it was nearly impossible to resist the temptation of drinking it up. My hands flared with an ice vapor strong enough to call goosebumps on the skin of anyone in a ten-foot radius of me, snowflakes dancing through my hair, encircling me in a cocoon of a blizzard. Drunk on magic, I sank into the tug of my newly released power, furrowing myself in the sweet whispers and promises of ice.

My magic was strong too, pumping through my veins alongside my blood. Much stronger than I had ever expected it to be, a burst of screeching wind proving as easy as flicking my wrist. If I ran into a blade, I half-expected frost to pour out of the wound instead of blood. But what forced my hand wasn't my drunken surges of magic. No, it was my growing fear that spurred my ice.

I kept an eye out for Alexei, but ever since the first attack, I had not seen him. I hadn't even realized I had lost him until a wizard by my side knocked me from the killing strike of a blade. It was only then did I notice I was in the center of the battlefield, Alexei no longer in sight. It took everything in me to continue, focus on the battle around me, but ever since then, each second that passed with him nowhere to be seen sent my anticipation rising like a flooding river. I tried to tell myself he would be ok, but everything Francois had told me came rushing back the instant Alexei vanished from my side.

Alexei's magic had never been so weak and growing weaker still with each passing day. I worried relentlessly. I had also lost track of Furn, but knowing the manners of the satyr, he probably had slipped out the second the fight began, nabbing a wine bottle on his way out while he was at it.

I ran into some trouble with a guard who seemed to recognize me, but with a fearful dodge, I evaded his whirling blade, locking his feet to the floor with a mound of ice, and continued running. All too soon, I couldn't stop myself from calling Alexei's name, but the thunder of battle drowned out my desperate cries.

Bodies littered the floor, the stink of blood and death wafting with the overwhelmingly sweet scent of magic, bringing a nauseous pull tugging at my stomach. I had never seen a dead body, let alone a man slicing another man open, and the sight threatened to make me retch all over the once pristine floor. My ears rang with the screams filling the castle, my boots leaving bloody footprints with each quick step, and my magic poured out of me with no control.

I just wanted it all to stop. I wanted to have Alexei and Sasha by my side, and I wanted to be somewhere far away, away from everything. Away from the castle, the king, and the crystals. Away from Cyrene and my brothers, Dulce, Payne. How had I possibly thought fighting our way out of the Embrasian castle would ever work? All I had done was sent countless wizards and Embrasian guards to their deaths. The revelation caused me to falter, my chest hitching from more than just running.

"Morrow!"

I skidded to a halt, panic banging against my chest so hard, I nearly toppled over. I whirled around in horror, locking eyes with the Magician I never wanted to get in the way of. The rest of my courage fled by the sight of him, seeping from my head like blood pouring from a stab.

"Should've known it was you," Marble sneered. "Do you ever give up?"

I struggled to pull air into my lungs as he approached, his hands glowing with a red vapor I could only distinguish as Fire Dust. My mind raced as he grew closer and closer, his steps casual and relaxed, like there wasn't a raging fight surrounding us.

I lifted my shimmering hands, my voice sounding just as pathetic as I felt. "Get away from me, or else I will—"

"You'll what? You'll fight me? Please, without your Kementari, you're helpless."

I shook my head, my hands trembling, determined to keep my dignity despite my fear. "If you think that's true, then I pity you, Marble."

"You pity me?" He released a laugh. "Show me, then. If you're so strong, bring me to my knees. Cut me open. Watch me bleed as the life escapes my eyes. Go on."

I took a hesitant step back, my face twisted in terror, but somewhere deep inside me, I wanted to do all that he had said, and I knew it wouldn't be hard. As simple as snapping a twig, in fact, and with the power in the air, perhaps even more simple.

But I couldn't bring myself to do it. I wanted it, gods, it scared me how much my fingers twitched to have his neck caught in my hands, but the mention of the Kementari name kept me stuck. I saw Francois, his life crumbled up by the actions of our parents, and yet he had enough control to continue on while the rest of his family turned on him. I saw Alexei, his unwavering fear of discovery, and yet, his constant need to help. They deserved to rampage, to spew their anger out on the world, but they remained unwilling. Unwilling to spread their fury, to lose control, to seek revenge. I wanted to see myself in them, and this was my chance.

"I'm not going to fight you, Marble. I just want freedom, like every other wizard in this country!" I cried.

"But you aren't a wizard!" Marble exclaimed, his voice devoid of its natural jubilance. "Why are you doing this, huh? What motivates your heartless self to ruin your life like this?"

"I'm doing this because people like you exist!" I shoved an accusing finger at him, my face twisted in a glare. "If you can't see that, then you're just as heartless as I am."

With a scream, he charged at me full speed, his hands aglow so bright, I thought I could already feel the heat of the Dust laced in his skin. I threw my hands up, an icy barrier blocking him off. The Magician burst through it without a trace of hesitation, sending ice shards flying at me, and before I even had the chance to run, he had his hands reaching to tear me apart.

I released a shriek as a blast sent me flying backward, landing on my back with a painful thud across the room, the breath knocked from my lips. I sputtered on gasps, scrambling to my feet in order to evade another attack. I jumped from an oncoming blast of fire, the heat licking my skin and singeing the tips of my hair.

My adrenaline kicked in once more, heightening my magic like kindling to a flame, my buzzing hands bursting with frost. I knew I wouldn't survive the fight without defending myself. I shoved my arms out, throwing a biting surge of wind Marble's way. I watched as his strange eyes grew wide, a scream escaping his lips as he stumbled to regain his balance. It was a small opportunity, but an opportunity nonetheless, so I took it.

Before he could right himself, I took off running again, but the second I turned my back, Marble appeared in front of me in a cloud of smoke. I screamed as he lunged, his eyes glowing brighter than his hands, holding a maniacal flare. The two of us crashed to the ground, me flailing desperately as my lungs drowned in panic. Marble attempted to pin me down. I moved too fast, however, and with a deep exhale of breath, a blast of frostbite flew from my cold lips.

Marble shrieked as his face numbed with a spreading frost that blistered his skin black and red. I recoiled at the sight, gasping as he clawed at his face in an attempt to stop the spread, running his Dust induced fingers down his cheeks, leaving bloody trails dripping from his chin.

His eyes flashed brightly before he clasped his hands around my throat, too quick for me to fight. I could feel the warmth of his blood staining my neck.

"Recognize this?" he growled, locking his fingers, digging them in my flesh.

Instantly, an agonizing burn spread through my body, a burn all too familiar. I screamed in pain, writhing under his touch. The ice vapor in my hands sizzled out, smothered by the unbearable heat. I choked on gasps, failing to draw in even a wisp of air, my chest contracting and expanding violently. Tears burned my cheeks as they fell down my face, steam rising from my eyes.

I clawed at Marble's hands desperately, his warm blood running down my fingers, but he didn't loosen his grasp. Instead, he only squeezed tighter. I tasted death on my tongue, the scent filling my nose, entangling in my hair, soaking my skin as its black cloak began to swallow my vision.

But, as if death had given me mercy, Marble's hands pulled away, leaving air to flow through my chest with another, different burn. My mouth hung agape in shock, the black spots in my vision fading ever so slowly.

Just as I was about to question what happened, a scream ripped through my disheveled thoughts, helping me regain my senses. I clamped my mouth shut, blinking rapidly to rid of the blurry spots floating in my eyes, and the sight that greeted me puzzled me.

It was Marble, but he had stopped moving, towering over me with his lips parted slightly, dull eyes wide, the glow in his hands gone. I blinked once more, and when I opened my eyes again, my gaze darted right to the long, silver sword sticking out of the middle of his chest, the blade mere inches from my face. Marble's blood dripped onto my cheek.

A pair of hands curled around me and pulled me out from under Marble, folding me into their chest so I could no longer see the scene that had just played out in front of me. Out of fear and confusion, I tried pulling away, a twinge of adrenaline returning to the pit of my stomach, but I paused as the person spoke.

"Don't look."

I managed to tear my head away, lifting my chin to see Alexei gazing down at me. A bleeding cut ran down his cheek, and his eyes appeared dazed, but other than that, he seemed untouched. Despite what had unfurled only a few moments before, I felt a wave of relief wash over me and I couldn't stop myself from melting in his arms, dropping all of my weight on him. He supported me entirely.

"She's injured. I don't think she can fight anymore."

Though I was exhausted, and the heat of the Fire Dust still scorched my body, I lifted my head to see who Alexei was talking to. My eyes found Sasha, who towered over the kneeling Marble, still frozen on the crystal floor. The prince's face twisted with a raging fury that marred his once childish features.

I watched as Sasha grasped the hilt of his sword and yanked it from Marble's chest, splattering blood across the floor. He lifted his foot and kicked Marble's back, sending the man crashing in a pool of his own blood. My stomach churned at the sight and I swiveled my head back into Alexei's chest, my own breath seeming louder than the cries of battle around us.

"Can't you order them to stop or something?" Alexei asked, shouting over the excess noise.

"I have no power over anything anymore," Sasha answered, the sound of his footsteps growing closer.

He gently laid his hand on my shoulder but pulled away quickly as I recoiled at the touch. I wasn't sure if I had meant to, or if what I had seen him do contributed to my actions, but soon, even the reassuring hands of Alexei brought a rising fear and disgust to my stomach.

"Are you alright, Ivory?"

"You—you killed him," I said, though it came out as barely a whisper.

"It was either him or you," Sasha responded. His voice had lost its childlike flare. "And I wasn't about to let it be you."

As if sensing my growing discomfort, Alexei eased his tight grasp on me, allowing me to take my own weight once again. Though as I stood, the ground beneath me spun in circles. I stumbled to regain my balance, waving the two off as they stepped forward to help. No matter what, I refused to become a burden after one little attack. I would fight, and keep fighting, until all three of us were safe outside the castle walls.

Or until I died.

"Let's get out of here," Alexei said, his lips quivering. "The wizards are holding their own."

"But—"

"No, Ivory. Whatever you're thinking, just stop. You're in no condition to continue, just let us do the rest."

I opened my mouth to protest, but before I could, his hand gripped my shoulder tight, sending a shock through my body, and he led me into a sprint after Sasha. My feet shuffled pitifully as I ran, Alexei's firm grasp keeping me upright. Sasha remained always paces ahead of us, his crimson-stained sword slicing down whoever got in our way. As my eyes filled with the blood Sasha drew, I realized the childish and naive prince we had met not so long ago was gone, and before me fought not a prince, but a leader. A general. The most justifying general I had ever seen.

As the Magicians attacked, Alexei's fire sent them scrambling to evade us, and while Sasha grew stronger in battle, Alexei grew weaker. It was subtle, but held so close, I could see the way his breath hitched with each blast, the exertion in his eyes, the wince in his face. Dread sank into my chest the longer it went on, and all I wanted to do was cut in, unleash my wrath upon every enemy in the room, but the simple task of keeping my eyes entirely open drained the small amount of energy I had left. My legs shook beneath me, each step more difficult than the last, but I had to keep going. I had to survive long enough to see Alexei and Sasha out. I had to.

But King Cathair had other plans.

His voice thundered like a cannonball, an order of refrain, so loud every Magician and guard faltered. Even the wizards, who appeared fearless just a moment ago, lost their previous ruthlessness. The fight paused, as if holding a breath, watching anxiously as the king finally made his appearance.

He came striding through the doors, flanked by four Magicians on one side and four guards on the other, his face twisted in an ugly snarl that matched his flaring eyes. The scar running down his cheek suddenly seemed a lot more prominent, reminding everyone in the room who he was, and the long sword of gold swinging menacingly at his side seemed to mock each and every wizard. His fists were curled in tight balls, his strides so long and quick, he crossed the floor in a matter of seconds. His armor chinked as he walked, ringing through the once booming battlefield.

Every head turned to see him, every eye redirecting, taking in his sudden and threatening appearance. I felt myself shrinking back and noticed everyone else was too, nobody wishing to get in the way of the king in fear of dire consequences. Everyone except Sasha.

"I've had enough of this!" King Cathair bellowed, his face red with anger, his voice trembling dangerously. "I will not have mutiny in my own kingdom! Who is behind this?"

Sasha immediately cut in front of me. Though the crowd remained silent, a few nervous glances were thrown in my direction. Alexei's clasp on my shoulder tightened, but the action was devoid of its usual reassuring feel.

Instead, it sent an image of my head rolling detached from my body in my mind. I clutched onto my stomach to keep from losing all the contents inside it, my face flushing so pale, it appeared a little green.

"It was me!" Sasha shouted, his grip on his sword unwavering as he stepped toward his father. "I planned this."

"Impossible!" Cathair spat, and without warning swung his hand across Sasha's face, sending him crashing to the ground, the slap reverberating through the room as his sword flew from his hand. "I will not have my own son lie to me!"

Sasha scrambled to his feet, his hand finding the sword he had lost from Cathair's blow, but as he pulled himself up, I glimpsed a flare of hesitation in his eyes. Suddenly, I saw Layton standing in the place of the king, myself in Sasha's. I knew I would never have the strength to tear a blade through my brother's chest, no matter how terrible he had been to me my whole life. I would've rather experienced death by his hand than murder on my own. And despite all the killing Sasha had already committed, having the face of the one who raised him on the other side of the blade was different.

My legs trembled violently, so violently I knew without Alexei's support, I would've already crashed to my knees. Clutched by the thorny hands of fear, my chest heaved as I hyperventilated, the scene before me stealing my breath in the most painful way. I yearned for it to stop, for time to slow just so I could process everything in front of me, just so I could have a second to think, to breathe. The feeling of helplessness was unbearable, and with it came a certain ruthlessness rising up through my panic.

I was willing to do anything to slow time, just to get me that one moment I desired.

"It was me."

A collective gasp rose from the crowd as my frail voice resounded through every ear. King Cathair locked eyes on me, his face displaying death and murder in his expression. I quivered just at the sight of it.

"How dare you return to my palace!" With a single hand, he reached into his scabbard and withdrew his golden sword, the blade shimmering.

"No!" Sasha cried, jumping to block the king.

"Step aside, Sasha." It came out more of a growl through his clenched teeth.

"You'll have to kill me first," the prince replied, spreading his arms wide open as he tucked his sword back in his own scabbard.

Idiot! Don't put away your sword! My thoughts went unheard.

"Don't tempt me, boy."

King Cathair's face showed no sign of hesitation, as did Sasha's, even as the king lifted his sword ever so slowly. Fear gripped onto my chest, the crowd surrounding us buzzing. I knew as soon as Cathair struck, the wizards would engage in full anarchy. Sasha seemed to understand this as well.

"Do it," Sasha urged, his hands still held out, leaving his chest and throat vulnerable.

As Cathair pulled his sword back to strike, I couldn't tell which of the two were bluffing. Or if they were even bluffing at all.

In a flash, Cathair dove, obviously catching Sasha off guard. The prince jumped back, but Cathair's sword never came in contact with his skin, instead slipping right past him. As Sasha stumbled, Cathair grasped onto his collar, shoving him in the hold of the guards behind him. They seized his sword, Sasha flailing, screaming to be released, but his cries went unacknowledged. My stomach dropped as they hauled him out of the king's way.

Alexei held onto me tighter as Cathair returned his fuming gaze to me, his boots echoing menacingly with each step. I watched as Alexei extended his shaking hand, his face contorted with effort before sparks flew from his fingertips. The flame was small, but it was all Alexei had left. He was almost out of time.

Cathair seemed undeterred by Alexei, his expression twisting into one of disturbing bliss.

"Now you, I can kill," he sneered, once again lifting his sword, but this time, I knew he would bring it to use.

Time seemed to slow as the king took his long steps toward us. Alexei's hand loosened on my shoulder, leaving me slipping from his once strong grasp, and despite his glaring eyes, I could feel his fingers trembling, hear breath go short and shallow. The flame in his hand flickered, sinking bac into his palm as if cowering from the oncoming king. I wanted to cowe it.

King Cathair's sword rose high, catching the air between the blad pointed directly to Alexei's chest. I didn't know how I did it, but wit of energy, I launched Alexei out of the way, sending him crashing t floor. I threw my arms out and took his place.

The sword slipped through my chest with ease, mercifully qui a scream in my throat as pain exploded through my stomach, a of stinging and burning I had never felt before. My arms dropp failing underneath me, my breath hitched. My thoughts, which had just been on Alexei, were now transfixed on the agony instead.

A scream tore through my ears, no, multiple screams. Who they belonged to, however, I couldn't distinguish, every voice slurring together in a dreadful ringing. My lips hung open as my body hit the ground with a painful thud. I wrapped my hands around the blade sticking out of my stomach, grunting as I yanked it out and dropped it. When I pulled away, I caught a glimpse of my hands, stained with a warm crimson, and pressed them against where the sword had entered my flesh.

I could hear death's sweet calling like the song of a lark, so relieving, I nearly cried. I wanted to reach out, take death in my arms in an embrace that stole away my pain. But a different calling kept me grounded to life, despite my wish to leave it behind.

"Ivory, no." The voice was almost sweeter than death's, drowning in a pained and melancholy sugar. "Don't you dare die. Please, please, not after I just got you back!"

Though my vision had already gone blurry, lights fading in and out, I tried searching for who the voice belonged to. The voice that could keep me from accepting death's promises. But all I saw through the blur was a distant shine of emerald green.

"Wait, wait, please! Let go—let go of me! Please, she's dying!" The broken words pierced my ears.

My shirt clung to my warm skin, hot liquid soaking through the fabric, piling on the crystal floor beneath me. My breath grew shorter, for each intake hurt more than the last, my lungs crying out for air, but I ignored their pleas. Tears rolled down my cheeks subconsciously, the only release from pain I could find.

I'm . . . dying, aren't I? This is finally it. So many close calls, all for . . . nothing.

I didn't want to lie to myself in my last moments, but I didn't want to admit the rising fear slowly making itself known. I had come so close to death, had felt the graze of its breath on my neck, but this time, I knew that if I closed my eyes, I wouldn't open them again.

So, I tried keeping them open, just for a last few moments, just for my final thoughts, but with the pain coursing through my body, my mind remained blank as ever. The need to rest my heavy eyes grew urgent, almost agonizing to resist.

Just as I felt my eyelashes hit the bags under my eyes, a hush swallowed the wailing screams in my ears, but I lacked the strength to tear them open to see what I had left behind. All I knew that, besides my pain, I had one other notion furrowed deep in the last functioning part of my brain.

I had finally paid off my debt to Alexei Kementari.

A life for a life.

40

The whistle of a train sang in my ears.

I shoved away the darkness crowding my eyes while the sound echoed somewhere beyond my hearing, the distant song calling me, squinting as the light of a candle fire illuminated my skin. I rubbed my eyes, finding my legs while I stumbled forward, inching my way through a long tunnel. With a lack of feeling, I felt weightless, like a feather drifting in the wind. Dulled, my senses did little to lead me.

I emerged from the hall into a kitchen that resembled the same one I grew up with. A cup of cold tea sat in front of my little wooden chair, the countertops just as clean as they were when I left them, the floor still creaking beneath my feet with each shuffle. I barely had the time to question my whereabouts before a voice cut through the deafening silence.

"How long are you going to stand there?"

I snapped my head up, noticing the man sitting on the other side of my chair for the first time. I scowled as I recognized him, his strange eyes, his purple and white cloak, round, jovial face. A cup of tea wrapped in his hand, Marble shot me a knowing look.

"Marble." I took a seat, his name like a curse on my lips. "Does that mean I'm . . ." My face blanched.

"No. Not yet, at least." He sipped from his cup nonchalantly.

"How are you here, then?" I asked, but it came out more like a demand.

Marble shrugged. "I might not really. I might just be a figment of your imagination, or maybe a memory. Gods, I could even be a manifestation of your magic. You never know."

I clasped my mouth shut, a wave of confusion washing over me. I didn't know what else to say, awkwardly watching as the former Magician sipped his tea without a care. He offered no other answer, and the longer we sat in silence, the more I realized he would remain silent as long as I didn't push for conversation.

I said the one thing I could think of. "I'm sorry."

"You're not the one who killed me." Again, he shrugged casually. "I lived a lot longer than you may think. With so much time lost to my own magic, it was well past my time to die. In a way, I should be thanking you, and apologizing."

"Oh." I reached out and grabbed the handle of my cup. I couldn't resist the question rising up in my throat. "How did you know when it was your time to . . . to . . ."

A chuckle escaped his lips. "Oh, you'll know."

"I will?"

He nodded confidently, but his certainty was lost to me, and as he refused to elaborate further, a silence settled in between the two of us once again. I tapped a finger to the wood table just for a source of sound. I nearly jumped when Marble spoke again.

"A part of you did indeed die, however."

My eyebrows scrunched up as his words processed in my hazy mind. "What do you mean?"

Instead of answering, he chuckled once more and ignored me as I asked again. When I asked a third time, irritation laced in my voice, he merely downed the rest of his tea in one gulp and stood, untying his cloak. I watched as he pulled it from his shoulders, setting it down on the chair before he turned away.

"Give Prince Sasha an apology for me, too." He lifted his arm, displaying the back of his hand to me as he began his way out.

"Wait, where are you going? What am I supposed to do?" I cried, panic processing for the first time. Despite my hatred for the wizard, I didn't want to be left alone, especially when it seemed he held all the answers I desired.

"I'm done with this life." He paused to swivel his head just so he could meet my eyes. "But you must stay. They're waiting for you, after all."

Again, he left me no time to question him, disappearing into the shadows of the house. I sat alone, sinking in the sudden silence, gazing blankly at the cloak he had taken off and left behind. The cloak that symbolized who he was, the one he wore so proudly, so loyally.

Somewhere in the distance, another train whistle resounded, far, far away. I thought I heard a voice of strange familiarity.

I pulled myself out from the chair, my feet ready to carry me as I stood.

. . . .

"We can't leave her here! What if she wakes to find all of us gone?"

"She won't. We'll be back before she does."

"How do you know? She could die if we're not here! You want her to die?"

"Would you get a grip? If she just so happens to wake up, the diamond dolls are here."

"Don't bring my dolls into this. She needs us!"

"You mean she needs you?"

"This has nothing to do with me!"

Just as I heard the two bickering voices inhale deep breaths to fuel their next shout, another voice beat them to it, cutting off their next enraged accusation. The voice, like the other two, held a distinct impatience and irritation. His sharp tone made even me want to clasp my mouth shut, even though I hadn't opened mine in the first place.

"Enough, alright?" The speaker released an exasperated sigh before he continued. "You've done nothing but fight ever since we got out of Embrasia! All this fighting is getting us nowhere!"

"What do you propose we do, then?"

"Do you speak to all your friends like that?"

"Would you shut up for one second?"

"Enough!"

I groaned as the third voice rang throughout the air, clutching my hands to my ears. The soft warmth of a blanket grazed my fingers as I moved, helping me realize the presence of the mattress underneath me. The three voices all simultaneously grew dead silent, and I could feel the weight of eyes on the back of my neck.

"Ivory?" For the first time, I realized the voice belonged to Sasha. "Are you awake?"

My answer came out more like a grumble. "Well, now I am."

As the sound of their footsteps grew closer, I fought to pry open my eyes, urging away the haze clogging up my thoughts. My whole body felt heavier than ever before, a weight like a stone sinking in my chest. I gasped for breath as I struggled to pull the blankets away, grinding my teeth while my face twisted in pain. My hand instantly found my stomach, where the cloth of gauze grazed my fingers when I reached under my shirt.

My vision cleared to find three faces peering anxiously over me in dim light. Sasha's golden eyes were plagued by lack of sleep, a bandage wrapped around his forehead. The identical eyes of Francois and Alexei greeted me next with pleading worry. For a second, I forgot the fact Alexei and Francois had not seen each other for years, and it took me a moment to realize how strange it was seeing him.

"Francois?" I rasped, blinking a couple of times just to make sure my blurry vision wasn't deceiving me.

The last I remembered of the wizard was his confident stride from my house in Cyrene, but as I stared up at him in that bed, I didn't recognize anything but his green eyes. He was neither Aven Calvo, the blind man, or the man I had met in the library. Instead, he was a rather short, scraggly young man, his skin as dark as Alexei's and his unruly hair so dark, it nearly appeared purple. Instead of the nice dark outfit I had last seen him in, he wore a simple white button shirt hiding underneath a Prussian blue vest, his trousers brown and his tall boots unlaced. His resemblance to Alexei was almost shocking, though his nose dipped a little more dramatically and his cheeks sunk in slightly more noticeably, but other than that, I could've mistaken them for twins despite their differing hair colors.

"Yes, it's me." A smile slid on Francois' lips, as if excited to finally show his true self to me.

I blinked again, directing my gaze on Alexei. A bandage covered his left cheek, his hair pulled back in an ungainly ponytail that had pretty much fallen apart. By the sight of him, a terrible throb in my chest pounded against my ribs and I hunched forward, wincing. As my senses returned to me, I couldn't fight the oncoming pain from the fight in Embrasia, my body weighing me down with my own exhaustion. I didn't know if my legs would even be able to support the rest of my body if I tried standing, but that wouldn't stop me from trying.

"What happened?" I asked, using one hand to wrap around my torso and the other to hold my aching forehead.

"Francois happened," Sasha replied, earning a glare from Alexei.

"How . . ."

"I told you I've been keeping an eye on you," Francois answered with a quirked eyebrow, a smile playing on his lips. "I thought you might've needed my help; it turns out I was right. And I was almost too late."

"What happened to Cathair?" I questioned with a gasp.

The three shared a look, but it was Sasha who eventually answered. He sat on the edge of the bed, nervously plucking at the threads in the quilt, searching for the right words.

"Well," he cleared his throat, "after you went down, something happened. There was a bright light, and Cathair flew across the room. Francois said it had something to do with, well, with your heart."

"What do you mean?" I asked, confused.

"When Cathair stabbed you, the blade pierced your heart. Well, not really. It pierced the, uh, it—"

"Oh, for the sake of the gods!" Francois cut in. "He hit the spell, but when he hit it, it fought back."

My eyes flung wide open in shock. "Is he ok?"

"He's fine," Sasha assured me. "Without him, we were able to overthrow the guards and Magicians. For now, Cathair's being kept in the dungeon. I . . . I'm in power for the time being."

For the first time, I noticed the golden crown that used to rest atop Cathair's head hanging from Sasha's belt, the diamonds gleaming uselessly. A flash of despair crossed Sasha's face, but with the blink of his eyes, it was gone.

"And, the wizards?" I inquired, leaning forward anxiously.

"They're fine," Alexei replied with a reassuring smile. "They were all sent home or to Naxos with a generous amount of apology gold."

I quirked an eyebrow, a flare of amusement lashing in my heavy stomach. I didn't care to question if apology gold was even a thing, relieved to hear the outcome of my stupid rebellion, but the feeling didn't last long. Flashes resurfaced in my head, the bodies and blood piling on the floor, Marble's slack body, the screams, the king. Everything that I encountered that day threatened to tear my once stable mind. I sucked in a deep breath, urging myself to push away the memories despite them fighting to take over.

My throat tightened, a swell of pain rising in my chest as tears pricked in my eyes. My breath hitched, the aching throb in my body raging. I groaned and clutched onto my chest tighter, releasing short puffs of air as tears slipped down my pale cheeks.

"It hurts," I choked out, trembling. "My—my chest. Gods, it hurts."

Alexei's warm hands found mine, entangling our fingers together. His sweet scent drifted into my nose, and for the first time, I couldn't take the aroma. I lost control of my tears, allowing them to stream down my face shamelessly as I gasped for breath. The three tried calming me down, whispering reassuring promises, but every word was lost to me. The flashes of the rebellion vanished by Alexei's touch, and all that remained in my thoughts was *him*.

Him who I fought so hard to protect, him who I ran to rescue every time he needed, him who I followed without hesitation, him who I found solace in after everything I had been through. I had never known home, but with him by my side, I finally understood. He was my home.

I found his eyes, my shoulders quaking as I sobbed, the swell in my chest rising like the tide. Words formed on my lips, but I didn't know how to say them.

"Alexei." My voice was broken. I reached out and took his face in my hands, and though my eyes swam with tears, he was still clear as ever. My lips formed words that wouldn't come out.

"Ivory," Alexei said as I struggled on my words, slipping from my cold hands, "it's ok. I know."

"No, you don't know," I insisted, babbling. "I—you—I mean, wait, I need to tell you something."

"You don't have to." Alexei withdrew from me, but I grasped onto his sleeve before he could leave. He sucked in a breath. "Please, don't. I'm sorry, Ivory. This is all my fault. All I've done is hurt you, so I understand if you don't want to stay with me anymore."

My stomach dropped and the throb attacked me once again. "No! I can't leave you!"

"Alexei." Francois reached out to his brother, but he waved him off.

"You can. I don't want you anywhere near another fight. You almost died, Ivory, and it could've been all my fault. I can't watch you kill yourself just to protect me," Alexei said, his voice shaking with each word. "You won't understand."

But I did understand. I shared the same desperate urge to keep him safe, no matter what the cost, just the thought of losing him like another stab wound. But I didn't know how to tell him. How was I supposed to let my feelings be known—these feelings that I had never felt before, so strange and foreign in my chest, so heavy, so painful, yet so strong.

"*Alexei*," Francois repeated, his voice sharper, his eyes flicking between me and Alexei.

"What, Francois? What could you possibly say to make this easier?" Alexei snapped, whirling to meet his older brother, his face twisted in both anger and anguish. Though his voice echoed loudly, every word broke like delicate glass.

Francois ignored his outburst, crossing his arms with a soft glare. "You might want to listen to Ivory. I have a feeling she has something really important to say."

I shot a confused look to Francois, but as our eyes met, I noticed a knowing glint in his expression. Almost like he knew what I wanted to say. Almost like he was urging me to say it. I gave him a confident nod of thanks before I addressed Alexei again.

"Alexei." It was a fight getting out of bed, but I didn't want to confess everything like a bedridden child. I wanted to stand before him, strong and proud, no matter how much it hurt. "I didn't let myself be stabbed just to let you go. I didn't start a wizard rebellion, or confront the Highwayman, or face sirens to never see you again. That day I left Cyrene, I didn't know what I was going to find, but I knew I was searching for something. And after all this time, I think I've finally found what I've been looking for."

Alexei's eyes shone as my words filled the space between us. When he spoke again, his voice trembled, but it held a certain feeling to it, a feeling of both defeat and passion.

"Do you really think I'm saying this because I don't want to see you again? I'd stay by your side through death and back if I could."

"Then why are you trying to get rid of me?"

"Because I love you!" Alexei exclaimed, throwing his arms out. He sobered, hanging his head, speaking softly. "And I know you can't understand. I don't want to do that to you, Ivory."

My chest tightened with the proclamation, his words echoing in my head like a chime. Through my shock, a flare of bliss rose up in my body, warm and fuzzy, like a sip of hot cider. I wanted to hear the word again, for once finding that I didn't hate it. No, instead it brought a bubbling glee rising in the pit of my stomach.

Love. He loves me. Alexei Kementari loves me.

In the midst of the moment, Francois cleared his throat purposefully loud, interrupting whatever was going on between me and Alexei. A warm blush rose to my cheeks as I realized both he and Sasha were still present, listening and watching everything.

"Actually," Francois spoke up, a mischievous grin playing at his lips, "she can understand. I probably should've told you this before you started talking, but Ivory has had her heart this whole time."

"What?" Alexei and I both shouted in perfect unison, the once tense moment completely lost to our surprise.

"Do you remember what I told you about breaking the spell, Ivory?" Francois asked.

I nodded. "An act of true love."

"Yes." Francois smiled. "You broke the spell when you traded your life for Alexei's. It was the perfect act of love."

I paused, my eyes growing wide with realization. The throbbing and pounding in my chest weren't the pain of my wound, wasn't exhaustion, wasn't everything else I thought it was.

"You—you mean . . . ," I trailed off as I pressed a hand to my chest, and for the first time since I could remember, a pulse filled my palm. I gasped and pulled away quickly, shivering from the beat.

A shudder of disgust ran up my back, a shudder I couldn't stop. There was something *moving* inside me, pulsing, beating, fluttering, pounding like a bird trapped in a space too small. Something alive. A heart.

My heart.

I met Alexei's gaze frantically, a surge of triumph rising in my stomach despite the disturbing thump-thump-thumping. His green eyes flashed, his anguished expression melting away, replaced with a small smile I could only describe as hopeful.

Finally, I could say it. Finally, I could mean it. Finally, I could *feel* it.

"I love you, too!"

41

"Gods, it's about time!" Sasha exclaimed, throwing his head back dramatically as a smile burst on his face. "You have no idea how long I've waited for you two to do that."

"What?" My cheeks flushed pink as I swiveled my head to face him, my eyebrows shooting up.

"Well, it was so obvious he loved you this whole time, he barely even tried to hide it," Sasha answered. "But Alexei here is just so oblivious, I thought he would never admit it aloud."

"Sasha!" Alexei shouted, a rose tint coloring his cheeks.

The prince's smile grew, a laugh bursting from his lips. I couldn't help but join him. I still wasn't entirely sure how love worked, but I knew it was something I shared with Alexei. Soon, Francois joined in on the laughter, and a few moments later, Alexei couldn't resist a few chuckles as well.

"Since when were you a love expert, Sasha?" Alexei asked, clearing his throat as he tried to hide the small chuckles he had let loose.

"Ever since I met you."

"Oh, hush."

The smile on my lips had seemed to take a permanent place on my face, my cheeks aching from all the sudden grinning, but I still couldn't ignore the real pain in my torso, the pain that wasn't just the heavy weight of my beating heart. I wanted to forget about the king's golden sword, but the stinging of the wound served as a constant reminder.

As the others continued laughing, my hands found my torso once again, my knees buckling from supporting my weight for so long. I stumbled back, sinking on the bed as a wave of dizziness attacked. I groaned under my breath, the smile that I thought permanent fading with quick ease.

"Ivory!" Alexei rushed toward me, his once joyous expression gone. "Are you ok? Let me see."

I pressed against the bandages harder, ignoring Alexei's request. Sharp waves of pain shot through my body like knives in my blood, the room spinning slightly. All traces of laughter disappeared. Sasha and Francois stepped forward quickly, worry drowning in their eyes.

"I'm ok," I mumbled weakly. "Just a bit tired."

"Then rest," Alexei insisted, pulling the covers back. His voice carried a certain urgency in it that made me want to comply, but something kept me from it.

I still hadn't had all my questions answered, and I wasn't going to allow myself to sleep until I knew everything that I wanted to know. Though I knew this was the worst time to be stubborn, I couldn't help but rebel against my body's pleas to shut my eyes and drift off, no matter how painful it was.

"Wait." I blinked a couple of times to rid of the blur beginning to take over my vision.

"What? Do you need anything? Do you need water? I can get you some," Alexei said, but before he could slip away, I caught his sleeve.

"No, I don't want water. I want answers," I said, and I didn't wait for whatever Alexei wanted to remark next. "Where are we?"

"Oh." A frown tugged at Alexei's lips, but he answered nonetheless. "We're back in Andros, in the shop."

"I thought the shop burned down."

"Well, we're in what's left of it. My living room's gone, and half my kitchen, not to mention my staircase might collapse at any minute, but it's good enough. The dolls have been trying to rebuild ever since we left," Alexei explained.

I nodded, finding relief in knowing my whereabouts. I couldn't help but slump back, glad to be back in the city of beautiful lights. I had only stayed one night in the city, but I felt like I had returned to a place I lived in for years. Nothing felt familiar about the walls sheltering me, but instead a certain sense of security I only felt in Andros filled my being.

"Let me get you some water." Alexei stood again, but I snatched his hand this time, quick and tight.

"I heard you arguing earlier," I said, my voice sharp.

Alexei's eyes darkened, his frown slipping into a scowl that he shot Francois. When he parted his lips to answer me, I expected his voice to hold anger, persistence, but instead, his words were soft and gentle, so much that I instantly wanted to listen and comply.

"You weren't meant to hear any of that. It was just something between me and Francois, and us only."

I wanted to accept this answer, to leave it be, but the memory of their voices prevented me from it. Whatever they had been arguing about was important, important enough that they would shout over it, their voices loud enough to call me from my unconscious state. The fact that I hadn't been meant to hear it convinced me to push further.

"You said something about leaving," I persisted. "Where are you going? Why?"

Alexei's face fell, a groan rumbling from his lips. "It's nothing, Ivory. Please, would you get some rest? You're practically falling asleep on me here."

"Am not," I grumbled, though the tug of sleep had grown increasingly strong, yanking its taut rope with every passing second. "Is this about your brothers? Please, tell me."

I could tell he was going to decline again, but before he could, Francois spoke up.

"She deserves to know, Alexei. You out of all people should understand."

Alexei's once soft expression disappeared, and with deliberate drama, he whirled around to meet Francois, his hands on his hips. "You mean like how you told her everything?"

"I wasn't going to send her back to Embrasia without telling her. She's a part of this just as much as we are," Francois replied, clenching his fists as he fought back a glare.

"No, she's not!" Alexei cried, a faint shadow of smoke rising from his body. He threw his arms out, taking a step toward his brother. "Nothing about this whole situation is about her. This is about us and them."

"You know that's not true," Francois snapped, his face pinched in a glare that rivaled Alexei's. "Ever since we cast that spell, it wasn't just about us anymore."

"And who's fault is that, huh?"

"You think I wanted them to cast the spell?"

"Well, you didn't do much to stop them!"

"Look what happened to you when you tried!"

"Enough!" Sasha and I cried at the same time, our voices filling the air between us.

The brothers paused and backed off, arms crossed like they were small children. If we were in a different situation, I might have laughed.

"I'm tired of all this fighting!" Sasha exclaimed, stepping in between Alexei and Francois, holding a glare of his own. "Do you have any idea how much time we've wasted because of you two?"

"Sasha—" Alexei began, but the prince cut him off with the sharp uplifting of his hand.

"No. This isn't just about you, Alexei. We're all in this together." He stopped to give the slightest of smiles to Francois. "I don't care how dangerous this will be, I'm not letting you go off on your own."

"Hey, Ivory here," I cut in before anyone could fit in another word. "Is anyone going to tell me what you're talking about, or will I have to guess?"

"Tell her, or I will," Sasha said to Alexei as he folded his arms across his chest.

Alexei pursed his lips before releasing a long sigh of defeat, his shoulders slumping slightly. When he turned to meet my gaze, I saw clear hesitation on his face. So much hesitation got my heart beating faster, and the feeling was not as simple as all the books described it.

"I thought you would be safer if you didn't know, but I know that's unfair. Especially after everything." He sighed once more, then reached into his coat and pulled out a folded piece of paper. "This arrived at dawn."

I accepted the paper, gingerly taking it in my hands, and unfolded it carefully. One word was written on the paper in messy black ink, splatters filling the white space.

Auxilium.

I glanced up at Alexei, my eyebrows furrowed together in confusion. It clearly wasn't my language, and just by one word, I couldn't tell which language it was. Unease dripped into the pit of my stomach as I read the word once more.

"What . . . what does it say?" I asked, my voice light and apprehensive.

"It says," Alexei released a breath, "help."

I winced as his answer entered my ears. Something told me it would mean something like that.

"Who's it from?"

"We have an idea, but it doesn't make much sense," Alexei answered, taking the one-word note from my hand and tucking it back in his coat pocket.

"What do you mean?" I asked, shaking my head.

Alexei's eyes flitted away from my gaze. "Well, Francois and I think it's from . . ."

Francois didn't wait for him to finish his sentence. "Mercedes."

I caught a gasp, the name of another Kementari catching me off guard. I knew little about Alexei's older brothers, Valentin and Mercedes, but what I did know had long planted a spike of unease in me. Alexei had tried hiding the fact he even had brothers for the longest time. Knowing that they had sealed my fate with their curse, I wished I had known of their names way earlier.

"Mercedes?" I tested the name in my mouth. "But why would he be asking for help? Especially from you."

"We don't know, Ivory," Francois answered, a frown tugging at his lips. His eyes were plagued by something more than just lack of sleep. "And there's no way of knowing unless we go find him."

"And here's where the arguing starts," Sasha muttered under his breath with a sigh.

"Let's say we answer his call." Alexei whirled to face Francois, an obvious scowl fighting to take over his face. "We find him, everything's all peachy, and then, before we know what's going on, he and Valentin are ripping our hearts apart!"

"But what if he really needs us? What if they've been found by those Magicians? What if this is the king's doing?" Francois countered.

In the corner of my eye, I saw Sasha wince, stepping back with a pained expression. Clearly, this sounded like something Cathair wouldn't hesitate to do.

"Cathair's in his own prison, where we put him and where he'll stay," Alexei insisted. "This is exactly what they wanted!"

"What is?"

"What you're doing right now!" Alexei cried, throwing an extended finger at his brother. "They want us to question and worry until we've thought up a bunch of ridiculous scenarios. They want to lure us into a trap!"

"But what if it's not? What if he's in real danger? What if he really needs our help?"

"I think we should go, Alexei," Sasha piped up, his face set with determination. "Don't you want to make amends?"

"Amends?" Alexei's eyes flared with anger. "The last time I saw them, they had half my heart in their hands. They've forced me to live with diminishing magic all these years, and now, you want me to *help*? Even if Mercedes did need help, I still wouldn't go. You want to know why? It's because nothing he can do will convince me he deserves my help after what they did to me!"

Before Francois or Sasha could fight back, I reached up and grabbed Alexei's sleeve, squeezing his arm tightly. "Alexei, I know how you feel, believe me, but ignoring a cry for help makes you just as bad as they were. You need to let go of the past, because that's the only thing keeping you from possibly regaining your family."

"But—"

"Please," I squeezed tighter, my eyes burning in his, "don't ruin your chance to forgive them. Don't ruin your chance for a family. It might be too late to fix mine, but you could still have yours. Don't let this chance go."

I could see Alexei's thoughts jumble in his eyes as he clasped his lips shut. I let his arm go slowly, running my hand down his sleeve until my hand found his. For a second, I thought I had made a mistake, but as I began to pull away, he gripped my hand tight, sending a rush of warmth through my body.

"Ivory," he grumbled.

"Go, Alexei. Help Mercedes before it's too late. I know you want to put this all behind you. I know you want to live without being paranoid. Go."

Alexei was silent for a long moment.

"Alright, I'll go." He released a sigh, while a smile burst on Francois' face.

As Alexei's head dipped, I found I wanted to hold his hands in mine, pull him close to me, anything to reassure him like how he always reassured me. My face flushed with heat by the sudden urge, an urge so foreign to me, yet so strong. It was unfamiliar, but somehow, it felt right.

Before I could convince myself against it, I quickly pressed my cold lips to Alexei's cheek. His head shot up as I rushed to pull away, my face glowing with a red tint. My heart hammered in my chest like a pesky bird trapped in a cage, and all I wanted to do was wrap a tight hand around it to suppress the raging pounds. But for the first time since I could remember, my heart wasn't still despite my wishes.

"Ivory," Alexei breathed, holding a hand to his cheek. Once again, I thought I might've done the wrong thing, but barely a second passed before his once defeated face beamed, a dopey grin spreading across his cheeks.

I nearly slumped in relief, anxious tension falling from my shoulders, a smile finding its way to my lips. I chuckled nervously, willing myself to ignore the stinging pain in my abdomen.

A laugh escaped his lips. "What was that?"

I tried to keep the confusion from my face. "You just looked like you needed one."

Again, he laughed, full and hearty, and I was glad to get rid of his dark attitude, an attitude that didn't suit his face, a face that seemed perfectly sculpted for smiles.

"Well, then thank you, my brave knight," he said, dropping in a dramatic and humorous bow that brought laughter to my lips.

"Anything for my wizard in distress." I gave a wide grin, practically beaming, my heart fluttering wildly.

"As much as I don't want to break whatever *this* is," Sasha interrupted, "I think we should set off."

Our smiles dropped, the light atmosphere ruined.

"You're right," Francois said, nodding. "We shouldn't disturb Ivory with all this. She needs to rest."

"What?" I exclaimed. "I'm coming with you! I'm not staying here!"

The three men looked at me like I had gone crazy.

"Ivory, you can't possibly expect us to let you come with. You can barely cross this room, let alone travel to Naxos," Francois said, his voice firm.

"I can!" I cried, and slipped from the bed, grinding my teeth as I stood. "I'm fine. I—" With a sharp spasm of pain in my stomach, I lurched forward, clutching around my torso with a groan.

"You can't." Alexei practically forced me back under the covers. "You just got stabbed, for the gods' sake! I know you don't like staying in one spot for too long, but please, promise me you won't leave this bed until we get back."

"But—"

"Promise me!"

I clasped my mouth shut, practically glowering. "Fine. I promise I'll stay here and be useless." I turned my head stubbornly as he tried to console me, but I refused to listen.

One part of me knew I was being irrational, but I couldn't help the anger boiling in my stomach. I wanted to confront the Kementari brothers just as much as Francois, but thanks to that blasted king, instead I would stay far away, in Andros with an agonizing wound in my stomach, lying helplessly for hours to come. And though I wanted to take Francois' word for it, I still couldn't help but agree with Alexei.

What if it truly was a trap?

"If we're not back by sunset, I want you to find help," Francois said, knocking me from my thoughts.

I turned to meet his eye. "Who? If you haven't noticed, I haven't made a lot of allies recently."

The three paused, their faces falling as they realized what I meant.

"Cecil," Sasha eventually piped up.

"Or Furn," Alexei added uncertainly.

I huffed. *I can't believe they're leaving me with the safety of the boy I barely know, and* Furn.

"But you won't need to," Francois said. "Everything will go smoothly, and we'll be back before sunset. Get some rest, let yourself heal."

I frowned, resisting the urge to cross my arms as I nodded unenthusiastically. "Fine, just . . . be careful."

"Of course." Francois nodded, and as Alexei and Sasha lingered, he left the room without a second glance back to me.

And just like that, it was just like before, the three of us alone together, an impending doom weighing down on us. Except this time, I wouldn't be able to join the fight.

Sasha stepped forward, fiddling with the hilt of his sword. "Ivory, I . . . I'm sorry."

"What are you apologizing for?" I tilted my head, eyebrows knitted together.

"My father. The Magicians. My whole kingdom," he replied. "And anything else on the list."

I allowed a smile to slip onto my face despite the situation. "None of that is your fault. You have no need for apologizing."

"But—"

I held up a hand to silence him. "You're my friend, Sasha. I know you would've never let any of that happen if you had a choice."

The corners of his lips twitched up, relief washing over him. "Thank you, Ivory."

"Just promise me you'll come back," I said with a sudden seriousness, my eyes narrowed.

"Nothing will keep me from it," Sasha responded, a confident grin spreading across his cheeks. He reached out and I took his hand, my smile returning as he gave it a tight squeeze. "I may not love you the same way Alexei does, but I do still love you. Remember that, ok?"

I nodded, hoping I hid my confusion well. I guessed I still had a lot more to learn about love than I thought. Sasha let go of my hand, slipping from the room with one last little wave to me. I didn't miss the wink he sent Alexei.

As he left, he also seemed to take away our conversation skills. Not a word passed either my lips, or Alexei's. I waited for him to say something, but instead, he kept his mouth shut, his eyes wandering.

"Alexei," I said, mostly just to break the tense and awkward silence, "will you be ok?"

"I'll be fine," he answered quickly, "don't worry about me. Don't worry about anything."

I shook my head, a chuckle bursting from my lips. "You know I can't do that. Worrying is my middle name, after all."

"No, it's not. It's—" He paused as he realized he didn't know.

I let loose one more chuckle. "Come back to me in one piece and I'll tell you."

"Then I'll do whatever it takes." Finally, a smile found its way to his lips. "But you better be in one piece as well."

I dramatically glanced down at my torso. "Oh, me? I'll be fine. Nothing better than a refreshing stab." I mimed jabbing a knife in the air, which sent Alexei losing his resolve to hide his laughter.

"Alright, alright." He fought to rid his face of joy. "I'm serious."

I extended my hand out for him, warmth spreading through my cold fingers as he took it in his. I brought his hand to my lips, bestowing an icy kiss on his skin. "I'm serious, too. Come back to me, ok?"

"I will." He nodded. A sigh escaped his lips. "I'd go to Cyrene and back a hundred times if I had to."

I wanted him to stay, cursing myself for convincing him to go. I wanted the moment to last forever, his hand in mine, his eyes only on me. If I could've, I would've tucked him somewhere safe and comfortable, perhaps my pocket, so I could carry him around wherever. Or perhaps I wanted to be the one in his pocket. Whatever the case, all I wished was one more minute, but it seemed the gods couldn't spare it.

Alexei slipped from my grasp, even as I held tighter. "I should go. They're waiting. The diamond dolls will help you with whatever you need, don't hesitate to ask."

Don't go. "Ok."

I watched him turn and stride out the door, but before he disappeared, he swirled his head around, his eyes finding mine. "I love you, Ivory Morrow."

I opened my mouth to cry for him to stay, but he was already gone, closing the door behind him, leaving me tethered to a bed by a king's sword. Grinding my teeth, I clambered from the sheets, groaning with each step. I nearly collapsed on the door, resting my ear against the wood. Their voices were almost impossible to make out, but with a childhood of eavesdropping, I managed.

"You got your sword?" Francois was asking.

"And a dagger."

"Good. Alexei, do you have that spell I told you to find?"

"Right here."

Francois sighed. "Then I think we're ready."

My heartbeat accelerated as I continued to listen to them finish their last-minute packing, and I thought my heart might've actually stopped for a moment the second the front door opened. The slam echoed in my ears, and despite how hard I leaned into the door, their voices couldn't be heard.

With a shaky breath, I cracked the door open, stepping into what was once Alexei's main room, now worn down to scorched wood and bare floor. It seemed the fire had swallowed Alexei's couch, desk, rug, hat stand, and about almost anything else that used to be there. I caught a gasp in my throat as I gazed upon Alexei's home.

"I knew you wouldn't stay put."

I jumped, which resulted in a sharp pain shooting up my chest. As I winced, biting down on my tongue to keep from crying out in pain, I glanced around to find the source of the light voice. My eyes found Francois.

"Francois," I said through clenched teeth, "I—I'm not—"

"Don't worry," he chuckled, "I won't tell Alexei. Take this." He threw a small vial my way, which I nearly didn't catch.

"What is it?"

"It should help the pain, but only until sunset. We'll be in Naxos, Enderrial Chateau, at the bridge of Nerandeux."

I blinked as the names became a jumble in my mind. "What are you—"

"The back entrance is hidden by vines and thistleburn bramble. More covered that way." With that confusing notion, he sent me a wink and vanished from the house.

I gazed, dumbfounded, where he once stood, questioning every word that had left his lips. I snapped from my stupor to glance down at the vial in my hands, glowing an intimidating purple, the liquid bubbled and churned.

"What in the name of the goddesses above?" I mumbled, turning the bottle over a few times through my fingers.

"I was told it doesn't taste very good." Another voice entered my ears, one that rang vaguely familiar. "But that shouldn't stop you from drinking it."

I whirled to find a little man sitting atop one of the shelves that were still intact, lounging over it like it were a sofa. I nearly choked on his name.

"Vince!" I cried, smiling. Never had I thought I would be so happy to see the chatterbox again, but something about him reminded me of someone else I knew. I held up the bottle for him to see. "Do you know what this is?"

"Yes. It's just as Francois said," the diamond doll responded with a simple nod. "I would plug your nose when you drink it, though. I've seen that potion once, when Alexei got caught up in a fight. He nearly threw it back up."

I resisted the urge to smile at the story, instead uncorking the bottle, keeping myself from letting its scent enter my nose. I clasped my eyes shut, threw my head back, and dipped the bottle over my lips, glad to have something to relieve the pain that held me back so.

I almost instantly regretted it, however, as the liquid fell down my throat like a combination of slime and mud, rancid like curdled milk. I forced myself to swallow before I could spit it out, my face puckered up in disgust. I gagged, afraid it would be me who threw the potion back up. But I kept it down despite it making my face glow green with sickness.

I let loose a curse word Layton definitely wouldn't approve of, shoving the cork back on the bottle as I wiped my lips, one last shudder running up my back.

"That was pleasant," I mumbled sarcastically, rising from my hunched form, my lips pursed together.

"How do you feel?" Vince asked, leaning precariously off the shelf.

I opened my mouth to respond, but as soon as my lips formed a word, a strange sensation bubbled up in my stomach. I coughed, stumbling a few steps in shock. With each step, more strength seeped into my muscles, my hazy thoughts cleared, the irresistible pain caused by the wound fading away. Drawing in breath soon became easy and pain-free, the dizziness disappearing like a flame in the wind. All the pain, gone.

Upon seeing my stunned face, Vince chuckled. "Worth the taste, don't you think? Too bad it'll only last until sunset, though you do have all day. You know, that's just enough time to get to Naxos."

Suddenly, with a clear mind, I realized what Francois had done.

"Vince, I need a weapon. And trousers."

42

Alexei

My hand still tingled with Ivory's kiss as I clasped onto the hilt of my dagger. I didn't want to imagine having the need to put the blade to use, but a sinking feeling in my stomach spoke unsettling words that said otherwise.

In Naxos, the smell of sweet magic filled the air like smoke, delicious smoke, but smoke, nonetheless. Even with my failing heart, flames sparked from my fingertips just by the aroma, and when I glanced over to Francois, I found his dark hair dancing with bright flames. He controlled it quickly, ushering the flames away with a simple swipe of a hand, while Sasha and I watched in awe. Suddenly, Sasha's trusty sword that had saved our lives in Embrasia seemed useless.

I swallowed roughly, attempting to contain my fear as we neared the bridge of Nerandeux. Perhaps if I prayed hard enough, the bridge would collapse under our feet. But, when we arrived, I found the bridge constructed from the same strong stained glass it seemed the rest of Naxos was made from, the colors swirling in the dawning sun, the shine mocking the crystal shimmer of Embrasia.

The design of the Wizard City reminded me far too much of the Embrasian castle, like the wizards had purposely created a colorful version of Embrasia. It seemed it left the same effect on Sasha, who had fallen silent the second we first glimpsed the massive gates of Naxos.

"There's Enderrial Chateau," Francois announced with a slight quiver to his voice.

The giant chateau was impossible to miss, spanning at least an acre or two long, and I dared to think it might've been only slightly shorter than the Embrasian castle. The stained-glass windows gleamed with deep blues and crimsons, like a sea swallowing a sunset, encircling in entrancing patterns of stars and swirls. The architecture was beautiful, a work of art brought to life in front of my very eyes, but my dwindling heartbeat stole my ability to gawk for long.

"You—you live there?" Sasha sputtered, the first words that had passed through his lips since we entered the city. I hoped I was at least hiding my shock better than him.

"Says the one who lived in a castle his whole life. Let's go," Francois replied dismissively, but the closer we grew to the chateau, the shakier my older brother seemed. His strides became slow and hesitant, his fingers spurring with nervous ash. I almost pitied him. Almost.

His nerves only encouraged mine. I was so close to turning around and dragging Sasha out with me, back to Andros, back to the person who needed us most. I couldn't believe I had left Ivory while she had to endure the pain of a stab wound alone. I grimaced at the thought of her struggling for each breath, her shaky hands, and weak legs. She had grown so strong in my presence and seeing her in such disarray sent my heart plummeting.

"We'll make ourselves unannounced, for now. There's an entrance at the back that nobody uses anymore," Francois said, his wavering fingers tugging at the cloak around his shoulders.

It's almost like he knows we'll be attacked. I kept my mouth shut despite the words bubbling up my throat. We had already argued on the train ride to Naxos as I tried to convince him we were most definitely heading to our doom.

"You know we can't take them if they attack," I had said to Francois while he was actively trying to ignore me. "They're stronger than you, my heart's failing, and Sasha has no magic."

Francois plucked at a loose thread in the train cushion. "If we can avoid Valentin, we'll be fine."

"Wait, wait," Sasha cut in. "You mean, we'll really get attacked? I thought this was a rescue mission. I would've brought a bomb or something if I knew we were actually fighting crazy wizards."

"He's not crazy!" Francois cried. "Valentin isn't gone yet. There's still a piece of the old him somewhere in his heart."

"And if there's not?" I questioned.

Francois tensed. He disregarded my question, which served as the answer. If Valentin couldn't regain control, we were as good as dead. Francois knew. I knew. And now, Sasha knew.

In my pocket, I carried a talisman, a mere spell of protection, but it was all I had left. I wished I had a disguise spell or at least an enhance spell, but I had been running low for quite some time, and with the fire, most of my remaining spells burned to ash.

As I glanced apprehensively to Francois while we clambered over overgrown shrubs and vine stalks, my longing to run heightened. With his uncanny resemblance to my mother, I didn't know if I would be able to turn my sword on him, if I needed to. Trust was a dwindling thing in my mind, and growing smaller still, but I wanted to believe he was on my side. Ivory's words replayed in my ears.

Don't ruin your chance for a family. It might be too late to fix mine, but you could still have yours.

How could I fix mine if they didn't want it to be fixed? If they would've rather seen me mangled and dead? Still, her words struck a chord in me. Though my mother was gone and my father nowhere to be seen, my brothers truly were my only family left. I knew I should've been doing whatever it took to get them back, but the fear of the last time I had seen them kept me from it.

I was so young, wearing Francois' hand-me-down coat that was two sizes too big for me. Nothing had been more painful than the way Valentin extracted my heart right from my chest, and I never forgot the empty dullness where my heart had just previously been. I loved Ivory's cold kisses, but I couldn't help but compare them to that moment when my whole body went numb without the warmth of my heart.

And if I didn't get back what they had stolen, I would soon experience that cold again. The thought sent a shiver up my back and I grasped onto my dagger tighter.

"Thistleburn," Sasha muttered beside me.

"What?"

"Thistleburn," he repeated, his eyes wide. "I've never seen it before in real life."

"It's just a bush." I shrugged. "Watch out for the thorns."

Francois pushed the vines away, revealing a concealed door that blended in with the rest of the mural on the walls. Sasha and I stepped through the thistleburn bramble, stumbling around the thorns, glaring over our shoulders as Francois called to us to be careful.

He caught up with us, making a face as thorny vines lashed across his cheeks, and reached out for the knob.

"Ready?"

Why does he have to sound so unsure?

"Let's just get this over with," I grumbled, displaying a countenance of indifference despite my pounding heart and spinning thoughts. How I yearned for my indifference to be real.

Francois' eyes flickered over me, as if searching for my hidden thoughts, and with a deep breath, gave his attention to the doorknob. His wrist moved painfully slow, inching the door open with the slightest push. The door slipped silently, revealing walls of stone and marble, tile floors shining with enough polish to coat the floors of the Embrasian castle two times over. Standing guard along the walls, statues of gods and goddesses perched upon tall, gold pillars glared down at us, their marble faces displaying unwelcome. The ceiling curved in archways, torches illuminating the hall.

My jaw nearly dropped because of the magnificent sight. While I had been forced to hide and run my whole life, fear and paranoia breathing down my neck, my brothers were living it up like kings themselves in lavish comfort. How had they possibly attained such a home?

Just as I began to express my confusion, Francois gestured to a sudden curve in the hallway between two weapon-wielding gods. I shuddered under their scowling faces as Sasha and I followed him like children following the pied piper. It killed me that I allowed him to lead me further and further into his home, my hand twitching to use the blade so tightly clasped in it. Next to me, the ruthless warrior Sasha had been during the Embrasian rebellion was nowhere to be found, instead, the nervous prince I had first met walked by my side. His knuckles flushed white as he gripped onto his sword.

I wished I had some way to reassure my unlikely friend, but I was in no position to pretend I wasn't just as afraid as he was. Weaving through halls and doors, we blindly tread the heels of Francois, ready to throw desperate attacks at any second, at anyone. I urged myself to ignore the beautiful glass windows, lifelike statues, and intricate design of architecture, my heart pounding faster and faster with each step that brought me closer to my brothers, who I had spent the last twelve years hiding from.

"Where are we going?" Sasha spoke up, and though his voice trembled, I could sense a type of strong irritation. "You're not leading us right to a trap, are you?"

"What?" Francois gasped. "Of course not! I thought you were on my side!"

"I'm not on anyone's *side*," Sasha spat.

"Then why—"

Before he could finish his sentence, a crash resounded through the hall. All three of us paused as a groan sounded from behind one of the many doors. We caught each other's gazes and rushed toward the door the voice came from behind.

Though I would've gone with the more subtle approach, Francois burst through the door, his hands aflame like fireworks, a battle cry on his lips. Sasha and I drew our weapons, following after him, but as we jumped through the threshold, we found Francois had paused, his eyes directed on something. I searched for what had so intently caught his eye and froze, a gasp caught in my throat.

Struggling to climb to his feet, a young man with incredibly dark hair, tan skin, and dim green eyes clutched his arms around his torso, his face twisted in pain. Though I hadn't seen him in twelve years, I felt like not a day had passed since I last saw him.

"Mercedes!" Francois cried, sprinting to meet our brother. He dropped to his knees beside Mercedes, wavering hands hovering over him. "Mercedes! What happened? Talk to me! Are you alright?"

My stomach dropped, the color in my face seeping away. I couldn't believe it. Francois had been right all along. It wasn't a trap. Mercedes really did need our help.

I ran to join Francois' side, taking a knee in front of my older brother. His forehead gleamed with sweat, his elegant mahogany vest wrinkled, his collar torn from his neck. Pathetic groans escaped his lips as Francois shook him, and I almost forgot he had tried murdering a child in her bed when he was twelve.

He pried his eyes open, eyes almost identical to mine, and through his pain, a look of confusion washed over his features.

"Lexi?" he sputtered through gritted teeth. He slowly pulled a hand from his torso and extended it to my face. "Lexi."

I waited for some type of attack, some dark magic to rip my cheek open, but instead, his fingers simply brushed against my skin before his hand fell limply back to his stomach. I released a breath I hadn't realized I had been holding.

"I'm sorry," he breathed out. "I'm sorry. Lexi, I . . ."

"Let's get him out of here," I said and moved to wrap my hands under his arms. "Are you going to just watch, or do you want to help?"

Francois snapped out of his daze, quickly assisting me lug Mercedes up. I heaved under his weight. Clearly, he had eaten as many cakes as he wanted over the past twelve years, yet his cheeks appeared sunken in, his bones protruding through his outfit.

He lived in a place grand enough to rival the Embrasian castle, his clothes more expensive than anything I could ever afford, yet his body seemed to match one of a neglected prisoner. His apology rang in my ears like a bell, his frail voice rebounding through my head mockingly. After all he had done, everything he had put me through, a simple sorry should've been nowhere near enough for me to forgive him. And yet, I still couldn't help the sinking guilt in my stomach for wanting to ignore his message.

A hiss escaped his lips as we pulled him up, his legs trembling as he tried supporting his own weight. Francois and I held on tighter, wrapping his arms around our shoulders. His head rolled, his chin hitting his chest.

He spoke, using the rash language Mom had taught all four of us when we were young. "*Auxilium* . . . Valentin."

"Valentin needs help, too?" Francois asked quickly. "Nod if that's what you meant."

Mercedes didn't nod. "*Effugium* . . . *ante* . . . Valentin."

Escape before Valentin.

Before we could react to his words, the door flew open behind us, and standing in the doorway, with the same shrunken figure, ebony locks, and disheveled waistcoat, the eldest of all four of us brothers stood, his eyes glowing a bloody crimson.

Valentin.

Suddenly, I realized what Mercedes had been trying to say. His words were meant to be a warning. Fear like no other crawled into my chest, wrapping around what was left of my heart in a painful embrace.

Valentin's lips curled into a sneer as he entered, striding casually toward us. "Well, if it isn't Alexei and the prince. Or, should I say king?"

His voice triggered a stream of memories that rushed back to me like a flood. I saw the four of us messing with a stray cat, sneaking it inside when our mother's back was turned. I recalled countless games and songs we made up to fill our time. I saw our secret hiding place in the attic, remembering the code names Valentin had assigned us. He was always Val, Mercedes was Des, Francois was Fran, and I was Lexi. As clear as glass, I could see the room we shared in our youth, our beds hanging in mid-air because of a spell gone wrong.

I blinked, shaking the repressed memories away. The Valentin I remembered was nothing like the one who stood before me. The Valentin I remembered was gone.

Francois let go of Mercedes, leaving me to support all of his weight, while he stepped in front of the three of us. He threw his arms wide open in an attempt to keep Valentin from coming any further.

"Leave them alone!" he shouted. "Or else."

Valentin's eyes sparked with excitement at the threat. "Or else what? You think you can beat me? If Mercedes couldn't, then how do you think you can?"

"You did that?" Francois sounded a little breathless, his voice broken. "Why, Valentin? Why can't you just forget—"

"Why? *Why?*" The spark of excitement disappeared terrifyingly fast, replaced by a dangerous scowl that took over his whole face. He threw a finger at me. "He betrayed me, Francois! Just like Mom! Just like Dad! And now, just like you and Mercedes."

"Take a look in the mirror, Valentin! Have you seen yourself lately? Your magic has eaten you alive! If you don't stop this, it'll kill you!" Francois cried. "I'm trying to help you. *We're* trying to help you!"

"I don't need—" But before he could finish his sentence, Sasha threw himself forward, sword raised.

Sasha swung at the wizard, and he would've actually hit him if Francois hadn't intervened. He jumped after Sasha, holding him back with a desperate cry. Valentin's eyes grew wide as he stumbled slightly, but the falter didn't last long. His fists burst aflame, aiming straight for Sasha.

"Sasha!" I screamed, but it was too late.

The blast flew across the room like a bullet, hitting Sasha square in the chest. The new king flew backward, collapsing to the floor in an unmoving heap just a few feet away from me.

Francois gasped, his guard completely down while Valentin aimed for him next. A surge of panic shocked my body into action. I lifted a hand, sending a stream of fire Valentin's way, the attack more difficult than ever before. I gasped from the effort of using just a little magic.

"Francois!" I cried, using the one second I had bought him to alert him.

Francois whirled to meet Valentin, his hands sparking as he charged. Though everything in my being told me not to take my eyes off the fight, I ignored the blaring warnings as I practically threw Mercedes to the couch behind me and rushed to Sasha's side. Dread intertwined with my panic, an awful weight in my stomach threatening to overwhelm me. But I knew I had to stay in control. I had to stay focused if I wanted to get us out alive.

"Sasha, get up. You have to get up." I shook him violently until a groan escaped his lips.

"Alexei?" he whispered. "Gods, I thought you were my grandma for a second there."

Of course, even close to death, Sasha's humor still remained. I wasn't sure if I should've been glad or clonked him myself.

"Don't go toward the light," I said as I pulled him up to his feet. He stumbled a bit but held his weight a lot better than Mercedes. "You're stupid, you know."

"Oh, yeah, I know." He nodded. His eyes rolled back, and he fell from my grasp, hitting the floor with a thud.

I scrambled to pick him up again, but a sudden shriek stopped me short. I glanced up to find Francois pinned by his neck, thrown against the wall with flaming hands.

"Fight me, Francois!" Valentin screamed and slammed him over and over to the wall. "I know you're stronger than this! Fight, you pathetic coward!"

I winced as I watched, urging Francois to fight back, but he did no such thing. He allowed Valentin to continue bashing his head against the wall. Even when a splatter of blood painted the wall, Francois refused to fight back. I realized, with a sinking dread, he was doing it on purpose. He wasn't going to fight back.

"I can't!" Francois shouted. A stream of tears fell from his twisted face. All of a sudden, another memory hit; Francois crying when he skinned his knee on the pavement. Valentin had slung him on his shoulders and carried him home, attempting to make him laugh. "You're my brother, Valentin! I can't fight you!"

My heart swelled, but Valentin gave no reaction, only slamming him once more. I watched in despair as Francois crumpled to the floor, blood dripping from the back of his head, his throat burned by Valentin's hands. Valentin prepared for one last blow, but before he could deliver it, I lunged at him.

My hands exploded in a last effort of weak magic as I threw a punch at my older brother's face, but he dodged me with terrifying ease, my flames just barely licking his cheek. I groaned slightly as I felt my heart skip a couple of beats. My fingers buzzed for more power, but I couldn't give it to them.

"After all these years," Valentin cried, "you finally return! And for what? To fight me?"

I bit back an insult. "What do you think you'll accomplish by killing us? Without us, you'll be alone. Truly alone."

"Good!" he screamed, and shot toward me, dangerous red flames rising from his skin. "All three of you betrayed me!"

With breath caught in my throat, I whirled to evade Valentin's oncoming blast, the heat nipping my skin. I stumbled, and with a grunt of exertion, called upon a small flame. All that was left of my magic.

I flung myself at him and the two of us crashed against the floor. He screamed as my pathetic flame scorched his face, and before I could dodge it, a hurtling blast shot at me.

I shrieked and scrambled away as my coat caught fire. I tore it off, my chest heaving, my skin blistering with the heat. Valentin jumped to his feet, already in a fighting stance, his hands sparking with his next attack. I wasn't sure how much longer I could've held him off on my own, but Sasha and Mercedes were unconscious, and Francois was bleeding from his head having already admitted he couldn't fight Valentin. I was alone, and my magic had run dry. A chill had already started to sink into my chest. Wouldn't be long until it swallowed my heart.

I needed help. Or, I needed to stall.

"That was my favorite coat, you know," I said through heaving gasps. Anything to give me time, no matter how stupid it made me look. My magic had completely dulled, a prickly cold seeping into my bones. My heartbeat had slowed dramatically, not half as fast as it should've been. I was running out of time. I needed to regain the other half of my heart. It was now or never.

I reached into my pocket and pulled out my last talisman, holding it up so Valentin could see. Out of anyone, he would know the power of a talisman. He would know the destruction a simple spell could cause. It was the first thing our father had taught us.

"I'll give you one chance to stand down, or else this whole building comes down with all of us in it."

Valentin's hands remained aflame, his face still twisted in a glare, but he didn't throw another fireball. "You wouldn't."

"Would I?" I grasped onto the paper for show, causing Valentin's face to fall for a split second. A flicker of triumph rose in my chest. "Let's make a deal. You give me my heart, and I won't destroy your house."

To my ultimate dread, a smirk slipped on Valentin's lips. "So that's what you're here for. Little Lexi wants his heart back. Well, you should have thought of that before you sided with Dad."

"I didn't side with Gethan!" I exclaimed. "Listen to yourself! How does killing a little girl justify what Gethan did? I only wanted to fix your mistake."

"My mistake?" He scoffed. "The only mistake I made was not killing you that day. You've hidden long enough, Alexei, but I've finally found where you've been all these years. I know where you're keeping her."

I bit back the fear that rose up in my throat, willing myself to keep my tone steady. "I don't know what you're talking about. I never saw that girl again."

A snicker escaped Valentin's lips. "You've always been such a terrible liar. She's managed to hide for twelve long years, but one fateful night, I finally found her. I sent the Incarti after her to finish what I had started, and yet she still escaped me again. And again, in Lockdale. And again, in Andros. I put two and two together. I've known you've been helping her this whole time."

My stomach dropped as I listened to his words. The whole time, it was Valentin sending the Incarti after us. I never realized why Ivory's brothers kept her locked up in Cyrene, I always just assumed they were demented, but the reason made terrifying sense. It was to protect her from Valentin.

And they never told her why.

Valentin's cracking laughter ripped me from my revelation. "Don't look so sad, Lexi. After all, she'll never have to go back to Cyrene ever again."

What was left of my heart plummeted. "What do you mean?"

"Right as we speak, the Incarti are tearing her limb from limb. Just. Like. She. Deserves." His eyes took on a brighter hue with each word.

My heart stopped, my knees buckling from underneath me as shock crashed onto me. My throat tightened. Cold tears threatened to spill down my cheeks as Valentin's laughter filled my ears.

How could I have left her? It couldn't be true. She couldn't be . . . dead. After everything we had been through, everything we survived. But a flash of pale, lifeless eyes entered my mind like some type of vision, and the image forced reality onto me. In the state she was in, she had no chance against the Incarti.

I clasped the protection spell tighter in my fist. If only I had left it with her, but instead, I had it, uselessly using it to trick my brother. It was my fault she was left defenseless. It was my fault.

"As much as I'd love to see this continue, it has already gone on long enough."

I wasn't sure if I even tried dodging his next attack. He swung his leg and hit me square in the cheek, sending me sprawled out on the floor, blood dripping from my nose. Waves of pain spread through my face, but I could barely get myself to care. If Ivory was dead, then what was the point? With her in my life, I had no need for what was left of my broken family, but now, it seemed I had lost everything. Valentin was too far gone. Francois and Mercedes might've been dead. And she, the only person I truly cared about in years, had been taken away from me. And it was all my fault.

I deserved to die. I deserved the most painful death Valentin could give me.

Valentin pinned me against the floor, his hands blazing as he wrapped them tightly around my throat. I gasped for breath, but none came, though my mind wasn't on breathing.

She just got her heart back. She's gone. Gods, I lost her, too.

I wanted to see her one last time, at least. Her snowy locks and crystal azure eyes. Her millions of freckles. Her snowdrop skin. I wanted to hear her laugh, like a twinkling bell of celebration. She would never laugh again. I would never hear her laugh again.

As my vision began to go dark, the pain drawing me from life, something whizzed in between me and Valentin. His hands slipped from my throat and I pulled in long, desperate breaths, tears staining my cheeks as my chest rose and fell violently. An agonizing burn spread through my chest like fire itself.

The two of us turned to find a silver arrow sticking up in the carpet just a few inches away from us. Our heads shot the other way, where the arrow came from, and my weak heart leapt in my chest.

340

Standing in the doorway, snowy hair piling down her shoulders, crystal azure eyes blazing, Ivory aimed an arrow right for Valentin's chest.

43

I missed. How could I have possibly missed? He's right there!

I had just barely made it, following the sounds of screams through the huge chateau until I finally found where Alexei, Sasha, and Francois were. Though as I burst into the room, all that greeted me was a sight I was hoping I never had to see. Francois and Sasha were down, unmoving. Alexei and a dark-haired man were struggling on the floor. As soon as I realized the man's steaming hands were strangling the life out of Alexei, I cocked an arrow.

And, of course, I missed.

The man pulled away from Alexei, leaving him crumpled and bleeding on the soft velvet carpet, turning to face me with a sadistic grin cracked across his cheeks. His beady eyes shone with a red glow, though he shared the same night hair as Francois and caramel skin as both his brothers. I swallowed the fear rising up in my chest as he ever so slowly approached me.

"So, you've come to join the party?" he asked, his voice slurred with the same deep accent that both Alexei and Francois shared.

I gave a tight smile as I prepared another arrow in my bow. "I didn't want to miss the fun."

The man chuckled darkly, but I didn't wait to listen for his next remark. I released the arrow, watching it fly in the man's direction, slicing through the air. But instead of driving into his chest, the arrow stopped mid-air and combusted. I tried wiping the shock from my face, fear digging its claws in my heart.

"You must be Valentin," I said evenly despite the terror raging in my body. I placed another arrow between my trembling fingers and drew the thread back. "I remember you."

My third arrow didn't get nearly as far as my other two, combusting just a half-second after I let it go. The small explosion caught my fingers, and with gritted teeth, my bow slipped from my hands.

It's not like it'll be useful anyway. I nonchalantly walked past my only weapon, my fingertips tingling with icy rage. I knew I'd have to resort to my magic anyway. However, I never expected that I'd have to fight alone.

"I don't want to fight you, Valentin," I said, and even dared to raise my hands in some type of surrender. "I just want to talk. We can stop this if we all just calm down."

"I am calm." He lifted a flaming fist for show, his eyes sparking. His hair flickered with flames, similar to the way Alexei's used to.

"If you were calm, your eyes wouldn't be glowing," I countered sharply. "All you have to do is control your magic, and we can all just go home."

"What do you know?" Valentin spat dangerously, his voice like a knife.

I swallowed nervously before I spoke again. "A lot more than you think. Look, I know how you're feeling, believe me—"

"Don't you dare compare yourself to me!" Valentin screamed, and before I could catch his next move, he was flying at me with hands blazing red and orange.

I scrambled to evade him, practically falling out the door and into the hall. The wizard rammed into one of the god statues, destroying it with only his body weight, sending marble pieces flying across the floor. I didn't have much time to gawk. Valentin's beaming red eyes caught mine, promises of murder painted in them.

I threw what I hoped was a blast of wind his way before I took off sprinting down the hall, my feet banging against the floor, echoing throughout the whole chateau. I couldn't possibly hurt him, but I knew that was all he wanted to do to me. There had to be a way to stop him without hurting him. And without dying in the process, of course.

As I dove behind the cover of a goddess statue, a blinding blast of lightning nearly struck my feet. I swallowed a scream, unaware Valentin could conjure lightning as well as fire.

"Come out, Morrow!" Valentin shouted with a hint of insanity. I had to get him to realize his magic was eating him alive before he lost himself completely. A part of the real him still had to be there, somewhere deep down. The part that loved his mother and father. The part that loved Alexei, Francois, and Mercedes.

I just had to find it.

My fingers trembled as I let loose a vapor of frosty mist, blowing it to fill the hallway. Soon, the mist hid everything in sight, and I thought I might've heard Valentin trip over something. Might've been wishful thinking, though.

"Coward!" Valentin's voice echoed through the hall menacingly. "All you've ever done is hide! Face me!"

I swallowed a ball of fear as I inched away from the statue, blindly making my way toward his voice. A spark ignited in the mist and a flame appeared from a hand, but as I ushered a gust of wind, it died out. Valentin scoffed as he repeatedly tried to call upon his fire, only for it to be snuffed out by my magic.

"This is how Alexei feels," I called. "How would you like your magic to fail you forever?"

"So, you want his heart?" Valentin snarled, whirling to face me. He threw a blast of fire, but it missed by a couple of feet, disappearing in the icy mist.

I darted to a different spot before I spoke again. "Listen, I know you think your family betrayed you, but if you could only see how much your brothers love you—"

"Shut up!" Without warning, fire spread across the hall in a flaming entourage, swallowing everything in its way.

I scrambled to escape the heat, all my focus on keeping my spell intact gone. The mist dropped to the floor, leaving the tile wet with melted snow, and me completely vulnerable. I nearly shrieked as another bolt of lightning just barely missed me by an inch. I needed another plan, quick.

And I might've had one. It was crazy, sure, but at least it was something. What plan of mine wasn't crazy, after all?

"Alright, Valentin," I turned to face him, my hands hovering in the air, "you want to kill me? Well, you're gonna have to catch me first."

I stomped on the tile floor, spreading an icy sheen crawling to cover every inch of the ground. Valentin stumbled with his blazing hands aglow, and as I whirled to run, my feet sliding gracefully on the ice, the gap between the two of us widened until I had created a safe distance.

My chest heaved as I sprinted across the ice, throwing blasts of biting wind behind my shoulder to douse the flames that flew after me. Heat licked my skin, calling sweat pouring down my face. Smoke filled my lungs like venom, slowing me down, snuffing out my icy magic with each passing second.

Lightning struck around me, destroying statues and paintings and pillars as I weaved in and out of hallways, Valentin's screams of frustration growing louder each time I evaded him. My fingers prickled to release a spell to stop him entirely, to lock his muscles in ice, spread to his heart and leave the same frosty residue he had left on mine. I wanted to make his heart cease.

I wanted to stop his heart. And there was only one way to do that.

The Highwayman had shown me how to do it the moment he did it to me. Ever since then, the spell taunted me, always there, always yearning to be used. It was crazed magic, cruel, dark magic, I knew. But I also knew just how simple it was to steal someone's heart.

Alexei had once told me magic came from the heart. Get rid of the heart, get rid of the magic. Get rid of the magic, get rid of the psychotic power it cast over Valentin.

All I had to do was catch him and not get burned in the process.

I sucked in a deep breath, diving behind the cover of a stained-glass wall, pressing myself against it. The crimson glass threw a glow over my pale skin as I shoved a hand to my mouth in an attempt to quiet myself.

"Where are you?" Valentin bellowed, his voice drowning in his own uncontrolled magic. His accent had somehow disappeared in the raspy roll of magic, leaving each word that left his lips distorted. I was running out of time.

The echo of his footsteps grew louder, sending the beat of my heart accelerating. I thought he would surely find me just by the loud thumping inside my chest. I swallowed the beat that had risen up in my throat, igniting my hands with a cautionary frost, preparing, waiting, waiting. Waiting. Waiting.

He stepped into my line of sight, his eyes widening as he caught a glimpse of me in the glass.

Now!

I threw myself from my hiding spot, shoving my arms out in an attempt to pull the magic from Valentin's chest. He cried out in alarm as the two of us crashed to the floor. Just as I released a wave of magic in him, a surge of electricity shot through my body.

I shrieked and collapsed, my fingers twitching around the orb in my hand as a burning agony traveled through my veins like a deadly poison. Steam rolled off my skin, my ears ringing, my mouth hung agape.

I blinked away the spots that had clouded my vision, spasms of pain keeping me tied to the ground. The smell of burning flesh entered my nose and it wasn't until Valentin shuffled next to me did I realize it was my flesh that I smelled.

Valentin groaned and crawled up to his feet, but as he stood, his knees buckled. He glanced around blankly, as if he had entirely forgotten where he was. He looked confused, like the same twelve-year-old boy he had been before his heart corrupted him. He held his forehead, blinking rapidly as he swayed. When his eyes fell on me, however, a loud gasp escaped his lips.

"Oh my gods!" Valentin exclaimed, his disoriented voice thick with Alexei's accent, laced with panic and desperation. "What happened? Are you ok?"

I grumbled in response as his heart rolled from my grasp, but Valentin didn't acknowledge it. Instead, he hauled me up, supporting my weight as my heart skipped multiple beats. I forced myself to focus, craning my neck to catch a glimpse of the man who had just tried to kill me.

His face was pale, his eyes wide and green as ever—as they should've been—the glowing, blocky red gone. Somewhere beyond my pain, a wave of relief washed over me. I did it. I saved Valentin. And got electrocuted in the process.

You win some and you lose some.

"Ivory!" a voice cried, echoing throughout the winding halls. The voice shook me down to the core, letting some haze clear.

I glanced up to see Alexei and Francois sprinting toward us, Francois with blood soaking his hair and hands sparking. Valentin paused, withdrawing a gasp that he caught in his throat.

"Let her go!" Alexei shouted, running full speed.

I fought to extend a hand as Valentin tensed. Francois caught Alexei's arm, stopping him from ramming into me and Valentin. His face blanched as if he knew what I had done.

"It's ok," I rasped.

Valentin didn't wait for them to process my words. "She needs help! I don't know what happened, but there's something wrong with her." He transferred me to Alexei, whose skin had grown almost as cold as mine.

I had spared Valentin from succumbing to his heart, but now that was all that Alexei needed. I just hoped I still had enough time.

"Ivory," Alexei hesitated, glaring down at me with a mixture of concern, relief, anger, and confusion all in one, "should I even ask?"

I cracked a smile despite my smoking skin and spasms. "It was Francois' idea."

Alexei shot his gaze to his brother. "What did you do?"

Francois winced under Alexei's blazing eyes. "I might've given her a dose of Ambrosia."

"You did *what*!" Alexei screamed. "Are you crazy?"

I reached up and tugged on a strand of Alexei's hair, hushing him as he continued to shout at Francois. "The potion is going to wear off soon, and I am not fainting before I know you have your heart back."

"What is going on?" Valentin exclaimed suddenly, cutting off whatever Alexei had planned to say. He had his hands clasped in his hair. Something was off with his green eyes, a sort of glaze in them. "Where are we? Where's Mercedes?"

"You don't remember?" Alexei questioned cautiously.

"Remember what?" Valentin replied, throwing his arms out in a childlike manner. Without the corrupt power of his heart, he seemed to be as harmless as the twelve-year-old he used to be.

Alexei and Francois exchanged worried glances that were nowhere near inconspicuous. I resisted the urge to stomp on Alexei's foot.

"Remember that I stole your heart," I said, lifting my head to meet Valentin's eye.

"You . . ." He reached to his chest, his face flushing, and a flash of realization crossed his features. "What did I do? How long has it been?"

Alexei pushed Francois forward in a not-so-subtle way.

"Well, uh." He wavered, scratching the back of his head. When he pulled his hand away, his fingers came back coated in blood. "What do you remember last?"

"I—I don't know. Everything is just a haze, but I feel like I'm supposed to know her." He stopped to gesture at me before continuing. "And I feel like something really bad happened. Where's Mercedes? Don't tell me he's . . ." His voice broke off, a look of anguish taking over his shattering expression.

"No, no," Francois quickly assured him. "He's going to be fine."

"And Sasha?" I rose an eyebrow.

"Who's Sasha?"

Alexei clamped a hand over my mouth before I could answer. "He's fine, too."

"And, you are?" Valentin nodded at me.

I extended a hand, offering a weak but cheeky smile. "Ivory Morrow. We met when we were kids."

"You spent so long under the corrupt power of your heart, it started to steal who you are. Your magic, your voice, your body, and even your memories. You'll remember everything eventually, but it'll take some time," Francois explained, a frown tugging at his lips.

Sure, he'd come to remember, but we were certain he wouldn't want to know the damage he had wrecked. Once his memories came back, he would have to face them head-on. And the frail, innocuous Valentin that stood before us seemed nowhere near ready to face his past. I couldn't imagine having to recall memories of attempted murder.

"You said something about Alexei's heart," Valentin said, the corners of his lips turning down.

The three of us paused. I glanced up at Alexei, but he seemed frozen, both dread and hope gleaming in his eyes. I bit back another spasm of pain. The stinging in my abdomen had grown increasingly pressing, but I wouldn't let myself succumb to the wound. I needed Alexei to be alright.

"Yes, Val," Francois finally spoke up, "and we need to know where you put it, if you can remember."

Valentin's face scrunched up in effort, his hand on his chin. Alexei anxiously leaned forward, the warmth in his grasp depleting with each passing second. He needed the missing piece of his heart, and he needed it now.

Something clicked deep in Valentin's eyes, the glaze subsiding. His expression darkened, his innocuous mien falling. He dropped his hand and caught Alexei's gaze, his lips pitching downward. For a moment, his memory seemed to have returned to him in a rush.

"I . . . I'm sorry, Alexei," he said, his voice falling soft. He tore his eyes away, wincing. "I don't have it. Mercedes tried taking it away from me and I—" His voice cracked.

"Where is it, then? What do you mean you don't have it?" Francois demanded. Panic drowned in his words, causing Valentin to wince once more.

"I destroyed it! That's why I attacked Mercedes, isn't it? He—he tried, but I didn't listen. Where is Mercedes?" Valentin babbled, the color flushing from his face. He glanced around desperately in search of his little brother.

"Mercedes will be fine, Valentin!" Francois exclaimed. "But Alexei won't! He *needs* his heart, and he needs it now!"

Valentin stumbled back as if Francois had struck him, his eyes widened, shaking his head. "I'm sorry, I . . . I don't have it. It's gone. Please tell me you still have some magic left."

All eyes shot in Alexei's direction. I swallowed nervously, my heart hammering against my chest. Alexei's lips parted, but no sound came out. Instead, he merely shook his head.

"No," Valentin whispered. "This is my fault, isn't it? I'm the one who . . ." He let the rest of his sentence die on his lips with the realization, withdrawing his gaze. His eyes found the stray heart abandoned on the floor. All at once, his flare returned.

"Alexei!" he shouted, making all three of us jump. He rushed to scoop up the glowing orb lying on the floor, holding it out with a desperate smile. "This heart has done no good for me, but maybe for you . . ."

"Wait, you can't just give your heart to me," Alexei said, shaking his head. He glanced at Francois through the corner of his eye. "Or, can he?"

"Technically, yes, but that would mean Valentin will lose his magic forever. Are you sure you want to do that to yourself?" Francois asked Valentin.

Valentin nodded. "I'm sure. Please, take it as an apology."

I pushed myself from Alexei's grasp, nodding in encouragement, ignoring the way my fingers twitched repeatedly. I didn't care losing a heart was like death for a wizard; Alexei deserved that heart just as much as Valentin didn't deserve it.

Alexei's eyes gleamed with emotion as he slowly held out his hand. Valentin transferred the glowing orb into his little brother's palm with such certainty, one would think he was merely handing over a trinket. Upon Alexei's touch, the orb let loose a stream of colorful sparks and ashes. He hesitated before he clasped his hands over the warm heart.

"Val . . . thank you," Alexei said softly.

A smile found its way to my lips as his shoulders relaxed, apparent and visual relief taking over his features. I watched as he gripped the orb tight and brought it to his lips and—

Nothing. Nothing happened.

My heart sank. The hope shining on Alexei's face disappeared quicker than when it came. He pulled the orb from his lips and tried again, but it remained apart from his body, sparking mockingly at the wizard.

Alexei dropped his hand, anguish taking over his face. "It's . . . too late."

Francois and I exchanged glances, our eyes wide. I held a hand over my lips, shaking my head. It couldn't be too late! Not after all we went through!

Despite my dread, burning anger rose up in my stomach, entangling in the icy crevices of my heart. My fingers sparked with heat, the same heat Alexei used to possess. I didn't care if it was too late. I wasn't going to let him lose his magic.

"No." I stepped forward, plucking the orb from Alexei's loose grasp. "It's not too late!"

Without warning, I shoved the orb through Alexei's chest, ignoring his gasp of surprise. I jumped on the tip of my toes, capturing his cold lips. I released the magical surge of fire I carried, pouring every ounce of power I could into him.

His eyes ignited like a star, magic swirling around us rapidly like a dancing blizzard. Flames licked up my skin and onto Alexei's, his hair just as bright as the embers. Sparks flew from the two of us like fireworks, hues of azure blue and sunset orange mixed with vibrant violet and yellow. My heart burned like an inferno, heat filling my chest, my lungs holding rampaging flames.

My flesh grew hot, smoke and ash rising from my glowing skin, but I didn't let go. I pressed my lips harder against his, allowing myself a few more seconds before I tore myself away. I stumbled, my vision going dark, all of the pain I had been pushing away flooding into me at once.

I blinked quickly, urging myself to stay conscious just a little longer. I needed to know if what I had done, whatever it was, worked. I needed to know Alexei's flame would never die out.

I sputtered on ash, somehow finding my feet despite my buckling knees, drawing in deep breath after breath, the chill in the air replenishing. The color had returned to Alexei's skin, his eyes shining with incredible light.

"Ivory," Alexei gasped, "how did you know how to do that?"

I fought against the darkness slipping into the corners of my eyes. "So, it worked?"

"Yes, it worked!" Alexei exclaimed, and the joy in his voice almost made me want to kiss him again, this time without the magic.

"Good, good," I muttered, my legs failing. "You might want to catch me."

And *then* I fainted.

44

"Do you think if I scream loud enough, I can get Francois to bring us cinnamon buns?" Mercedes asked nonchalantly.

He lounged on the sofa next to me, fumbling with the braid Sasha had done for him, wearing a pair of silken pajama pants. The deadly wound he had received from Valentin no longer oozed pus, but it remained bandaged, and he, like me, remained bedridden.

The two of us were left the worst from the fight against Valentin, and our recovery passed slower than I could imagine. The days of medicines and bandages turned into weeks, and it wasn't long until the weeks became months. At first, our focus was merely finding the strength to support our own weight again, but as the time passed, we found ourselves spending most of our hours conversing and trying to enjoy each other's company.

Despite the fact Mercedes had tried to murder me as a child, it seemed his fight with Valentin was enough to shake his corrupt magic and let him see just how insane his brother had become. He had been having doubts, but as he tried expressing these doubts to Valentin, his brother responded by attacking him. However, long after that fight, his magic haunted him, whispers of revenge keeping him up late at night. It wasn't long until he decided to give up his heart, just as Valentin had done.

Both brothers remained heartless, which meant magicless. The fear of losing themselves proved too great for them to handle.

Mercedes and I found ourselves in the same situation, our bodies plagued by fatigue and all sorts of cuts and bruises that left so many scars. So instead of succumbing to awkward silences, we decided to agree on a mutual liking for each other, just so we wouldn't die out of our own boredom.

The conversations started out civil, and dare I say caring, but that sort of talk didn't last long. We discovered each other's snark pretty quick, but I had to admit he was clever. And quite funny, but I would never tell him so.

Mercedes was quicker to recover, probably because he wasn't stabbed as well as fought the psycho Valentin had been, but I wasn't that lucky.

"Can't you just give me that potion again?" I once asked Francois out of pure desperation. It was only two weeks into my recovery, but it felt like eight.

"All that potion does is replenish until the next sunrise. Once it wears off, the body goes right back to how it was before. Your body won't heal if you take it again," Francois explained patiently.

I responded by throwing a pillow at him.

But there were some potions he allowed me to drink. None of them sped up the healing process, but they helped me through the worst of the pain. The one I had grown to rely on the most was the same potion I had taken in the Mandrake with Marble and Crystal. It knocked me out faster than any punch, and the slumber was the only respite I could get.

Sleeping was the only way to keep the memories of *everything* at bay. The memories of the siren's song, the fey carrying me off to their realm. Marble's nightmare eyes, his Fire Dust hands, his dead, bleeding body embedded to the crystal floor. Memories of Layton, Dean, and Dulce, of the wizard rebellion I had sparked right in the center of the Embrasian kingdom, the gold blade that slipped through my chest so very easily. Flashes of lightning haunted me, my fingers still twitching even as the months passed.

I couldn't face all the memories at once. So, I hid from them, kept them trapped somewhere deep in the crevices of my mind. My body might've been healing, but it seemed my brain persisted to keep itself broken and disheveled. Lying in bed for hours upon hours became easier, frighteningly easy, and my will to eat diminished steadily.

Even cinnamon buns no longer appeared appetizing.

"You literally just ate five waffles," I finally answered Mercedes.

He sighed and stretched, a few of his bones popping with the movement. Since the fight, my hands never stopped twitching, and his bones now had a strange pop to them every time he moved too quick.

I watched as he slipped from the couch, holding his weight just fine. We both knew we didn't need to be on constant bed rest, but Francois and Valentin insisted we let ourselves heal just a little longer. For the first time since I met Alexei, I was allowed to rest, but rest was the last thing I wanted. All I really wanted was to jump out the nearest window just for some adrenaline.

But a sudden care for what Alexei would think of that kept me from it. The first month or so, he plastered himself to my side, always there with bandages or medicines or anything else I could ask for. He escaped the fights with little harm, which was an ultimate relief to me, but I could sense the guilt it caused him. The previous experiences he went through haunted him just as it haunted me, darkening his light eyes. He had been so close to losing his magic forever, and flashes of the Embrasian rebellion taunted the both of us. He also had to deal with telling his brothers about their mother.

Mercedes hadn't talked for a couple of days after Alexei explained what he learned during our time with the former king. Their mother, Scarlett, didn't abandon them to become a general in the king's war. She left because it was the only way of obtaining the papers to allow her sons to live wherever they wanted. I could only imagine how Valentin and Francois took the news.

Though soon, I knew Alexei couldn't stay by my side forever. His house was in shambles, his dolls and business abandoned. I urged him to return to Andros, to finish rebuilding his shop, reopen and get his life back. I wouldn't allow myself to keep him back.

"But what about you?" he had asked.

I glanced down at the bandages wrapped around my torso and gestured to the scars of lightning running up my shoulders. "I'm not going anywhere."

"I can't just leave you here," he argued, shaking his head. "Nothing good ever happens when we're split up."

I offered him a smile, folding his hand in mine. "We're not in danger anymore. Francois is here. I'm sure he won't let anything happen."

It took me a few more days, but I eventually cracked him. He returned to Andros, leaving me in the biggest chateau I had ever seen with the three boys who had tried to murder me as a child. But I wasn't complaining. It was awkward in the beginning, as I couldn't meet Valentin's eye for a while, but soon, I got used to his presence.

As Valentin's memories slowly returned to him, it seemed to affect his mental health pretty quick. His sunken body didn't get much better, the bags under his dull green eyes growing darker and darker. Though he apologized countless times to everyone, sorry seemed forever on his lips, haunting him, he never believed he could ever be forgiven. Mercedes and Francois were quick to forgive, but it took me a little more time.

The relationship between the two of us wasn't perfect. It was tense and slightly awkward, full of unrequited glances, stutters, and nervous shuffling, but I felt that perhaps, with time, a *lot* of time, we could become unlikely friends. I was in love with his brother, after all. He was stuck with me whether he liked it or not.

Alexei finally had his family back, and I hoped that maybe they would be mine, too. I spent hours thinking of Layton and Dean, but their names didn't warm my heart. I always thought that if I ever gained the ability to love, I would love them right away, like a switch in my brain telling me that that was what I was supposed to do. But, I didn't.

At first, I still didn't understand it. They were my family; I was supposed to love them. They raised me and yet they kept me hidden from the world, letting me grow with my mind full of lies and deceptions. The effects of their isolation taunted me even though I knew I was free.

One part of me wanted to run back to them, to let them lock the locks, chain the chains, bury me in lies that made everything better. And the other part of me never wanted to see their faces again.

I wrote many letters, all of which ended up thrown across the room in a fit of rage or crumpled up with my tears staining the ink. None of them were sent. And I wasn't sure when I would be brave enough to send one. If I would ever.

To make matters worse, just a few days after Alexei left for Andros, I woke with dark hair spurting from my roots, and when I had frantically beseeched Francois, he told me quite a confusing notion.

"It's because your heart has heated up," he explained. "The curse is disappearing, and your real features are coming back. Just look at your eye."

I ran to a mirror and was horrified to find that my eye indeed had changed. My left eye, no longer pale blue, held the same chocolate brown my brothers' eyes contained. Every time I glanced at myself, I was met with a constant reminder of them. We shared the same blood, after all, but the fact that I looked nothing like them had become a relief. With strands of dark hair and one brown eye, I thought I would never be able to shake what they had done to me.

Sasha, however, was an entirely different story. He got himself bandaged up, downed a potion, and with some heartfelt goodbyes, returned to Embrasia in a rush. His kingdom was left in disarray, a castle full of traitorous Magicians and guards, citizens with no knowledge of what had happened. Through his letters, we learned Cathair, with a bit of coaxing (and perhaps a little more), agreed to pass his crown to Sasha officially. Sasha ended up sitting through two coronations, one in the dungeon with his father, and the other publicly.

The countless wizards we had rescued and fought alongside flocked to the castle the same day King Sasha dismissed the staff of Cathair. In a more recent letter, we found Furn had become Sasha's not-so-royal squire. I could only imagine how that went down.

Embrasia had changed for the first time in decades, and with Sasha as king, it wouldn't be changing back for a long time. Wizard papers and identification were abandoned, entry to Embrasia free. The Council of Naxos and the king of Embrasia signed a peace treaty, and finally, the conflict between the Embrasians and the wizards died out like a flame in the winter wind. A new era had begun under Sasha's reign, one where wizards and humans could live together in peace.

During my recovery, Sasha had come to visit me several times, joining in on the conversations between me and Mercedes. Sometimes we would listen to him panic about the stress of being king or rant about his old complications with his father. He had once recounted our Highwayman adventure with exquisite and slightly over-dramatic detail, recalling me flying in the underground burrow riding a flaming horse and him taking on a hundred men at once with only a rock and a sling.

After such a story, Mercedes begged to be taken on an adventure like ours, and even though he still walked with a slight limp, I may or may not have cast a mirage spell to make it look like he was sleeping soundly through the night in order to fool Francois. The two returned from their adventures with more stories than the last, their hair tousled, and sporting more bruises than I could count, always coming back with a new weapon or two.

A knock interrupted whatever remark Mercedes wore on his lips, flinging me back to the present. Francois walked through the gold-rimmed door, followed by the boy I hadn't seen in weeks, wearing his signature magenta coat, his long hair swishing perfectly, diamonds hanging from his ears.

"Alexei!" I cried, practically flying from the comfortable spot on the sofa to wrap my arms around him. My heart gave a jolt with his sudden presence. I squeezed as tight as I could manage, smirking as I heard his breath catch. The warmth of summer stuck to his skin like sugar to a strawberry.

He laughed as he attempted to suck in a breath. "You must be feeling better."

I let go slowly, taking as much heat from him as I could. Since his heart had been completed, the warmth he used to carry seemed like kindling compared to now. My hands lingered on his cheeks, cupping them firmly as his smile grew.

"I missed you," I said, my own freckled cheeks aching from all the smiling. "What are you doing here?"

"I came to take you home," he answered simply. He paused, a quizzical look passing over his features. "You have mismatched eyes."

My smile dropped at the reminder. I looked away bashfully, fumbling with the strands of dark hair that had appeared over time. "Yeah, it—it has something to do with the curse, or something and—"

"I like it."

My head shot up. "You do?"

He put a hand to his chin, nodding. "Yeah. I should do the same, don't you think? Brown is so in right now."

"No!" I exclaimed.

He burst out laughing. "Alright, fine, I won't."

I allowed a grin to slip its way back to my lips. "You said something about home. What do you mean?"

"Oh!" His eyes sparkled, and he took my hands in his. "I forgot to ask. Do you want to live with me?"

Behind us, both Francois and Mercedes facepalmed. The slaps echoed in the stunned silence I left.

A chuckle escaped my lips, my heart fluttering wildly. "Live? With you? In Andros?"

"Yes, well, you don't have to if you don't want to, of course, but I thought that it might be good, I mean, nice, you know? We built an extra room for you, just in case, with lots of windows, and—and plants and—"

"Can I just kiss you now?"

"Is that a yes?"

"Of course it's a yes!" I exclaimed, and threw my arms around his neck, connecting our lips.

"You do know she's still on bed rest, don't you?" Francois interrupted.

The two of us pulled away, throwing glares like daggers at the wizard. In the corner of my eye, I thought I saw a mischievous smirk run across Alexei's face.

"What a shame it would be if someone were to jump through that window," he said, nodding to the open window on the other side of the room.

"Don't you dare—"

But we were already gone.

Epilogue

The snow twirled in an intricate dance, falling from the dark sky like stars themselves. The cold bit my nose and ears, tinting them pink. Summer had passed quickly, and winter embraced the city of Andros with blizzards and icicles down every road. Coated in a thick blanket of fresh snow, lights illuminated the city, casting a multicolor glow against the endless white. In the distance, music floated in the air, traveling to my numb ears atop the balcony of Alexei's shop. A calm beat in my chest soothed my nerves.

I leaned up against the railing, a cloud of warm air puffing from my lips, unblinking. Thrown into a pensive trance, I could easily ignore my shivering fingers clasped so tightly to the rail, the pressure of time snuffed out in the back of my head. My feet ached, my cheeks like that of a rose, strands of dark hair twisting in the wind.

"There you are. I've been looking all over for you." A warm voice pulled me from my trance.

I turned and smiled as Alexei took my side, the gems on his tailcoat clinking with the movement. Practically radiating with heat, I felt drawn to him like a moth to a flame.

"It's so . . . beautiful," I said breathlessly. "I've never seen anything like it."

Alexei chuckled and faced the city, staring at it with scrutinizing eyes. I leaned against his shoulder, his warmth scaring away the cold that had furrowed deep into my skin, and returned my gaze to the sea of lights surrounding us. He intertwined our fingers, an action that still gave my heart a little jolt even after spending summer and spring together.

"Everyone's waiting for us—" he paused as a frown took over my lips, my fingers twitching in his— "but I suppose they can wait a little longer."

I sighed, tearing my gaze away to meet his eyes. "I just . . . don't want to forget this."

He nodded silently, tucking me under his arm. I smiled, soaking up his warmth as I listened to the low song of the singing wind, the chime of bells, faint crackling of fire. Smoke rose from the chimneys of each home, the smell of pine and gingerbread fresh in the air.

"You know," he glanced at me through the corner of his eye, "it's like this every night."

"It is?"

"Here in Andros it is." Alexei nodded. "You seem like you've never seen snowfall before."

"I haven't. It doesn't snow in Cyrene, and there are no lights and galas and music and dancing."

"Oh." His face fell slightly.

I reached into my pocket and pulled out an envelope, stamped and signed with the names of my brothers. Dean had always been my favorite, so I wrote his name first, Layton's following shakily after. I held it up so Alexei could see, glad the cold had already forced my hand trembling.

"Are you sure?" he asked softly.

I took a deep breath and nodded before burying the letter back in my pocket. Their faces no longer sparked anger, instead something different. Something like pity. Though I had made up my mind on the letter, I still didn't know if I would ever return to Cyrene. I wasn't sure if I could.

There were a lot of things I wasn't sure of.

I thought I would get better with time, but as the bright summer days and rainy spring nights passed, I still faced countless sleepless nights. Sometimes, at random, my heart would fall into a frenzy, pounding against my chest like it yearned to jump free. Nightmares of the distant gleam of a blade haunted me. Small spaces seemed to close in on me. A flash of lightning was enough to rattle me.

But no matter how many nights I spent awake, how many nightmares forced me out of bed, how many times Alexei had to reassure me the walls weren't shrinking, he was always by my side. And I was always by his.

"If you want, I can pull some chairs out here." Alexei's voice ripped me from my thoughts, slowing my racing heart. "And I could bring blankets, too. Oh, and hot chocolate! Does that sound good?"

He didn't wait for me to answer. "We can put on a bunch of socks, like a bunch. And, if you want—"

"Shhh," I interrupted, holding my hands to his cheeks. "I'm gonna kiss you now, ok?"

"Ok." He smiled.

I rose to the tips of my toes, gently pressing my lips against his. A rush of warmth spread through my body, a rush I felt every time we kissed, sending my heart in a spin. I could feel his smile through the kiss as he wrapped an arm around my waist, pulling me closer.

"You've *got* to be kidding!"

Alexei and I jumped apart, turning to face a livid King Sasha, who stood in the doorway, glaring with his hands on his hips. His crown rested lopsided on his head of barely tamed caramel hair.

"We're all downstairs waiting for you!" he exclaimed. "We're going to be late!"

"We were just getting some fresh air," Alexei replied with an innocent grin.

"Sure you were." Sasha whirled around. "I'm not going to be late because *someone* wanted fresh air."

Alexei and I laughed as we followed him inside, a blast of warm air greeting us, making my flushed skin prickle. Reconstructed with the same diamond the Embrasian castle was made of, Alexei's new staircase must've been at least two times grander than the last, the railings lined in gold.

Downstairs, we found Valentin, Francois, and Mercedes waiting by the door, dressed in the most elegant attire they could find, their fingers decorated with jewels. Valentin had even brushed his hair and Mercedes had somehow been persuaded to keep his favorite sword behind.

"There you are." A smile spread across Francois' cheeks.

"How long were you out there?" Valentin asked with examining eyes. "You two look freezing."

Alexei and I glanced at each other, laughing softly. His nose took on a pink hue, snow decorating his perfect hair. Glowing with mirth, his brilliant emerald eyes gleamed.

"We were just enjoying the weather." He grinned.

"Well, you can enjoy the blistering cold at the gala, alright?" Sasha was losing his serious demeanor word by word, and by the end of his sentence, the smile he had been holding back revealed itself.

"I thought you didn't like these holiday parties. You said so yourself yesterday." I smirked, crossing my arms knowingly.

"I don't, but I like my people. They all know I'm going to be there," Sasha replied with an uplifting of his finger.

"Look at you, Mr. Good King." Alexei nudged Sasha, earning the slip of a chuckle from his lips.

The rest of us snickered as Sasha punched the wizard's shoulder, laughing. He might've been king, but somewhere deep down, he was still the same childish prince I had met so long ago.

A loud chime echoed from beyond the shop, ringing with a sing-song tone. As a collective group, we all paused to hear it.

"The six o'clock bell!" Sasha shrieked, and threw the door open.

A blast of biting wind entered the house, beckoning through my hair and skirt. The faraway music of the gala reached my ears even from the shop. I tightened my scarf before grabbing Alexei's hand. He glanced down at me with a smile, sending a rush of heated magic billowing up in my chest. A thousand twinkling snowflakes drifted from the gray sky through the night of music and celebration.

As six, we entered the snowfall.

Kylee Minus

Kylee Minus published her debut novel, *Heartburn*, during her sophomore year of high school. She lives in Southern Illinois with her parents and three older siblings. She's written many stories that will never see the light of day, but she's always dreamed of publishing a book someday. *Heartburn* is her first novel and she plans many, many more to come. When she's not bothering her twin sister, she devotes herself to writing, reading, running, drawing, and watching cartoons.

Made in the USA
Columbia, SC
07 September 2019